Angel™

City Of
Not Forgotten
Redemption
Close to the Ground
Shakedown
Hollywood Noir
Avatar
Soul Trade
Bruja
The Summoned
Haunted
Image
Stranger to the Sun
Vengeance
Endangered Species
The Longest Night, vol. 1
Impressions
Sanctuary
Fearless
Solitary Man
Nemesis
Monolith
The Essential Angel Posterbook
The Casefiles, Volume 1—The Official Companion
The Casefiles, Volume 2—The Official Companion

Buffy/Angel crossovers

The Unseen Trilogy
    Book 1: The Burning
    Book 2: Door to Alternity
    Book 3: Long way Home
Monster Island
Seven Crows
Cursed

Available from Pocket Books

Buffy
the Vampire Slayer™
ANGEL™

heat

Nancy Holder

An original novel based on the hit television series by Joss Whedon and David Greenwalt

POCKET
BOOKS

London   Sydney   New York   Toronto

First Pocket Books paperback edition June 2005

POCKET BOOKS
An imprint of Simon & Schuster
Africa House
64–78 Kingsway,
London WC2B 6AH

Printed and bound in Great Britain

10 9 8 7 6 5 4 3 2 1

A CIP catalogue record for this book is available from the British Library

ISBN 0-7434-9251-X

This book is for my daughter, Belle, who says, "If it's going to be fun, there has to be some screaming."

ACKNOWLEDGMENTS

My sincere thanks to Joss Whedon, David Greenwalt, Marti Noxon, David Fury, and the staffs, casts, and crews of *Buffy* and *Angel*, especially Sarah Michelle Gellar and David Boreanaz. A warm salute to the Pocket Posse: my wonderful Simon & Schuster editors and editorial assistants, past and present: Lisa Clancy, Liz Shifflet, Micol Ostow, Lisa Gribbin, Tricia Boczkowski, Patrick Price, and Beth Bracken. To my Most Honorable Agent, Howard Morhaim, and his intrepid assistant, Mara Sorkin, I kowtow in your general direction for all your help and support. Thanks to First Daughter Rebecca Morhaim, for the smile you put in your father's voice when we speak on the phone. To Lisa Morton, thank you for the gift of the Chinese films, especially *The Terracotta Warrior*. To my friends and family, my gratitude and my love.

PROLOGUE

In the Ice Hell:
Where Time and Dreams Are Frozen

In the vast caverns of the Ice Hell, the massive red body of Lir, the great demonic warlord of the dimension of Sol, strained for freedom.

It had done so for more than a thousand years.

Nearby, its savior, the dragon Flamestryke, slept on in his enchanted stupor.

Three things were needed to free them both: the Orb, the Heart, and the Flame.

Lir had worked for centuries to obtain them.

And now, despite the foolish machinations of the Powers That Be to keep them from him, Lir saw his chance at last.

The next cycle of heat was here; the Year of the Hot Devil was ascending. Joss sticks of Chinese magicians whispered, *Hell is coming.*

And the King of Hell will destroy us all.

If Lir could have smiled, he would have.

He knew that if he was patient, his laughter would shatter worlds.

Los Angeles, February 8, 2000

They say that vampires burn in the sunlight the way evil men burn in hell: tyger, tyger, burning bright, who can take that much pain?

Who should have to?

Buffy the Vampire Slayer staggers among the ruins of Sunnydale. Smoking buildings, huge piles of rubble. The street is a mosaic of asphalt, cement, and body parts. Blood rushes into the gutters.

The Sun Cinema blazes behind her; the burning marquee reads A SUMMERS PLACE *until the flames lick at the S and it disappears. Then the entire sign goes up in flames.*

Armageddon has come, and it has struck the Slayer down.

The earth sizzles under her heeled boots. Her hair is silver with ash; her cheeks are tinged with soot and blood; and her black tank top is burned half away. Her black trousers are ripped on both sides from thigh to ankle so that they hang in tatters like a Celtic warrior woman's skirt.

She staggers, hand over her heart, as she bends down to pick up a tattered teddy bear. Tears are for victims and people who have time to cry; Buffy surveys the bear's damage with dry eyes and trembling hands.

I bleed for her.

Her Slayer senses pump up, and she knows she is not alone; she turns her head and stares straight at me. Her eyes widen, and I know it is almost too much for her to see that I have come.

That means it's over.

"Oh, my God, Angel!" she cries.

She flings open her arms.

And I move from the dancing red shadows.

I lost my soul to have you, I tell her as I approach, as I drink in her beauty, richer than any blood I have ever tasted in my long life.

Then I lost my humanity. For twenty-four hours I was a man, your man, and then I gave it back, to save you. I would do anything to save you.

I love you, Buffy Summers.

But I can't save you, my love.

No one can.

Not even I.

I move from the red shadows into the smoky day; the sun blazes red in the sky, but it is there.

It is there.

And it burns me as I walk toward her. My hair ignites first, and then my shoulders; then my arms and hands, and finally, my face.

Tyger, tyger, the flames shred my body with razor-sharp incisors, but I move toward Buffy, moth to the flame. Candle in the firestorm.

One burning soul reaching toward another . . .

Tyger, tyger, she screams, and runs toward me, shrieking, "Angel! No! Go back!"

But there is no going back. I love her. I cannot live without her another night, another hour, another flame-bright breath.

Since it's all over, I'll die with her.

That pain sears me far worse than this one.

Carrying a torch, becoming one . . . what is the difference, if I can't be with her on the last day of the world?

"Angel!" Buffy screamed.

She ran to him and threw her arms around his burning silhouette as the red sunlight devoured him. Then her hands went through him, and there was nothing left but ashes. A hero's funeral, a hero's cremation, and his ashes sifted through her fingers to sprinkle the sidewalk. The fierce fiery wind picked them up and carried them away.

"No!" Buffy cried, staring at her empty hands, then screaming at the sun. "No, no, no!"

"Angel!"

"Sssh. Buffy, it's all right."

Buffy bolted upright. Wearing a loosely belted black silk robe, his hair tousled, Angel sat on the edge of her bed. He wore a look of tender concern. Without saying a word, she grabbed his hand and touched his cheek. He was there. He was fine.

"Oh, my God," she murmured, pressing her fingertips against his temple, his lips.

"Bad dream?" he asked.

Unable to tear her gaze away from him, she moved into his arms. He held her tightly. Then she leaned her head back and offered her mouth to him. He sighed happily and pressed his lips against hers. She did not close her eyes; his long lashes brushed his cheeks as he drew her close and held her.

The vein in her neck pulsed.

His fingertips found the thin straps of her baby tee; he

4

slipped them off her shoulders and molded his long fingers around her upper arms, tracing the contours of her clavicles and the hollow of her throat with his thumbs.

"I dreamed that you died," she told him as he laid her back against the pillows. "You walked into the sun to kiss me."

"I would do that," he whispered, nibbling her earlobe as he unthreaded the belt from his robe and dropped it on the floor. "I burn for you constantly, Buffy. My heart is on fire. Feel it."

He took her hand in his and placed it on his chest. Intense heat scorched her palm.

"Ouch!" she cried, pulling away.

But he caught up her hand and held it there, his larger hand over her smaller one. Earnestly he said, "Feel the heat. What does the poem say? 'Some say the world will end in fire.'"

He kissed her hard, his mouth ungiving, as her hand burned. Blisters broke out on her palm and across the knuckles. The pain was awful.

"And it will end in fire, Buffy. In fire."

"Let me go," she demanded, struggling.

"But it's worth it, isn't it?" he whispered, pushing her back against her pillows. "It's worth burning for?"

And it was. Oh yes, it was, all that joy and pleasure and melting and heat . . .

All that dying, and heat . . .

"I've been so cold without you," she whispered back. "Angel, I've been freezing to death."

"Some say the earth will end in ice," he murmured.

"I prefer the fire," she replied, searching his face. "I do, Angel. I do."

Then she and he burst into flames, red-and-orange flames shooting to the ceiling; they writhed and undulated together, death claiming them; fire claiming them; their love claiming them. . . .

"Oh, my God," Buffy moaned.

She opened her eyes.

She was in her bed in the dorm room she shared with Willow. Willow's bed was empty. Sweat poured down her forehead, and she was alone; flopping onto her back, tears spilled down her cheeks and she realized she was crying. The grief came hard. Her body spasmed with each gut-wrenching sob.

She rolled over and buried her face in her pillow. The walls in Stevenson Hall were thin; she didn't want anyone to hear her. It was hard enough hiding her secret life as the Slayer without attracting more attention by sobbing as if her heart had just broken.

This was the sixth night in a row she had had this dream. She didn't know why she was dreaming about Angel and burning alive. She did know from years of experience that her dreams were often prophetic. Six times definitely meant something.

And these dreams were tearing her apart.

However, my heart's fine. More than fine. Riley lives there, and I'm good with that. Angel is of the past . . . except for the last six nights of nightmares. And, okay, dreams now and then, but that happens with breakups, right?

When she was finished crying, she glanced at the digital clock on the nightstand separating her and Willow's beds. It was three a.m.

It's so hot. We're having another Santa Ana and here we are without any air-conditioning. Maybe Will and I should go stay with Mom until it cools down. Mom would like that. Me too. Except with the slayage and the classes, going back and forth from Revello would chew up so much time. Plus, no big smoochies with Riley over there . . . so, better to stay here. In the heat.

She rolled over with a sigh and closed her eyes.

They say that vampires burn in the sunlight the way evil men burn in hell: tyger, tyger, burning bright, who can take that much pain?

Who should have to?

The Slayer dreamed on.

I love you, Buffy Summers.

But I can't save you.

No one can.

Three a.m.

A great time to practice law, if you work for Wolfram & Hart.

"This body is excellent. You have done well," Qin said to his attorney, Lilah Morgan.

"Thank you, Celestial One," Lilah told him, bowing low.

He smiled at his reflection in the steamy mirror. Wavy black hair, a sculpted face, perfect white teeth. Broad shoulders, skin the color of toasted almonds. Two-thousand-dollar suit, five-hundred-dollar tie.

He had come in as Marc Lee, a reclusive Chinese billionaire. Now he would be Alex Liang, the young and handsome Chinese-American multimillionaire, and a longtime client of Wolfram & Hart. Alex Liang had factories in Korea, Malaysia, and China. Branch offices in Japan, Australia, China, and head-quarters in Los Angeles. He was worth so much that no one knew exactly how much that was.

Except for the senior partners at Wolfram & Hart.

Thus it had been a huge cause for concern when the original

Alex Liang let it be known that he was dissatisfied with his relationship with Wolfram & Hart and was seeking to cut off his association with the firm. Lilah, who handled his account, had not wanted that, of course.

Meanwhile, upper management had recently signed on Qin, the fabled Yellow Emperor of China. Although Lilah was not privy to all his plans, she had managed to steal portions of the firm's dossier on Qin and read them lightning-fast before she had to return them.

It seemed the emperor was something called a Possessor—a being that hopped from body to body in order to preserve its life. As she understood it, Qin's peculiar needs sucked the heat out of the host body he inhabited until it actually froze. This freezing was a problem for him, and had been ever since he had been born, in 210 B.C.

Spotting an opportunity to get rid of a bad client and provide services for a new one, Lilah Morgan had conspired behind Alex Liang's back to give his mortal body to Qin. Upper management had approved, and Lilah was praised for her cleverness and initiative.

"Here are Liang's credentials," Lilah said, approaching the great Chinese immortal. She was afraid to touch him, but she didn't reveal that as she placed Liang's birth certificate, passport, and several driver's licenses on an ornately carved jade dish. "And a snapshot of his financial situation." The report was contained in a large wooden box, which she began to heft from a cart she had wheeled into the room.

The new Alex Liang snapped his fingers. At once, the ungainly demon-monkey creature that had accompanied him scampered toward the box and grabbed it. The monkey-demon was a hairy, ugly thing, about five feet tall, with a stubby snout and curled fangs. Its eyes were completely black, and they gleamed with malicious idiocy. Lilah had no idea why it was there, and she was worried that it might relieve itself on the brand-new Persian rug she had placed beneath her desk.

"No, no," Liang said to the monkey-creature. Wagging his finger, he nodded at one of the six Mongolian bodyguards who had also accompanied him, wordlessly ordering the man to take the box. Like Lilah and the monkey thing, none of the guards had been allowed to witness his transformation. Lilah had been sorely tempted to try to tape the event, but he had warned her not to pry.

It was a warning she had decided to heed.

"You will deliver a female with Dark Blood to my address?" he queried.

"Of course." Lilah inclined her head. Now that he had successfully accomplished his body-hop, he wished to have the same service provided for his lover, the immortal woman named Xian. She was also a Possessor. Lilah was hoping to accompany the unlucky female host she had in mind to the fabulous underground temple Qin was constructing near Universal Studios.

"My guards will accompany her," Qin informed her. "No one else." He looked at her pointedly. Then he checked his watch. "I have some business with Mr. Manners."

Shucks. I won't get to see the temple after all.

She inclined her head. "As you wish, Most Honorable Qin."

"Call me Alex." He flashed her a bright, false smile. "And make sure Xian's new body is hot. I like her hot. And Chinese."

"Hot." Lilah nodded. "And Chinese. Of course."

He gave her a condescending wink. "That's my girl."

Then he reached out a hand and patted her butt.

9

Lilah gritted her teeth and smiled. "Of course I am."

"Our business is concluded, then. I'll tell Holland how well you performed your assignment."

"Thank you. It was an honor, Most Honorable Qin," she replied, bowing low.

"Of course it was." He cocked his head, appraising her. "A pity you are not Chinese. I would be tempted to arrange for Xian to take your body. You do possess Dark Blood, did you know that? It's very rich, very strong."

I have Dark Blood? I'm not sure if that's a good thing, Lilah thought. *Maybe that's why I ended up working for Wolfram & Hart. The senior partners must know I have it.*

With a flourish, Qin swept toward the door. One of the guards picked up the body bag Lilah had provided per his instructions. It had been lying on her couch, and she assumed that Qin's old body had been stashed inside it.

"Would you like a gurney for that?" she asked the Yellow Emperor.

"No."

Then he left, taking his guards, his body, and his disgusting pet with him. As soon as the door slammed shut, Lilah got down on her hands and knees and sniffed her carpet. *Damn it.* Her nose wrinkled in disgust at the odor of urine. The ugly monkey had peed on it.

Then she checked her couch. Thankfully, there were no stains and no odor from the cadaver.

At least he dies clean—which is more than I can say for a lot of our other clients.

Crossing back to her desk, Lilah buzzed her secretary. Her name was Janet Ming and she was so hot, she practically set her chair on fire every time she sat down. Even better, she carried Dark Blood in her veins. Lilah had sent a vial of her blood to be analyzed in the Wolfram & Hart labs. Janet hadn't thought a thing about it; most Wolfram & Hart contracts had to be signed in blood, and withdrawals were a common occurrence among the staff.

"Janet, would you come in here a sec?" Lilah asked her sweetly on the speakerphone.

"Of course, Ms. Morgan," Janet replied.

"Good. Oh, and page janitorial."

"Yes, Ms. Morgan."

Lilah disconnected, opened the top drawer, and pulled out a hypo. As she pressed on the plunger to make sure there were no air bubbles, a pang of regret made her sigh.

Janet was the best damn secretary she had ever had. Replacing her would be a challenge.

"But I'm always up for a challenge," Lilah murmured. At the sound of the opening door, she hid the syringe behind her back and turned to face Janet. The petite secretary was carrying a Chinese-style cup of steaming green tea.

"You're here so late," she said to Lilah. "Thought you could do with a little pick-me-up."

"Oh, you're so good," Lilah grieved. "Please put it on my desk."

As the beautiful woman complied, Lilah stuck Janet in the back of the neck with the hypo and caught her as she fell.

Three hours later, the fabulous young woman named Janet Ming was no more. At least, not on this earthly plane.

The Possession had not gone smoothly, however. Sometimes it was difficult for Xian to Possess her new body. This had been one of those times, a fact that Qin did not hold against the exquisite Lilah Morgan. There was no way to tell when it would be easy and when problems would arise. Qin's court sorcerer, Fai-Lok,

11

was researching it. But he had not yet unraveled the mystery.

Freezing was a problem for both Qin and Xian, and it was growing worse for both of them. They had to body-hop more often now, and it was becoming difficult to find people with Dark Blood to Possess. His request that Xian hop into a woman of Chinese descent was based on personal preference, not necessity. But Dark Blood was a requirement. Without Dark Blood, there could be no Possession.

Be that as it may, the body-hop had exhausted Xian, and she was going to be out of commission for the rest of the evening. Qin tried to amuse himself with observing the construction of his vast temple complex, but he was restless. So he took his personal bodyguards and one of Alex Liang's many limousines on a long tour of L.A.

He grinned as he surveyed the streets from behind the tinted and heavily warded windows. What an evil city! What dissolute inhabitants! As Fai-Lok had promised, it would be a perfect site to initiate his war against the humans who infected this plane.

In three years, it would be the Year of the Hot Devil, the sixth since his dynasty had fallen to brigands and thieves. All signs pointed to victory this time. He had failed five times; he would not fail again.

He cruised the neighborhoods, traveling from the luxurious high-rises to the seedy downtown district. Whores plied their trade; neon signs blinked and flashed. He smelled drugs, but no opium.

"Pull over," he said to his limo driver, who had no reason to suspect that he was not driving that night for his old boss, Alex Liang. The presence of unfamiliar bodyguards was no cause for alarm. Wealthy men changed security staff as often as they traded on the stock exchange.

The man did as he was asked, and Qin turned to his body-guards, saying, "Wait here. I want to walk alone."

The six men seated on either side and facing him frowned as one, and he laughed and said, "I'll return in half an hour. If I don't, you have my permission to look for me."

They were not assuaged in the least, but Qin didn't care.

He got out and started to walk, enjoying the click of his heels on the pavement. He loved being alive. He loved the advances of civilization. He had to admit that there were advantages to having been forced from power two-thousand-plus years ago. It had allowed him to move like a maverick through time. He had learned how to change and adapt, to shed his outdated habits and ways of doing things as easily as his bodies.

He paused at a crosswalk and looked around lazily, idly wondering which way to go. He decided to hang a left. A single car drove past. He loved the sound of its tires.

A sign to his right read JERICHO ICE HOUSE. He heard a radio and the noises of someone moving around.

He walked into the alley and found the back door. It was unlocked; he pushed it open and went in.

A man was bending over an open container. His back was to Qin. He reached his hand toward the container . . .

. . . and started shaking. Then he began to scream.

Fascinated, Qin cocked his head.

The man glowed from head to toe, a living ember. Then his skin blackened and cracked apart, revealing veins of glowing heat.

With a bellow of agony, he ignited, becoming a human torch, and toppled over, crackling and sizzling. If he wasn't dead, he would be, soon.

As Qin watched, a beautiful woman sat up inside the box and looked at the charred skeleton with a worried look on her face.

13

Her cheekbones were flared, and she had a ridge across her brow. Her hair was long and red, like fire.

Demon? he wondered.

She was panting; her back was glowing—no, wait, it was not her back, it was her spine—and when she saw Qin, she got out of the box and raised her palm.

Something emerged from her and blasted straight at him. It hit him square in the chest, flinging him backward.

By the God of Thunder!

He felt heat, tremendous heat, deep inside his body. For a moment his new heart threatened to cook, and his blood to boil. And then, whatever it was that made him who he was, whatever it was that gave him the terrible freezing problem, cooled the blood until it was luxurious and warm and pleasant.

He felt fantastic. Different. Changed in some way.

The woman was clearly shocked. Wide-eyed, she backed away from him, shaking her head and looking down at her hand as if contact with him were burning her in turn.

"You . . . you should be dead," she said. In English.

He replied, also in English, "In a way, I am."

Then he advanced on her, catching her wrist, and demanded, "Who are you? What are you?"

"I . . . I . . ." She yanked on her hand, looking wildly around, then back at him. "Is Jhiera coming?"

"Who?" he asked.

"Oh, no," she moaned. She yanked again, starting to panic, gritting her teeth as he held her fast. "I thought she would be here. I've made a mistake!"

"No, you haven't," he assured her. "Come with me. I can offer you sanctuary." He gripped her other wrist and moved in close, his body against her. "That heat. Give it to me again."

14

"Please!" the woman cried, struggling against him. "Let me go!"

"Give me heat," he urged her, hoping to agitate her into attacking him. "Heat. I crave it. I need—"

"Let her go," a voice behind him commanded. "Now."

Without releasing his captive, he turned to see a woman rather Asian in appearance, her hair dark and her eyes nearly black, but with the same strange ridges on her face as the woman in his grasp. She was wearing abbreviated leather clothing, revealing a taut, muscular body. She was clearly a warrior of some sort.

He took a step toward her, towing the other woman with him.

"Don't come any closer," the warrior warned him, shifting her legs as she assumed a defensive posture. "And let her go."

He glanced down at his hand around the wrist of the red-headed woman. Then he smiled lazily at the dark-haired woman said, "Or you'll do what?"

As an answer, she raised her palm, as the other woman had done, and slammed more heat energy into his body. The force sent him flying, and his hostage ducked behind the other woman. *Sublime! By the God of Thunder, I am renewed! Transformed!*

Deliciously warm, from head to toe, the parts of him that had begun to cool crackled as if with a blast of dragon's breath. Health and longevity coursed through him. Heat rippled off him in waves. He looked down at his hands; his skin was red and glowing.

He touched his face. His demonic aspect had erupted, revealing horns and fangs.

He grinned at her.

Her reaction was even more comical than the other woman's. Goggle-eyed, she blurted, "You're not human."

"That makes several of us, here in this city," he replied, putting on his human face again Then he cocked his head and said, "And I think you and I need to talk." He held out his hand. "My name is Qin. What's yours?"

Uneasily, she crossed her arms over her chest. "Jhiera," she said stiffly. "Of Oden Tal."

CHAPTER ONE

Los Angeles, Three Years Later

There are all these stories about holes.

Dig one deep enough, you're supposed to reach China.

Dig a little less, there are tar pits, tunnels, subways systems, sinkholes, and caverns.

Graves.

Tombs.

Also, hell.

Just down the hill from Universal Studios in Los Angeles, there was a Metro stop. Escalators and stairways traversed the warrens of subway lines as passengers debarked the shiny red trains. Most of the passengers were people who couldn't afford cars, but the occasional movie executive rode now and then, for the novelty; a college professor or two, to make a statement about ecology; and the occasional minion of an evil overlord, late for the big ritual to herald in the Year of the Hot Devil.

Eric Chu hurried out of the northbound Metro. He was covered in sweat; Los Angeles was in the grip of a heat wave. The heat was important to Qin, evil master of all he surveyed, to whom Eric had pledged his eternal loyalty. The Santa Ana was declared a favorable portent. The joss had been tossed, the stars consulted: The time for action had come.

It was also important to Eric's true master, Fai-Lok, Qin's court sorcerer. The word had been passed: Fai-Lok was about to make his move against Qin, and his loyal followers had to be ready to strike twenty-four/seven.

Which, okay, apocalyptic warfare, history midterm . . .

Eric wore baggy shorts and a UCLA T-shirt. He carried a small black leather satchel stamped with the chop of the Ice Hell Brotherhood: a diamond of ice surrounded by flames shaped into lotus petals. Inside the satchel lay his precious red ceremonial robe.

Fai-Lok had ordered all his followers to sew protective golden amulets into their robes by the light of the full moon to ward off all forms of harm to the lower belly, where the life force, or qi, was centered.

Eric had sewn in a couple of extra amulets. He needed a lot of protection. What he was doing was dangerous in the extreme. Though he had sworn a blood oath of allegiance to Qin's tong, the Ice Hell Brotherhood, he had secretly thrown in his lot with Fai-Lok's supersecret Hellmouth Clan. Eric had a very simple reason for doing so, and her name was Maria del Carmen Maldonaldo Alcina. She was his chick, and she was *hot*.

Fai-Lok had revealed that in the brave new world Qin planned to create, there would be no human beings left alive except for

18

those of Chinese ancestry. Maria's family was Hispanic. If Qin succeeded in his plan, Maria would be toast.

He couldn't let that happen.

Using the magicks that Qin's magicians had taught the members of the Ice Hell Brotherhood, Eric took a breath, waved his hand, and became invisible.

In the Metro stop, columns were decorated with painted tiles illustrating the founding of Los Angeles. No one else but Eric could see the ornately carved door in the center column that glowed and shimmered like a desert mirage.

With a hand no one else could see, he pushed it open.

He couldn't prevent the vertigo that overwhelmed him as he stared downward into nothingness. Swallowing hard, he took a step into space.

Invisible forces cradled him in their palms. He felt their solidity and relaxed a little. Then he stood with his legs spread to balance himself as they carried him downward.

Below him, his brother monks in their scarlet robes were assembling for the ritual. From this great height their eager murmuring reminded Eric of bees.

The temple blazed with color—carved-jade columns; the vast football-field-size floor a free-form mosaic of fire and smoke; a huge elaborate balcony overlooking it all, the work of master craftsmen who had been killed upon its completion. The colors were crimson, bright orange, and the deep red hue of a fresh kill. Row after row of ancient statues of six-feet-tall Chinese warriors in their battle gear reached from the floor to the cavernous ceiling a hundred feet into the air, aligned in carved shelves like chess pieces. Their faces were obscured by rolling, oily black smoke. A harsh burning scent permeated the room, a languorous undertone to the many competing odors of incense, perfumes, and terror.

19

Statues of dragons carried enormous braziers in their heads. Charcoal and wood simmered inside, making their eyes glow. Modern outdoor heaters were stationed everywhere, and the heat was nearly unbearable.

Eric touched down and ducked into one of the corridors and ran to the banks of lockers provided for the monks. Quickly he unzipped his satchel and donned his robes, placing his street clothes and satchel into his locker. He was sweating like a pig and felt a little sick from the heat.

The great gong rang out over the cavern as Eric joined the throngs. He craned his neck to stare up at the balcony carved from stone, where Qin would soon appear to the masses.

Rows of monks and beautiful maidens dressed in red robes proceeded onto the balcony, dipping hands protected with barbecue gloves into bowls of glowing embers, which they scattered on the stone floor. Qin's gig came fully accessorized with loyal followers. God, if he ever found out what Fai-Lok was up to . . . Eric shuddered and tried to stop imagining the various ways Qin might torture Fai-Lok to death.

Fai-Lok, and all his friends and relatives. And followers . . .

High-ranking politicians from several Asian nations and innumerable celebrity guests swept in next, as well as the upper echelon of the Ice Hell Brotherhood. They were surrounded by bodyguards carrying Uzis across their chests. Many of the guards were Mongolians, said to be Qin's original ancestry.

Soon, more than a hundred bodies filled the overhanging balcony. Almost a thousand monks watched on the floor below.

Then, more enormous heaters were pushed onto the overhang by bald slaves who looked like professional wrestlers. Eric was continually astonished at the Great Immortal's need for heat.

"The Most Celestial Qin approaches!" boomed a voice over the PA system. "May he live a hundred thousand years!"

The roars around Eric were thunderous as more bald slaves appeared, carrying a gaudy sedan chair through the applauding crowd on the balcony. A man wearing the golden Dragon Mask sat on the chair, waving to his followers. It was the great Qin.

The sedan chair was fashioned of gold and jade, made to resemble a flying dragon. Eric had been told it was a copy of the original, which had been destroyed in the Great Fire that had leveled Qin's palace a millennia ago.

All the onlookers fell to their knees and kowtowed, foreheads pressed to the floor, palms outstretched.

Wearing a perfectly cut tuxedo, still Possessing the body of multimillionaire Alex Liang, Qin adjusted his Dragon Mask and greeted his followers with outstretched hands. Then he snapped his fingers and the sedan chair of Xian, his lover and soul mate for centuries, began its journey to the center of the overhang from the opposite side.

Xian was beautiful today, in a brilliant red Versace gown and rubies around her neck and at her ears, her ebony hair pulled up and coiled around her immense Dragon Crown of emeralds and jade. He had first placed that crown on her head—a different head, of course, but still very Chinese—in Cathay, in 1632.

But Xian remained Xian. She was hot-tempered and lustful, relentless and driven. Her life energy—her qi—blazed like a comet. Even at this distance, he could feel it. It fed him.

Though he still Possessed Alex Liang's body, Xian had been through four female bodies since then. Xian's freezing problem was worsening. And unlike Alex, the blasts of heat energy from the Oden Tal women had not helped prolong the Possession of any of her host bodies. In fact, it had fatally damaged Janet Ming's, forcing Xian's into an emergency body-hop that had nearly ended her life.

Fai-Lok will figure it out, he thought, smiling at Xian. She dipped her head in reply. *I have to concentrate on my destiny.*

At a clap of his hands, two towering Dragon Thrones appeared from recesses in the floor of the vast balcony, rising up on hydraulic lifts. Qin and Xian rose from their chairs and climbed onto their thrones, towering above their followers.

As Qin switched on his body mike, he stood and stretched out his hands. The cheering stopped at once. His followers were well trained, and they knew what to expect if they disobeyed his commands.

"My brothers, my dear brothers," he said, beaming at the monks, at the courtiers, and at the bodyguards. "Welcome. Our time is at hand. The stars speak to us of success. Let's usher in the Year of the Hot Devil!"

The crowd went wild. He let the sound wash over him, basking in their adulation. The ones who didn't love him were terrified of him.

Works for me, either way.

"We have been promised a victory!" he shouted. "We will rule this dimension again!"

He raised his hands above his head, urging the monks to scale new heights of frenzy. The walls shook. The balcony vibrated.

It's a great day to be a power-hungry demigod!

A sweating, quaking Eric tried to cheer along with the other monks, but his throat was sandpaper.

What the hell am I doing? he thought as he stared up at the man who wore the Dragon Mask. He looked at the presidents of countries standing alongside world-famous Asian movie stars. At dictators and princes. *I'm just a Chinese kid from Glendale. I don't care what Fai-Lok has planned for the*

Hellmouth Clan. We can never hope to defeat this guy. He's all-powerful; he probably knows about us. He's probably going to round us up during this ritual and . . . and kill us!

He had to get the hell out of there.

Panicking, he turned away from the balcony and tried to push through the crush of monks. No one could give way; they were packed in tight. Faces stared back at him in horrid fascination as he realized he was creating a scene.

"Dude," one monk hissed. "What the frick is wrong with you?"

Eric was spinning out of control. He turned left, right, bruising shoulders as he did so, jostling guys who pushed back at him, one muttering, "Chill, man," and another, "Do you want to get us all killed?"

"You there! What are you doing? Where are you going?" Qin demanded, his amplified voice ringing in Eric's ears. "Who is that man? Bring him to me!"

The cheering of the throng died away. The room fell silent.

Everyone—*everyone*—looked at Eric.

There was a stir of abject terror among the monks. Few approached the Dragon Throne and lived.

Three monks crammed around Eric grabbed him. They were pale and nervous, as afraid to come near Qin as Eric was.

Then one of them muttered, "Sorry, bro."

The second one blinked rapidly, as if he was about to pass out, and hissed, "Brought it on yourself, you moron."

Eric went numb, feeling little as they dragged him through the crowd.

At the right front corner of the great cavern, a heavily armed, expressionless guard took Eric from his relieved captors, who bowed low and scurried anxiously back into the crowd. The big beefy man pushed Eric into an elevator and stood behind him. The two whooshed upward toward the balcony.

Oh, my God, I'm going to die, Eric thought. *I pissed off Qin. But I won't tell him that Fai-Lok is a traitor. I won't say a word about the Hellmouth Clan.*

Hell I won't! I'll spill my guts if it'll save me. . . .

As the elevator door opened, he heard Qin's voice booming across the cavern. The reverberation added to the atmosphere of total power, and Eric closed his eyes for a second to keep from throwing up.

". . . and now I'll show you the secret weapon that will help restore us to greatness! Our allies will bring us the heat that we need to burn away the chaff and leave the wheat!"

The guard pushed Eric out of the elevator, forward through the mass of people on the overhang. *Help me, help me, please,* he silently begged each face he saw. But they stared back at him haughtily, impassively, with no trace of pity.

Better you than me, their expressions said. *You dumb bastard.*

Then he was thrown to the floor. It was superheated, and blisters formed on his skin. He clenched his teeth, unknowingly biting through his upper lip until he tasted blood.

Freaking, he stared down at an approaching pair of high-heeled black leather boots. He raised his head.

A dark-haired, dark-eyed woman appraised him. Her face was very human, save for a vaguely reptilian ridge on the sides of her face. Her eyes were almond-shaped; she looked Asian, like him.

One of the guards jerked him to his feet. The woman reached out a hand. She looked straight into his eyes, and for a moment he thought he saw there the compassion of the Goddess of Mercy, Kwan Yin.

Then something happened. Something billowed out from her palm and slammed into his body.

There was a collective gasp on the balcony.

Inside, his heart felt . . . warm.

Then hot.

Hotter.

He screamed with agony. The pain was unbelievable. It flashed into his arms and legs, and then his torso and his stomach and his heart . . . his heart . . .

I'll tell you everything, he begged, unable to speak. His insides were melting. *I'll tell you! I'll tell you!*

Then Eric Chu's heart burst into flame. His blood boiled. His skin crackled away; his eyeballs burst.

He was dead long before he became a cinder.

Which may have been due to the amulets he had sewn into his robe.

Or may have not.

In any case, note was taken by one and all, including the other followers of Fai-Lok, seeded among the thousand monks gaping at the spectacle, sickened and terrified.

I love it, Qin thought, pleased, as the young monk burned from the inside out. The kid's skin split and glowed; it happened fast, but it was lovely, like the fireworks of centuries past. Burning from the inside out. *I'll never get tired of this kind of death.*

With a wave of his hand, he encouraged the monks to voice their approval of the kid's death. The cavern shook with their shouts as one of their own went up in flames.

One of Qin's Mongolians stepped forward with a simple broom and a dustpan. He swept up the boy's ashes and deposited them into the nearest brazier like so much mess.

Qin grinned at Xian, who pressed one long, lacquered fingernail against her brilliant red lips. Her eyes gleamed. She was as turned on by the experience as he had been.

It's going to be awesome when we go to bed tonight. . . .

"This woman's people have pledged their loyalty to us!" Qin announced as he pointed to his lovely executioner. She raised her fist above her head and stood at attention, moving to salute every corner of the cavern.

"First we'll burn Los Angeles to the ground! Then we'll savage the rest of this country and I swear as your leader that before the Year of the Hot Devil is halfway over, we will conquer this dimension!"

The monks went berserk. They stamped on the floor and pounded their fists, screaming his name as if he were a rock star. "Qin! Qin!"

If he closed his eyes, he could imagine he was back in China, on the original Dragon Throne, in his glory days, when he had burned all the books in the library and all the men who had hidden them from him. Thousands of books, thousands of scholars.

I thought so small then, he reflected, amused.

"We will strike down our enemies and burn them into ashes!" he continued. "And we'll start with Angel and the Slayer!"

Then he ripped off his Dragon Mask as the demon blood rose in him and took over. His large, green horns shot from Alex Liang's head. His face elongated and became green and leathery; his eyes slanted into two thin lizard-slits that glowed scarlet. Fangs sprouted and curled, the points of the lower ones grazing his batlike snout. His demon hair grew white and lustrous, burying the short, wavy black hair of his host.

Xian changed, too, becoming his demonic consort. Her hands were talons; wings sprouted from the back of her dress. She stood on her throne so that the masses could see her in all her terrible glory.

The masses cheered and applauded, chanting, "Qin! Xian! Qin! Xian!"

They cheered for nearly an hour.

In their midst, a young man named Dane Hom sweated and spoke to the demon god Lir, who lived inside his mind: *I am yours, Dark Lord, I and your other followers. We still serve you, and only you.*

Then he closed his eyes and added, *Keep me from the flames, I beg of you. Save me from the heat.*

And from the icy confines of his body's prison, and the vast reaches of his ruined dimension of Sol, the great demon Lir replied: *I will save you. Listen for my orders. Soon you will march.*

Soon everyone but you and the others will be ashes.

Angel, standing in the Universal City Metro station, waiting for an informant to arrive on the next subway train, cocked his head and thought, *Am I hearing something?*

Then a dark-skinned kid with a cranked-up boom box sidled up next to him and wheedled, "Hey, man, you got a extra quarter for the Metro? I lost my wallet and I need to go pick up my paycheck. I don't want to miss the train, because they're holding the check for me and—"

"The ticket machines are upstairs," Angel cut in. "Trains come every ten minutes."

"Oh, right," the kid blurted, with a look that said, *busted.* "Right."

He stood beside Angel until the train came, and then they both boarded the fifth car together. Angel sat down beside a window and put his Roberto's plastic take-out bag on his lap. It was no business of his if the kid was scamming a free ride. The fine was high, though, if he got caught.

Where's Aristide? he wondered, gazing around at the other passengers. He didn't see the Frenchman anywhere. Aristide was supposed to provide some information on a vampire who had been draining people who worked in L.A.'s garment district. "Fashion victims," Aristide had joked.

Angel had not so much as cracked a smile.

Someone told the kid to turn off his boom box, which he did. Then he glanced over at Angel, frowning past him to the window. He moved his head left, right; Angel realized he was looking for Angel's reflection in the window.

He looked straight at the kid.

The kid blinked and said, "Oh. Um, hey. Hope I got the right train. Where you going?"

"Hell, probably," Angel told him.

"Ha." The kid grinned. "Hey, me too, man." He bobbed his head. "Gonna be crowded down there."

"You got that right," Angel replied.

Something in Angel's look must have weirded out the kid. He looked away and started singing softly to himself, which made Angel wonder about the yelling that he had almost heard.

Subterranean? he wondered. *Or something from that kid's boom box?*

"Who were you listening to?" he asked the kid.

"Kane," the kid replied. "Awesome group. Lead dude used to be a lawyer."

"Huh," Angel said. He tapped his fingers on the sack—tacos, a present for Fred—and thought, *I'll ask Lorne if he knows that group's work. See if there's something on a CD that sounds like what I heard.*

The kid looked at Angel and said, "Are you a lawyer, man?"

Angel frowned at him. "Do I look like a lawyer?"

"No," the kid confessed. He looked a little shy. "You just act like you know what you're doing."

And there was a moment where the kid let down his bravado; and Angel remembered being that young and that confused. What it was like to have to put on an act just to get through the day.

He saw that the kid's low-slung jeans were frayed, and his running shoes were ragged. He noticed how thin the kid was.

My father told me every day that I wouldn't amount to anything.

And he thought of Connor, and his guts twisted inside.

The next stop was coming up. *Aristide's not going to show,* Angel realized. *I'll double back and get my car.*

As he rose, he handed the plastic bag to the kid and said, "Have some tacos."

The kid looked surprised; he stammered, "H-hey, it's cool, man." But when Angel kept his hand extended, he took the sack.

His eyes darted to the contents, and Angel saw the hunger there. He saw this kid wondering how he was going to get through life. If he had the stuff to survive on the mean streets, get out, and get it going.

As the subway slowed, he got up and exited the train. Walking away, he glanced over his shoulder.

The kid was laying into a taco as if he hadn't eaten in a week.

Sunnydale

Sunnydale High School had had an evil coach before. Mr. Marin, the swim coach, had exposed his Sunnydale Razorbacks to a weird steroid that turned them into fish monsters. Coach

29

Larry Wong figured he was simply carrying on a fine old tradition by exploiting his ballplayers for his own personal gain.

That meant recruiting most of the football team and their friends into the Hellmouth Clan, a secret society dedicated to declaring war on the Slayer.

"We are the future!" Larry had exhorted them. "We're a team, on and off the field. The Slayer's only in the game for her own personal glory. She won't keep any of you safe from any of the bad stuff that happens around here! Remember what happened to the old high school? It'll happen again, if you trust her!"

The kids bought it. Larry had been diligently building the Hellmouth Clan until there were more than a hundred members. Most of them were Sunnydale High School and U.C. Sunnydale students. A few were college hangers-on and disaffected youth, the kind who bagged it and left town without too much advance warning. All of them were afraid of dying. Larry promoted diversity in the secret tong, since his master, the sorcerer Fai-Lok, had assured him that there would be no discrimination in the new world order. That was the reason Larry joined up. Fai-Lok had convinced him that in the final battle between the Hellmouth Clan and the Ice Hell Brotherhood, the only hope for non-Chinese human beings was the Hellmouth Clan's victory. "The Chinese-only card is Qin's, not mine," Fai-Lok had told Larry. "I'm your only chance to have non-Chinese friends and loved ones spared from certain death."

Though Fai-Lok was a sorcerer, he looked like an ordinary Chinese guy. Larry knew that appearances could be deceiving. The Slayer herself was a delicate little thing. But he'd seen her in action. She could snap a fullback's neck with one hand if she felt like it.

At least, that's what Larry kept telling his fullbacks.

The two had first met two years ago, in the Sunnydale pub called the Lucky Pint. Fai-Lok, Qin, and Xian had arrived in town to investigate the lay of the land . . . and to see just what kind of power the current Slayer possessed.

They found her to be formidable. It was going to be a challenge to take her out.

Qin—*also a normal-looking guy, but Xian, whew! What a babe!*—had invited Larry to found a local cell of the Ice Hell Brotherhood, and he had agreed. Then Fai-Lok approached him later with his private deal, which meant replacing the Ice Hell Brotherhood with Fai-Lok's own secret society, the Hellmouth Clan.

"I'm going to let Qin believe we're going to distract the Slayer with her own local war while he takes over Los Angeles," he told the coach. "But the truth is, I'll launch our war from here. I have operatives in the home cell of the Ice Hell Brotherhood who will seize possession of Qin's secret weapon and transport it to us. It's the dragon, Fire Storm. There is nothing more powerful on earth than this dragon. And she's going to fight for us," Fai-Lok continued.

He convinced Larry. Larry got busy and built the Hellmouth Clan into a large network of minions. He was a good recruiter—coaches had to be—and he was feeling very satisfied with the game plan.

Then about a month ago Fai-Lok changed the rules.

"The Year of the Hot Devil has begun," he said to Larry on the phone one night. "By the Full Moon of Fire Storm, you need to have a hundred sacrifices ready."

"*Sacrifices?*" Larry had repeated, his voice cracking.

"You're getting off easy. In China, we have to use a thousand to get the portal generated."

31

"But what about the Slayer?" Larry protested. "She'll start investigating. What if she finds out about us?"

Fai-Lok chuckled. "Be resourceful, Coach. Take the homeless, the runaways. People no one will miss. Not even the Slayer."

"The Slayer doesn't work that way," Larry argued.

"Don't be so idealistic. She's human. She can't save everyone. She has to prioritize."

That was when Larry balked and tried to get out. But it was like being in the Mafia: Once you were in, you were in. There was only one way out—and that was as a sacrifice himself.

So Larry did as he was ordered.

He had less than three months to round up a hundred people to kill.

He got busy.

Her name was Roxanne Ruani, and she had just had a terrible fight with her boyfriend, Johnny Heybeck. Johnny wanted her to help him rob a liquor store, but she was done with drinking. And stealing, too. Her probation officer had gotten her into a 12-step program, and she was doing great.

"Jerk," she muttered to herself as she stomped out of the Fish Tank, where she and Johnny had gone to shoot pool. She was a little anxious being around all the booze, but Johnny had some bets to collect on and he said he would be lonely without her.

But the guys Johnny was waiting for didn't show up, and he was busted flat. No coinage meant bad visitors would be coming for him, and he started sweating. And drinking. In her 12-step program, they warned people about HALT: don't get hungry, angry, lonely, or tired.

They should have added T for "terrified for your life." That was real incentive for getting wasted.

After a few beers, he came up with the liquor store idea. Roxanne told him no way, and he told her to get the hell out of his life.

So she was doing just that, crying and walking down the street in the roughest part of Sunnydale, feeling stupid and sorry for herself and wishing something would happen to magickally whisk her away from there.

Then a nice-looking man slowed down his car and unrolled his window. He stuck his head out of the window and said, "Are you in trouble?"

She recognized him. She had seen him around town. He was the football coach at the new Sunnydale High.

Figuring he was safe, she nodded. "I am in trouble," she said. "Can you give me a lift?"

"Of course."

He opened the passenger door, and she slid in. Sensing a willing ear and a lot of sympathy, she opened up about Johnny and began to cry.

"So . . . no one knows where you're going right now?" he asked her.

"No. No one cares. My parents are scumbags. I'm on my own tonight. That stupid Johnny!" She cried harder.

"Okay. That's good," Larry told her. Then he put a rag over her mouth, and she sucked in some kind of fumes; as she struggled she started seeing double, and then she saw nothing.

When she woke up she was locked in a metal cage about the size of a dump truck in an underground cavern. She was trapped with about twelve other people, strangers to her. They were homeless types, scrawny and smelly, and they stared at her with dull eyes.

"Where the hell am I?" she cried, lunging at the bars.

"I think it *is* hell," said a toothless old man who smiled wildly at her. He rocked himself back and forth, staring straight at her. Then he nodded. "Yep. Hell."

Roxanne started screaming until a figure in a red robe appeared from the darkness and barked at her to shut up. It was a guy, and he sounded like he was about sixteen. The other people in the cage warned her to stay the hell away from him, and to do exactly as he told her.

"He's the Devil," the toothless old man explained. "He'll beat you senseless. I came in here with twelve teeth," he told her. "Now I got none."

"Why? What's going on?" Roxanne asked him, sobbing.

"We were evil.". The man's smile grew. "And now we're payin' for our sins, little sister. Glory hallelujah, Devil's gonna chew us up and spit us back out. It's the way of the world."

He cackled maniacally.

"It's gonna be a hot time in the old town tonight."

CHAPTER TWO

Sunnydale

It was slaying time, and the living was . . . on fire.

But not in a good way.

For slayers and other living things, it was hotter than hell in Sunnydale. The desert-scorched wind of a Southern California–style Santa Ana raced through the town like a crazed demon with a torch. Havoc was on the menu. Mayhem was for dessert. It was so hot that spontaneous combustion was not out of the question.

In the nearby woods the underbrush smoked, taunting the bunnies and squirrels with the threat of a wildfire. Closer to Revello Drive, heat nibbled on the few wooden shake roofs left in town, though most had been replaced with tile. They were tinderbox delicacies, ripe for firestorms. There was no water to wet them down. As often happened in Southern California, water was being rationed.

As happened just as often, no one had taken measures since the last water rationing to prepare for disaster. No one had put in sensible landscaping to keep the threat of totally scorched earth away. Like people in any other self-respecting Southern California town, Sunnydalians loved their lush, green lawns and big honkin' shrubbery. Try to talk them out of it, feel the heat.

It was fall, but it burned like high summer. There would be no frost on the Halloween pumpkins in the little town that perched on the mouth of hell, just rotting fruit that drew flies. The Santa Ana sucked the last of the moisture from the earth, ripped out tumbleweeds and spit them ricocheting down the streets like dried-up porcupines. Bloodred autumn leaves withered as they dropped onto parched expanses of crackling brown grass and skeletal bushes.

Heat boiled off the streets and steamed in the air. Sunnydale was not a nice place to be, and people were getting pissed off and mean about being there. Even the forces of darkness were meaner, although, unlike human beings saddled with mortgages and jobs, they could just pick up and leave if they wanted to. But it was too hot even to think about.

Night brought no relief. People teetered on the edge, and a lot of them frankly jumped right over the cliff of civilized behavior, screaming all the way. Tempers didn't just flare; they ignited. Lovers didn't stop at quarreling. The ER was overflowing with stab wounds and bullet holes. Babies . . .

. . . better not go there . . .

Fans whirred uselessly; kids thought about payback. Dogs snapped at fleas and whined to be let in, to be let out, to be left alone.

It was a hot time in the old town tonight. The Devil cruised Main Street with his cool *Matrix* shades on, the top down, and Buddy Holly on the radio: "Goodness, gracious, great balls of fire!" All dressed up with places to go. Ghosts capered like smoke. Vampires got brutal. Demons reveled, knee-deep in the hoopla. The joint was jumping, and to make matters worse, tonight was a full moon. As bad as things ever got in Sunnydale, they got worse when it was full-on lunar madness.

God, just to have a break in the weather! Anyone who could get away with it slogged indoors and collapsed in a frosty shell of sweat and air-conditioning. That included the cops. It was going to take a major disaster to move those patrol cars tonight; their wheels were melting on the parking lot asphalt. Hell, the civilians got to stay at home or cool down in the bars. It was a Tuesday, must-watch TV night in Sunnydale. Iced tea, ice-cold beer, frozen margaritas, and good shows; EMTs were anxious: The threat of a rolling blackout would affect more than the Nielsen ratings if TV's and air conditioners went out. . . .

Buffy Summers, the Vampire Slayer, was not at home with iced tea, cool air, and her grumpy kid sister, Dawn, who had too much homework. Sweaty and also grumpy, Buffy crept through the Shady Hill graveyard. She was on patrol, and on her guard. Even before the Santa Ana, there had been a distinct increase in Hellmouth activity of late, and several nights of patrolling had turned up nothing to account for it. Oh sure, Buffy had dusted the occasional vamp and cut the head off a demon or three, but the victims were outweighing the villains, and that was bad news in the Slayer biz.

There were more dead and far more missing than usual, and tonight was no exception. Twenty minutes earlier, she had discovered the body of a very old man with his throat torn out, his eyes bulging, and his mouth pulled back in a rictus of pain and

37

terror, as if he had died thinking, *Wait! I'm supposed to go peacefully in my sleep, not like this, not like a savaged animal!* The sight of him had pushed Buffy over her own personal edge. It was time for a little retribution, Slayer-style, and she was not going home until she found whatever had killed that man, and made it very, very sorry, as in dead.

Death was not new to Buffy Anne Summers. Death was her stock in trade, the burb all slayers called home; though when Buffy had been Chosen, she had been calling L.A. home. Until her first Watcher, Merrick, arrived, she hadn't known anything about Watchers or Slayage. Bloodsucking vampires and demons had been the stuff that bad date movies were made of, not lifestyles.

That had all changed; Merrick had trained her as best he could before he was killed. She remembered the stomach-churning adrenaline rush of her first few kills; the horror of seeing an actual dead body. She burned down the gym at her old school, Hemery High, and her parents got divorced. All that was trauma enough. Staking vampires went beyond the beyond. She'd had nightmares. And she'd tried to get rid of them by quitting her slaying gig when she and her mother had moved to Sunnydale.

But slayers don't get to quit. They are the ultimate tragic heroes. They are dripping with symbolism about the champion's quest, not to mention dripping with green demon blood from some yicky lopped-off tentacle or exploding eyeball or something.

Slayers are Chosen, and they don't get unchosen.

That was a lot for a fifteen-year-old to handle at the time, in addition to algebra; but Buffy's next Watcher, Rupert Giles, had helped her accept her destiny and she had grown up. Now Giles was out of the country, and death had become the big comfy couch of her existence. But the rush of death-dealing was still there, and she felt it now, zinging in her blood. As she kept her focus and maintained red-alert status, her heart was still soft enough that wrongful death still moved and infuriated her.

The old man had not deserved to die that way.

Guess there was a reason I came back. Again.

Somewhere in the distance, someone was singing. Buffy listened to the high, thin voice, all fingers crossed that the singer was who—or what—had killed the old man. Buffy was hot, she was tired, and she was ready to kill something.

The singer crooned, "I've got peace like a river in my soul, in my soul."

Doubtful, Buffy thought, stake in hand. She wasn't sure if the thing she was stalking was a vampire or a different kind of demon, but it was highly unlikely that it had anything in its soul.

It was far more likely that it didn't have a soul at all. The old man had died a brutal death.

Not that the ensouled were incapable of such savagery. It was just that, this being Sunnydale, the probability that the killer was supernatural and soulless gave far better odds.

The wind whipped up, a wave of heat slicing across Buffy's cheek like a knife blade that had been held over a fire. In an almost prescient gesture, the Slayer shifted her foot to the right as she crept forward, just missing a crackle of leaves that would have announced her presence to her own particular prey.

And there it is.

In the moonlight, a little girl wearing a rotting dress sat atop a tombstone, swinging her legs back and forth as she sang the simple tune, repeating the same line over and over to herself. She appeared to be about three, in human years. Her lacy dress was a tattered mass of cobwebs and bits of fabric caked with dirt, very old-fashioned, maybe turn-of-the-century. She looked Asian, with almond-shaped eyes and high cheekbones, her hair a puddle of ink spilling over her head and across her shoulders. Whether the moonlight bleached her complexion, or her face was chalk white, Buffy couldn't tell.

As Buffy moved closer, the girl lowered her head. She was cradling something between her hands, gazing intently at it. As the child toyed with the mysterious object, something snapped and Buffy froze, assuming for a moment that she had accidentally stepped on a branch and betrayed her presence.

"I've got peace like a river . . ."

Buffy's eyes narrowed as she saw what had happened. The sound had been the breaking bones of a finger: The girl was holding a withered human hand. She had just cracked its forefinger, the arthritic knuckle a rocky bulge as if she were using the digits to count something, like daisy petals in the old rhyme that lovesick girls murmur to themselves: He loves me, he loves me not.

Then she giggled without looking up, and raised the hand palm-forward as if in greeting. As Buffy watched, the broken forefinger rose upward like a cobra and beckoned directly at the Slayer, urging her to approach.

So the girl knew Buffy was there.

Okay, Buffy thought, *bring it on.*

"*Ssssslayer,*" the girl whispered in a gravelly, menacing tone, distinctly different from her childish singing voice.

"Yo," Buffy responded.

"*Ssssslayer, it is time.*"

"Time for you to die?" Buffy hefted her stake in her grip. "Again?" She was fairly certain she had a vampire accessorized with a magickally animated Hand of Glory in her sights; but when the little girl raised her face and stared at her, she wasn't vamped out. Her eyes were completely black, but otherwise, she looked fully human.

That didn't mean Miss Muffet was not fangy. It didn't mean anything except that she probably still hadn't revealed her true face to the Chosen One. Buffy kept steady on her course; vampire or otherwise, she was gonna kill that little monster. Inhuman evil radiated off the girl like shimmering waves of heat; she was fair game for slaying, and Buffy really needed to take out something so she could go home happy. The old man needed avenging. Heat and failure both made for a cranky Slayer.

"Time for *you* to die, again," the girl replied, still with the gravelly voice. Maybe someone else who watched less TV would be impressed, but Buffy had seen that little girl in the soda commercial speak with the voice of Joe Pesci, and what was scarier than that?

"He is coming," she continued, "and we are gathering."

"Gathering? At the river?" Buffy asked her. "Who's coming?" *Might as well ask first and slay later.*

Willow could use some information about what was going on; so far, they had found no mystical convergences or special dates on the calendar to explain who was turning up the heat in the Hellmouth, so to speak. Anya had put forth the theory that demons got antsy in hot weather just like everyone else.

"Then they should just chill. Lie out, work on their tans," Dawn had argued, then quickly looked at Xander, Anya's former fiancé, and added quickly, "Joke. I fully accept the idea that Mr. Sun is not my friend. No tanning. Very unhealthy for human beings as well as vampires." Xander had been on everybody's case about wearing sunblock ever since his aunt in San Francisco had had a suspicious mole removed from her back.

"Who's coming?" Buffy asked the girl again, impatiently;

things were about to become very unhealthy for the creature on the tombstone, and in the movies, at least, the monster gave up the secret just before the hero killed it.

As if to answer, the girl reached up and pulled down the forefinger again, then snapped the middle finger in two. Then she moved to the ring finger and broke it just as deftly. The three fingers dangled downward, rippling in the wind.

"All three of them. For the two." She smiled. "And we are preparing the way for the one. 'I've got peace like a river . . .'"

"So . . . you're holding a revival?" *Three. For the two. And a one.* "Or maybe a math class?" As she spoke, Buffy surveyed the mounded grave covered with brown grass in front of the tombstone. Undisturbed. So the little girl had not risen from the grave—at least not from this place. But was there a vampire lying in the dirt beneath her feet, waiting to launch itself at the Slayer when she got close enough?

The girl smiled as if she could read Buffy's mind. Her face was angelic, her eyes large and dark.

"Why were you singing that hymn?" Buffy asked her.

"I don't know," the girl replied airily. "I just like the words. Although, to be truthful, I don't remember what it's like to have a soul."

Soul-free after all. Score one for the Slayer. "It's okay—for most," Buffy amended. "Some people, it wigs them." She thought of Spike, whose anguish had pretty much driven him crazy. She thought of Angel . . . and felt a pang.

Best to not go there. Not tonight. She had been dreaming of him so often lately, and missing him more than usual. . . .

"We who are soulless have an advantage," the girl said. She tapped the place where her heart should be, might not be. With demons, it was hard to tell if they had humanlike hearts in humanlike places—whether or not they wore human appearances.

42

"Advantage being, no conscience," Buffy filled in for her. "Everything is black and white. Or rather, all black."

The girl nodded. "Evil feeds us, and we feed it in return. And we have big appetites."

"Yeah, I'm betting you're a member of the evil Big Plate Club," Buffy shot back. "No leftovers to send to China."

"Oh, there's plenty of evil in China," the girl said, chuckling. She tilted her head. "More than you can imagine."

All right. A hint, Buffy thought, taking mental notes. *Something about a two and a three and something about China. And food. With five you get kung pao shrimp? Kung pao chicken?*

"Is that so?" she asked the little monster. "I have a pretty good imagination. But how about giving me a hint?"

"Uh-uh-*uh*," the little girl said, wagging the hand at her. "That's all you get." Then she laughed and added, "As they say, talk to the hand. You know whose hand it is, don't you?"

The old man. Damn. I hate being right.

"Why?" Buffy asked, shortcutting to the next logical question.

"We're all about magick," the girl said. "Those are all the hints you get."

Then, without warning, the creature flung the hand at Buffy, did a backflip off the tombstone, and started to run. A regular person might have been startled and let the girl get away. But Buffy was not a regular person.

She was the Slayer.

Working on a pun about going mano a mano, she batted the hand out of her way and rushed toward the tombstone, executed a deep squat, and broadjumped the six feet of brown grass before it. She landed on top of the headstone itself, and sprang at the girl. She tackled her and brought her down, hard.

43

A roar of fury behind her and the thunk of the heavy gravestone announced the emergence of something from the dirt. Something had lain in wait for her, and she'd jumped right over it.

Score two for Buffy, and all the bad guys can do is sing badly and complain.

The girl writhed in Buffy's grasp. With her frenzied movements, her rotted clothing and flesh began to drop off—*ewww*—but Buffy kept grabbing past the rapidly decomposing outer layer to the bloody layer beneath; then the layer beneath that, then her bones. Within seconds, the girl was nothing but a gristly skeleton with big black eyes, shaking and struggling; then she began to convulse. From her jaws streamed frothy drool like a dog with rabies, and her eyes turned milky white.

"He is coming," she announced in her little-girl voice. "He is the one! He will set his armies lose and overrun you! You will die!"

"Who's coming?" Buffy demanded, keeping hold even though she really, really wanted to let go and get a Handi Wipe out of her pocket.

In the next moment, the bones fell apart in Buffy's hands. The jawbone dislodged, and the upper half of the girl's skull chattered wordlessly in Buffy's grasp. The eyes dried up, and the skull was like some kind of windup toy from a joke shop, upper teeth clattering maniacally against Buffy's hand.

"Ouch!" Buffy shouted, dropping the skull.

Then something leaped from the top of the gravestone onto Buffy's back. The Slayer did a forward roll through the bones of the little girl, bringing the thing with her, then sprang to her feet.

The monster held on.

"Got your back!" cried a familiar voice.

It was Spike, who now had both a soul and a good sense of humor as well as timing. Despite the heat, the blond-haired vampire was clad in his duster, which rushed about him like great black leather wings as he circled behind Buffy and grabbed at the thing that was attempting to choke her. Staring down, Buffy registered moss-covered finger bones across her throat, clamping hard, and Spike's hands clamping over them. *Dead and deader.*

"Coming!" the thing shrieked like a bird of prey. "Teee-heeeee!"

"What is coming?" Buffy managed, although it sounded more like, "Mtt ms mmgmg?"

The stranglehold was loosened as Spike ripped the hands away; Buffy whirled around to see that it was an adult skeleton he had yanked off her and he was flinging it to the ground. He started kicking at it with his big, heavy boots, scattering the bones as Buffy cried, "Stop! No!"

"No?" He looked puzzled, gave the thing one last forceful kick, and gazed at Buffy.

She knelt down beside the skull of the attacker and bellowed at it, "Who is coming?"

But whatever animating force had filled the skeleton had left it. It lay inert beside the scattered bones of the little girl, which also did not move or speak again. It was over.

Silent night, sweltering night. Not so calm . . . blazing bright.

"What's going on?" Spike asked, shifting his gaze from the fragments to the girl he loved.

"Nothing, now." Buffy wiped moss off her neck and grimaced at it, trying to rub it off on the gravestone. "Thanks."

"My pleasure. Wot's this, then? Hand of Glory?" Spike asked, picking up the dead man's hand. He held it out to Buffy. "Souvenir for Red?"

"Spike. Willow doesn't use those." *I don't think.* However, she took the hand from him and said, "Follow me."

If the hand belonged to the dead old man, returning it to him was the best she could do for him now. Though his murderer had been . . . neutralized, the Slayer had found no satisfaction in taking her out. All Buffy had left were some questions, too much adrenaline, and the beginnings of a sinus headache. Santa Ana's did that to her.

As dry winds whipped up graveyard leaves, she crunched over them without a thought for the noise. Spike trampled along beside her, his profile etched against the darkness by the moon. It was not altogether displeasing to see.

"Let's go," she said, retracing her path toward the body of the old man. Recalling the man's throat wound, she narrowed her eyes and said, "You didn't attack anyone, did you?"

Spike looked wounded.

"Okay." She shrugged. The girl had pretty much boasted about the crime.

Spike sighed and said, "Another dead man. Far too many of those in this town." He took the hand from her and sniffed it.

"Yuck, Spike." She grimaced at him. "Show some respect. Or at least, don't be gross." Then she cocked her head, leveling her gaze at him. "Were you following me?"

"You oughtn't patrol alone," he informed her, stuffing the hand in the pocket of his duster. "Things are getting out of . . . *hand* round here." He grinned at her. "You need a *hand* with your work."

"One more pun and I'll give you the *finger*," she shot back.

The left side of his mouth pulled up in a lazy grin, and he patted the pocket affectionately. "Did you know that one of Dru's sisters told her that her baby fingers would fall off, same as her baby teeth? Then adult fingers would grow from the stumps. Put the old girl into a lather, all right. That was probably when all the madness started, not from Angel. Captain Forehead takes all the credit, but I think she was a bit dotty to start with."

His smile grew a bit more affectionate, a bit more wistful. "Wonder how she's getting on."

"If she comes here again, I'll kill her," Buffy said blandly. "There. Look." She pointed at the body. A scattering of leaves had drifted across the old man's face, one landing directly on his opened, bloodshot eye. Buffy felt a sharp pang, was very sorry—for one fleeting instant—and then sealed all that up inside so she could continue to do her job. Death was her constant companion, and she was used to making room for it in her life.

"It's his," Spike confirmed, gesturing to the man's right arm. It ended in a pulpy mess at the wrist.

He pulled the hand from his pocket and laid it beneath the wrist, shifting it an inch or two, nodding as if to confirm that this was indeed the missing bit. "What was she doing with it?"

"Same as you said about Willow. I think she was going to use it as a Hand of Glory," Buffy replied, watching as Spike knelt on one knee beside the man. "To do magicks."

"Maybe so," he agreed.

The moonlight shone on his hair, and she thought of the moon-drenched night when she had found him in the church. Spike had been at the zenith of his craziness then, utterly tormented by the soul waking up inside him. He had gone through hell to get that soul, for her. So that he could be the kind of man she would love.

Emotion for him welled in her now. It was love of a sort, but it was a gentle and sympathetic feeling. Not the kind Spike wanted—the kind with heat in it. The kind lovers share.

47

"What?" He glanced up at her, and she shrugged, not answering, not looking away either. Her life was so strange. Her heart, stranger still. Everything in her wanted to put her arms around him and do . . . what? Say what?

"What?" he asked more sharply, blinking at her.

"You guys were in China a hundred years ago," she ventured. "You, Angel, Darla, and Dru."

"The Boxer Rebellion." He sighed heavily. "Now that I've got a soul, I don't feel quite as wistful about those days." He looked downcast. "Killed a slayer, y'know."

"I haven't forgotten," she assured him. "Angel had his soul then."

Though the mention of Angel's name clearly hurt, Spike flashed her a haphazard grin. "Darla was furious with him. He wouldn't feed. I was caught up with my victories. Struttin' with bloodlust. I was new." He gazed at her, his lids hooded, his smile growing more ironic. "The Chinese say, 'May you live in interesting times.' Startin' to think that's a curse, not a blessing."

"I know the feeling," she replied sincerely.

They shared a moment. Okay, two. They were warriors both, extraordinary beings who had broken the rules even of their unruly existences, and defied heaven, if there was such a place. Two rather ordinary people once, a Valley girl and a bad Victorian poet, filled with the insecurities of their youth and their times; and now . . . there were no definitions for what they had become. Buffy was the slayer who had died twice, altering and confusing the slayer lineage: Kendra had been called, and at her death, Faith.

Spike was a vampire who had not been cursed with a soul, as Angel had been. Yet something inside his demonic nature had permitted him to love deeply enough to demand one.

48

They were alike in that; together, in their way, in their aloneness even from their own kind. There had never been a slayer like Buffy. There had never been a vampire like Spike.

A third moment then; and Buffy found herself thinking of the poem Dawn had to learn for English class. It was by Emily Dickinson, and it began, "I'm nobody! Who are you? Are you nobody, too?"

Wish I could be. Wish Spike was.

"What?" he said again, and his voice was soft.

Buffy stirred. It was time to move on.

"That bony ghost or reanimated thingie or whatever an old friend of the family, by chance?" she asked him.

He shook his head. "And I think she was more properly a wraith. A ghost that can take solid form."

"No," she told him. "I've come up against ghosts I could break before. Just like I broke her."

He shrugged. "Don't suppose it matters much. You killed her fair and square."

"I'm going to ask Willow to check it out."

"Good," Spike said.

Buffy looked at the old man, at the leaf on his eye. She reached down and picked off the leaf, which crumbled like so much dust between her fingers. He stared at her, seeing nothing. There was an old wives' tale that the last thing a person saw was recorded on his eye, and that if one knew how to look for it, one could see it. That one could see a murderer if the victim had seen him—or her—as well.

All Buffy saw now was that this man was dead.

"I wonder if he has family looking for him. If we should leave him here for someone to find or take him someplace else. Or bury him. After all, we're in a graveyard. It'd be convenient."

"Hold on." Spike rummaged through the man's pockets.

Buffy knew that in his pre-soul days, even after the Initiative put in his chip, Spike had looted the dead in search of money and cigarettes. "Look."

He held up a California state ID card, the kind that was issued if someone didn't have a driver's license. In the state where the Chevy was the state bird, one had to be a bottom-feeder or too old to drive not to have a license. "Take a look."

He showed it to her. The man's name was Elmer Freiwald. His address was the Sunnydale Rest Home, which was close by. How creepy, to have a rest home near a graveyard. Of course, with an even dozen cemeteries inside the city limits, it was kind of difficult not to have a rest home near one of them.

Or a butcher shop.

Ewww, not even thinking about that . . .

"Might have a daughter comes to see 'im on Sundays, brings the grandkids," Spike suggested, replacing the card in the man's pocket.

Or he might have spent every Sunday wishing that his daughter would come to see him, Buffy thought, feeling pensive.

"Okay," she said, "then let's take him closer, leave him where they can find him. Whoever that is, they'll probably need therapy afterward."

"Right."

Spike took off his duster and handed it to Buffy, then hoisted the man over his shoulder, fireman style. Buffy crouched down and grabbed up the hand.

The hot wind whipped up; above their heads, the dry branches rattled together like knucklebones, like the damned rolling dice. Buffy could almost hear voices:

My money's on the Slayer.

My money's not.

Armies of evil are coming.

Put me down for armies of evil, two to one.

"You're quiet tonight," Spike observed as they made their way out of the graveyard. "That little girl get your tongue?"

"Tired," Buffy replied. "Hot." She looked at Spike, who carried the dead man easily, as though he weighed less than kindling. Lightweight deadweight. "So. Maybe a wraith."

"That, or something else magickally animated, I'm guessing," he suggested. "Magick's in the air." He raised his face toward the moonlight; he looked as if he were made of alabaster. Or French vanilla ice cream. "I can feel it. Can you?"

"All I feel is the heat," she said. She reached up and swiped perspiration from her brow. "It's hotter than hell."

"Actually, it's not," Spike replied, flashing her a devilish grin. "But it's close."

Los Angeles

Jhiera of Oden Tal was furious. She stalked into Qin's private chambers as the First Chamberlain of the Ice Hell Brotherhood trailed after her. When the terrified servant crossed the threshold of the forbidden room, he flung himself to the floor and cried, "I could not stop her, my lord!"

Qin was lounging with Xian in the hot tub, which was surrounded by three white-hot iron braziers stoked with charcoal. The room was like a blast furnace.

Jhiera said, "This is not what we agreed on!" She strode to the side of the hot tub. "How dare you use one of my women to perform your macabre little sacrifice!"

Qin smiled languidly at her. He linked hands with Xian and said, "Come, join us."

She picked up a small jade dish of pickled sparrows' tongues and flung it at the wall. It smashed most dramatically. Her arrogance thrilled him.

"I'll gather my women," she informed him. "We'll leave this dimension immediately."

He chuckled. "You can't. The city is crawling with Vigories. You'll never get past them, even if you try to use portals. You and I both know you're dependent on me to provide protection for you and your followers." His smile grew. "It's an ancient form of Chinese statecraft. Keep your friends close, and your enemies closer."

"I was not your enemy!" she shouted at him. "We had a bargain!"

He looked pained. "I notice your use of the past tense. Are you my enemy now? I would hope not. Once I have use of Fire Storm, I will turn it on the Vigories. I will dethrone your father, and you will rule Oden Tal. As you so long to do." His eyes glittered as he leaned forward into the steam, inhaling it.

"Believe me, I know what it is to long to rule a vast dimension. We will both get what we want, Princess Jhiera."

"I do not long to rule," she shot back, putting her hands on her hips. "I long to keep my women free."

"You can only do that by completely altering the existence of your kind," he pointed out. "You know you must crush the opposition. There will be no peaceful coexistence between you and the established order. You will have to destroy your civilization in order to achieve your ends."

Jhiera set her jaw. "No. I am not the Bringer of Chaos."

"But you are." He shrugged. "Don't feel bad. I am too. But I promise a new world. A better world. For those who are close to me."

Grinding her heel into the pieces of jade on the floor, she narrowed her eyes and glared at him. "I was a fool to trust you."

"Please, Jhiera. You never trusted me," he countered. "But trust is not necessary between us."

She shook her head and began to pace. Her muscles rippled; her dark eyes blazed. Heat practically radiated off her. He loved to watch her move. She was like a slinky cat.

Then she stopped. "What did you promise Shiryah to ensure her cooperation with the ritual?" she demanded.

The princess spoke, of course, of Shiryah, the Oden Tal female who had burned the young man for Qin at the ceremony. He had asked her to do it, and she had complied without a single question. Pity; a waste of youthful energy, that boy's grisly and agonizing death. But discipline must be rigidly enforced. Qin had learned that in ancient China. The boy had broken ranks for some reason, and that could not be tolerated. How could he hope to mold these young men for battle if they couldn't even maintain their composure during a peaceful gathering?

Qin waved a lazy hand. "I didn't have to promise her anything. She's like the rest of your kind. A man-hater."

Clearly he hit a nerve, for she raised her hand as if to fling heat his way. Then she lowered her arm. "Lies!" she spat. "I am no murderer! I did not come to you to kill for you, Qin. I came for one reason only: to help liberate my women."

He tilted his head and regarded her with a wounded expression. "Dear Princess, have I given you any reason to believe that I will stand in your way?"

"You will not command my women to kill for you again," she said. "Or I will gather them and we will leave."

She turned on her heel.

"Where are you going?" Qin asked pleasantly.

"It is none of your business," she replied coolly. "I do not answer to you."

She slammed the door behind herself.

"Well," Xian said, amused. "We'll have to have her followed."

"Of course. Those are my standing orders," Qin replied. Then he called out, "You can come out now, Shiryah. She's gone."

The Oden Tal female stepped from behind one of the braziers. She looked moderately frightened, but more titillated, really. Her dark eyes, her fanned cheekbones—she resembled Jhiera very closely. They might have been sisters.

"Your mistress is angry with you," Qin said.

Shiryah sidled up to Xian, who reached out a hand and touched her scantily clad hip. Shiryah beamed at her and moved her body in such a way that Xian's hand caressed her.

"She's not my mistress anymore. Xian is my mistress." She smiled at Qin. "And you are my lord."

"Such loyalty," Qin drawled.

"Such affection," Xian added, trailing her fingertips along Shiryah's skin. "Such warmth." She smiled meaningfully at Qin.

"We've been hunted all our lives," Shiryah told them both. "Jhiera simply wants to raise the stakes. She joined forces with you merely to escalate our war. But you offer a new world where we will be safe."

"I'm so glad you understand that," Qin said sincerely. "Once I control this dimension, I'll shut all the portals that lead from Oden Tal to here, and the Vigories will never be able to invade this dimension again." He regarded Shiryah, his eyes shining with excitement. "Fire Storm can do it. She can destroy the portals once and for all. But I need to unfreeze her before I can use her. And to unfreeze her, I need the special heat your kind can produce."

"I understand," Shiryah said. She took a breath. "If Princess Jhiera orders us to go back to our home dimension, I'll disobey her and stay. I'll unfreeze Fire Storm myself. I can do it as well as Jhiera. I have the same power in my *k'o.*" She made a half-turn, showing them her ridged spine, which began to glow.

"She will call you a traitor. She will hunt you," Qin observed. "She won't permit you to stay behind."

"You will protect me." Shiryah smiled at the two of them. "As you love me."

"As we love you," Xian said. She gave Shiryah's hand a little tug.

Coquettishly, the Oden Tal female climbed the three stone steps that led to the lip of the hot tub. Then she took off her skimpy black leather clothing and stepped into the churning water.

She winced. "It's very, very hot," she told them.

"Yes." Qin held his arms out to her. "It is."

Sunnydale

It was almost sunset, and Troy Kelly was glad. He'd been painting the interior of a condo at the Sunnydale Spanish Landing condo complex all afternoon, and the paint fumes were making him sick. He was aching to lay down the paint roller, go outside, and have a smoke.

He heard something in the corridor and smiled, figuring it was his boss, Bill Franks, telling him to pack it in. *Quitting time. Right on.*

"That you, Bill?" he called.

There was no answer.

Anticipating a reprieve from painting, he finished up the section he was working on. He was going to have his cigarette, then load up the paint, get it back to the shop, and tonight, he and his girlfriend were going to the Sun Cinema to see a sneak of a new flick starring Nathan Fillion. She'd won the tickets from a radio station.

He heard the noise again. He stopped, cocking his head, and said, "Bill? You out there? Should I pack it in?"

He was confused. Someone was shuffling around out in the hall, but not coming in.

Damn. It might be kids, he thought. Sometimes bored high school students would sneak in and vandalize his jobs, just to be freakin' evil. More than once he'd been called back to paint something he'd just finished. No skin off his nose; he got paid twice. But it was the principle of the thing.

"You'd better not be looking for trouble," he said ominously.

He put down the roller and walked into the hall. He looked up, down.

A flash of red scooted around the corner.

"Hey!" he shouted.

Troy gave chase, heading down the corridor and hanging a right.

He ran smack into two guys wearing some kind of baggy red robes. They were both teenagers. One of them, tall and dark-haired, grabbed him around the waist while the other one stuck a gun in Troy's face.

"What the hell are you doing?" Troy shouted.

"I'm sorry, mister," the dark-haired kid murmured.

Then someone stuck a needle in Troy's arm, and the world wobbled away. His knees buckled, and as he passed out, the dark-haired kid said, "That makes ninety-five."

"This sucks," the other kid said.

Los Angeles

Were we in love?

Angel stood on the roof of a high-rise downtown office building and gazed out at the vast, glittering tears of Los Angeles

56

reflected in the skyscrapers and the black satin night. Most of the windows in the office buildings were dark. Something that might surprise tourists was that Angelenos, as a rule, went to bed early. For actors, makeup calls came at dawn; and the money guys who followed the stock market had to rise early, when New York revved up.

But the streets below still swirled with gold and rubies as headlights and brake lights crisscrossed Sunset and Hollywood; Angel could see the Chinese Theatre and, farther on, the Magic Castle, headquarters for members of the international magicians' fraternity.

He didn't know what he was looking for; he was restless and antsy. The hotel, huge as it was, had felt too small to contain him, although that didn't make sense. The Hyperion had just lost another tenant: Cordelia had left again, to stay with Connor. His son.

Were we in love?

Cordy had become his love. He had managed to move on beyond Buffy, finally, although he knew, deep in his sad and dark soul, that the brightest moments of his life had flared and died: the part of his long existence that he had shared with the beautiful blond slayer. He could handle that, most of the time; but when he was low like this, he found himself thinking of his soul mate, and missing her very much.

A human man might have thought it odd to seek comfort from one lost love in the memory of another. But Angel had lived a long time. Feelings were far more complex than most people had time to comprehend. In his youth, matters between men and women were simpler. Love was a luxury few indulged in. Life was harder, and people married in order to share its burdens and find some pleasure along the way. Women were forced to be dependent on men.

He smiled wryly. Ironic that he had wound up with the three most independent women he could think of: Darla, Buffy, and Cordelia.

Were we in love?

Oh, yes.

In his way, with each of them.

But Buffy . . . she was the one.

He stared out at the city, his coat catching a wave of wind. Streetlights and headlights wept, while Angel, dry-eyed, stood vigil.

In the hotel, Fred stared wide-eyed at the wall. She lay on her side, away from Charles Gunn, and wondered if he knew she was awake.

Wondered if he would try to touch her.

She swallowed back tears. Her throat was tight, and she felt cold inside. As if when Charles broke Professor Seidel's neck, all the warmth in her body had been sucked out of her—along with Seidel's body—into the dimensional portal Seidel had opened to get rid of her. With the floor of the professor's office bursting apart in a dervishing maw meant to devour her, she had watched Charles murder a human being.

He killed him so I wouldn't do it. Charles did it to keep me . . . innocent.

But she wasn't innocent. She wasn't giggly Fred, who came back from Pylea a little off, a little goofy. That Fred was done. That Fred had died.

The Fred who lay in this bed beside Charles was someone she herself didn't know. It was as if she were a new being inhabiting her body. She didn't feel right inside her skin. She didn't feel right beside Charles. Nothing was right anymore. It had all gone very wrong.

58

A tear formed in her eye, but did not drop.

Then Charles cleared his throat. She tensed, thinking he was about to say something.

He remained silent.

Fred stared at the wall.

Wesley Wyndam-Pryce got up from the bed in his flat. The stitches pulled across the slash on his biceps, a souvenir from the day's battle against a nest of Sisters of Jhe. He and his crew had successfully taken them out; the world was safe again, for the moment.

He studied the tousled hair streaming across his pillow, the feminine shape outlined by the thick Egyptian cotton sheet.

I risk my life to beat back the forces of darkness, and then I sleep with the enemy. . . .

He trudged into the kitchen, poured himself a glass of champagne from the silver Wolfram & Hart ice bucket, and toasted the full moon. He sipped thoughtfully, seeing his reflection in the window. The scar across his neck was visible in the light, a visible reminder that he was no longer part of Angel's inner circle, not a member of that strange, extended family.

He thought of sweet and lovely Fred across town; Fred, who was different now. More like him. Tainted, one could say. Not tainted like Lilah, certainly. Not that dirty.

He glanced in the direction of the bedroom.

No, not like Lilah.

Lilah could kill twenty college professors, rouse him to frenzied passion, and sleep afterward like a baby.

He wondered how well Fred slept these days.

With a heavy sigh, he finished off the glass. As he turned to place it on the counter, Lilah appeared in the doorway, wearing one of his shirts and nothing else. Her toenails gleamed with bloodred polish. She was heartstoppingly, breathtakingly beautiful.

"Save me any?" she purred, slinking toward him. Her perfume was musky and spicy, mingling like incense with her body heat.

He smiled grimly and gestured to the bottle. "Help yourself." She sauntered up to him and put her arms around his neck. Lilah smiled brightly at him, her dark eyes flashing, her hair tousled and wanton.

"I intend to," she told him, pressing her lips against his, her body against his. The warmth fanned from his lower belly, and she nuzzled him, eager for the heat.

And Wesley responded, needing warmth, craving it, because his world was cold and he was freezing; and he despised her for giving it to him almost as much as he despised himself.

CHAPTER THREE

Sunnydale

The night was sweltering, and the Most Honorable Fai-Lok, the Number One Court Sorcerer and confidante to the Most Celestial Qin, was comforted, at least, by that. To his everlasting irritation, he had lost Possession of the body in which he had traveled to Sunnydale less than a day ago. He had contacted the local leader of the Ice Hell Brotherhood, who was to bring him a fresh body to Possess, but not until tomorrow night. Until then, Fai-Lok had to be content with Possessing one of the terracotta warriors set up for the exhibit in the parking lot of the Sunnydale Museum of History. It was not a pleasant experience . . . but the heat made it easier to endure.

Banks of klieg lights illuminated the rows upon rows of fully armed warriors and warhorses, all rendered to Fai-Lok's specifications a millennium before in burnt orange and gray terracotta clay. They had marched against Qin's enemies, an amazing and horrifying horde of death.

Each had been painted with the Dark Blood of Qin himself; then Fai-Lok had employed magickal forces to provide a perch for the *p'ai,* or lower soul, of the demons and human brigands, cutthroats, and thieves called to fight for Qin on the human plane. That *p'ai* remained within the figures, making it possible for Fai-Lok to Possess them, but it was not the same as dwelling inside a living, breathing human being.

What glorious times those had been when he had created this army! The stink of fear, the blaze of terror! If all went well, this Year of the Hot Devil would see these soldiers terrorize the soft, modern people of today . . . and topple Qin from his throne forever.

He had set his plans in motion decades ago. Using Qin's vast network of minions in the Ice Hell Brotherhood, Fai-Lok had planted sufficient evidence about the terra-cotta warriors for an archaeologist to finally take note of their discovery.

From his perch inside the general leading the grotesque army, he surveyed his temporary domain. The grounds of the Sunnydale Museum of History had been transformed into a miniature recreation of the burial grounds of his liege lord, Qin.

No one realized that the fabled emperor had never lain among the treasures of his grave.

He had never died.

Qin had been the most merciless warrior to conquer the vast feudal lands of the Asiatic steppes. History had bestowed glory on the name of Genghis Khan, but Qin had surpassed the Mongolian warlord on all fronts: military might, cunning, and cruelty. He had been the first leader to alloy all the fractious clans and tribes and societies and families into a single entity. Mighty Qin. Mighty China.

But I was the power behind the throne. I was the one who gave him the edge.

I, whom he never valued. He treated me more like an errand boy than his court magician. I, who gave him the thousands of terra-cotta warriors who insured his victories.

As the magnificent army had been uncovered, the world had taken note. Fai-Lok's pride was difficult to contain. The digging team cleared out some of the vast warrens of rooms of several hundred of the figures, exposing them to light in order to warm the dormant *p'ai* within.

Meanwhile, Fai-Lok magickally warded the deeper-level cavern where the true prize still lay hidden beneath the earth, soon to be moved to her launch site in anticipation of his treacherous plot: the beautiful and ferocious dragon, Fire Storm.

My secret weapon . . .

Reacting to the energy of Fai-Lok's hot emotions, the terra-cotta general he Possessed shifted on its armored foot. Its bearded face and heavy brows contorted into a lustful grimace identical to that of battle fury, then tilted slightly. The topknot of hair rippled.

Its armor, though clay, glinted in the harsh glare.

Above Fai-Lok's head, colorful banners of orange and yellow whipped in the midnight heat. The full moon gleamed, and he thought of Xian, his secret love, with a sharp pang of lust. Her complexion had been likened by many a court poet to the luster of the moon, of a pearl. Beautiful, indeed, from her silken black hair to her exquisite feet.

Qin had never realized that she had been unfaithful to him

with Fai-Lok. He had believed that both of them were as loyal to him as the planets were to the sun.

In this Year of the Hot Devil, we will strike him down. I will march my army against my master. And I will rule this plane of existence with Xian at my side.

My minions have successfully stolen the Orb, and Larry Wong has received possession of it.

We are nearly ready.

The thought gave him heat. He shifted again, alert to the approach of a human being.

"Hello?" called a distant voice, and the statue's hideous smile widened. Blood pounded in Fai-Lok's ears of clay; it was soul-blood, the richest of the life forces, and it thrummed throughout Fai-Lok's incorporeal body, until the statue itself pulsed as if with a beating heart.

"Is anyone there?"

The statue's head turned the merest fraction of an inch, Fai-Lok guiding it slowly with the force of his will. As its lips parted, fangs showed.

In front of the topknot, horns pushed out of the clay head: They were magickal manifestations of the evil that Fai-Lok was, distilled down through the centuries until, if one could actually see what he had become, it would be a burning ember of demonic evil, quickly set ablaze. Fan it with another evil—with temptation, or with sin—and its power could ignite the entire museum.

Stay calm, he ordered himself as footfalls echoed within the hollows of his terra-cotta vessel. His nerves sizzled with urgency; his soul-blood roared with furious desire. *Do not betray your presence.*

Do not kill this peasant.

But the residue of the *p'ai* of the warrior clung to the insides of the statue, and as it mingled with Fai-Lok's own higher soul, the very grains of dirt that made up the clay strained for death-dealing.

The statue began to tremble and smoke, its feet jittering against the carpet laid over the parking lot.

"Hello? Is anybody there?" Tilisa Laurens called out again from the steps.

Damn, what stinks? She stood in front of the main entrance of the museum, surveying the parking lot filled with Chinese statues. She tried to sound brave, but she wasn't, very. She was new in town; she had only taken the museum guard gig because her cousin Lorenzo told her that her biggest problem would be staying awake all night.

"Take something to read," he'd advised her, handing her his stack of comic books. "Here. I got the newest *Fray.* They won't let you watch TV on the job, but you can read."

She'd passed on the comic books. All she had taken with her tonight was an old issue of *Jane* and some stationery to write her best friend, Isabel, back in L.A. Neither had held her interest. She had been skittish, anxious. The museum kept shifting all around her, things making noise.

As she walked from one turnkey station to the next—the security guard equivalent of the Stations of the Cross—the stuffed bear beside the exit sign seemed to snap to attention. She almost saw him swipe at her with his paw. In the glass case beside the fire extinguisher, the Aztec sacrificial knife flashed as if an invisible hand had caressed its razor-sharp blade. The sad, dark eyes in the row of scary religious paintings . . . were they watching her?

Things seemed to move just as she looked away. Every time she turned her back, it was as if the exhibits took one baby step toward her. It was like working in a fun house. Only it wasn't very much fun.

When she told folks here in Sunnydale that she'd gotten the gig, she had gotten some awfully strange looks. Now she was beginning to wonder if Lorenzo had played down the risk factor because he needed her share of the rent. To pay her share of the rent, she needed a job.

I didn't realize I really was going to be working in a haunted museum. . . .

There it was again, a little scraping sound. And the smell. Something burning. Should she set off the fire alarm? What if it was nothing? Would they fire her for calling the fire department for no good reason?

Better check it out first.

Crap. Just what I don't want to do.

Steeling herself, she took a breath and reached for her gun. It wasn't loaded, although she had been given bullets to use in case of an emergency. The thing was, she wasn't supposed to load her weapon unless she was sure she was in trouble. That was what her boss in Museum Security had drummed into her, and though it hadn't made any sense to her at the time, she hadn't worried much about it. She had figured she would never *be* in trouble in the Sunnydale Museum of History.

Maybe it's kids, she told herself as she listened to the muffled noises coming from the rows of Chinese statues. *Setting something on fire.*

The exhibit stretched the entire length and width of the parking lot. Each life-size figure was different, with its own facial features, hairdo, armor, and battle gear. They were very muscular and stocky, a truly imposing army, and she didn't like to look at them. They freaked her out. When she'd told Lorenzo about them, he had teased her unmercifully; and

Tony, one of his stupid friends, had told her some weird story about a time that a statue in the Sunnydale Art Museum really had come to life.

"Wahahaha. And it killed everybody who worked there!" Then Tony had finished swigging his Colt 45 and let out a truly disgusting beer burp. And the other guys had nodded and laughed.

Lorenzo's homeboy Jac J had taken up the story. "No one was left alive. It killed 'em all and sucked their blood."

Dorks, Tilisa thought, absently running her hand down a couple of her beaded braids. *Trying to scare me, messing with my mind.* After that, she'd asked for the graveyard shift just to spite them.

Stupid me. I let them get to me, that's all it is. There's nothing haunted about this place. There's just my imagination.

"If you don't come out, I'm going to call the police. The real police," Tilisa added. She fished in her dark blue uniform pocket for the Baggie containing her six bullets. Her hand was slick with perspiration and it shook a little; and she exhaled slowly, irritated with herself for being such a wuss.

Maybe it's Lorenzo's stupid-ass friends. That'd be just like them. Well, mad as I am, I still can't shoot any of 'em.

"Come on now," she said firmly. "Game's over."

Silence.

She moved her gaze from the statues to her bullets. Should she load her gun?

There. Something had moved. A statue slightly taller than the others that was posed slightly in front of the front row. A leader of some kind. Or was it a trick of the light?

Statues don't move.

She tried to swallow, but all the moisture in her mouth had turned to dust. Standing on the perimeter of the parking lot, she sweated beneath the powerful lights. The Santa Ana wind flapped the scarlet and crimson banners of Chinese characters hanging on long poles, flicking shadows over the heads of the warriors.

It's the wind. It's making them knock against one another. And I'm smelling someone's barbecue. I'm outside, for God's sake. That's all it is.

Satisfied—well, not really, but as close as she could get to satisfied—she turned on her heel, eager to return to the air-conditioned museum. She ignored the prickle of fear at the nape of her neck and kept going.

There was a louder noise behind her.

Just the wind.

She was surprised that the people who had set up the exhibit today hadn't taken better precautions about placing the statues too close together; they'd drummed into her how much each soldier was worth. Also, that they were outside. There was supposed to be an awning over them, but the delivery had been delayed; it was supposed to be here tomorrow, before the exhibit officially opened next week. Still, it was amazing to her that these priceless figures had been exposed to the elements.

The Chinese government had been very worried about releasing the three hundred figures into Sunnydale custody, citing how they were irreplaceable antiquities. Some guy in L.A. had talked them into it, or bribed them, so the other guards were saying. Whatever. It wasn't her problem. Still, it impressed her that some people had the ability to ignore the wishes of an entire foreign government.

There was another noise, a sort of muffled thump. Tilisa's chest tightened. Why, oh why, hadn't she applied for a job at the Double Meat Palace? She'd thought the security guard job would be more of a career path, lead to bigger things, maybe

even like becoming a bodyguard for rock stars or something . . .
not that she'd told Lorenzo that. He'd just laugh at her.

There! Did something move?

Swallowing down her fear, she hurried her pace, jogging from
the lot to the path that led to the front steps. Her gun was still in
her hand. The Baggie of bullets was in her other hand. Sweat
was pouring down her forehead. Her heart was pounding.

She reached the first step.

Another thump, this one closer.

"That's it. I'm calling the cops," she announced, her voice
shaky. "Right *now*."

Closer.

Her scalp prickled.

Closer still.

Oh, God. I'll just turn around and . . .

But she couldn't. She was too scared to turn around. It was
stupid, but she was really freaked out. The whole place felt
wrong. It felt dangerous.

*I didn't grow up in East L.A. without some survival skills.
And mine are telling me to get the hell out of here.*

And another.

That smell . . . stronger.

She broke into a run.

Okay, I'm on the second step, third . . .

There was a heavy scraping sound, like thudding footfalls, as if
something massive was chasing her up the steps. Something that
was gaining on her and she did not have the nerve to turn her
head and look; the door was just ahead of her. She stretched out
her hand. Her gun was still in one fist, the bullets in the other.

It was right behind her. She could feel the air moving against
her back.

She scrabbled for the door; it was reinforced glass, and she hadn't locked it. All she had to do was push it open and then she could lock it behind her. Just reach out her hand and give it a push. Her fingertips brushed against it.

Home free.

Something brushed the tip of her ponytail. She shrieked.

Then it grabbed her around the waist, yanking her away from the door and tossing her easily against the stairs. She grunted, shocked, losing her grip on both gun and Baggie. Her forehead hit the edge of the cement step. She had no time to register pain; she was flung over onto her back so hard that for a moment everything went gray.

Grunting, she forced open her eyes.

She was staring into a face.

But what a face.

It was one of the clay soldiers, but it had changed. Its features were contorted, as if it was laughing, transforming into a hideous demon grin. Its mouth was fanged; horns had sprouted from the clay, it was so crazy-looking, so wild. . . .

This is not happening, she thought, plummeting into shock. She realized in the recesses of her mind that she needed to struggle, had to get away. But it was as if one part of her brain understood that and the rest simply could not understand what was going on. *It is not happening.*

But it *was* happening. The creature's mouth spread wide in a grin, and white fangs flashed at her.

It was happening, as she balled her fists and tried to smack it, hard, then realized that its hands were wrapped around her wrists. It was lowering its face toward hers. She smelled . . . smoke. And something foul. Something that was dead and rotten. Warmth washed over her, the stench of fetid breath clogging her nostrils. The statue was crushing her wrists; pain shot through her arms and into her fingers.

The banners flapped. The face leered.

"P-please," she rasped. There were eyes glaring through the statue's eyeholes, long and green and reptilian. Something was inside the soldier, wearing the clay like an outer skin.

"No. No, no, no, no!" she begged, shaking her head from side to side. Her heart trip-hammered against her ribs. Her back throbbed.

It paused as if it understood her, and hope flared inside Tilisa. Her brain worked overtime to reassure her. She was going to be all right. This was a joke, or a misunderstanding. Someone was wearing a mask.

"Okay. You got me. W-we g-good?" she stammered.

The statue laughed. It threw back its head, and the wildest, craziest cackle flew out of it like a bird, and Tilisa screamed in reply.

She screamed as hard as she could, praying that someone would hear her.

Then it slammed its forehead against her face, hard. Her nose cracked like a rifle shot. The pain was so intense that she couldn't scream. Instead, she gasped, sucking in the blood that gushed down her face. Blood splashed over her eyes, and she couldn't see; it burned. Everything burned.

It was happening!
It really was!
To her.

Los Angeles

It was Santa Ana time, and the hot winds were whistling down the canyons of the skyscrapers near the sprawling Liang Museum of Art. Though Gunn was sweating, inside he felt cold, old, and ready to pack it in. Three in the morning, the streets

71

were depressing, almost as depressing as the bad neighborhood he had once called home. Boy hustler there, flashing him a sullen expression that betrayed his fear; young girl bunched up against the streetlight, fifteen—if that; probably a runaway.

The few faces on the street this time of night reminded him of him, back when it was the war wagon and his sister and his homeboys fighting off the vamps and tracking down food.

Things had changed. His sister was dead—staked by Gunn himself after she had been vamped. Then he had left the streets for Angel's crew and a new kind of family. But then George, his old second in command, had died. The rest of the crew shunned him after that.

Then he fell in love with Fred, the beautiful woman they had saved from Lorne's home dimension of Pylea. Wesley had been in love with her, too, but she had actually picked Gunn over English . . . and that was even after Wesley's nerd 'tude had started wearing off and he had actually become kind of cool.

So there Gunn was, with the woman he knew was the one . . . and then he killed someone looking to hurt her . . . and now, there were ashes where his heart should be. Nothing warm touching him.

In the middle of a Santa Ana, he felt like he was encased in ice.

Maybe if I got me a long black coat, Gunn thought dispiritedly. *Hell, I ain't no vampire fashion victim. . . .*

Angel was moving ahead of him; they were on patrol. Lorne had told them that word on the street—under the street—was that something was going down with the big exhibit from China. Someone was going to try to steal some of the statues, or vandalize them, something like that. Made sense; a big bunch of celebrities had shown up earlier today to protest the exhibit. There were a lot of human rights violations in Tibet, courtesy of the Chinese government, and that mattered to some rich and famous people in the movie industry. They didn't want Los Angeles coin paying to exhibit Chinese art, especially when it was a bunch of terra-cotta warriors buried with some warlike dude who had wiped out all kinda indigenous people.

Gunn wasn't sure exactly why Tibet was so important to people like Richard Gere, but now that he had seen a bigger picture working with Angel, he, well, he knew there *was* a bigger picture. Time was, he would have resented actors with big bucks seizing on a cause that was so far away, when little sisters and brothers went hungry all over Los Angeles, hustled for food, struggled on a daily basis just to stay alive. But he had come to understand that doing good came in all sizes and shapes. The more good was done, the looser the grip evil had around the throat of humanity.

And for some folks, the price to be paid for doing good had nothing to do with dollars. Not exactly cash-heavy, Gunn paid best he could. After all, souls were priceless, and life could be awfully damn cheap.

His life was pretty much all he had to offer.

Angel turned around and glanced at him. The vampire looked as glum as Gunn felt, and no wonder. Last spring, Angel and Cordelia had been moving toward each other, about to finally, really connect. Then Connor captured his father, chained him up, locked him into a metal box. He threw him in the ocean, where Angel rotted all summer, starving and going out of his skull.

Meanwhile, Cordelia became a higher being, but then came back with amnesia. Despite the fact that she had no memory of him, she was very attracted to Angel, and the sparks began arcing between the two of them all over again. It had been pretty incredible to watch.

Then Lorne had helped her get her memory back, and it was all downhill after that. She remembered that she'd been ascended; and that with her elevated viewpoint, she had witnessed all the terrible things that Angel had done the times he had been Angelus—a soulless, evil monster who loved torturing folks for as long as possible. Cruelty had been Angelus's game, and Cordy had seen all his worst moves.

That had been too much information for her to handle. Gunn got that: There was something inside her soul that said, *I'm not the kind of person who could love someone like that.*

So she had split, packing her bags and moving out of the Hyperion. Now she was staying with Connor, of all people. Connor, who had trapped his own father and sank him to the bottom of the Pacific. Granted, the kid had been warped by the bastard who stole him as a baby and raised him in the hell dimension.

Man, I woulda killed Holtz if he hadn't already gotten himself offed. . . .

No. No more killing. Fred and I would still be okay if I hadn't killed Professor Seidel.

"You okay?" Angel asked quietly as he dropped back, checking on his partner.

Gunn shrugged. Angel shrugged back, a bitter smile flashing across his features. This patrol was obviously a waste of time. Nothing was going down, and they might as well—

A scream pierced the night.

In unison, both men broke into a run, Gunn briefly catching up with Angel as the vampire took a moment to pinpoint the location of the scream. Angel gestured to the left, and Gunn nodded. The scream had come out of the museum complex.

And there was another one, louder and more frantic than the first.

Tanked with vampire strength and stamina, Angel raced on ahead. He shot around a corner, disappearing from view. Gunn heard the clink of chain link and figured Angel was scrabbling up and over a guard gate.

He followed after, just in time to see Angel drop to his feet inside the gated compound of the museum's courtyard. Angel yanked hard on a padlock while Gunn scanned the area over Angel's shoulder. There were bushes and statues and lots of folks fighting with one another.

A redheaded woman and a blond woman were screaming and beating on a man. Two or three other guys were running out of the main building, and two more people were fighting. Another one burst from around a very ugly bronze statue. Gunn's warrior brain toted up the head count: five guys. Two— make that three—women. The third one had short dark hair, and black markings like tats over one eye and across the side of her face.

Angel swung the gate open for Gunn and ran toward the fight. Gunn came up right behind him, eyes on the action. Adrenaline surged through him like a shot of Jolt. He was on; he was ready.

As he moved closer, he saw that three of the men weren't human. They were some species of demons with ridges on their foreheads. They were flanking the two Asian men and the three women, who on second glance might also be demons, with flared cheekbones and gaunt features.

The younger Asian man and the female with the tats were kung-fu fighting a demon assailant together. The other two women weren't as battle-savvy, but they were managing a few roundhouse kicks that at least prevented the other two demons from taking them down.

Angel shouted, "Jhiera!"—which was a word that made no

sense to Gunn. Angel hesitated a few seconds, as if he wasn't sure which side to join. Then the vampire grabbed one of the two demon guys fighting the blonde and the redhead and sent him flying, side-kicking another one with his right foot and clipping him behind the knees. As number two went down, number one got back up. Angel planted his right foot on the ground, then executed a roundhouse that caught the first one under the chin. He went back down.

"I warned you people!" Angel shouted at the short-haired female. "Not in my city!"

"Angel, they're trying to kill him!" Tat Chick shouted back as she gestured to the man beside her while at the same time slamming her booted foot into the chest of an oncoming attacker. Four more ridge-heads had appeared, though from where, Gunn wasn't sure. The dark-haired woman's assailant was also a ridge-head; the man who he was trying to kill was Asian and all human, if Gunn could trust appearances.

And I haven't started trusting appearances yet. . . .

Maybe Angel did. Whatever the vampire's reasoning, he doubled up his efforts to take out the quartet of male aliens surrounding the females and the two human men. That was good enough for Gunn; he joined in, flying up behind the nearest alien and double-fisting him over the head.

His target lurched forward but did not fall. Whirling around, he swung at Gunn, who thought bemusedly as he ducked, *Huh. These guys look kinda like Klingons.*

"Watch out for the women!" Angel shouted, and Gunn raised a hand as if to say, *Copy that.* But he privately thought the women were doing just fine and didn't really need any help. They were kicking ass just like Charlie's Angels.

Then the woman with the facial markings held up her hand, and some kind of energy stream shot from it. Gunn figured she had a concealed weapon; its ammo vibrated like a silver bubble, then slammed into one of the alien men. The man catapulted backward into Gunn, and they slammed to the concrete. Gunn took advantage of the moment to pummel the dude into unconsciousness before he got to his feet.

"Not here!" Angel yelled, rushing Tat Chick.

Gunn studied the woman as Angel threw his arms around her from behind; she struggled to throw him off, then doubled forward to bring him over her back with her momentum. That was an old trick in Angel's book—Gunn's, too—and the vampire was ready for it. Angel countered, yanking her off her feet, and flung her to the ground as she fired off the weapon again. Only, Gunn still didn't see a weapon.

The older Asian man, who didn't seem to know how to fight, took a roundhouse from one of the remaining three alien males; he groaned and hit the pavement, trying to break his fall with his hands and then screaming as his wrists cracked under the force of his body weight. Gunn heard the breaks and grimaced in sympathy.

"Get him out of here!" Angel shouted to Gunn.

Gunn bent down, gathering up the man around the chest, and urged him to his feet. The man's hands dangled uselessly; his knees buckled, and Gunn hoisted him up and threw him over his back. He darted toward the open door, thinking to use it as a shield. Then another stream of energy coursed past him, and the door burst off its hinges.

He charged across the threshold, spotted a sofa in the sparsely furnished room, and laid the man down on it. Then he turned on his heel to rejoin the battle.

Against the moon, something swooped downward, sailing a few feet above Gunn's head. It was leathery and winged, about the size of a small horse; it looked to be some kind of flying reptile, long, greenish-blue, and scaly, with a blunted nose and large, almond-shaped eyes, and a mane of leathery flanges that extended down its back and ended in a tail. As it rocketed closer, it spouted some fire at him, just like in the movies. Gunn dodged it by bending back *Matrix*-style, but Gunn was no Neo: He fell flat on his ass.

The fire missed him completely and splattered on the cement walk in front of him. Within a second the concrete was completely eaten away, revealing smoking dirt beneath.

Man, that's no ordinary fire!

The younger Asian man broke away from the fracas and raised his hands, gesturing and speaking to the creature. It cocked its head as if listening, then dove down beside the man and hovered there about three feet off the ground. Yelling to the short-haired woman, he slung one leg over the creature's body, extending his arm toward her.

From her place on the ground she looked up, spoke in a foreign language that sounded like Chinese, and crabbed toward him. One of the Klingons rushed her; she turned and shot at him over her shoulder—*where is her power coming from, her damn hands?*—and the attacker sailed across the courtyard, slamming into some kind of butt-ugly brass statue.

"Gunn! Don't let her get away!" Angel shouted as two of the demon guys grabbed his arms.

"Got it!" Gunn yelled. He scrabbled up and bounded forward, yanked the body of the nearest unconscious Klingon into a bear hug, and used it as a shield as he moved between the woman and the man on the flying snake-thing. She hurled more energy beams at him, and they slammed into the torso of the demon that Gunn was holding. The force dropped Gunn in his tracks again.

Man, this is getting old.

As Gunn threw the ridge-head down, he saw that Angel had managed to subdue one of the last two assailants and was repeatedly slamming his fist into the face of the other. The other women had taken on the remaining Klingon. He lunged right at Tat Chick, hoping she'd have to take some time to reload or recharge or whatever it was she had to do before she could turn him into subatomic Gunn particles.

No such luck; she looked to be locked and loaded. She raised her hand, palm out. With a survivor's well-honed sense of timing, Gunn flattened himself on the sidewalk as a surge of energy blasted within inches of his bald head. Reflexively he closed his eyes; when he opened them again, he saw something he did not see every day but had seen quite recently: a dimensional portal was flaring open about six feet above the courtyard. Blue and shimmering, it rushed like a whirlpool as it broke into the night. Then it wobbled downward, growing, all the while pulsating with blue light. It became stationary about fifteen feet away from Gunn . . . and about ten feet from the woman.

She yelled at the other women. The redhead lay crumpled on the ground, inert. The blonde raced toward the portal while Tat Chick went after the one on the ground and helped her up and started her running.

The blond one dashed through and the redhead was about to leap after her when the last Klingon grabbed her around the waist and pulled her down. He had something in his hand—*a knife!*

The demon male slashed at her; the knife blade sliced across her back. The black fabric of her top separated along her backbone.

Whoa, check that out, Gunn thought, doing so.

Her spine was ridged, as if it had grown on the outside of her body instead of the inside. Skin-covered bones stood out in sharp formation like mountains on a relief map. That backbone would make it tough to lie down.

Even more interesting, it was glowing a deep rosy red, as if it were on fire. Only thing Gunn could compare it with was jacked-up evil demon eyes, or the charcoal-orange tinge of superheated metal.

With a shout, the male let go of her and backed away, despite the fact—as Gunn figured it, anyway—that he could have stabbed the woman a couple of times and put her out of commission. The sight of her backbone obviously terrified the dude.

In his eagerness to get away from her, the Klingon stumbled and dropped to his knees. Steam rose from the woman's body, rising like smoke toward the night sky. The man shouted again, in a language Gunn didn't understand.

The guy's shouts changed to screams. Then he began to glow. His skin darkened and blistered, then cracked; his eyes began to bubble, and he burst into flame.

As Gunn stared in revolted fascination, Tat Chick grabbed the woman's arm and hauled her toward the portal. They were nearly through it when Gunn pushed himself from the concrete toward it, executing a flying tackle that went wide as Tat Chick and the redhead leaped into it.

The portal slammed shut and disappeared. Switching objectives, as warriors did in the field, Gunn whirled back around to check in with the guy on the flying lizard.

But the dude was gone, and so was the lizard. Enveloped in the sickening odor of burning flesh, it was just Gunn, Angel, and some dead or unconscious guys.

"Angel, what the hell?" Gunn asked.

Then one of the Klingons groaned.

Angel crossed over to him, dropped down beside him, and said, "What are you all doing in my dimension?"

"She's back," the Klingon said, in accented English. "The Bringer of Chaos is here!"

"Noticed that," Angel retorted, giving Gunn an ironic look as if to say, *Can you believe this crap?*

But Gunn was at a loss; he had no idea who any of these people were, nor why Angel knew them. Angel said to the demon, "So you guys were hunting them down again? Didn't work before. Why'd you think it would work now?"

"Back to do worse," the Klingon continued. "To deal death."

"She dealt death before," Angel said.

"And you let her go," the Klingon accused him. "What she brings . . ." He groaned again.

Gunn got up and crossed the courtyard, hunkering down beside Angel. The guy was in bad shape, bruised and beaten, his eyes nearly swollen shut. Blood ran from his mouth, and his skin was ashen. Not burned, just very gray.

"I know what she brings," Angel said. "I've seen it."

The demon's eyes were beginning to cloud. He was dying. He choked, shaking his head, and grabbed Angel's forearm as he gazed steadily into the vampire's eyes. "No. It's going to be bad for you, here in this dimension. She brings it through for him. You can't imagine . . ."

"Try me," Angel suggested. "Who was the guy on the dragon?"

"He is the one. Allies," the man said. "War . . ."

Gunn remembered the guy he had rescued. He said to Angel, "Be right back."

As Gunn rose, Angel's dying guy made a choking noise. Writhing, he grabbed Angel's forearm, clinging to him, the blood gushing from his mouth.

"War!" he cried.

His back arched, and he went limp. His eyes stared glassily as his head lolled to the side.

Frowning, Angel lowered him to the ground.

"Dead?" Gunn asked, and Angel nodded.

Sirens sounded in the distance.

Damn.

Gunn turned toward the room where the older Asian man lay, then realized they were out of time.

As one, he and Angel rose, surveying the carnage as they trotted toward the shadows leading out of the courtyard.

Blue and red lights bounced off the stucco walls.

"Y'know, it's damn interesting," Gunn said, gazing in the direction of an oncoming squad car as he and Angel hid in the shadows, waiting for them to pass. "Cops in L.A. show up only for the weird stuff. Regular person could bleed to death before they'd cruise on over, much less turn on a siren. Something like this goes down, they're here before you can say 'Wolfram and Hart.'"

"I've noticed that too," Angel said. A second squad car flashed by. "Wonder if our lawyer friends tip 'em off."

Gunn gestured to the carnage. "Is it too complicated for you to explain to me who these people are?"

"Now, yes."

A third car bolted past them. Car doors opened, slammed shut. Footsteps pounded the cement. Radio phones yakked and squawked. Discovery was underway; there would be more cars—a lieutenant, an ambulance, a medical examiner; maybe some reporters whose stories would never get printed.

Gunn wondered what the police would conclude about the crime scene. There was never anything on any news program or in the *L.A. Times* about all the weird shit that went down; Angel said it had been the same in Sunnydale, where vampires were explained away as "gangs on PCP," and demonic sightings were chalked up as the result of hallucinations caused by gas leaks. People didn't want to look at the seamy side of reality. They just wanted to pretend it didn't exist.

"Lorne's information was good," Gunn observed as they walked toward Angel's car, which was parked about six blocks from the museum. "Something was most definitely going down."

The young hustler and the runaway girl he had seen earlier had disappeared. Gunn was glad they had a measure of survival instinct. Most folks had no idea just how mean the streets of Los Angeles really were.

"Yeah," Angel replied as he started to drive back to the hotel. He fell silent again. Brooding. Which was not too noteworthy, because Angel was usually silent and brooding.

When Angel glanced overhead, Gunn realized it would be daylight soon. He was suddenly very tired; his adrenaline rush was winding down, and he wished Fred would be home at the hotel waiting for him. Most likely she was there, but not waiting for him. Most likely she'd be pretending to be asleep.

"So those guys," Gunn pressed. "Demons, I'm guessing."

"Vigories of Oden Tal," Angel confirmed, glancing at him. "They came around before your time."

"Working with you, you mean," Gunn filled in. "Before that time."

Angel nodded. "The leader of the women, the one with the short hair and the markings. She's Jhiera."

"And she's a Vigory?" Gunn asked.

"No. The men are the Vigories. They hunt the women. Jhiera's the princess of her dimension, and she's trying to protect the women, get them out of there and into a safer dimension. Ours. The men . . . castrate them. They clip a

83

place in that ridgey backbone that pretty much lobotomizes them."

"That backbone that can set guys on fire." Gunn grimaced.

Angel nodded, meeting his gaze. "That backbone."

"Baby's got spine," Gunn quipped. "So she's a freedom fighter. And those guys were trying to shut her down." He frowned at Angel. "Why did you try to stop her?"

Angel shifted gears, gave the rearview another glance. "You saw what happened. There were two human males in that fight. I told her if she killed any more men in my town, I'd kill her. Even if they were Vigory men."

He hung a left and looked back over at Gunn. Someone short melted into the shadows; Gunn figured it for another runaway. Too many on these mean streets. Even one was too many.

Angel said, "You saw the way that guy cooked. That's the way they kill."

"Works on human males too?" Gunn made a face. "That why their men clip their backbones? Disarm 'em, so to speak?"

"Jhiera said the heat problem was only temporary, while the women sexually mature. She said they can't control it then. I thought she meant it would eventually fade away. But here she is three years later, still using it." Angel shook his head, looking very angry. "I warned her not to bring her battle back here."

Gunn slid a glance at him as he checked the rearview mirror again. Angel sounded a little off, and he wasn't sure why. There was more going on here with this situation than the dude was letting on. Which would not be a new thing. Angel played it close to the vest.

And why did he keep checking the rearview mirror? To see if Jhiera was coming after them?

"Why the museum?" Gunn asked him, trying another tack.

"We had word something was going to happen tonight. You think it was an ambush?"

"Of us?" Angel asked, and it was clear from his tone that the same thought had occurred to him.

"Yeah, us," Gunn retorted. "Maybe she set it up so she could take you out. Keep herself safe while she brings the battle back to L.A. Well, relatively safe," he added, massaging his jaw. "Guys in her dimension know a few moves."

"A trap." Angel frowned, going all broody again. "I wouldn't put it past her."

There it was again, that odd catch.

"Vigory dude said something about dealing death. Maybe he meant your death." Gunn thought of something. "That Asian guy I saved? He was okay. I mean, he probably has two broken ribs, but he's not stir-fry the way that other Vigory guy is."

"Then he'll wind up in a hospital," Angel filled in. "An ER."

Gunn nodded. "Nearest one is St. Alexis."

Angel turned on his blinker and made another left. Then he glanced up at the sinking moon. The sky was beginning to lighten.

"The sun's going to come up pretty soon," Angel said. "There's a sewer tunnel near here. I'll drop myself off, and you go on alone. I'll get back to the hotel underground, and you can check out the hospital."

Gunn nodded as Angel swerved to the curb and got out. Gunn himself climbed out of the car and walked over to the driver's side as Angel moved away to the center of the street. As if it were a lightweight TV prop, the vampire removed the manhole cover from its location in the asphalt, laid it down, and climbed into the sewer entrance. He sank from view, sliding the cover back in place.

Satisfied that his boss was safe from the sun, Gunn signaled and pulled away, hung a U, and headed for St. Alexis.

CHAPTER FOUR

Los Angeles

The ER of St. Alexis was a madhouse, which was usually what ERs in L.A. were like on Saturday nights. Also Sunday nights. And Mondays at three in the afternoon. Kids screaming, guys writhing around on gurneys with gunshot wounds. Car accidents and domestic violence. Tears. Profanity.

What a lot of people didn't realize was that ERs usually smelled bad. Urine, body odor, vomit. The stench of catastrophe. Folks in ambulances thought to themselves, *If I can just make it to the hospital, I'm gonna be okay.* Then they got there and realized there were still no guarantees.

Gunn calmly wove his way toward the main desk; a harried-looking man with silver-gray hair glanced up at him and said, "Yes?"

"Looking for my . . . cousin," Gunn said softly. "Chinese man. He fell and broke both his wrists. My aunt said they brought him here."

The man ran a hand through his hair and said, "We've had a real crush—"

"There was a fire or something," Gunn prompted. "This other guy my Chinese cousin was with got burned."

"Oh." The man perked up. "The Hangar 18 guy." An intrigued smile flickered across his features.

Gunn knew then that he had the correct ER for sure. Hangar 18 was supposed to be the secret government location of some alien bodies retrieved from a crash sight out in Roswell, New Mexico. The burned Vigory must have been brought in and he was "the Hangar 18 guy."

At Gunn's placid expression, the man lost the smile and said in a professional tone, "Your cousin's probably still in the ward behind us. He was just brought in. I can try to find him for you." He looked very eager to get in on this weird scene.

"It's okay," Gunn said placidly. "I'll have a look, if you don't mind."

"If he's not back here with us, they might have already taken him to orthopedics. Or radiology." The guy was eager to help, wanted to stay involved. Not good. Gunn couldn't conduct his investigations with this guy looking over his shoulder.

"Thanks." Gunn moved off.

He ambled down the center of a large, rectangular space cordoned off with blue curtains. A hospital bed was stationed in each cubicle, most of them surrounded by distraught onlookers and briskly efficient people wearing navy blue scrubs. Gunn knew his emergency rooms, knew that the really bad cases were wheeled off into surgery as soon as they came in. The folks in these beds had been triaged as the ones who could suffer for a while without dying.

In the nearest beds he saw lots of bloody bandages. Lots of brown faces, black faces, white faces. No Asian faces. People looked at him expectantly, as if hopeful that he was there to do something about their injuries, their pain, their fears.

Gunn moved on.

He went down the next row of beds. Nothing there, either.

Then he saw him. Asian guy, all alone, except for a pretty white woman in scrubs who was checking an IV running into his arm. Gunn dawdled out of her range, waiting to see if she might leave. Sure enough, she gave the IV another look-see, then picked up a clipboard and flipped pages as she walked away, her back to Gunn.

As soon as she was gone, Gunn calmly approached the man. Gunn leaned over, scanning the man's singed face to see if he was conscious.

He was. The man's almond-shaped eyes rolled toward him, and his blistered lips parted. He blinked and said, "You." His voice was thick, the single word slurred. They had put him on something for the pain. Two broken wrists, Gunn would want something too.

Gunn nodded. "Me."

The man's eyes drifted closed.

"What happened?" Gunn asked him, trying to keep him conscious so he could answer questions. "Who were those people? Who are you?"

"Tsung Wei," the man murmured, lids flickering. "Museum's curator."

"That's your name?"

The man did not reply.

"What were you . . . ?"

His eyes closed, and his lips went slack. He was not dead, just passed out from his medicine. Gunn pulled his wallet from his pocket and fished out an Angel Investigations card. He wrote "Charles Gunn" on it and walked over to the dirty, bloody pile of clothes on a chair beside the man's IV stand. He fished around for the guy's dark gray business trousers and found his wallet, opened it, searched for a card.

Pay dirt. There were several identical ones, reading DR. TSUNG WEI, CURATOR, ASIAN ANTIQUITIES, LIANG MUSEUM OF ART.

Gunn took one, replacing it with his own, and dug around some more. A good investigator never passed up an opportunity for additional information. Credit cards, Blockbuster Video card, dude worked out at Gold's Gym. But nothing else that could give Gunn any information about what had been going down at the museum at that time of night.

He had just put the man's wallet back in his pants and laid the pants back down, when the woman in scrubs returned. She looked at Gunn sharply and said, "Sir, please wait in the waiting room. This area is for medical personnel and patients only."

Gunn thought about mentioning the other people gathered around patients' beds, but he knew she was more worried about his proximity to the guy's clothes than to the guy. He figured he wasn't going to be able to loiter very well—she'd probably go alert the hospital security team about him—and wasn't going to get any more out of Dr. Tsung Wei this morning, anyway.

He felt bad. Felt he'd been sloppy on this recon. He turned on his heel, walked out of the ER, and headed for the morgue. Sir-fry guy would be in there.

But the room number of the morgue wasn't listed on any of the directories provided for civilian perusal. So he sidled up to an ebony-skinned man in scrubs with a name tag that read

JACKSON, got streetwise, and said, "Hey brother, I'm supposed to go to the morgue."

"Basement. Two-A," Jackson supplied helpfully. He grinned. "You going to check that weird dude out?"

"What weird dude?" Gunn asked, all innocence.

Jackson's brows shot up. "One dressed up like a movie extra. The crispy alien," Jackson said. "Come *on*. Where you been, bro? It's all over the cafeteria."

Gunn raised his brows. "Huh. News to me."

"Go check it out," Jackson urged. He lowered his voice and leaned forward, narrowing his eyes. "It's freaky."

Great. The buzz was on. Gunn figured his chances of getting into the morgue beneath the radar were gone.

Still, he had to try. There was an attendant seated at a desk beside a nondescript door labeled 2A. Gunn nodded at him and said, "Jackson sent me down."

The dude scowled at Gunn. "Well, he can kiss my ass," he snapped. "Free tours are over." When Gunn stared back, all blank, the attendant said, "You tell him he brings one more friend or 'date' down here, I'll get him fired."

Damn. If real life was like a TV show, he'd go find a spare doctor's coat, a pair of glasses, and a clipboard, return, and sail on past this guy. But this wasn't TV, and real life was not that simple.

He turned around, aware that the attendant was memorizing him, and decided to go back to the ER. But his "friend" who had been at the desk before had been replaced by a blue-haired old lady in a pink smock with a badge reading VOLUNTEER pinned to it.

"I'm here to see Dr. Tsung Wei. The museum curator who came in with two broken wrists. He been transferred to a ward yet?"

"You family?" she asked harshly.

"Yes," he replied, just as harshly.

She gave him a suspicious look and placed her hands on a keyboard on the console. "Please spell his name."

Gunn complied.

She typed it in awful damn slow, and then raised her blue-gray head and snapped at him, "He has requested no visitors."

"But he doesn't know I came into town," Gunn said smoothly.

Her blue eyes cracked like ice cubes in hot water. *"No visitors."*

Again, were this TV, he would have had someone with him to distract the old bird while he peeked at her monitor and snagged the room number. But again, it wasn't TV.

"Is there anything else?" the woman demanded frostily.

"No. Thanks. You've been more than helpful," Gunn told her, biting his tongue.

The sun was completely up by the time he entered the Hyperion, which had become both Angel Investigations' headquarters and living quarters for Angel, Cordy, Fred, and Gunn after Angel's first office had blown up. Lorne had moved in next. Then folks had scattered over the summer. They had cleaned out Cordelia's old apartment when they thought she wasn't coming back and Connor lived in a rat's nest of a warehouse, and in Gunn's book, that boy was a rodent. And now Cordy was there with him, which was twelve different kinds of wrong.

Wesley still had his own place, of course. All to the good, 'cause he was not welcome here, that was for *damn* sure. Not after the whole kidnapping Angel's son thing.

"Charles! My God!" As soon as she'd seen him, Fred had left Angel's office. She was hurrying toward him, and it was like some great moving scene where all was forgiven.

Except that she stopped about three feet away and crossed her arms over her chest.

"Angel just went upstairs," Fred told him. He said that some princess of another dimension is back in town and setting people on fire!"

"Yeah. That's the short version." God, he just wanted to take her in his arms. He'd killed that bastard Professor Seidel for her. To make it so she wouldn't have to . . . and now she could hardly stand to look at him. Christ, she'd seen Angel at his most demonic back on Pylea, distracted him from killing him and Wesley by offering him animal blood. But Gunn was more of a monster to her now . . . and all because he had wanted to spare her from seeing if a killer lived inside her own skin.

"She can automatically ignite people?" Fred asked.

Gunn shrugged. "Men, mostly. Where she comes from, the men put down the women in a real harsh way."

"So the women incinerate them?" Fred looked shocked.

"Yeah. Pretty much. The ones who run with Jhiera, anyway."

"Wow. Payback's a . . . thing to be researched," she said unsteadily, her cheeks reddening as she looked away.

Payback was kind of a dirty word between the two of them at the moment.

"Plus, they've got portals," Gunn added. "You might look into that. Since . . . you know about that."

The past hung heavily between them. Fred murmured, "Yes, Angel mentioned portals."

Charles Gunn felt as if the floor were opening up again. There was part of him that just couldn't buy that Fred was not in his arms right now, head tilted up so she could see him, making sure he was okay and letting her love wash over him.

But that was the way it was. That was their reality.

"I don't have much else on her." He made a face. "She's a good fighter. Even without the *Firestarter* groove goin'."

She nodded, her beautiful eyes huge. She was breathy, the way she got when she was upset. "I'm also going to do some research on . . . on burnings and things like that." Blanching, she gestured toward the computer in Angel's office. "I'm-I'm glad you're okay."

Thank you, baby, he thought sincerely. *Even for just that, thank you.*

"Check on a guy named Dr. Tsung Wei too," Gunn told her. "He's a curator at the museum, there when the attack went down. He's at St. Alexis. I talked to him, but I didn't get much out of him before he passed out."

"Okay," she said. "He's, um, going to be all right?"

"He has two broken wrists, so he might not be so good on the piano for a while. Other than that, he got off light, compared to the other guys there." He stifled a yawn. "I'm wiped. I'm catching a few, then I'll be back up to see what the what is."

"Oh. Okay. That's Angel's plan too." Her cheeks blazed red as she lowered her gaze. "Um, sleep well."

"Thanks."

He brushed past her, smelled soap and perfume, and longed just to touch her hair. But he did nothing; he simply took the stairs one at a time and trudged down the hall.

Taking off his shoes, socks, shirt, and jeans, he climbed wearily into bed.

And did not sleep.

Downstairs, Fred's heart pounded dully as she flicked on Angel's computer and typed in "Tsung Wei." Her eyes glazed with tears as the search engine moved into action. She wanted to go to Gunn and tell him it was all right; she was over watching him

93

grab a man's head and twist it, hard; over hearing the *crack* of Dr. Seidel's breaking neck. Over watching Gunn throw his corpse into the interdimensional portal that would serve as his grave.

But she wasn't. It was as if the feelings inside her had gotten stuck. She was frozen solid, and she couldn't even pretend she felt anything at all.

Dr. Tsung Wei, Liang Museum of Art came up, and she began to scan the information. After rereading the first sentence for the third time, she became aware that someone was standing behind her.

Let it be Gunn, she thought; but it was Angel, who said, "Hey."

"I thought you went to bed," she told him, turning around to face him.

"Not yet." He hesitated, looking hard at her. "You okay?"

"Yes," she blurted too fast. She touched her hair. "Don't I look okay?"

"You . . . everybody's on edge."

His dark brows knit over his eyes. She could remember a time when standing this close to Angel would turn her to butter. She had been completely infatuated with the man who had refused to behead her back on Pylea. A guy does something like that, you develop feelings for him. But Angel and she weren't in the cards. It didn't have anything to do with the whole vampire thing. She just wasn't sure anymore if there was *anybody* in the cards. Or if she was even playing with a full deck anymore.

"It's been . . . eventful lately," she replied. "With this burning princess. And, um, all the people coming and going, and . . ."

His grim smile indicated that he caught her drift. He thought she was talking about Cordelia. He ran a hand through his hair and sat on the corner of the desk, gesturing to the monitor. "Dr. Tsung Wei. That the man Gunn saved?"

She jerked. "Uh-huh. He works for the museum." She clicked on the link. "I'm just about to retrieve some more information."

Angel nodded as if he were listening to her, but he said, "I figured Jhiera would listen to my warning. I told her I'd take her down here if she killed any more humans, and I will."

That seemed to satisfy something in him. Then he was just about to leave as the link connected and a photograph of a very handsome Asian man filled the screen.

He blinked. "That's the guy who flew away on the dragon."

She read the caption below the picture. "He's Alex Liang. He's a really rich guy, even for a rich guy. The museum is named after him."

"So he was at his own museum tonight with Jhiera. And he has a pet dragon. Not named Puff, I'm willing to bet."

Without acknowledging his little joke, she scrolled down.

"Dr. Tsung Wei is the curator of Asian art at the museum. He oversaw the installation of five hundred terra-cotta warriors from the Qin Dynasty. The Los Angeles exhibition is one of five exhibitions of warriors being held concurrently throughout the world. A second exhibition's being held in Cleveland; a third, in Frankfurt, Germany. A fourth, in Tokyo. And a fifth is just now being installed—" She looked at him.

Angel leaned forward. "In Sunnydale," he finished for her.

"Sunnydale," she echoed.

"And we have an attack from another dimension, and a man flying off on a dragon." He cocked his head. "I wonder what Sunnydale's got."

"You'll probably want to discuss this with Buffy," Fred said anxiously.

He nodded. "What time is it?" He checked his watch. "A little early. I'll let her sleep." He gestured to the screen. "What else is there?"

She clicked on another link. "Tsung Wei had traveled to China to oversee the shipments of all five exhibitions to their prospective museums."

"And he was on the museum grounds tonight with Alex Liang and Jhiera," Angel observed. "What about the Sunnydale exhibit?"

She clicked on the appropriate link; the curator in charge of the exhibit was Alan Johnson. There was a photo of him; he was standing beside one of the figures with a big smile on his face, his arm around the clay shoulders as if he were showing off a fine old friend.

Bet he dies, Fred found herself thinking.

"I . . . I think I'll get a cup of coffee," she ventured.

"Okay. I'll do some more research," Angel told her, taking the seat she vacated. He leaned forward. "I'll start with Alex Liang."

"Good idea," she said.

Truth was, she was exhausted. She hadn't gone to bed all night, but if she went upstairs, it would mean being there with Charles.

She didn't want to face him. Didn't want to face herself.

I was going to kill someone. I had it in me to commit murder. Seidel had it coming.

But oh, my God, Charles might have been killed tonight. If he had died . . .

I should go up there.

Her heart tightened, and she remained frozen in place.

I can't.

Instead, she got her coffee and took it out into the garden.

She sat with the steaming cup on the arm of her chair, watching the day begin.

Something's very wrong here in L.A., she thought. *Again.*

Sunnydale

Buffy felt bad about leaving the dead old man on the grounds of the rest home. It was hot, and he was not going to look—or smell—any prettier an hour or two from now. After a brief conversation with Spike, they decided that the best place for him would be where the shadows would linger, while at the same time not being so hidden that it would take a long time for him to be found.

As they arranged his hand beside him, Buffy murmured, "Rest in peace."

"Piece-*es*," Spike intoned somberly.

After they were satisfied with the old man's location, they put some distance between themselves and the corpse. The air was devoid of birdsong, as if even the crows and jays were too tired to sing.

Spike said, "Gettin' hot. Gonna get sunny soon. Gotta head out."

"Thanks for showing," Buffy said sincerely. "You helped me out."

He gave her a lazy grin, the one that began with his lowering his face, then tilting his head just so, and grinning wryly as he glanced up at her through his lashes. She knew that look so well.

"You could've taken 'em both without me."

"True. I could've taken 'em both if I had to," she replied. "It was nice not to have to."

His answering look said what his voice did not: that it had

been very nice to be there with her, for her. To lift some of her duties from her shoulders, if for just a little while. To keep the Slayer company on her lonely path.

"Get some rest," he said to her. "You look tired."

"True. I mean, I *am* tired." She glanced up at the sky; swirls of deep purple were bleeding into the midnight blue. The sweltering night would sizzle into an overheated day. Vampires who ventured out for even a second or two in the overbright sunshine would end up as flaming torches.

"You going all the way to your room at Xander's?" she asked him. "You'd better hurry. You haven't got much time before the sun comes up." She made a face. "You don't want to be Kentucky Fried Vampire."

"Not gonna chance it," he told her. "You're right. It's a bit of a hike."

He gestured to the graveyard. "Gonna stick around here. Locate a musty crypt, sack out. Haven't had much alone-time lately."

Translation: He and Xander couldn't stand living together.

"Just wish I had the one with me old telly. I'm behind on my soap." He smiled dreamily. *"Passions."*

"Doesn't Xander have cable?"

"He blocked it," Spike said with disgust. "Activated some childproof *chip* in the box with some blasted code. Always cursed with chips, I am." Spike narrowed his eyes. "Said he'd release it once I did my fair share around the place." His voice shook. *"Dishes."*

"Fair is fair, Spike. After all, you live there rent-free."

He looked terribly affronted. "I don't use dishes. Don't touch 'em, ever. I drink my blood straight out of the carton."

Gross. She made a face. "You leave your wet towels on the floor."

He huffed. "And speaking of dirty linen, is there anything about my living circumstances you *don't* know about?"

"A few things." She smiled at him. "C'mon, Spike. Be a good roomie."

"For you, I would be," he told her. "Xander needs a little goose now and then. Keeps his blood circulating. Keeps him young."

"Keeps his blood pressure up," Buffy countered. She glanced back up at the sky. There were washes of lavender where the deep purple had layered over the dark blue. The sun was on its way.

"You need to go in," she cautioned him.

He grinned again. "Worried about me, luv?"

"Yes," she said frankly. "Go. Rest in peace." She held up her pointer finger. "Just one. Piece."

"Same to you, Slayer."

He gave her a salute, then drifted off among the thirsty, tired trees. Buffy watched after him, then turned to go home. She was tired and listless, wished she had even something as silly as a soap opera to catch up on. She didn't feel particularly better for having destroyed two evil things.

But at least we might be on to the cause of the increased mayhem, she thought, cheering a smidgen. *That little girl's gabfest means I've got something to bring home to Professor X.*

In a crypt in the Shady Hill Cemetery, two figures in red robes held down a struggling girl who had the bad luck to jog too close to their hiding place. A third injected her with the serum Coach Wong had distributed among the teams he'd sent out to nab "fresh recruits."

Sam Devol, the fourth member of the team, peered through the grate of crypt and whispered, "Okay, the Slayer's gone. Let's get the hell out of here."

He looked back over his shoulder at the girl. She was unconscious.

I don't know what Coach wants with her, but this is wrong, he told himself. *What the hell am I doing here?*

It had started a few months ago. There was trouble at home—his parents, bickering a lot. Someone calling and hanging up. His dad staying later and later at work. When school started, Sam shined on his parentals' dance of stupidity; he had enough to deal with, with classes and Principal Wood, who was always riding him. His only outlet was football. Coach Wong seemed to get how much pressure there was on him, sensed he was aching to work it out on the field. Coach started singling him out during practice, giving him a few words of praise or encouragement. Wong made Sam feel like there might actually be a point to all the hassles.

"Life's a journey, Sam," Wong had told him in the locker room. "You're a warrior. Your path might get rocky, but you've got the stuff to battle your demons. You've just got to believe in yourself."

The man's words were like water in the desert. Sam had blossomed under Coach's guidance.

Then one night, after practice, Coach had invited him to a private meeting with some of the other guys. "A special group," Coach had explained. "I've been watching you, Sam. You're special too. Special enough to join us."

He had led Sam to the bleachers, where about a dozen other players were grouped together. Something was up, and they were in on it. Coach had a pile of red robes in his arms.

Coach revealed the truth about Sunnydale: Buffy Summers, the guidance counselor, was really something called a slayer.

"Buffy was supposed to come to Sunnydale to protect everyone," Coach explained. "But the Slayer lost her path. She's not on the hero's journey anymore. She's off on her private revenge trip. If she really cared about humanity, she'd form an army and get down to business.

"That's why we've created the Hellmouth Clan. To save our world and everyone in it. We're here to defeat the evil forces that the Slayer is ignoring. It won't be easy. And some of it won't be pretty.

"But we're warriors," Coach continued. "We will fight, and we will prevail."

Sam was dazed. There was more: Coach told him about magicks and demons and a dragon, and showed Sam enough to convince him. He summoned fire, and wind. He made a ball of blue flame glow between his hands, then hurled it at the field, where it caught the turf on fire until the sprinklers put it out.

"C'mon, Sam, be one of us," Kim Rademacher urged him. Kim was the placekicker. "We're Sunnydale's only hope."

Sam shook his head. "I just can't believe it."

"I'll prove it to you," Coach Wong told him.

So Coach had taken a small party of them out on recon—in one of Sunnydale's many graveyards—and Sam had observed the Slayer in action. Without breaking a sweat, she staked a vampire, which then exploded into dust!

"She's awesome. She's a superhero!" Sam had blurted.

"Then why is there so much crime in Sunnydale?" Coach had asked him. "She only goes after demons and vampires— and why? Because they killed her mother. It's a personal revenge trip, just like I told you. We'll make the streets safe for everyone."

Coach had shown him crime stats, clipped articles from the paper. He showed him Joyce Summers's obituaries, both of which reported that the lady had died of natural causes— one said heart attack, one said stroke—but Coach insisted that that was a cover-up. Yes, a lot of crimes were committed in Sunnydale, and apparently the Slayer did nothing about those.

"The police are for handling crime and stuff . . . ," Sam had ventured.

"The police can't keep up," Coach argued back. "They're short-staffed, there's budget cuts, just like at school. You know how it is.

"That's why the Slayer came here. To help. Only she's not doing her job."

After a while, Sam had to agree. And he was in.

All the way in.

And now . . . he was beginning to realize just how badly he wanted back out.

"That's the fastest anyone has passed out. I hope she isn't going to die. They don't count if they're dead." Kim Rademacher looked hard at Sam. "You okay, man?"

"Sure," Sam said unsteadily. "You?"

"Sure."

But Kim didn't look any more okay than Sam felt. He looked like he was about to hurl. Or scream.

Maybe I can talk to him, Sam thought. *See if we can get ourselves out of this mess. Maybe if we told the Slayer . . .*

The two linebackers who had held the girl down for the shot hoisted her up. One of them flopped her over his back, firefighter style.

"I'll get the truck," Sam volunteered.

"It's cool. I'll do it," Kim said slowly, giving Sam another hard look.

He doesn't trust me, Sam realized, and despaired. *That means I can't trust him. I'm alone in this. I'm screwed.*

Why did I ever listen to Coach Wong? He's the real evil of Sunnydale.

And what we're doing . . . that makes me evil too.

Dawn, as in the time of day and not Buffy's sister, had just occurred when Xander gave Buffy a beep on the horn and pulled his car over to the curb as she crossed at Main. She waved at him and headed over to his car. He was Sharp-Dressed Guy in his suit, which meant he had a client meeting, and he looked hot. Hot as in sweaty around the edges and wishing he'd opened a surf shop instead of going into construction. In Antarctica.

"Hey," he said, rolling down her window as she opened the door. Radiohead was blaring on his speakers. "A security guard was killed at the museum last night. Her cousin works for me. Called me on my cell to tell me he wasn't coming in."

"Bummer," Buffy said feelingly as she picked up some folded blueprints and put them in the back.

"It's okay. I don't need a carpenter today, anyway." Without missing a beat, he added, "Sounds like a job for SuperBuffy."

"Xander, you fired me off the last job I worked in construction," she reminded him.

"Not that. A guard was viciously attacked. The only evidence is a broken terra-cotta statue crushing her into oozy bits. Y'know, those Chinese guys."

Buffy blinked, thinking of the little girl. *There's plenty of evil in China.* "Chinese guys?" she echoed. "What Chinese guys?"

"The terra-cotta soldiers from ancient China," Xander explained patiently. "Or rather, from current-day China, 'cause ancient China, well, that's a thing of the past. C'mon, Buffy. You know, the big art exhibit."

"Oh. Haven't paid attention to the art objects, Xand. I've

been a little busy," Buffy replied. "What with the increased demon activity, I haven't read a paper or checked my online news in, oh, a year."

"Which is so very different from all the other years," he drawled.

"Busted. Not current-events Buffy," she said. "The stuff I need to keep track of doesn't go so well with the fast-food commercials."

"Which is why I listen to talk radio, and channel surf at night," Xander quipped. "Just in case something slips past the censors."

"And in this case, statue-smashing made it," Buffy mused. "Thanks."

"I live to serve." He made a happy face. "You want fries with that?"

"I don't indulge this early in the morning." Buffy climbed in and belted as he turned down his music and pointed to a large cup near the dash.

"Then have some refreshing Big Gulp," he invited.

She brought the massive drink container to her lips and sipped on the straw as they pulled away into the early morning commute traffic.

"I'm thinking this has demon activity written all over it," Xander told her. "Word—ah, neat, the man with the extended metaphor!—is that the statue that smutted this girl was not where it was supposed to be. Rumors are flying that it chased her." He looked at her. "Crazy much?"

"Like Alcathla," Buffy said anxiously. That was the demon-statue Angel had brought to life with his own blood. To stop Alcathla from sucking the entire world into a hell dimension, Buffy had had to run a sword through Angel's heart and send him straight to hell instead. He had come back insane from the torture.

104

"Not Alcathla," Xander reminded her. "Alcathla go bye-bye. Besides, this statue is Chinese."

Buffy took another sip of soda and savored the tangy after-taste. "Right. Sometimes it's hard to keep all the demonic statuary separate."

"Harder still to keep track of? Demonic date-uary." Xander flashed her a half-smile. "Mate-uary."

"Don't worry, Xander," Buffy said kindly, handing him his drink. "Someday you'll date a human girl."

"Yeah, when hell freezes over," he grumbled good-naturedly.

"And she won't even try to kill you, I'm betting."

"My money is on misadventure," Xander told her. "Nope. I'm a demon chick magnet, and that's all there is to it."

"Speaking of demons, Spike is going to try to remember to help around your place more," Buffy told him.

Xander mock-shuddered. "I can feel hell gettin' colder. Buffy, he's such a pig. He uses all my best coffee cups for his blood-and-Wheatabix sundaes and then—"

She gazed sorrowfully at him. "He lied to me. He said he never touches your dishes."

"Yeah, never touches 'em to wash 'em."

"I'm sorry. I'm the one who decided he should live in your closet." She yawned.

"Guest room," he corrected. "And, yeah, he's only there because you asked me. So, let's leave it at 'lucky him.'"

It was not the first time Spike had lived with Xander, and Buffy knew that Xander really was capable of saying no, if that was his final answer. She felt a wave of affection for him in her tired bones and leaned her head back on the seat. Life certainly did have its odd twists and turns.

"Thank you," she said sincerely.

"You're welcome," he replied, equally sincerely.

Her head was getting heavy against the seat as Xander wove through the traffic. He was a good driver; she had never mastered it. Whistling to himself, he drove quickly to the museum. The storied building had also been the temporary home of a mummy who had come to life, namely, the beautiful Inca princess Ampata, who had been in love with Xander.

Poor Xander; he truly was a demon chick magnet.

Street traffic was crawling past the building and the parking lot in front, everybody rubbernecking to see why the joint was jumpin'. The parking lot sat some distance from the curb, set off by expanses of grass and shrubs. Sunnydale black-and-whites had roared up and stopped haphazardly in front of the lot, testimony to an emergency response. Two of the squad cars still flashed their red and blue lights. As Xander rolled slowly past with the rest of the parade, a uniformed police officer stationed in the middle of the street gestured for them to keep moving.

"Bad news travels fast," Buffy said quietly. As she pushed the button to open her window, she craned her neck to survey what lay beyond the foreground of cops and vehicles. Sawhorses had been set up around the perimeter, spanned by yards and yards of yellow plastic tape stretched across them. The tape read, in big black letters, POLICE LINE. DO NOT CROSS.

Contained within stood rows of statues of sturdy guys wearing topknots. Each one stood about between five and a half and six feet. What she could see of their faces looked fierce and determined. They wore breastplates; some carried shields. They did not stand in battle poses, but with resolution and determination, as if awaiting orders to launch an attack . . . on Astro Turf, or something like it.

Living? Possessed? It was difficult to get a good look at them, as yet another squad car drove up and two of Sunnydale's finest climbed from the vehicle.

"Rats," Buffy muttered. "Can't infiltrate."

"Figures," Xander said, studying the scene through the windshield, keeping track of the cars around him. "We'll have to check it out later."

"Yeah," she concurred. Then she yawned tiredly and moved her neck from side to side, wincing at the sharp crack that spoke of balled-up tension or maybe the need for a visit to the chiropractor that she couldn't afford.

Xander reached forward and turned up the air conditioner. "I'll see what I can find out from Lorenzo," he offered. "Maybe you should just go home and get some sleep."

She slumped in the seat. "First I have to tell Willow what I saw." She looked over at Xander. "We have some possible leads on why things have been going all wacky lately. Old dead man. A psychotic, disintegrating zombie Chinese girl with a Hand of Glory; a wheezing animated skeleton; and suspicious statue death."

"'And a partridge in a pear tree,'" Xander sang. "Was this a scavenger hunt?"

"The Chinese girl said something about evil in China. And gave me some numbers." She held up her fingers. "One, two, and three."

Xander nodded sagely. "Aha! I detect a pattern."

Buffy grunted.

He went on. "Y'know, the Chinese are big into joss sticks. They throw these little sticks that have numbers on them. Then you look the numbers up in a book. Then it tells you your fortune. Like tarot cards, only instead of shuffling a deck, you toss your joss."

"Toss your joss. I like the sound of that," Buffy said. "Anybody up for joss tossing?"

"It does have a certain ring," Xander agreed. "Maybe Will can find something about it on the Net. Anya might have salvaged some joss paraphernalia from the Magic Box when it went up."

Buffy nodded, gazing back at the museum as they passed it. "Lorenzo staying home from work?"

"Yeah. Maybe we can go by later, extend our sympathies and grill him for information."

Buffy nodded. "Good idea." Then she groaned, suddenly remembering that she had employment. But at least it was a day job without a cow hat. "It's a work day. I have to go to the school and help the students with their problems."

"Call in sick. It's almost true. Tired is like being sick, only without the nasty flulike symptoms."

She opened an eye. "Xander, I just got this job. I can't have Principal Wood thinking I'm unreliable."

"Buffy, he won't fire you for one sick day. Besides, he knows he'd have a hard time replacing you."

She pursed her lips together and gave him a look. "Because no other adult in Sunnydale would work for what he pays me."

Xander looked pleased that her earth logic was his earth logic. "Exactly. Unless they can't get employed at the Double Meat Palace. And hey, free food."

She shook her head wearily. "Just drive me over to Hellmouth Central, Xander. I must be schoolbound. Who knows? Maybe somebody will come in to talk about the murder. I could glean information."

"Or fall asleep at your desk, and then he might really fire you."

"I won't fall asleep," Buffy insisted, closing her eye again.

Then she started to snore.

Smiling fondly at the Slayer, Xander drove Buffy home. Buffy occupied a place in his heart no other woman did: First he'd had a crush on her, then an unrequited love. He had been her goofy sidekick. Now he could sense the mutual respect that had grown out of their growing up. Lovers and fiancées might come and go, but what they had . . . that was a lifetime thing.

Problem with that was, one or both of their lives might be painfully short.

He was pulling into the driveway when Dawn sailed out the front door with her books in her arms, looking relieved and giving him a wave. She hurried up to the car and looked down on her sleeping sister while yanking open the door.

"Hey! You could have called," she said to Buffy as the Slayer muzzily woke up. "I was worried about you." She glanced at Xander. "It's like those movies where the guy says, 'I'm going out for cigarettes,' and then he, like, totally splits."

"Only Buffy doesn't smoke, so you should have been suspicious right off," Xander told her.

Dawn shrugged. "She said she was going out patrolling for a little while. Not all night."

"I'm sorry, Dawn." Buffy yawned. "Forgot the cell phone."

"And your toothbrush," Dawn retorted, waving her hand in front of her nose. "Did you kill anything? And then, like, devour it?"

"I'm not sure. I think she was already dead." Buffy swung her legs out of the car. "But I didn't devour her." She looked up at her sister. "Listen, Dawnie, someone got killed at the museum last night. A security guard, young, female, just moved here. If the other kids at school talk about it—"

Dawn brightened. "On it. Not for nothing am I called Harriet the Spy. Or rather, Dawn the Spy." She scrunched up her nose. "Actually, I'm not called Dawn the Spy. No one knows I spy."

"Good. You're a good spy." Buffy stood up and put her hand

on Dawn's shoulder. "It was a girl named . . ." She looked at Xander.

"Tilly or something," Xander supplied. "Laurens, like her cousin. Lorenzo."

Buffy gave a little moan. "Lorenzo Laurens? That's so sad. What are some parents thinking with the names?"

"Are you staying home from school?" Dawn asked Buffy.

"Yes, because she stayed out all night," Xander interposed. Then he added, heading young sis off at the pass, "You, however, will be going."

Dawn raised her brows, all innocence and hope. "If I say I stayed up all night, can I stay home too?" At Buffy's stern expression, she added quickly, "Stayed up all night worrying about you?"

"Nice try," Buffy drawled. "Where's Willow?" Willow was usually the official driver-to-school.

"Inside. She looks tired too. Too tired to drive, probably." Again with the hope.

Buffy turned to the man with the wheels. "Xander? Can you help?"

"'Help' is my middle name. Well, actually, it's Lavelle. But I'm happy to drive her to the unhallowed halls of learning," Xander replied as Dawn made a sad face. "On my way to my meeting, which I should rush to attend." He smiled at little sis. "Dawn, shall we?"

"But we have a quiz in history," Dawn whimpered.

"Then you should have stayed up all night studying," Buffy said cheerily. She loaded Dawn into the car and gave her a little wave. "Night."

Dawn crossed her arms over her chest. "Humph."

"Save it for your history teacher," Buffy told her. She shut the door and gave Dawn another cheery little wave.

Dawn remained farewell-free as Xander backed out of the driveway and headed toward the newly rebuilt Sunnydale High. Relieved that her sister hadn't put up more of a fight about getting out of the quiz, Buffy headed toward the occasionally rebuilt Summers residence.

I remain the champion of cutting school and having no marketable skills to show for it, she thought. *Thank goodness.*

Buffy let herself in through the kitchen, where Willow was hunched over a portable fan, daubing her cheeks with a wet paper towel. She was dressed in a filmy, calf-length, wine-colored skirt and wine-and-moss-colored sleeveless top, and she looked good. Ever since Willow had gone veiny and evil, her fashion sense had continued to improve.

"Okay," the Wicca said at the sound of the closing door. She began to straighten. "I'll get my keys"—she glanced over her shoulder—"only now I won't, because you aren't Dawnie in need of a ride to school."

"I am Buffy in need of a few hours of sleep." Buffy gestured with her head in the direction of the driveway. "She snagged a ride with Xander."

"Good, because I don't want to move a muscle." Willow turned her face back to the fan. "It's hotter than hell."

"Spike says not." Buffy opened the fridge and got out a half-gallon of orange juice. The sensation of cool air against her face was wonderful, and it was with real regret that she closed the fridge.

She half-raised the container toward Willow, who pointed to a glass on the table that was already half-full.

Wow, half-full. I'm an optimistic person, Buffy observed, happy with that thought.

She poured herself the OJ, set down the container, and sat at the kitchen table. Combing her fingers through her hair, she leaned back, sighing, loving the moment that contained no violence, death, or detached body parts cooking in the morning sunshine.

"Spike went patrolling with you?" Willow asked anxiously.

"Showed unexpectedly," Buffy assured her. "And he was a help." She moved her shoulders and cricked her neck. "I saw something a little odd tonight. This decomposing Chinese girl who spoke English. And sang. Also, a really big skeleton that tried to choke me to death." At Willow's look of alarm, Buffy added, "It didn't."

"That's good." Willow frowned. "Were they together? Do you know if magicks were involved? Things have been very active lately."

"She made some kind of crack about there's lots of evil in China," Buffy told her. "Then Xander and I just tried to investigate this death at the museum. Did you hear about it yet? A guard was smushed by a statue. Also from China—the statue, not the girl." She thought a moment. "Or maybe the girl was also Chinese. I don't know. I'm just assuming there."

"Anyway, there was a death," Willow concluded.

"Two." Buffy held up her fingers. "An old man near the rest home, and this guard at the museum."

"Okay." Willow took that in. "Also, sad."

"I was hoping you could do some research. Maybe with Anya."

"Sure. Now that she isn't a vengeance demon, we can do that." Willow picked up her orange juice and moved to the table, taking a seat across from Buffy. "Chinese. Did either of them say anything else? Has the statue made a statement?"

"The statue has remained mum, at least as far as I know. And, yeah. The little girl said something about the three and the two."

Willow pondered that while she sipped her juice. "Hmm. Anything about a one?"

"Sorry, my bad. Also a one," Buffy informed her. "A three and a two and a one." She drank some more orange juice. "I think three and two are preparing the way for a one."

"There's one statue," Willow said, daubing her face.

"One that moved. There are like a jillion statues." She thought a moment. "She said 'we' are gathering in anticipation. Of the two, I think. Oh, and something evil's coming and it's time for me to die. Again."

"Maybe it's the two deaths last night," Willow said.

"Probably that." Buffy gathered up her blond hair and twisted it into a chignon, holding it off her neck and closing her eyes. "She also sang a hymn. *I've got peace like a river in my soul.*"

"Hmm."

"However, I do believe she was soul-free. Also, not the best singer."

"Vampire?" Willow asked, then added, "Even though our vampires seem to be ensouled these days." She thought a moment. "Not sure about the singing. Spike did okay when we went all musical."

"Our *vampire* is a special case." Buffy wondered why she made a point of correcting Willow on her choice of a plural noun. After all, Angel was ensouled too.

Maybe because he's not one of "our" vampires anymore.

But I've been dreaming about him. About being with him . . .

. . . Wow . . .

"Buffy?" Willow queried.

Buffy jumped guiltily. "Huh?"

"I asked you where Spike went."

She collected herself, smoothing her hair and clearing her throat. "Out of the sun. Into a crypt."

"He have any thoughts?"

"Some. Nothing very helpful, although, happily, coherent."

"That is happy," Willow agreed. "Going crazy really takes it out of a person."

"Xander suggested you look into joss tossing. Joss sticks. Maybe Anya has some."

"Could be," Willow agreed. She gave Buffy a quick nod. "I'll get right on it, Chief. I'll call Anya and see if she wants to go over the research at her place. She rents. Utilities are included."

"Air-conditioning," Buffy realized. "Wow."

"Yeah." Willow's voice was hushed, reverent. "Air-conditioning."

Buffy took another sip of juice and pressed the glass against her forehead. "God, it's so hot. I remember when Mom used to yell at us for forgetting to close the windows when she ran the air conditioner. Now we can't afford to run it at all."

"Things will get better," Willow assured her. She lowered her voice and added, "Before I started my recovery program, I used to fantasize about divining the winning numbers for the lottery. I would have been on that 'three and two and one' thing like a flash, see if we could win the Double Lotto with it."

"That would be so wrong," Buffy said wistfully.

"Yeah. Sorry about that."

They smiled wryly at each other. Then Buffy drained the glass and stood up slowly. "I'm going to collapse for a while. I shouldn't be this tired. I'm the Slayer and I only killed two dead things."

"It's the heat," Willow suggested.

Buffy moaned and headed upstairs. She took a quick shower and washed her hair, then pulled on some boxers and a fresh baby tee.

She had just slid under the sheets when the phone rang. She

whimpered once, then realized it might be Principal Wood checking in on her. She picked it up and muttered, "H'lo?"

She saw Willow on the threshold of her room and nodded at her to come on in.

"Buffy." It was Angel.

Buffy's eyes widened. Her heart did . . . something. Like skipping or maybe thundering. She wasn't sure. They didn't call each other much. It was easier that way. But the dreams . . .

They were repeats of dreams she had had three years ago: Angel confessing his love, and then fire, all around . . .

Her body, igniting, with heat and passion . . .

Angel with her, the way . . . the way they had been once, only once. She dreamed of him, of that. Of his touch, and his body . . .

"Buffy?" Angel said.

She realized she wasn't speaking. She managed to make the sounds come out.

"Hi. Angel," she croaked.

Willow looked intrigued. She walked into the room and perched on the side of Buffy's bed. Buffy grimaced, and Willow patted her hand.

"So. Um. What's up?" Buffy asked Angel, when he didn't say anything more. She figured this was difficult for him too. The speaking thing.

"Terra-cotta statues," he replied. His voice was husky, a bit strained. "You've got some too."

"Chinese?" she asked, looking at Willow. "Warrior guys?"

Willow processed that.

"Warrior guys," Angel said.

"We think one of them just killed a security guard at the museum," she told him. "What are yours doing?"

"Huh." Angel sounded surprised. "So far, ours aren't doing anything. Fred linked our exhibit with your exhibit."

"You have an exhibit," she repeated for Willow's benefit.

"At the Liang. Gunn—a guy I work with—"

"I know who he is," Buffy told him.

"Right. He and I went over there, checked it out. We had a tip that something was going to go down. Jhiera was there. Old nemesis. Sort of."

"Jhiera?" Buffy echoed, looking at Willow, who shook her head to indicate her ignorance of the name. "Liang?"

"Museum," Willow supplied, under her breath. "Art."

"The Liang Art Museum?" Buffy asked Angel.

"Jhiera was at the Liang Museum. And so was Alex Liang. Museum is named after him. Rich businessman up here. He was with Jhiera, and they got attacked by some Vigories of Oden Tal. Those are interdimensional warriors. Yes, art."

"Who's Jhiera?" Buffy asked.

"She's their princess," Angel filled in. "About three years ago, we fought over some guys she was killing. I told her to stay out of Los Angeles."

"She didn't listen to you," Buffy likewise filled in. "And she's back."

"Right. I think she's involved with Alex Liang somehow. And he's behind the five exhibitions of these warriors. So, I'm assuming he's evil."

She nodded even though he couldn't see her. "We had a Chinese ghost who kept saying the one we were seeking was here. And something about a one and a two and a three."

"A Chinese ghost?" he repeated.

Buffy filled him in. "She came equipped with an attacking skeleton," she finished. "Willow and Anya are going to look into it."

"Good. Let me know what they find out."

"I will."

About the three other exhibits," Angel continued. "They're in Cleveland, Tokyo, and Frankfurt, Germany. Does that mean anything to you?"

She was puzzled. "Cleveland, Tokyo?" Then she closed her eyes and said, "Cleveland *and* Tokyo. I knew that."

"And Sunnydale," he finished.

She looked at Willow. "They have exhibits too."

"Tell Angel I said hi," Willow said.

"Willow says hi."

"Hi back." His voice was warmer now. It was almost like he was comfortable talking to her.

"Angel . . ." Buffy trailed off. *Do you miss me? Do you dream about me too? About making love to me? Oh, Angel . . .*

"Yes, Buffy?"

"Do you have any connections in those places?" she said quickly. "Maybe we should warn them."

"There's a guy in the hospital we're going to try to work with," Angel told her. "Museum curator."

"At the Liang," she said.

"Right. His name is Dr. Tsung Wei, and he was in charge of all the installations. Either he's a pawn or a bad guy. We're going to figure that out after you and I hang up."

"Sounds like a plan."

"Sorry I woke you." He hesitated. "I could have called later. . . ."

"I was up," she assured him quickly. "Will and me. We were up, both of us. Just us."

"How's Dawn?"

"Great," she said. "Well, except for carrying on the fine Summers tradition of not studying. Let me write down that guy's name." She opened the drawer in the nightstand and fished out a notepad and a pen.

"T-S-U-N-G, new word, W-E-I," Angel told her.

"Got it," she informed him.

"Okay, then. I'll let you know what we find out. In the meantime, watch your back."

"You, too, Angel." She took a deep breath, really not wanting to go. Knowing she had to. "Bye."

"Buffy . . ." There was a pause. Buffy caught her breath. Then Angel said softly, "Take care."

The words were spoken so quietly, so gently, and yet, they slid through her heart like a knife.

We had to do this, right? she wanted to say to him. *We had to part, stay away?*

She cleared her throat.

"Thanks. You, too, Ange . . . Angel."

They disconnected.

Buffy set down the phone, looked anxiously at Willow, and said, "I'm *so* not supposed to care, but who the heck is Jhiera?"

CHAPTER FIVE

Sunnydale

Dawn slunk down the halls of Sunnydale High, ears pricked for gossip about dead security guards. In the distance she saw R. J., the quarterback whose letter jacket had put her, Anya, Willow, and Buffy under a love spell. Unlike his brother, who had lost the magick when he'd, well, lost the magick, R. J. still had a couple of dozen girls drooling over him, although of course the jacket was history. Xander and Spike had burned it in her very own fireplace.

And I cannot imagine ever having a fire in that fireplace again. It is so hot.

The girls—seniors, dressed like hoochie mamas and wearing way too much makeup—were hanging on every single word R. J. said, as if he had just invented the English language.

Dawn rolled her eyes. She was *so* over him.

In fact, so over him that she accidentally ran directly into the chest of Principal Wood, who had been walking down the hall from the opposite direction.

"Oh, my God!" Dawn squealed, embarrassed. She dropped her books; they plummeted to the floor—and on Principal Wood's nicely polished loafers—like boulders of knowledge. She began to dive after them.

"Miss Summers. Ouch," he said, then halted her progress toward the floor with a polite tap-tap on her shoulders. "Please, allow me. I'll get them."

"Oh, I'm so sorry. And my sister's sick," she added, covering her mouth in total humiliation as Principal Wood squatted on the floor and picked up her books "She's way barfing."

Her biology notebook had flopped open, and there for him to see were the doodles and notes she and Roxanne Ruani had passed back and forth during the highly informative and very funny sex-ed movie she'd seen last Tuesday. Things she did not *want* the principal of her entire high school to see.

He either didn't notice or was amazingly polite as he closed the notebook and placed it on top of the stack of books he had made. Then he scooped them all up and said to her, "Have you considered a backpack?"

"Yes. I have one," she said quickly. "Only, it was inside the house and I saw Xander and Buffy driving up from . . . the doctor's office . . ." She slowed down. "Because of, you know, the sickness. That she has. And Xander offered me a ride."

He eyed her. Gosh, he was cute. It was embarrassing to think that way about a guy as old as he must be, but there it was.

"What's wrong with Buffy?" he asked her.

"Rash," she blurted.

"A heat rash?"

"Yes. Heat."

He tsk-tsked, looking sympathetic. "Those can be miserable. Tell her I hope she feels better."

"She will. Once she stops, um, itching," Dawn said brightly. "The itching is just making her batshi . . . crazy." She swallowed. "I think she barfed because of the heat, also." She wished she could just fold herself up and climb inside her own jeans pocket, away from his deep brown principal's eyes that seemed to see everything. "Um, I have to get to class."

"Of course." He handed her the pile of books. "I'll cancel her appointments. She has a bereavement case today. I think it's her first."

"Bereavement," Dawn echoed, her heart skipping a beat. "As in, somebody dying?"

"Yes. A student's cousin, just moved here from out of town," he said. "But I can't really discuss that. It's confidential."

"Of course." She bobbed her head. "Because, that means you can't talk about it."

"Right." He smiled faintly, then raised his brows. "The bell is going to ring."

"Right." She flashed a crazed smile at him and scooted around him, practically running down the hall.

Robin Wood looked after the sister of the Slayer. He didn't for a moment think the Slayer was ill.

Wonder what Buffy's been up to.

Wonder if it's something I can help with.

He wasn't sure it was time yet to let her know who he was. He couldn't gauge how she would react. He had gone to a lot of trouble to land this job at Sunnydale High, with the hope of assisting the Slayer in her ongoing battle against the forces of darkness. If she rejected his offer of help, he wasn't sure what he would do next. Sunnydale was located on a hellmouth, a focal point for evil, and activity had stepped up of late. Robin figured Buffy Summers could use all the help she could get.

No guarantee she'll see it that way, though.

No one knew that Robin Wood was the son of Nikki Wood the Vampire Slayer, who had died before he was old enough to go to kindergarten. No one realized that Robin had engineered his transfer to Sunnydale to join forces with the current Slayer in her battle against evil . . . if she would let him.

No one suspected a thing . . . least of all, Buffy Summers.

He continued down the hall to his office. The secretary, Ms. Khabazian, looked up from her desk in greeting.

"Cancel Emilio Laurens's appointment with Ms. Summers," he said. "But keep his hour with Dr. Hildalgo." Dr. Hildalgo was the school's staff psychologist. As an employee of the Sunnydale High School District, he had a lot of experience counseling students with loved ones who had died.

The dark-haired young woman nodded. Then she said, "By the way, the museum wants to know if we plan to proceed with the field trip to the exhibit. Next Wednesday," she reminded him helpfully. "Assuming the police are finished with their investigation by then."

"Hmm. Good question," Robin replied. "I'll have to think about that."

Ms. Khabazian smiled wryly. "With a murder scene to gawk at, you know the kids will be dying to go. So to speak."

"So to speak." He opened the door to his office, went in, and shut the door.

I wonder if Buffy's found out anything about this death, he thought.

The police hadn't shared anything substantive except that a probable homicide had occurred. One of the school security guards with an inside track had informed Robin that they weren't even sure of that; that it may have been that the strong Santa Ana wind had knocked a statue over, crushing the young woman in a terrible freak accident—but an accident nonetheless.

And anyone who believes that . . . is a typical resident of Sunnydale, the happy town swimming in denial.

He sighed and pressed the speaker button on his phone for the secretary.

"Assuming the police give us an all-clear, we'll be going on the field trip," he told her. Denial extended to parents of his students. And if he knew teenagers, they'd all find a way to get over there and check the death site for themselves. Better to do it in an organized and orderly fashion, keep them together, try to keep them safe.

"Okay. I'll let them know," she said.

He disconnected, and glanced at the whiteboard behind which he had hung his impressive array of weaponry. One press of his finger and the whiteboard would whir upward, revealing glittering knives, swords, brass knuckles, and even a mace—just like in some superspy James Bond flick.

Is it time for me to let Buffy know who I am and what I want? he wondered. *We've only known each other a short time. But demonic activity is up, and I know she could use some help.*

He set that aside for the moment and settled in for his day. He was paging through his schedule of appointments when the speakerphone buzzed. It was Ms. Khabazian again.

"I've got Sam Devol here," she informed him. "He was caught smoking in the bathroom again."

Robin smiled faintly and shook his head at the intrusion of the mundane into his private and far more exciting business. Sam, Sam, Sam. His perennial detention attendee. If there was a rule, Devol would find a way to break it.

"Send him in," Robin told the secretary.

• • •

The hot hours of the hot day were filled with activity at the Sunnydale Museum of History. Police investigators dusted the statue in which Fai-Lok resided, looking for clues to explain the death of the insignificant female guard. With her terror and her agony, she had brought great heat into his being, and he was revitalized, though he remained still inside his statue.

"Man, she reeks," said the Sunnydale Medical Examiner. He had swiped some kind of fragrant cream beneath his nostrils, forming a white mustache.

The man reminded Fai-Lok of Bai Ju, the supreme leader of the Ice Hell Brotherhood at the home temple back in China. Bai Ju was the one who was charged with the magickal transport of the dragon, Fire Storm.

Little does he realize I have an operative who will thwart his mission to send the dragon through the portal to Qin in Los Angeles. Fire Storm will land in Sunnydale. The Orb will call her here. And she will destroy the home base of the Slayer.

Suddenly a ghostchild appeared on the periphery of the crime scene. This particular manifestation was a little girl dressed in old-fashioned Christian missionary clothing from the days of Queen Victoria. The laces and velvets of her dress were rotted and covered with mold. She was at the moment unaware of him, though, of course, his soul-blood was what had drawn her to this place.

Fai-Lok frowned, displeased that his essence was being siphoned off to feed one such as she. The Hellmouth served as a beacon for the forces of darkness; because he was a creature of magickal darkness, he attracted them as well. His vital force called to souls who still walked; they capered and hurried along the conduits and corridors frequented by the dead, drawn to him. He could not always control them, and he had not anticipated this creature's appearance on such a day.

He saw her scanning the area for him with her dark, almond-shaped eyes, sensing his energy if not his precise location. It was not a propitious moment to reveal his presence, though it was a temptation to appear to her if only to order her to go away. With great force of will, he kept his exterior demonic appearance concealed, remaining invisible as he maintained his Possession of the statue.

After a time, she faded away, looking forlorn. Such a creature was evil and reveled in mayhem, more like a demon than the phantoms born in Europe and America. Chinese ghosts hunted human beings and brought them down like wild animals. He wouldn't be surprised if the little girl had killed a few people since arriving in Sunnydale.

After several long hours, the medical examiner began to slowly remove the fragments of the dead female's body. Flies were buzzing around it by then, and the hot sun made her stink worse, if such a thing were possible. Fai-Lok wasn't a weak-hearted man, but he was a refined man, and the stench wore on him and made him irritable.

He began to wonder why Tsung Wei hadn't done something to speed up the police investigation. By now, the curator of the Liang Museum in L.A. should have paid off the right people here in Sunnydale to cover up Fai-Lok's little misstep.

Had I only known how ineffectual he was . . . the murder of one insignificant guard should not create such a scene. I am a Possessor; I need to have heat.

Murder creates a lot of heat.

Fai-Lok shifted, feeling thwarted and ill-tempered. For now, he was trapped inside the statue, even though it was becoming psychically painful for him. The *p'ai* energy inside the terra-cotta warriors was brittle from misuse. The lower souls of Qin's fearsome armies had been magickally captured and imprisoned

125

during the time when Fai-Lok had served Qin in his original corporeal form.

If he listened closely even now, he could hear the screams of the soldiers he had butchered as their souls were shredded, their upper souls fleeing into the sky before they realized that they had been shorn of their *p'ai*. The *p'ai* gave them movement and volition; without it, they became wraithlike, pitiful shadows drifting on the winds, howling and mournful, filled with impotent rage.

The little ghostgirl was not such a one. She was a true ghost, a reflection of herself as she had been in human form. Fai-Lok had no idea who she was, but he knew that his energy would begin to draw even more strange supernatural beings to this place. Amplified as it was by his proximity to a hellmouth, Sunnydale would soon become the home territory for hundreds, if not thousands, of terrifying monsters the Slayer had never even dreamed of.

He was amazed that the police remained after the sun had set. Such hard workers! So dedicated! Like efficient bugs, they planted little flags where the various shards and bits of girl had lain, taking endless numbers of photographs. The mood among them shifted from bouts of macabre humor to silence and back again. He remained within the body of the statue, peering out the eyeholes without revealing his presence through his demonic aspect, as he had done with the guard. He kept himself invisible, and so was not detected even after being poked, prodded, and examined all day long.

Dr. Alan Johnson, the Sunnydale Museum of History curator, arrived to observe the scene. He had been out of town, and only just returned.

"Great, just great," the man muttered, wiping his brow with his handkerchief. "Tsung Wei will have my head."

Johnson turned to one of the police officers, the tall man with close-cropped blond hair. "Just the one statue was destroyed, right?"

"Yes, sir. And the one girl killed," the officer replied, clearly suppressing some anger at the other man's misplaced priorities.

"That sucks," the man muttered. He hovered at the edge of the yellow police tape, looking distinctly uncomfortable. His gaze swept the lines of statues, the milling officers. It was a chaotic scene. "Might I . . . ?"

"Sorry, Dr. Johnson. This is a crime scene. I can't let you go in," the tall officer told him, holding up a hand.

"Huh." The curator drew back from the officer as if he had touched a hot flame. He glanced at the museum building with a wistful expression. "I suppose the whole place is off-limits right now, too?"

"We'd prefer that you didn't go in right now, sir," the blond man said.

"I'm responsible for all the exhibits," Johnson pointed out. "I need to see if anything was stolen."

"We have people inside, looking for clues," another cop told him in a far more sympathetic tone than the blond cop's. "We'll do an inventory eventually, but top priority is the death."

Johnson wiped his brow again. He looked very worried. "I just got this job. There aren't a lot of positions in this field." Folding his handkerchief, he stuffed it in his pocket. "It was this or teaching art history in Kansas." He made a face.

"Ms. Laurens was an only child," the blond police officer replied steadily.

"You probably think I'm an insensitive jerk," Johnson shot back. "I *am* aware that someone got killed."

The short officer gave the blond one a look. The blond one said, "I'm sorry, Dr. Johnson. It's just that she was killed very brutally." Then he smiled faintly and added, "I'm new here too. Just transferred down from Simi Valley."

Johnson's voice softened. "Welcome to Sunnydale."

"Same to you, Dr. Johnson," the policeman said.

They smiled sourly at each other.

Fai-Lok was displeased. It occurred to him that he ought not to have murdered the girl.

I was hungry.

She was . . . there. . . .

One of the officers received a call on her radio phone. She spoke for a few moments, then hung up and walked over to the medical examiner.

Fai-Lok listened carefully.

"That was about Tsung Wei, the Liang Museum curator. He was attacked last night on the Liang Museum grounds," she informed her colleague. "He's in the hospital."

As the M.E. removed another section of the victim from beneath Fai-Lok's statue, he replied, "Sounds like a coordinated action."

"Sounds like," she confirmed. "There were signs of vandalism at the L.A. museum as well. A fire on the grounds, deliberately set."

Had Xian and Qin also made mischief up in Los Angeles? If so, Qin would be more forgiving of Fai-Lok's misadventure.

We must be more discreet. These humans might not see our hand, but there are others who might.

The Slayer.

Angel.

And I cannot afford to anger Qin.

Our plan calls for me to summon our demon friends from the Hellmouth and use them and the terra-cotta warriors to distract Buffy Summers. Then Bai Ju is supposed to send Fire Storm to Qin.

That is the plan.

But Xian and I have another agenda.

Fire Storm will come to me here in Sunnydale. We will pretend it is an accident, and we will persuade Qin to allow Jhiera to come here to thaw her out.

And we will turn Fire Storm against Qin and mount a war against him.

We will triumph. I have seen it in the joss.

He smiled in anticipation.

Then he lost hold of the Possession.

It happened in an instant, and he was not ready for it. One moment, he was still warm inside the broken statue; the next, he hurtled through time and space and the dark places between them.

Space was a freezing vacuum, culling every speck of warmth from him and crystallizing it into panes of nothingness. Space was the enemy; without borders and boundaries, his mind would lose definition, his soul would blast apart.

Then, briefly, there was a sense of something else with him, something close by that was more powerful than he could imagine. An Other . . .

What is this? Who are you? he demanded, terrified and invaded.

The only answer was a long, low chuckle, of such evil proportions that he could barely comprehend it.

And then, it was gone.

And then . . . he forgot about it. Completely and utterly, as if it had never happened.

His attention returned to his predicament; he shuddered with the cold as he soared past flickering ice-blue and deep purple shadows of times and places and the elongated faces of the dead—men, women, children; the thousands upon thousands of ancient Chinese dead he had helped Qin slaughter. The thousands he had killed since then, personally, and with the help of the Ice Hell Brotherhood—Russians, Japanese, British, Americans.

Their rituals required sacrifices.

Many of them.

Then he shot past solid shapes and into the ether, the black hole in the dead center, blackest heart of space. All was soundless and formless there, sucking in all time and space and form and movement; for a moment, he was blind and deaf, could taste nothing, smell nothing. He had no body and no grasp of his senses. For a single blink, he had no thoughts.

He was . . . *not*.

Suddenly his mind snapped into focus, followed by his senses. There was nothing to see for the next few moments: Then he flew past the shadows and the dead faces, the hungry dead and the angry dead, all the screaming and all the lamenting, as he returned to the plane of human existence in Sunnydale.

Chilled, he hung disembodied in the air, hovering like steam while he looked for a body to claim. The freezing made returning to a fresh warrior body an unappetizing prospect. He could continue to hide among them if he had to, but he was clearly growing less able to stay inside these prisons of clay.

None of the police officers carried Dark Blood, which bewildered Fai-Lok. He had assumed that most of the police force in Sunnydale would be quite evil and corrupt, but the earnest folk dusting statues and taking photographs of blood splatters were innocent souls in the extreme.

He began to grow colder. Slowly the police departed, a few lingering behind; then one was posted as a guard. As the others trailed away, the man stood alone, uneasy; and he paced and checked his radio phone over and over, betraying his anxiety.

The night settled in. The stars glittered. The orange and yellow banners flapped in the hot winds.

The air was warm, and Fai-Lok was grateful for that. There was a time when he had dreamed of learning to control the elements, cloaking China in an eternal summer. He had not succeeded in mastering the heavens. But with Jhiera on their side, fire would come to this planet, and it would be glorious.

After a time, the single police guard uttered a strangled cry. Then he whirled in a half-circle, staggering. Without further warning, he slid to the ground as if his bones had been ripped from his body. Surprised, Fai-Lok stared down at him, searching for signs of violence.

I didn't do that. Did I?

The man's eyes were closed. He was breathing. Not dead, then. But what had happened to him?

All was silent for another few seconds. Then a young woman with red hair stepped cautiously from the shadows. She was young, and quite lovely. Dressed in shades of burgundy, she crouched beside the young man, regarded him with great satisfaction, and curled her fingers at him like a Siamese dancing girl. She peered at him again, nodding to herself. Then she gestured behind herself, urging someone else to join her.

Recognition dawned on Fai-Lok as she gracefully rose. *She's Willow Rosenberg. A modern witch, and a follower of the Slayer.*

More people crept stealthily from the stand of trees on the west side of the parking lot. One by one they stepped into the glare of the klieg lights illuminating the frozen army of Qin. Fai-Lok knew each of the faces of the interlopers from JPEGs that Coach Wong had posted on their private Web site.

The dark-haired young man wearing a loose short-sleeved shirt over a T-shirt was Xander Harris, second in command to the Slayer. Next came Anya, a twice-changed vengeance demon. She wore her hair swept up, and was clothed in a filmy blouse and a short blue skirt. None of the three could be Possessed. None carried Dark Blood, although Anya's essence spoke of a whisper of it. It was not enough to sustain him, though. Pity.

It was not so much that being demonic carried Dark Blood with it, but that Dark Blood was a symptom of an enhanced capacity for evil. There were humans who carried Dark Blood—such as Qin's former attorney, Lilah Morgan, late of Wolfram & Hart—and demons who did not.

Fai-Lok had assumed that the blood of evil would surge through at least one of the bodies of the Slayer's band. Their actions spoke of their ease in traveling from good to evil and back again. Look at Anya, who had become a vengeance demon twice. Yet there was very little Dark Blood in her being.

Curious.

I'll have to forage for Dark Blood, then, he thought unhappily. *Move through the night like a wraith myself, and locate someone to Possess.*

Then Fai-Lok's soul-blood pulsed warm and electric as he sensed what he was looking for. He brightened.

Oh. There!

One who carries Dark Blood!

It was Spike the vampire, still a tall young man with platinum-blond hair. He strode from the trees as if he had no fear of anything in this world or the next; he briefly joined the others, then strolled toward the rows of terra-cotta warriors. Despite the hot weather, he was dressed all in black and wore heavy boots that clomped on the perimeter of the asphalt parking lot. Without missing a beat, he hoisted one leg over the yellow plastic police tape that read SUNNYDALE POLICE DEPARTMENT. DO NOT CROSS.

He glided quietly toward where the smashed statue had lain, touched the surface, and sniffed his fingers.

Spike, who had been in China. Spike, who had killed a Chinese slayer. Interesting that he was back in Sunnydale. Coach Wong had not informed him of that.

Fai-Lok was fascinated by Spike, by the eddies and flows of darkness that swirled within the essence of the vampire.

He has strong Dark Blood inside him. He's practically evil incarnate. And yet, he has a very strong soul of goodness. . . .

At the first possible moment, I will Possess him. It should prove to be exhilarating. And exhilaration warms me. . . .

Fai-Lok was hungry for the heat that resting inside a creature like William the Bloody would bring. Why, to be inside Spike might be a bonfire.

His appetite urged him to make the attempt here, now. It would be sweetly warm, deliriously hot!

I'll do it!

Anticipating the wonderful sensation, he cast his glance toward the vampire. He could almost hear the voice of sweet Xian warning him not to act rashly. According to her, his impetuousness was his greatest weakness, and the reason that he served another instead of ruling as master himself.

But I want that heat!

As if her voice whispered to him on the Santa Ana wind, Xian's voice echoed in his mind: *But do you want the consequences?*

Not only would it be dangerous to attempt such a thing in front of a witch of the caliber of Willow Rosenberg, but these were the friends of the Slayer, who were used to battle. He must do nothing to alert them to his presence.

And yet, he was already growing cold. . . .

"Well, let's see if we can find out what kind of monster killed Tilisa Laurens," Willow Rosenberg said aloud. "Then maybe we can see if that death is related to the others we've been having around here."

Then Buffy the Vampire Slayer herself emerged from the darkness with a crossbow in her arms. She walked with the stealth of a tiger, deliciously feral. The unmistakable mantel of power rested on her shoulders; he was drawn to her energy, but alas, she had no Dark Blood inside her.

Greetings, Most Honorable Slayer. May you die for a hundred thousand years.

By the Goddess Kwan Yin, whom he did not worship but by whom he had often sworn when he was in his mortal life, Buffy Summers was quite lovely. The pictures of her that he had seen on his laptop had not done her justice. She had beautiful, shiny blond hair that tumbled over the shoulders of her turquoise tank top. She wore black trousers of some sort, and boots with short heels. Silver rings gleamed on her fingers and thumb, and tiny hoops, several, in both her ears. She was quite slender, and her eyes were dark and enormous.

What an exquisite warrior. He was moved by her beauty. Xian in her original form had been like that—a combination of ruthless fighter and delicate maiden. Of course, Xian had been bred to be a courtesan. Buffy Summers had been bred to be a killing machine.

I must take care around her. I must never forget who and what she is, no matter how lovely I find her to be.

"Human blood," Spike announced, holding up the piece of pottery he had been smelling. "An' somep'n else I have never smelled before." He looked puzzled.

"Could that be the exciting fragrance of . . . deodorant?" Xander Harris asked him snidely.

Dislike between them, then. Are they rivals for the Slayer's affections? Coach Wong has said nothing about that.

"What do you mean?" Buffy moved past Xander and crouched beside the blond man.

"It means Spike needs to take showers more often," Xander rejoined.

Spike handed the shard to her. "There's something in this. Some kind of, I dunno, smell-vibrations. Like something was there and isn't now." He shrugged and clasped his hands, resting his elbows on his knees.

"Smell vibrations?" Xander repeated. "Are you on something, Spike?"

"Magickal residue," Spike said, quite irritated.

"Does it affect short-term memory? Like remembering to empty your smelly ashtrays?" Xander sniped.

"Leftovers of an animation spell?" Buffy asked Spike. "Like a spell that could have animated the hand that little dead girl was playing with?"

How curious. How interesting, Fai-Lok thought, eavesdropping with great delight. *They have met the ghostchild. And they are on to my presence inside the statue. I must take care.*

"No clue. That's Red's department, inn't?" Spike extended one long finger and pointed it at Willow.

"Will?" Buffy said, handing the shard to the witch. Willow solemnly took it and placed it in a brown paper evidence bag similar to the ones the Sunnydale police had used.

"I think you're right, Buffy. Maybe she used the animation spell to move the hand, and then later the statue. So then the statue came to life and attacked Lorenzo's cousin," Xander said.

"And it ate her up," Anya murmured pensively. "Poor innocent security guard."

"Dawn said her cousin thinks that too," Buffy told them. "That it was the statue. He'd heard the rumors about all the other coming-to-life museum exhibits. Lorenzo's cousin was scheduled to come in for bereavement counseling. While I was asleep."

She looked quite disturbed as she spoke. Fai-Lok had no idea why, nor what the witch's gentle pat on the Slayer's arm might signify.

"You needed your rest," Willow said. "I'll do some spells when we get home. But I think you guys are on to something."

"Are you going to check for traces of psychic transference?" Anya asked her.

Willow nodded. "With a Krevalsky's Titration."

"I'd try a Hardwick's Denaturing Spell too," Anya offered.

"Good idea," the witch replied. There was tension between her and Anya, as there was between Anya and Xander. Fai-Lok was interested. Aside from the return of Spike, there had been developments in the relationships among the Slayer's band of which he had not been kept apprised.

"We should do one of those demon-finding spells too," Anya suggested. "Without getting all sexy," she added, glancing at Willow.

"Sexy. Wouldn't want that," Xander muttered. "But I'm betting you'll find lots of new demon faces in town."

"So much new activity," Willow said, nodding.

"Thinkin' about starting up a demony dating service," Spike drawled.

"Oh, because you're so good at dating," Xander said. "Drusilla, Harmony—"

"Buffy," Anya interposed.

"Hey, we never dated," Buffy blurted, then looked awkward and glanced away. "No one here is good at dating, okay?" she said. "And we're not here to talk about dating demons. We're here to talk about killing them."

"Slayer's right," Spike grumbled. He raised his face to the

136

wind. "Weird smell. Like blood, only . . . only it's in the air."

"That's where smells come from," Anya said.

"Different." Spike shook his head.

"Like how?" Buffy glanced from him to Willow, who knit her red eyebrows and regarded him intently.

He kept sniffing. "Dunno. But it's strong around here." He squinted and stared upward.

"Magickal blood? The blood of something we can't see?" Willow posited. She glanced around, as if searching for clues in the night sky. Fai-Lok drew back into himself—a reflex only, as he could not be seen. He hovered, impressed by the speed with which they made their deductions. Clearly, this group had experienced many, many supernatural occurrences here in their hometown.

It will be fascinating to see how long they last against what is to come. I'm almost sorry they will die.

"Tell us again about the little cannibal girl," Xander suggested to Buffy while the witch spread her fingers and closed her eyes, as if searching the air for clues.

"Cannibal. Not sure of that. And, well, she . . . looked like that," Buffy said simply, pointing in the direction they had come.

The ghostchild had returned, wearing the face of her mortal life and the rotting clothes in which she had appeared to Fai-Lok. She flitted among the trees, dancing in a circle and singing in Chinese. Fai-Lok knew the words; it was an old funeral dirge.

Then the child said to the Slayer, "Greetings to you. The One we await lurks near you."

"Really?" Buffy looked first to her, and then to the others. "Is that a fact? Show me."

The girl spread her fingers and motioned all around them.

She twirled slowly in a circle. "He is near. He will send for the Flying One. Send through the Honorable One."

Oh, dear. What have we here? Fai-Lok was shocked. *She means me. She's talking about Fire Storm coming through the portal. How does she know that?*

Best to silence her, if he could. The trick, of course, would be to figure out how to dispatch her while he was incorporeal. Even if she had not been a ghost, he wouldn't have been able to Possess her—she was female, and therefore slave to the yin qualities of the universe. He was male, yang. Yin and yang existed separately, and could not mix. So there was no hope there of silencing her by taking her over.

"Send for who?" Willow asked her. "Who will he send through?"

"Actually, that should be 'whom,'" Anya murmured.

"Anya," Xander warned.

Anya shrugged and gave her attention back to the girl, who folded her hands across her chest and sang, "I've got peace like a river in my soul." Then she ticked her glance at Spike. "You don't know who I am, do you? I was a little girl in China when you were there with Drusilla."

"Bloody 'ell," Spike said slowly. "You're what, a vampire?"

She giggled at him.

"I am a ghost now," she said. "I was killed violently during the Boxer Rebellion and I walk now, seeking revenge on the living." She pointed at the Slayer. "You know what that feels like, don't you?"

"Talk some more about the evil in China," Buffy ordered her. She took a threatening step toward the girl, who retreated with a little run back into the woods. "What's coming through? Who is 'he'?" She jerked her head toward Anya and asked, "Or whom?"

"No, who is correct," Anya told her earnestly.

"He is here!" the girl cried. As a hot wind shook the tops of the trees, she raised her short arms upward and threw back her head, laughing. "Master!"

I've got to shut her up!

Fai-Lok swooped close to her; she sensed him and turned her head in his direction. The red-haired witch clearly took note and began to chant a spell. Fai-Lok didn't know what it would do, but he realized he might be in danger of discovery, so he shot upward to a higher distance, until the figures on the ground looked like Chinese puppets.

Something happened then; he wasn't sure if the ghostchild said or did something to provoke the Slayer, but Buffy Summers went after her. The ghost shot into the woods; the Slayer followed after, crashing through the underbrush. The ghost leaped straight into the air; Buffy jumped onto a rock, yanked back a tree limb, and catapulted herself toward the girl.

Fai-Lok wondered if the Slayer knew that the girl could not be destroyed; though her form was solid, she truly was a ghost. Any number of times she could be torn limb from limb, and yet she would come back.

The witch was still chanting; Buffy continued to pursue the ghost, who had scrambled up into a treetop and was shaking her fist at the Slayer and laughing. Fai-Lok realized that the little phantom was insane; something had happened to her prior to her death that had wrenched her senses from her.

While she taunted the Slayer, Spike circled around and approached her treetop sanctuary from the opposite direction. He was stealthy; Fai-Lok appreciated the way he moved. *Like a predator.*

Like me.

Then the witch moved her hands in front of herself and

arched her back. The sky shifted around Fai-Lok, wind whipping. A flash of lightning zigzagged past him, striking the ground near the terra-cotta warriors and singeing the carpet on which they stood.

It was all Fai-Lok could do not to move into the lightning to soak up its heat. He was horribly tempted. His very essence ached for warmth. He was nearly overcome with his hunger. Again, he forced himself not to give in to momentary relief.

Another flash of lightning smashed into the treetop where the little ghost was perched; she screamed and tumbled from the foliage and dropping gracelessly to the earth only a few meters from the Slayer's feet. She tucked in her arms and head and rolled; Buffy darted after her and shot her in the leg with the crossbow she carried.

The ghost shrieked and flailed. Then she wrapped her hands around the wounded leg and tore the bolt from her flesh. Buffy took advantage of that moment to dive after her.

"Need a hand again, luv?" Spike called from his position behind the ghost and the Slayer.

"She's not your luv!" Xander bellowed.

Spike rolled his eyes and darted forward.

And in that moment, something terribly cold washed over the vampire. It was as if someone had draped him in cold netting; it was so cold that it made his knees give way. He fell to the ground, gasping, eyes huge, trying to see what was attacking him.

He moved in a circle, saying, "What is it? Where is it?"

"What are you talking about?" Xander cried at him, pointing his fist at Buffy and the little girl. "Right there!"

Then ice seeped into his skull. His soddin' brain went numb. . . .

"Hey!" he shouted, grabbing his head.

Just as suddenly, the sensation vanished.

Fai-Lok withdrew. *This one cannot be possessed. He has no heat in him at all.* Yet he continued to watch the vampire.

Spike shook his head to make sure the pain was gone, then to clear his mind, and stumbled to his feet. He staggered forward, feeling as if someone had slammed him in the head with a motorcycle. Made of ice. Okay, not a motorcycle.

Spike looked over each shoulder and behind himself; then he realized Buffy was still tangling with the little weirdo.

He hurried over to help her, but his balance was off-kilter. Buffy looked up, a torn-off arm in one hand, a free-ranging leg in the other, and said, "What the hell is this thing?"

"Chinese. They're so off," Spike grumbled. "It's all that opium they smoke. Makes 'em go wrong before they die. Then you're left with inferior material for curses and suchlike."

He waded in and grabbed at the girl, discovering to his dismay that he had pulled the girl's head off her body. Thoroughly repulsed, he stared at it, and said to the girl's face, "What the 'ell are you going on about?"

"He is here, the master! The master is here!" she shrieked.

The she tried to bite him.

"Bloody 'ell!" Spike shouted, dropping her. As it landed, it exploded with the splatter pattern of an overripe cantaloupe. "Eww!"

"Spike," Buffy began, then seemed to think the better of it. She gazed at him as she dropped the rest of the little girl to the ground, making a face at her hands. So to speak. "What happened to you back there, with the jerking and the ow? Bad chipness?"

"Huh." He blinked. "Hadn't though o' that. Could be." He pondered. "Didn't hurt, though. I just felt cold."

"You felt cold," Xander said with disgust as he trotted up to them. Willow and Anya brought up the rear. "On the hottest day in hotville ever."

"Maybe you're cursed," Anya ventured. Then she looked confused. "Except that on a night like this, being cold would be a good thing. So it's not a curse." She shrugged and smiled at Spike. "Maybe it's the beginning of a curse."

"A precursor," Xander quipped.

"Exactly. Maybe his head is going to freeze solid," Anya said enthusiastically.

"We can hope." Xander looked at Willow. "Opinions, Mr. Spock?"

She narrowed her eyes and thought hard. "Strange things are happening, Doctor McCoy."

"Yes," Anya said, vigorously nodding her head. "Strange things."

Spike looked over Anya's head at Buffy. "And those two are the brains of the outfit."

"Hey," Anya protested.

"Strange things even for magickal things," Willow continued. "Magicks have a logic and a consistency to them. They're governed by laws and rules, the same as anything else."

"What part of this is the strangeness?" Buffy asked.

"That thing is a ghost, but it's . . . it's something else too. Its resonance is off." She looked at Anya. "Like it's being created by something or someone else."

"Like the holodeck," Xander threw in excitedly, then blushed and muttered, "I didn't say that."

"It kind of *is* like the holodeck, though," Willow told him. "As if it's composed of energy seeking a form."

"Isn't that what a ghost is?" Buffy volunteered.

"Sort of. But this seems like a construct or something." Willow waved a hand. "I'm having trouble expressing myself. Let me see if I can define it more accurately before I try to explain it to you guys."

"Okay, but what about what just happened to me? The cold thing?" Spike demanded.

Willow gazed at him appraisingly. "It could be that the ghost tried to inhabit you."

"Aww. I liked it better when we thought his head might explode," Xander grumbled.

Spike glared at him. Then he turned to Willow and said, "So, you'll be doing the research, eh?"

On the ground, the police officer Willow had enchanted stirred. Spike glanced down at him as the man murmured, "Onion rings."

"That's our cue to vamoose, right, Will?" Xander asked her. "Or you going to re-whammy him?"

"He's going to have a headache as it is," Willow said sympathetically. "If I knock him out again, he'll feel knocked out. I don't want to cause pain with my magicks."

"I think we should go home," Anya piped up. She glanced around uneasily and lowered her voice. "Next thing you know, there'll be bunnies."

"Can't have that," Spike said under his breath. He looked at the others. "Demon girl's right. I, for one, am calling it a night."

"It's almost time for the duty shift to change," Buffy observed, glancing at Anya's watch. "There'll be new police officers showing up to guard this place. Besides," she added, "Dawn's home alone."

"Gotta hit the old Chisholm Trail," Xander said. "Let's ride off into the sunrise."

"Okay." Buffy glanced around. "But we're not done here. Not by a long shot."

"You're right," Willow agreed. She waved her hands at the unconscious cop. "I'll give us a ten-minute lead. Then he'll wake up. I don't want him to get fired for sleeping on the job."

"That's nice, Will," Buffy said.

"And for your information, I do not wish to be called 'demon girl,'" Anya muttered at Spike.

"Demon woman," he said. She glared at him. "Demon person."

"I'm not a demon. I was de-demonized by D'Hoffryn. Who is now trying to kill me," she reminded him.

"Huh. Maybe this is something D'Hoffryn cooked up," Xander opined.

"I'm thinking not," Willow told him. "Anya's not in the mix."

"But I'll look into it. We'll get to the bottom of this."

The friends blended back into the trees, heading for parked cars and home . . . and, hopefully, some answers.

The sunrise threatened the horizon, and with it, the heat was renewed. But it was not the weather that warmed Fai-Lok's heart.

Just as the Slayer's band left, two young men drifted slowly from a different area of trees toward the murder site. From his vantage point, he could see their Asian features. More importantly, he could smell the Dark Blood of the taller and more handsome of the two.

An older man brought up the rear. Fai-Lok recognized him at once. It was Larry Wong, leader of the Sunnydale branch of the Ice Hell Brotherhood. The symbol of the Brotherhood had been tattooed onto his biceps. He carried a ceremonial knife behind his back, and he walked stealthily and uneasily as the three reached the parking lot.

The taller youth spotted the unconscious police officer. The older man walked over to him, put his hand into a silk bag tied to his drawstring pants, and sprinkled an herb over the man. It was wang-bo root, which caused dreamers to dream on.

"Fries with that," the police officer murmured.

Good, good, Fai-Lok thought happily. *At last, some competence!* His spirits soared. He would reward Wong for a job well done. Perhaps by giving him a position of authority in the new world that was to come. Or perhaps by killing him swiftly once the time came.

The trio approached the huge army of terra-cotta warriors. Wong waved his hands as the two younger men opened small vials of magickal essence and wafted them in the heated air. The potions tantalized the *p'ai* forces within the warriors, urging them to action.

A few of the statues shifted in reply.

Good, good, Fai-Lok encouraged him. *Rouse them.*

"My Lord Fai-Lok?" Wong called softly. As he spoke, he took a small mirror from his satin bag. The glass was etched with arcane Chinese characters. Like all such mirrors, its magickal properties had been sealed over the fire of the cremation of an enemy. Wong said to the taller youth, "Hold this, Jason."

The youth took the mirror from Wong; then Wong laid the knife across the boy's wrist and murmured the appropriate magickal incantation. With a quick flash of the blade, Wong slashed open his vein.

"Hey! Ow!" the boy shouted, trying to jerk away. But Wong held him tightly. The blood spurted onto the mirror, coating the surface.

Then the blood turned clear, and Fai-Lok's face appeared.

Wong and the two young men fell to their knees.

"I am here," Fai-Lok's reflection announced. "I am ready."

"Yes, Lord Fai-Lok," Wong intoned.

He nodded at the shorter boy, who grabbed the knife from

him, threw his arm around Jason, and pointed his knife toward his lower abdomen, where his qi resided.

"Coach Wong?" Jason cried. "What the hell are you doing?"

"You're going to be a vessel for Lord Fai-Lok," Coach explained. He raised his head toward the sky. "My Lord Fai-Lok!" he cried. "Accept the body of Jason Wu!"

Fai-Lok shot down into the struggling body. He heard the heartbeat pounding in his ears; felt the living Dark Blood singing in his veins. He tasted the boy's soul.

Then he assumed his demon shape and bit into it. The slow, thick *p'ai* was like gristle. That, he left alone. It was the upper soul he needed to tear out of Jason's essence.

It was lighter than air, a sweetness tinged with the sourness of dark energy. Fai-Lok got his jaws around it and yanked it from the *p'ai*. Jason Wu screamed and struggled, shrieked and begged.

Fai-Lok held the upper soul in his jaw, and then he flung it as hard as he could into the ether.

Jason Wu stopped screaming and collapsed to the ground.

Fai-Lok stepped into his form, assuming it, stretching and adjusting it to fit as his own higher soul poured into the empty space left by Jason's. He smelled steam, tasted smoke.

After a few more minutes, the Possession was complete.

"Excellent," he said to Wong, who sank to his knees and kowtowed. The other boy, the shorter one, had passed out.

"Welcome, Lord Fai-Lok," Wong murmured. "I am yours to command."

"Yes," Fai-Lok said. "Good. Where is the Orb?"

"In the cavern. I'll show you." He kowtowed again. "We are ready to begin the war."

Fai-Lok grinned down at him.

"Then let's begin it," he replied.

• • •

From his vantage point in incorporeal space, the consciousness of the great demon, Lir, surveyed the proceedings in the hellish town of Sunnydale. His son, Qin, busied himself with his temple in Los Angeles. The traitor, Fai-Lok, dreamed of bringing Fire Storm to the home of the Slayer, and then attacking Qin from the north.

Lir knew that Qin had sought to find him, and had wearied of the search. Perhaps it was simply that the halloing was also part human, and therefore subject to the frailties of that race.

No matter. Lir felt no affection for him. Qin would die with all the others who crowded this world.

He had waited millennia for the correct time to strike. Qin had no idea that his demonic father dwelled partially in his own mind, guiding him to the actions Qin and his followers had put in place. The Hell Ice Brotherhood and the Hellmouth Clan were two parts of a triad, and the third point was the Lodge of Sol. That point worshipped him, Lir. Knew of him. He had given knowledge of himself to their leader, Dane Hom. The Lodge of Sol would retrieve the Flame. When the other two of the triple arcana were likewise obtained—the Orb and the Heart—Lir would be able to free his body from its Ice Hell, and there would be such fire that it would never burn out in this dimension, until it was cleansed.

Then he would bring his own followers here—demons from other places; wild creations of his own—and he would raise his fists to the Powers That Be and smash them into bits, as he had witnessed the demon Vocah destroy the Oracles, speakers for the Powers.

The balance will end. I will prevail.

It has begun.

Lir watched, waited, planned.

Exulted.

CHAPTER SIX

Sunnydale

Tara was so cold. She was whimpering from the chill; her little hands were like ice. Her lips were tinged with blue, and she was shivering.

So as the rains poured down, Willow put a warm blanket over the grave of her beloved soul mate. The blanket was lavender, and the same runic symbols were painted on it that Willow had once written across Tara's back . . . in another dream. . . .

Frost crackled as the thick, fluffy blanket stretched across the grave, melting crystals beneath it. Just as quickly, the moisture refroze.

Tara's white marble headstone read BENEATH YOU, A WARRIOR SLUMBERS.

Through tears, Willow blinked. Now the headstone read
SOME SAY THE WORLD WILL END IN FIRE . . . SOME SAY IN ICE.

Those were lines written by Robert Frost, one of Willow's
favorite poets.

*I was so alone, until Tara. I didn't know why I couldn't hold
Oz. I didn't know why I couldn't feel warm . . . but in her arms,
there was so much heat. . . .*

From the pile of blankets beside her in the suburban
California cemetery, Willow reached for another one, unfolded
it, and spread it over the mound of frigid earth.

*Birth her again. Please, Goddess, cradle her in your arms
and make her warm and alive. I can't bear the cold world without her.*

Shaking, she raised her eyes to the brittle, dark sky. Gray,
sloppy clouds scudded. A dirty slash of yellow jagged through
them, spearing them in their centers; the rain poured down
from the wound, hard and driven. With another crash, and a
roll of heavy thunder like the lowing of an animal in labor,
she was back in England, in Giles's country home, staring
across the moor. Her hands were balled on the sill; the window hung open as the unfeeling rain whipped across Willow's
face.

She had a razor blade at her wrist.

*Giles doesn't know. No one knows how messed up I still am.
Should I do it?*

*If there is no way to redeem myself . . . Tara is dead. She is
dead.*

She is dead.

The rain . . .

. . . is the Goddess, bereft.

*This razor isn't sharp enough to cut away all the pain I feel . . .
oh, Tara, my love . . . I'm so cold without you. If Xander hadn't*

stopped me from destroying the world, it would have ended in fire. And hell would be a comfort to me now, because this cold is more than I can bear . . .

. . . and Willow blinked awake in her room in Buffy's house, tears of pain and tears of sweat streaming down her face. She was intolerably, insufferably hot.

She turned on her side and stared at the sweltering duodera pine branches outside her window. The moon hung low, as if it were too tired and overheated to reach its zenith.

A fan whirred gently; the window was open, making her feel vulnerable to attack. Willow had warded all the entrances to the Summers residence, and she had learned a long time ago that closing a window didn't do much to keep out anything in Sunnydale that wanted to come in. Still, she remembered when Angel had gone all evil and climbed into Buffy's room, sketching her in the night just to drive her crazy.

Willow felt off-balance, remembering her nightmare, and all the nights that she had worried about Tara lying in the cold, cold ground. The graveyards were hot now. The Hellmouth was boiling up evil and serving it on sizzling platters.

And Tara was still dead.

Listless, Willow got up to get a glass of water. She walked unsteadily, like an old woman. She was shocked at how weak she felt.

As she reached the threshold of her room, she heard weeping. It was coming from the direction of Buffy's bedroom.

Buffy?

Gingerly, Willow tiptoed down the hall. Yes. Buffy was sobbing, low, deep groans that only a good friend or a sister would be able to hear.

Willow crossed the hall again and peeked in on Dawn. She

was still asleep. Willow pulled her door closed and crept back to the Slayer's door.

She pushed it open.

The room had been Joyce Summers's room, and in the darkness Willow could still see it as it had looked six years before, when she, Willow, had become Buffy's first friend in Sunnydale. Willow had been so hungry to have a friend, a real friend; and she had gotten a quasi-Mom in the bargain. Willow's own mother had intricate political agendas to work on, still did. Buffy's mom had worked too much at her art gallery, though she had taken time to ask Willow how she was . . . and asked vampires if they wanted little marshmallows in their cocoa.

"Hey," Willow murmured, sitting gently beside Buffy on the bed, as the Slayer sobbed in her sleep. "Buffy. Wake up."

The Slayer woke with a start. She bolted upright, dazed for a moment, then focused on Willow. The look on Buffy's face was one of shocked disappointment, which she lost as she rubbed her eyes and said, "Will, what's up?"

"You okay, Buffy?" Willow asked.

"Sure." Buffy's eyes widened. She was such a terrible liar. "What's wrong?"

"Nothing. Well, except that you were . . . crying again," Willow confessed. "Same dream?"

"Yes." Buffy sighed, shifted, glanced downward. "I was dreaming about Angel, and the fire. Just like before."

Moonlight filtered through the curtains, casting Buffy in soft focus. Willow could almost see the fifteen-year-old girl again. Lifetimes had come and gone since then.

"I was dreaming about Tara," Willow told her. "Again. I do it a lot."

"Oh. Will." Buffy touched Willow's hand.

Willow covered Buffy's fingers with her own. "I just . . ." A teardrop slid to the tip of Willow's nose and hung there until she wiped it away. "I just miss her a lot." She shrugged. "I can't seem to get past the feeling-bad part."

"You will," Buffy assured her. "I still miss Mom." She smoothed back her hair. "And Angel. And Riley." Her grin was wry, crooked, and filled with pain. "Much with the missage."

"Much with the missage," Willow agreed.

"We'll keep busy. You and Anya will figure something out about the monsters. Then we'll kick some butt."

"Yeah." Willow yawned. "I'll call Anya in the morning. We'll do some work."

"Wild work," Buffy said. She smoothed away Willow's hair exactly as Joyce Summers once had done, and Willow's heart grieved the loss again.

"You going to be okay?" Willow asked.

There was a naked look on Buffy's face for a moment, as if to say, *I'm not sure I've ever been okay*, but the Slayer flashed a wan smile at her and moved her shoulders.

"Sure," Buffy said. "We both should get some sleep."

Willow nodded. She didn't add that she had no idea if she would be able to fall back asleep.

She went back to her room and stared up at the ceiling, sweating.

Los Angeles

His name was Honnar, and as the portal closed, he gasped and got to his feet. He was actually here!

Back on Pylea, he had not known how to open the portal through which his cousin had traveled to the land of Los Angeles. Almost every evening, he walked to the spot Landok had shown him, and dreamed of this very moment. And then the portal had opened as if the gods had granted his wishes!

But . . . but what happened here?

He gazed mournfully at the place where the demon karaoke club called Caritas had once stood. He knew its location by heart. Most, but not all, of the rubble had been cleared away, and all to show for the mystical place was a sign on the ground that said, CARITAS.

Honnar was six feet tall, a demon of finely toned dark green skin and red glowing eyes. He was an Anagogic demon from Pylea, and a distant relative of his, Landok, had told him stories about Krevlorneswath, also known as Lorne. Honnar knew that Lorne had traveled to this plane of existence because he had also inherited the Trait of Shame, which carried with it a love of music and the ability to sing.

All Honnar's plans for stardom . . . he had pinned them on Lorne and Caritas. He had never actually expected to be able to go there. And now the place was gone.

Violence was such an ugly thing.

And . . . *oh, my stars* . . . speaking of violence . . .

Two demons with bumpy faces leaped from the shadows. The pair raced straight for him, the taller demon raising a hand and bellowing something in a language Honnar did not speak.

They skidded to a halt; the demon said something to him in the same unknown tongue. Honnar, who had studied long and hard in order to be able to converse with Krevlorneswath in the dialect of English Landok said he favored, blurted shakily, "Hey, hi hi! How are you today? What a lovely outfit!"

The demon stared at him, so Honnar tried again. "Peach is your color!"

"You are not from Oden Tal," the demon finally said.

"Uh, I am Honnar of Pylea."

The attackers scowled at him. Honnar shifted anxiously.

"He resembles the ally of the vampire. The green one," said the shorter demon.

"I came here to go to Caritas," he said.

The demon shook his head. "I don't speak Spanish. Only English and the language of the Vigories of Oden Tal."

"You are not a Cow," Honnar said anxiously. "I thought Cows ruled here?" He swallowed. "Are you a friend of Angel? Friend? Of Angel and his followers?"

"Not likely!" the demon shot back.

The other demon glared. Honnar got even more nervous.

Landok had explained to Honnar that the Cows of Pylea were actually in charge in this dimension, and that some of them were antagonistic toward other races, particularly demonic ones. He had also shared tales of Krevlorneswath's adventures with him, including one about how using his Trait of Shame had actually saved his life.

"You'd better come with us," said the shorter demon, grabbing Honnar's arm.

In a panic, Honnar threw back his head and belted out the highest note he could.

"Eeeeeeeeeeeeeeee!" he yodeled.

The pair immediately clapped their hands over their ears. Groaning, they dropped to their knees; the shorter of the demons began rolling on the ground.

And Honnar whirled around and raced away as fast as he could, turning back only once—just in time to see a purple demon with three horns protruding from the crown of his head and a figure swathed in black clothing leap down from the rooftop beside the empty Caritas lot. They raced at the two ridge-faced demons, who were still suffering from Honnar's high-pitched musical note.

As the ridge-faced demons staggered to their feet, the

demon and the black-clothed figure pulled out long, curved blades and slashed the pair across their throats. Green blood spurted everywhere.

Honnar kept running.

Sunnydale

A couple of hours after Angel's call, Willow went downstairs to the kitchen to call Anya. Bedhead Dawn was in the living room with a bowl of cereal on her lap, watching cartoons. She gave Willow a little smile and ate a bite of cereal. Willow smiled back.

I need coffee, she decided as she dialed Anya's number. She got the beans out of the freezer and put them on the counter. She was halfway to getting the grinder out of the cabinet when Anya answered.

"Thought we could do that titration together," Willow said.

"All right. I'm not doing anything else," Anya replied. "I'm not making any money, that's for sure."

Because I destroyed the Magic Box, Willow filled in.

"I'll be over in about half an hour." Willow hung up, and made her coffee.

Los Angeles

"Fai-Lok," Qin said into his magic mirror, raising a brow at the young man who stared back at him. He was lounging on his bed in the Los Angeles temple of the Ice Hell Brotherhood. "How you've changed."

His Number One Court Sorcerer inclined his head. "I had to Possess someone new," he informed him. "It's a good body. Young and vigorous."

"Don't let Xian see it," Qin ordered him with mock severity.

"You know how she favors handsome young men." He meaningfully stroked the face of Alex Liang. "This one pleases her, but yours is more—how do they say it these days—buffed out."

"You also know she loves only you, Most Celestial One," Fai-Lok replied.

"We have a problem," Qin said, moving to the point. "The museum curator, Tsung Wei. He is heavily guarded, and I need him killed. Even invisible assassins have been unsuccessful."

"Someone is protecting him, then," Fai-Lok mused.

"I came to that conclusion on my own," Qin retorted. "I do have a brain, Fai-Lok."

The reflection of the sorcerer bowed low. "I meant no offense, Great Qin. May you live a hundred thousand years."

Qin ignored the apology. "Who can be protecting him? The vampire Angel? Does he have a strong magicks user among his followers?"

"They are all rather amateur," Fai-Lok replied. "Unless he has acquired a sorcerer or a magician of whom I am unaware." He added hastily, "And I'm sure that's not the case."

Qin chuckled. Fai-Lok had been with him for over a thousand years, but still never missed an opportunity to remind his master of his many gifts and talents.

"Shall I cast magicks against him?" Fai-Lok asked helpfully.

Qin turned his glance from the mirror to the row of magicians kowtowing before him. Dressed in regular Western clothes, they might have fooled anyone on the streets of Los Angeles into believing they were businessmen. But they were powerful sorcerers descended from families brimming with magickal talent. And all of them had failed to eliminate the powerful shield of protection guarding Tsung Wei.

"Yes, cast magicks against him," Qin said.

"Very well, Most Celestial One." Fai-Lok bowed low again.

"That is all," Qin continued, putting down the mirror. He glared at the sorcerers trembling before him. "If he succeeds, your lives are over."

In the recesses of Qin's mind, Lir laughed at his offspring's stupidity. He, Lir, was the one who was guarding Tsung Wei. He entered the minds of the assassins and confused them, rendering them ineffectual. Now he would lift the clouds of confusion, thus making it appear that Fai-Lok had succeeded where these men had failed. Then Qin would execute his vanguard of magicians.

Qin's ruthlessness would make himself even more vulnerable to attack.

It was just as well Lir had no love for him.

He did not deserve to live.

After his court sorcerers were escorted away by his First Chamberlain, Qin summoned Jhiera to his chambers. As he waited for her arrival, he threw some scraps of meat at the dragon that had carried him away from the battle at the museum. It lounged on his king-sized bed like a big dog, its wings folded demurely as it chuffed and snapped at the morsels. The acolytes had jumped to when he'd requested that three large steaks from Ruth's Chris Steakhouse be fetched for the sweet thing, which resembled a miniature of Fire Storm, but was an entirely different species.

There was only one dragon like Fire Storm.

The acolytes here are excellent young men. When I rule this dimension, I will kill them immediately, rather than prolong their suffering.

"Well," he said in accented English as she appeared on the threshold. "Things are a little complicated, aren't they?"

Jhiera turned in profile as she huffed and crossed her arms, showing off her amazing ridged spine. She looked at him sourly and said, "Complicated? This entire operation is a travesty. If I had it to do over, I would never have allied myself with you."

How dare you! he screamed at her silently. *I am Qin, and I will not be addressed in such a manner!* But he presented her with a placid exterior, smiling with the young Asian man's mouth, and said, "Don't forget. My fighters are the only things standing between you and the Vigories of Oden Tal."

It was true. In the last few hours the number of Oden Tal warriors on the streets of Los Angeles had increased. Qin had dispatched his own forces of demons and skilled ninja-style assassins to do battle with them wherever they could be found. Jhiera was quite aware that her situation was growing ever more precarious . . . and that Qin still had the upper hand.

Otherwise, he was certain she would not have patched things up with Shiryah so easily.

"Have you discovered yet how Angel knew we would be at the museum?" she pressed.

"There was a leak," he said. "It will be plugged."

"Do you still suppose Tsung Wei double-crossed us?" Jhiera asked.

"We suppose nothing," came a voice from the bathroom.

Xian emerged, her fluffy white hotel bathrobe belted loosely around her lovely, recently acquired body.

"We're alive because we suppose nothing," she continued, sliding into Qin's embrace. He nuzzled her, warmth rising in his body, then looked invitingly at Jhiera. She had ignored all his invitations to join them in the carnal act; she ignored him now as well.

• • •

Qin gathered up Xian's hair and pressed it to his nose, fascinated by the wispy, silky texture, mesmerized by the fragrance of the shampoo Xian had used. He thought of Fai-Lok's youthful appearance and wondered if he should Possess a new body, one younger than Alex Liang's. But the identity of the millionaire served his purposes very well. It was rather late in the game to pretend to be someone else.

"Tsung Wei shouldn't be a problem much longer," he told her.

"He will make an excellent sacrifice," Xian said, purring against him, entwining her arms around his neck. Jhiera was unmoved.

"If Shiryah burns him, I will kill her," Jhiera announced.

"She won't," Qin assured her, realizing that the Princess didn't know of his foiled attempts to send assassins to Tsung Wei's hospital room and murder him in his bed.

"I will do it," she said again, and for a moment he thought she was offering to burn Tsung Wei herself. "I *will* kill her if she burns another man for you."

How dare you! he flamed. *How dare you! I'll tear you to pieces for your insolence!*

But to her face he said, "She'll behave. You are her leader, after all."

Jhiera said nothing. She narrowed her eyes and glared at him as if she was thinking the same thing he was.

Jhiera of Oden Tal had outlived her usefulness as well.

"You'll be okay," Fred said anxiously to Angel and Gunn. Behind her, in the lobby, Lorne was directing the Furies in the re-warding of the Hyperion. Jhiera had apparently enlisted Alex Liang in her battle against the Vigories of her dimension, and fresh violence was breaking out all over Los Angeles as each side raised the stakes. The same demons—former regulars at Caritas, his karaoke bar—who had told Lorne that something was going down at the museum also told him with eyewitness accounts of Asian guys and demons beating the tar out of the ferocious, burly Vigories of Oden Tal.

Jhiera's campaign was the only explanation Angel and company could provide for the mysterious terra-cotta exhibits in Los Angeles and Sunnydale and the three other cities. Tsung Wei had been instrumental in setting up all five of them. According to Buffy, there had been no more strange deaths at the museum in Sunnydale—no statues coming to life, no crushed security guards—and Angel had to wonder if the reason was because he had run into Jhiera and Alex Liang at the Liang Museum.

"We're not on Jhiera's side," Angel reminded Fred as she handed Gunn a battle-ax. "We're not in that fight."

"Maybe she'll come after you, just in case, Angel heart," Lorne said anxiously. "Sic Alex Liang's ninja guys on you so you won't distract her."

"Sounds like she's got more pressing issues than us," Gunn observed, as he hoisted the ax across his shoulder. "But I'm with Angel on the situation. The bad guys must have figured out by now that we've linked Alex Liang with the clay soldiers here and in Sunnydale. Tsung Wei's a loose thread they have to cut."

Fred looked very anxious. "Then they'll try to stop you from talking to him."

"Yes," Gunn replied, his face softening at the evidence that she still cared about him. He wasn't sure how, or how much, but her concern was like her warm hand on his shoulder, instead of his humongous ax.

"And we'll try to stop them from killing Tsung Wei," Angel added. He turned to Gunn. "We'd better head out."

"Roger that," Gunn said.

"Ooh," Fred muttered, stepping forward. "Angel, it's bright out. . . ."

"I'll keep the top up," Angel assured her. "We need to take the car so we can transport him once we've got him."

"You have your cell phones, darlings?" Lorne asked, pantomiming a phone call by extending his thumb and little finger and placing them against the side of his face.

"We're packin'," Gunn replied.

Angel felt in his trouser pocket. "Got it." Not that that meant much. Angel was hopeless with cell phones.

"All right," Lorne said, nodding. "Hold on a sec." He looked over his shoulders. "Girls?"

The Furies smiled over at him, and the Anagogic demon pointed to Angel and Gunn.

"Give them a little pixie dust, too, will you?"

The trio waved their hands toward Angel and Gunn and chanted. Sparkles appeared in the air and settled on Angel's head and shoulders like faerie dandruff. Gunn got the same treatment.

They both thanked the Furies, and the three swooned, as per usual, in Angel's general direction. Then Angel and Gunn headed out toward the hospital, and the weakest link in the mystery so far.

The enormous red body of Lir, Lord of the Ice Hell, shifted in its frozen prison as his mind sent out its call. Certain this dimension's inhabitants were subject to his control from the great vastness of his own ruined dimension, and he had yet to discover why that was the case, he contented himself that it was so.

The millennia had provided him ample opportunity to find

minds who would listen to his thoughts, beginning with that first guard in the Ice Hell, who had transported his upper soul to the Yellow Land above his prison. Then he had whispered to Qin's father, Wei Lo; and so on down—to Dane Hom, hidden for the nonce among Qin's followers in Los Angeles, and soon, he would speak to others . . . perhaps to the senior partners of Wolfram & Hart.

That would warm me considerably, he thought. *And now, I will allow Tsung Wei to die. I lift the clouded thinking I have visited on his would-be assassins. I will suggest to Qin that he send the Shadow Monkey, who once devoured members of his household back in ancient China.*

And I lower more clouded thinking onto the workers at the hospital, who will see no evil, hear no evil, report no evil. . . .

It was dawn at St. Alexis. A busy time, for many people die in the night. The hours between midnight and three are dark hours for the living; more heart attacks claim victims in those hours.

As orderlies made the rounds with body bags on their gurneys, Tsung Wei lay drowsing. He felt no pain, and very little anxiety, despite the fiasco of the preceding evening. It was the medication, he knew. If he squinted and concentrated, he could make out the shape of the drip that hung beside his bed, a fuzzy glow against the thin curtains covering the rising sun.

Angel, the vampire guardian of Los Angeles, should not have known about his meeting with Jhiera and Qin. Had someone in the Ice Hell Brotherhood betrayed the cause? Had Tsung Wei's clever assistant pieced together snippets of phone calls, pawed through his trash?

No matter, no matter, Tsung Wei thought, drifting along with the drugs. *Angel will fail. They will all fail. No one can stand up against the First Emperor of China.*

I am on the winning side.

He chuckled with pleasure, unsure if he made a sound or if he was so high on painkillers, he only imagined it. Caught by a whirl of vertigo, he jerked and opened his eyes.

Tsung Wei gasped.

A monster leaned over him. Its face was an elongated blank except for two serpentine eyes, each a glowing emerald green; where a mouth and nose should have been, a large, gaping wound pulsated, blisters all around it. The eyes blinked with intelligence; narrowed with purpose as it leaned closer to Tsung Wei.

The curator gasped again. The room spun. He could not form words, or manage a scream. The face reminded him of a scroll from Qin's earthly reign of a hastily painted image he had seen with Chinese characters accompanying it.

I, keeper of accounts for the household, have seen this monster. It creeps in the night to devour the enemies of Most Honorable Qin, may he reign a hundred thousand years.

There were no other scrolls written in that particular hand.

The face leered at him; and Tsung Wei realized that, despite the fact that he was in peril of his life, he had drifted away on his cloud of drugs.

The creature opened its mouth.

Vertical rows of teeth glistened with mucus, and the monster made a horrible sucking sound as it lowered its mouth toward Tsung Wei's face.

The curator groaned, faintly, unable to move. His lids flickered shut, then open; he felt his heart pounding a little harder, but not hard enough to alert anyone who might be monitoring his vitals at a nurse's station.

The mouth drew closer. The stench was terrible; it was of the grave.

I did not tell Angel about the warriors, Tsung Wei tried to say. But now he wished he had.

Drool dribbled in a rope from the creature's mouth, touching his cheek. It burned the skin; bubbles appeared; the slime ate through his flesh and dropped against his jaw, worked its way through the bone, and then the teeth. And then his tongue, and then his palate.

The drugs kept his heartbeat steady. He thought drowsily, *I'm going to die . . . it's going to eat me . . . it will hurt. . . .*

But even the pain slid away from him as he attempted to latch on to it. But why latch on to it?

Because without it . . . I'm . . . dead. . . .

His languorous heartbeat continued to betray him. No one was going to come; no one was going to save him.

One of the monster's sharp fangs sliced into Tsung Wei's left nostril. It penetrated the flesh; Tsung Wei sensed the pain as a strange, cold pressure. He was numbed up.

I need to hurt . . . I need to feel . . . I need to show distress. . . .

The fang sunk more deeply, another joined it, then tugged. Tsung Wei was reminded of a dental visit, having a tooth removed. . . .

The backs of his eyelids were bright red; he tried to open his eyes and found he couldn't. After a time—who knew how long—he realized that his eyes were open.

They were covered with blood.

A nurse will come. . . .

Then he imagined he was back in Frankfurt am Main with Gisela Von Bischoften; Alan Johnson from the Sunnydale Museum of History; Head Curator Satoshi Matsumoto from the Tokyo Museum in Ueno Park; and Asian Antiquities

164

Curator Doris DeWitt from Cleveland. They wove through the historic old town district called Sachsenhausen, crawling from tavern to tavern. German beer songs, German beer. Some faceless dignitaries from the Chinese government had accompanied them. They had not sung, had not drunk. The museum curators were exuberant. They were each going to get some Qin Dynasty terra-cotta warriors!

None of the other curators knew that a fabulously wealthy man named Alex Liang had made all the arrangements with the Chinese government to arrange the five exhibitions. None of them knew that Alex Liang believed that he was the reincarnation of Qin, the First Emperor of China. Tsung Wei was not certain of that, but he did know that Alex possessed astonishingly magickal powers, such as have been claimed by the ancient Chinese. His court sorcerer Fai-Lok had animated a warrior for him, and called forth demons who kowtowed to Alex and called him Qin. Fai-Lok had shown Tsung Wei all this, and more.

So much more that Tsung Wei had sunk to his knees and called Alex Liang Master . . . musing privately that perhaps it was Fai-Lok who should be the one he worshipped, and he was the one who wielded the magicks.

"I will spare you, Mr. Wei," Alex had told him cheerfully. "I will give you a place in my new world order."

Even then, drifting through his memories, Tsung Wei hadn't been sure if Alex was all he claimed to be. But the suitcases of money—in several denominations that included euros, American dollars, and Japanese yen—had stilled any questions he might have posed. Seven million dollars, all for him, Tsung Wei. Seven was a propitious number, indeed.

For that sum, he had only to track all the exhibits and to grease the wheels of local governments if there were bureaucratic difficulties. There had been a couple, mostly having to do with fulfillment of security concerns so that the statues could be released into the museums' custody. Sunnydale was especially problematic, since the museum planned to stage the exhibit out of doors.

"Sunnydale must have soldiers," Alex had told Tsung Wei on the phone. "Bribe whomever you need to."

Tsung Wei had obliged.

And now, I am dying. . . . Who is killing me? Is it Alex Liang?

There was more numbing cold. More tugging.

He saw red no more.

My eyes.

My face.

I must struggle. I must scream.

But he lay frozen and drugged, drifting and dreaming.

This is a fine joke, he thought. Then he sobbed with terror. Or would have, if he still had a voice box.

Drifting and floating on a sea of medication, his body slowly consumed; the monster devouring him—Tsung Wei sensed its presence, as he could no longer see, smell, or taste. One faculty after another consumed, digested . . .

. . . I'm supposed to go to a wedding today, he thought dizzily. *They're registered at Pottery Barn. I'll go later. . . .*

. . . Wait, I can't, I'm dying. . . .

Then something new happened to him and he thought, *Who am I? Where am I? What's happening? What—?*

Figuring he was too recognizable at the hospital, Gunn stayed with the car while Angel went inside to find Tsung Wei. The thing was, he was having as much trouble as Gunn had had locating the man.

Angel shifted his weight impatiently as the older man behind the visitors' desk at St. Alexis slowly typed in *Hemingway*.

"No, T-S-U-N-G W-E-I," Angel said, pointing to the screen.

"Oh." The man scratched his chin. "I'm a little new at this, son. Just be—"

He frowned at the empty spot where Angel had been.

And now Angel was wandering down the halls of the orthopedic ward, checking charts on doors and poking his head into each room. He was grateful that he required no invitation to enter, since hospitals were public buildings. Otherwise, this could take a long, long time.

He reached a closed door—number 217 A&B—and saw a chart hanging on the door. *Tsung Wei.*

Pay dirt.

Angel lifted the chart out of the plastic pocket in the center of the door and slid it into his black leather jacket. Then he opened the door.

The first bed was empty.

The second was awash in blood.

The window just beyond it had been shattered.

His cell phone rang. Angel grabbed it out of his trouser pocket and flicked it on.

"Yo, something just trotted into an alley, accent on some-*thing*," Gunn reported. "So I drove around and I'm seeing a window all popped out."

Damn. "You didn't see it happen?" He looked at the shattered window frame. "I can't go too close. There's no curtain."

"You up where the window's busted?"

"Yes." Angel rapidly assessed the scene. "We must have just missed it. Whatever took him probably chopped him up."

"No one there is freaking out?"

Angel looked over his shoulder. "Must be magickally

cloaked." He moved to a monitor beside the bed. It was still registering Tsung Wei's vitals. "As far as the nursing station's concerned, Tsung Wei's still snug in his bed, with a heartbeat and stable respiration."

"I'll go after whatever went into the alley," Gunn told him. "I'll put my phone on vibrate only. Think that'll be safe enough."

"I'll catch up," Angel replied, then heard a noise and jammed his cell phone in his pocket.

It was just an orderly in the hallway, wheeling a supply cart as he whistled to himself.

Time to get out of here, Angel thought.

Hoping that the darkness of the alley would shroud him from the guy he was tailing, Gunn took off in the convertible. Meanwhile, Angel hurried out of Tsung Wei's room and made his way through the hospital, avoiding the daylit windows.

He emerged beneath an awning, then spotted taillights and followed Gunn into the dark alley. Gunn had stopped the car and was getting out.

"Hey," Gunn said as Angel drew up beside him. "So when I was staring at the window, I didn't see a thing. Then the air wobbled, and this shape appeared."

"Portal?" Angel asked.

"Or it can appear and disappear. I lost track of it."

"Look." Angel pointed at a manhole cover in the center of the street just beyond the other end of the alley. The large, round cover had been removed. "Looks like it went into a tunnel."

He pulled off his coat and wrapped the ends around his hands. Draping it over his head, he raced toward the circle of blackness in the center of the street.

When he reached the ladder, he gave the coat to Gunn, who held it over his head. It was an act of trust; if Gunn let go, Angel would cook.

Angel descended into the darkness and stink. He heard sloshing in the distance and hurried after it, mildly relieved to realize that where he stood, at least, there was no standing water. The sewer tunnel was dry, so far.

Gunn's footsteps clanged softly as he came down behind him. Gunn murmured, "Wish we'd had time to move the car. Any fool could connect some dots between it and Tsung Wei's disappearance if they had a mind to."

"His bed was soaked in blood. It was human," Angel said. He was still carrying the medical chart. "I've got his chart," he told Gunn, who couldn't see in the dark. Angel could. "I doubt it's been updated to include a massive bleedout."

They moved on, Angel grimacing as his next footfall splashed into foul water. Gunn grunted, but kept pace with him.

The sloshing continued on in the distance. Both men hurried toward it.

The sewer water swirled around Angel's calves. He grimaced. A year ago, Cordelia had picked out these trousers, trilling in her happy way about the great deal on woolen blends she had found in the garment district. Lorne had gone with her; the stuff he'd come back with on that foray had worked well for him during his captivity as a headliner in Las Vegas. Years of sewer-traveling experience told Angel that they were probably ruined now; no amount of dry cleaning would make them fresh again. It wasn't the pants he mourned, but the sudden, weighty feeling that Cordelia might never shop for clothes for him again. He felt a pang, but kept his mind on the task at hand.

He and Gunn moved in the darkness. Then the sloshing

receded. Either they were losing their quarry, or it had gone into another tunnel—or escaped via an exit.

Or it had realized it was being followed, and had stopped moving. And was waiting for them. With a dozen of its closest friends.

Gunn didn't slack, didn't slow, but he did mutter, "Best be ready to rumble."

"Right," Angel agreed. He gestured, even though Gunn couldn't see him. "There's a fork coming up. Stop for a minute."

They both froze. Angel craned his neck, listening hard. He detected a whisper of noise to his left, although it was very faint, and he was not at all sure it was being made by their target.

"Left," he told Gunn.

"Okay."

They slogged forward, Angel leading the way as the tunnel divided into two sections. He took the left. Sniffed. Nodded.

"They came this way," Angel said. "I smell the blood."

"Any chance the dude's still alive?" Gunn asked, but Angel knew it was a rhetorical question. They wouldn't know until they caught up with the thing they were trailing.

Up ahead, something glowed in the darkness. It was a rectangular shape, and it shimmered like a flashlight on glitter. It hovered, fixed in space, light from it winking and shimmying in a not-unfamiliar way.

"Portal?" Gunn queried.

"I'm thinking portal, yes," Angel replied.

"You should let me go first," Gunn said.

"No way," Angel shot back.

They sloshed toward it. Then the tunnel floor dipped, and both of them stumbled a few steps forward, unprepared. The water swirled around their chests. Gunn muttered something vulgar, and they worked their way toward the jittering portal.

Then it noticeably dimmed.

"We gotta hurry," Gunn said.

"Afraid you're right," Angel muttered.

Both of them began to swim.

"Remind me to get a better gig," Gunn drawled. "Something that don't include sewers, blood, or demons."

"That lets out becoming a lawyer," Angel retorted.

The glimmering weakened another notch.

Angel swam faster. The rectangle was flush with the brick wall of the sewer. He reached his hand toward it—

—and his fingers slid through the brick surface and into the light.

On the other side, he felt incredible heat. But it wasn't so bad that he couldn't stand it.

He said over his shoulder, "Wait here."

Then he pushed himself through the gleaming rectangle.

And Gunn came tumbling after.

Angel caught him just in time, with a stabilizing arm across his chest; they were standing on a narrow catwalk that Gunn had started to overshoot. As Angel made sure he caught his balance, he stared down below.

A hideous creature had just dropped off the last rung of a ladder attached to the catwalk. It was part baboon, part monkey, all nightmare. It reeked of the same blood Angel had smelled in Tsung Wei's hospital room.

Guess that's that, Angel thought grimly.

"Don't think this is in any of the L.A. guidebooks," Gunn whispered. "Whoever did the interior design is a big fan of the P.F. Chang's restaurant chain."

Gunn was right. Enormous, oversized statues of Chinese demons rose above enormous, oversized pots—*heaters?*

cauldrons?—boiling with smoke. And over it, the stench of carrion. And smoke, and ashes.

Death, Jhiera style.

"Damn, it's hot as hell in here," Gunn said.

"Not quite," Angel said vaguely, still looking around. The floor was a startling mosaic depicting a fire. "But from the looks of it, someone wishes it was."

There was a sudden rush of footfalls, hundreds of them. From recesses in the darkness, figures in red robes began appearing. They looked human; they smelled human. They were assembling with great urgency, their voices hushed and excited.

Where Angel and Gunn stood, the two were completely exposed if someone happened to look upward. As the chamber floor filled with more robed figures, the chances that he and Gunn would be spotted increased exponentially.

Then a gong sounded. Gunn and Angel squatted, trying to make themselves as small as possible. The gong rang out again, and again, the vibrations echoing off the walls.

People began assembling on a balcony directly across from Angel. Figures appeared on the balcony, and a muscle jumped in Angel's cheek when he spotted Alex Liang, who was escorting a dark-haired woman in black leather clothing that revealed a ridged spine. She was way too comfortable walking beside him. She had her arm wrapped around his waist, and he stopped walking and kissed her full on the mouth. Some of the onlookers murmured in response, and the two kissed harder, the man pressing himself around her. "Jhiera," Gunn muttered.

"Jhiera," Angel said, with equal disgust.

He wanted to stick around and see what was happening, but there were too many eyes in the room. It was too risky for him and Gunn to remain where they were. They were dangerously exposed.

Frustrated, Angel knew they had to retreat.

He looked at Gunn, who sighed and nodded.

Angel turned back around. Nothing gleamed in the solid rock wall, and for a moment he thought the portal had closed. Experimentally he stuck a hand out and it slid right through the rock, as if the wall were nothing more than a rear projection.

He went through.

Gunn followed.

They were back in the tunnel, and the portal on their side had vanished. Angel extended his hand and this time, hit solid rock.

"That creature ate Tsung Wei," he said to Gunn. "I could smell it on him."

Gunn muttered, "Damn. And you saw Jhiera, right? That was her?"

"I saw her." Angel cocked his head. "Something was different about her, though. I can't say what."

"She had that canary-eating grin, is what," Gunn replied angrily. "Plus the tongue action. She was awfully friendly with Liang, wouldn't you say?"

"I would say." Angel was pissed off. He'd thought Jhiera was all about the mission. It was obvious she took time out for a little pleasure . . . with a man who had his enemies either barbecued or eaten raw.

The two waded through the water, not bothering to swim this time.

"Okay, what was that place?" Gunn asked Angel.

"Not sure. Secret underground temple?"

"Sounds good," Gunn drawled.

Angel thought a moment. "I was at the Metro station in Universal City, thought I heard something deeper underground. I wonder if it was these guys."

"I remember that. You were looking to hook up with that informant." Gunn considered. "Huh. We haven't even had time to worry about the Fashion Victim sitch."

"They don't appear to be connected," Angel said.

"Maybe it was a coincidence," Gunn continued. "Tsung Wei forgot to pay his secret underground cult membership dues."

"Or they were afraid he was going to talk to us."

"Or that," Gunn agreed. "Possibly a more likely scenario."

"Let's tell Fred, see what she can come up with. Maybe we can figure out how to open the portal at will."

"Yeah, and get a cloaking device," Gunn said. "Damn, Angel, there's so many bad guys in L.A., you'd think they'd unionize."

"They did." Angel smiled faintly at him. "They're called the Motion Pictures Arts and Sciences Academy."

There are so many advantages to being a multimillionaire, Qin thought pleasantly, as his Number One Bean Counter, a human man hired for him by Wolfram & Hart, came forward with a number of large-ticket invoices for him to approve. Indicating that Shiryah should step aside for a moment, Qin signed the first one, which was a food bill, and chuckled. He wondered if this lackey knew that he, Qin, was the first emperor in all of the Yellow Land to standardize currency? His coin of the realm had been a circle with a square stamped out of the middle. Square hole, round peg.

"Thank you, O Most Celestial One," the accountant said, his voice shaking a little. Fear was good.

"You're welcome. And now . . ." He held out his hand to Shiryah and spread out his arms as his pet monkey-demon lumbered across the catwalk toward him. Its face was smeared with blood, and that was wonderful news.

"Ah. Good." He made a mental note to thank Fai-Lok for his

magickal intervention—and to have Shirya incinerate the incompetent magicians in his employ. "Now, let's begin a new era in terror," he said to Shiryah. "Who shall we burn first?"

Then a voice shouted, "My Lord Qin! There have been intruders!"

One of the many faceless monks who served him scrabbled across the crowded mosaic floor. "They came in through that portal!"

The young Chinese man jabbed his hand in the direction of the catwalk. "It was two men!"

"What?" Qin was astonished. "Why didn't the alarm go off? Where are the guards?" He leaned forward. "How do you know?"

"I-I-" The monk skidded to a stop. "I *saw* them. Just now." He looked around. "Didn't anyone else see them?"

Was this more incompetent magick?

He would have to deal with that later.

He clapped his hands and nodded at one of his enormous Mongolian guards. "Get your men! Go after them!" he cried.

Angel and Gunn had reached the end of the tunnel, to stare up at a drab shaft of light emanating from the manhole. Angel figured it for normal street light.

Gunn said, "I'll go first, bring the car over so you can climb right in. Not much traffic around here. We can probably get away with it."

"Cops might be there," Angel warned him.

"If anybody at the hospital has even noticed they're missing a patient," Gunn drawled. "Nursing shortage. Dude could lie there and rot, no one would come."

Gunn took the stairs and poked his head up at street level. He said softly, "Angel, it's dark out."

"What?" Angel looked up at him. Gunn glanced back down, looking freaked out. "It's nighttime."

"But we were only gone an hour," Angel said. "At most."

"Guess not," Gunn said. "Guess we entered some kind of time warp."

"Wouldn't be the first time," Angel muttered.

Gunn climbed out. Angel followed, and the two strode into the alley, where Gunn had left the car.

Angel said, "We're definitely going home with the top down. Way we smell."

"Good thing Fred and I aren't . . . taking a shower," Gunn finished awkwardly. He looked away from Angel.

They were about five feet from the mouth of the alley when shapes exploded from the manhole and raced toward Angel and Gunn. Then a second wave hurtled downward from the rooftops on either side of the alley just as Angel and Gunn raced into it.

One landed on Gunn; a veteran fighter, he responded with a roll to the side, managing to leap to his feet with a sharp kick to his downed assailant's ribs.

Damn! More Klingons!

Vigories to the right of him, the left of him; and behind him demons, big Chinese dudes, and some guys dressed like ninjas, all coming at him.

Angel had different visitors: a band of demons all the same. They were dark gray, and their faces were batlike: snub-nosed, with sloped foreheads and fangs protruding upward from their lower lips. Their bodies were squat, sinewy as they flung themselves toward Angel; their heads were no taller than the center of his sternum. Barechested, their short fingers ended in talons, and they fought with the grace of Wu-Shu Shaolin warriors.

Vamped out, Angel gave as good as he got, employing the ancient and secretive Indonesian martial art called Pentjak Silat. The demons stuck to traditional Chinese maneuvers, concentrating on slicing at him with their talons as they attacked in two's and three's.

He took a moment to assess Gunn's status. The veteran streetfighter was going hand-to-hand with a single Vigory, but that was only because the attacker's buddies were still dusting themselves off from the leap off the roofs. Soon, Gunn was going to be overwhelmed.

Angel jumped forward and grabbed one of the demons around the neck. Then he grabbed another and slammed their heads together. Without bothering to assess the damage, he went after another pair while at the same time executing a left sidekick to protect his flank.

He grabbed two more.

There are dozens of them!

Then he heard a shout from Gunn and the blare of a car horn. It came from the other end of the alley; as Angel glanced up to see what it was, demons and Vigories went flying in all directions.

The car barreled over more attackers and screeched to a halt. It was a car he didn't recognize, but a driver whom he did: green skin, red eyes and horns, Lorne jumped out, waving, and shouting, "C'mon, kids! Let's get the hell out of here!"

What about my car? Angel thought protectively as he dashed past his beloved convertible. But he leaped into the shotgun side of Lorne's borrowed wheels just as Gunn half-jumped, half-rolled into the back.

Within seconds, Lorne took off again, burning rubber as he peeled out and jetted down the alley.

"Careful, there's a hole there," Angel said, pointing at the unsealed manhole.

"Hey, great timing, man," Gunn added from the backseat. "How'd you know to come and get us?"

"Cell phone," Lorne said, hanging a sharp left. "Do either of you kiddies know if those guys know how to hot-wire a car? 'Cause your wheels are still back there, Angel-cakes."

Angel sighed.

"I didn't call you," Gunn said. To Angel, "Did you call him?"

"No," Angel replied.

Lorne cocked his head. "Actually, you kind of did, Angel. You must have accidentally hit your autodial at some point. I've had you on speakerphone for hours and hours. Course, I missed a lot of it, because apparently you two went underground."

Angel pulled out his phone. Sure enough, it was still connected. He remembered then that he had jammed it into his pocket when he had heard the orderly walking by.

"Cordy will have my head about the bill," he said without thinking. Then he sighed and turned the phone off. "What am I saying? She won't even know about the bill."

"Proving that simple adage about clouds and silver linings," Lorne said. "Aw, don't sweat it. Cordelia will be back and yammering at you for a raise before you can blink your big dark vampire eyes."

"Yeah, man," Gunn chimed in. "And we should argue the bill. We were in a time warp," he told Lorne. "We figured we'd been gone maybe an hour."

"That's a huge N-O," Lorne said. "Lucky for you. It's sundown and it's safe for all good vampires to walk the streets— well, figuratively speaking."

Gunn leaned forward. Angel saw the other man's frown in the rearview mirror. He didn't see himself. "Those Vigories must still be after Jhiera. And now they've got help from some demons."

"Maybe they're bounty hunters," Lorne suggested. "The little squat ones looked especially avaricious. They're probably booking agents in their own dimension." He wrinkled his nose. "And, *pardonnez-moi,* boys, but you two smell worse than bad reviews."

"Sorry," Angel muttered. "Sewer."

"Well, lucky thing I hot-wired a drug dealer's car," Lorne went on cheerfully. "We know he'll have the bucks to invest in some air freshener. So. Now that we've put some distance between them and us . . . what have you two boys been up to?"

Gunn looked at Angel. Then he said, "Big secret underground temple of death and interdimensional nooky?"

"Ooh, a bordello of evil? Try to remember everything you can about it," Lorne told the two of them. "We'll see what we can find on the Net."

Gunn cricked his neck, working out the kinks. So to speak. "Chinese curator, Chinese temple, Jhiera and Alex Liang and lots of heat . . . I'm seeing some pretty big clues here."

"They came after us because we got through one of their portals," Angel said. "I wondered why no one came after us after the museum battle. I figured Jhiera was steering as clear of us as possible."

"Huh. You think she's set herself up in town as some kind of queen?" Lorne asked. "Or as a talent manager?"

"Too high profile," Angel replied. Then he frowned. "Maybe you're right. Maybe she's lost it. Started out with a noble cause, tasted some power . . . it's hard to resist."

They blasted toward the Hyperion. Angel called Fred to make sure she was all right.

"Oh hi, Angel," she piped. "You're okay! We were worried, with you being gone so long and the phone going on and on and on. Um, is Charles all right too?"

"Yes. You want to speak to him?" Angel asked, glancing up at Gunn's reflection.

"Um, sure, yeah," she said diffidently. That surprised Angel, but he made no comment, just silently handed the phone to Gunn.

"Hey, ba . . . Fred," Gunn said.

Lorne said, "I'll see if I can get some more info on these folks. Underground, Chinese, demon-oriented. Probably some kind of tong. Secret society," he filled in for Angel.

Angel processed that. "They were all wearing the same color of robes. Red."

"A nice lacquer red, or a chrysanthemum?" Lorne asked. Then, at Angel's look, he sighed plaintively and said, "And to think I assumed you were a primo fashionista when I first met you."

"Just a guy with a coat," Angel finished for him.

Stepping from the shadows, Honnar of the Deathwok Clan stared at the car that zoomed past him. Unless his eyes deceived him, Krevlorneswath was the driver!

"Hey!" he cried, waving his hands.

He began to run down the street, then hung a left just as the car did.

Whoa.

What he saw made him think twice about any kind of singing career—here or in any dimension.

Qin had left the balcony to monitor the pursuit of the intruders. Now, in his private quarters, Shiryah and Xian stood behind him as he spoke via a radio phone with the leader of the demons he had sent after the intruders.

"The Vigories tell me it was Angel, the vampire, and his

180

human ally, Gunn." The demon's voice crackled over the phone, which had been magickally boosted in order to work so far underground.

Shiryah turned to Xian. "He's trying to kill us too! Not just the Vigories!" she announced, clinging to the Chinese Possessor.

Xian looked at Qin and said, "You promised the Ice Hell Brotherhood that we would burn Angel to cinders."

He looked up from the phone and smiled at her. "Then I had better deliver." Returning his attention to the phone, he said, "There's been a change in plans. I'll be sending additional forces your way. A lot of additional forces."

"Maybe Jhiera will make peace with you," Shiryah said to Xian, sounding hopeful.

"Maybe." Xian kissed her. "But it doesn't really matter, Shiryah. You're with us now."

"Yes." Shiryah smiled.

A little tentatively, Xian thought.

The Lornemobile turned down the street that led to the Hyperion at the same time that Angel's phone went off again. As he answered it, Lorne said, "Oh, dear. Have we got company."

"Angel?" It was Fred. "The hotel is being attacked!"

Black vans were pulling up around the hotel; dark figures dashed toward the entrance. Others were scaling the garden wall.

"It's a full-scale assault," Angel said. "We're definitely in the game now."

"Fred's in there alone," Gunn blurted, yanking open his door.

"Easy, big fella," Lorne cautioned, laying a restraining hand on Gunn's shoulder. "Let me get closer. Don't forget we had it warded."

Angel could see every movement despite the darkness. There were easily three dozen figures darting toward the hotel entrance and fanning around the sides.

Then a portal opened up on the front lawn, and a dozen Vigories of Oden Tal poured out of it.

Gunn traded looks with Angel.

"What's going on? Do they think Jhiera's in there?" Gunn asked.

"I have no idea," Angel replied. "Not my biggest concern, at the moment."

Lorne said, "I think we need some backup, don't you?"

There was a beat. Angel clenched his jaw and scowled at the former host of Caritas. "You mean Connor?"

Lorne's face softened as he smiled and shook his head. "*Au contraire, mon Ange.* I was thinking of Wesley." He took the cell phone. "Fred? Honey? You okay?"

Her voice came through very softly. "The wards are holding. So far."

"Okay. Stay on the line," Angel told her. He handed the phone to Gunn, who said, "Fred, talk to me."

Over their conversation, Lorne said to Angel, "I've got his number."

"Do you," Angel said flatly. With great reluctance, he handed over his phone.

Lorne was quiet a moment as he punched in some numbers. "Yeah, hi, chief," Lorne said into the phone. "Listen, we just ran into some Vigories of Oden Tal and assorted demons that we think are minions of an evil millionaire, and they're attacking the hotel. With Fred in it. All alone. We're driving up to the front right now."

Then Gunn said, "*Fred? Fred?*" He said anxiously, "She got cut off." He started punching in numbers.

Meanwhile, Lorne listened for a moment, then started nodding. "Wow. That's really great. Also, very unexpected by some parties. *Muchas gracias.*"

He disconnected. "Wesley will be dropping by in a few. With his new demon-hunter friends."

Angel stared at him. "Why?"

"I'm thinking gift horse, mouth, let's fight now and talk later. Plus, well, Fred," Lorne added gently.

"No way," Gunn grunted as he redialed again.

"I'm not sure if you're expressing surprise or saying you don't want his help, but yes, way," Lorne admonished Gunn.

They pulled to the curb, and the three leaped out. There was no sense parking any closer. It would give away the element of surprise, which was about the only thing they had going for them.

Mixed among the Vigories and the demons were humans in black ninja clothes. The fact that the demons, at least, were still having some trouble getting into the hotel assured Angel that the wards the Furies had put up were still holding. But he knew from experience that those could go at any time.

"We got a strategy?" Gunn asked Angel.

"Fight hard." Angel shrugged. "Don't die."

"Everything I ever wanted to know about living on the streets, I learned in kindergarten," Gunn said. He smiled faintly. "Wish I didn't have to fight in these nasty clothes."

"You do reek," Lorne said helpfully. He rubbed his hands together. "What say I perform a nice high C and get their eardrums bleeding?"

"Yo, wait," Gunn cut in. "If you break the windows, they might be able to get in."

"True. That might nullify the wards." Lorne looked frustrated.

"All right, we'll have to go with the 'fight hard, don't die' option. Which is not exactly my favorite song."

"The old standards usually work," Angel bit off. "Let's go."

There were bad guys racing everywhere, plenty for everyone to hit. Angel led the attack; the grand avengers got noticed awfully fast, and before he knew it, he was ramming his fist into a snub-nosed demon at the same time that he slammed his elbow into the midsection of a Vigory. The Vigory grunted and grabbed his wrist, trying to break it, but Angel whirled around and brought his fist, still doubled, hard against the Vigory's temple. The Vigory fell to his knees. Angel kicked him in the face, and the Vigory tumbled backward.

He picked up a demon and hurled it at three others. They went down.

He moved on.

"Gunn?"

"Yo! I'm good!" the streetfighter yelled.

"Lorne?"

There was no answer. Alarmed, Angel shouted, "Lorne?"

Still no acknowledgment. Angel couldn't see the Host's green face anywhere in the blur. He registered that distressing fact, then turned all his attention to the important business of not getting killed.

There were a hell of a lot of opponents to choose from. Which meant that every punch he threw landed somewhere and did some damage. Problem was, for every assailant he took out, another seemed to take his place. He kept on in; there was nothing else to do.

And things were not looking good.

"Angel! I'm falling behind!" Gunn reported.

Then from behind Angel, someone let loose with submachine gun fire. A Vigory froze in place, then toppled over, blood gushing from a wound in his back. One of the stubby-snouted demons was next, crumpling in a writhing heap on the grass. A young Asian guy was next. Then another. Humans were dying.

Whoever wielded the submachine gun was mowing a path toward the front entrance of the hotel. *For me to get in,* Angel realized. He rammed past the survivors the shooter had missed, and wrenched the front door open. He didn't look back as he raced into the lobby. He did remember to shut the door, in order to keep the wards intact.

"Fred?" he shouted, dashing into his office, looking behind the reception desk.

The lower floor was deserted. But no one had followed him in. The wards were still holding.

He hoped Gunn and Lorne were still holding as well.

He took the stairs two at a time, going by instinct to Fred's room. In times of trouble, it was her sanctuary.

He found her there, scribbling equations on the walls with a marking pen clutched in her right hand. In her left fist, she held a Bavarian fighting adze like the one Wesley favored.

"Hey," she said shakily as she saw him. She was trembling. "What's going on?"

Angel came to her and put his hands on her shoulders. "We don't know. But I have a feeling we're about to find out."

Outside, the gunfire was intense. Angel heard some shouts and a wild scream of pain. He smelled fresh blood. Lots of it.

"I wasn't hiding in here," Fred told him, her eyes huge with fear. "I . . . I was holding out for reinforcements. For you guys." She lifted her chin. "I'm ready to join the fray."

He smiled faintly. *Dear Fred.* He touched her cheek and said, "I think we're good. I think the fray is over. You stay here. I'll go see what's happening."

• • •

What was happening was the arrival of Wesley and his men. Gone was the foppish Brit who had come bumbling in from the cold, the silly rogue demon hunter who had pathetically struggled to please. Lean and focused, Wesley directed his hunters to pursue a dozen demons who were trying to scale the garden wall. With crossbows and guns, the men picked them off easily. The demons left trails of green blood on the hotel's exterior walls.

Cornered, the attackers were rushing the entrance, and Wesley stood in front of it, massacring them with his advanced weaponry and his ruthless determination.

"Inside's clear," Angel told him. "Got wards up. No penetration."

"Good," Wesley said. "Fred is safe?"

"Fred is safe."

Beyond Wesley, Gunn dragged an Asian man toward Angel, with Lorne bringing up the rear. There was red blood on Gunn's forehead and green demon blood on his cheeks.

He said to Angel and Wesley, "This dude's talkin'."

Angel opened the door to the hotel, and Gunn dragged the man in. Wesley resumed shooting. Lorne hurried around him, crossed the threshold, and slammed the door shut.

The man fell to his knees, prostrating himself before Angel.

"Don't make me talk. They will kill me," he begged.

"Who?" Angel demanded. "Who will kill you?"

The man shook his head wildly from side to side. Then, as Angel bent down to question him further, he bit down hard on something. His body jerked; his face went white; and foam began to gush from his mouth.

"Suicide pill!" Gunn shouted. He dropped to his knees and tried to pry open the man's mouth.

But it was too late. The man convulsed once, twice, and then collapsed. Gunn checked his carotid artery.

186

"Dead," he said disgustedly. "So if he was afraid they would kill him if he talked, what did it matter?"

"Torture," Wesley replied, biting off the word as he came into the hotel. Angel knew Wesley had some experience in that area, both on the receiving end—Faith had tortured him—and on the giving end: He had tortured Justine, Holtz's accomplice.

"Well . . ." Lorne looked back at the battle. "There will be other survivors. Probably."

"There'd better be. We need some answers," Gunn said.

Angel narrowed his eyes. "Perhaps Jhiera can provide us with those."

CHAPTER SEVEN

Sunnydale

Willow picked up the tuna-salad sandwich Anya had prepared for her and paged through another one of Anya's charred books from the Magic Box. It was a volume on magickal tiders and titrations, in ancient Sumerian. The Hardwick's Denaturing Spell had been a flop. They were moving on to the Krevalsky's Titration.

Will tapped a word as she tried to remember the English translation.

"This means either 'fat' or 'factual,'" she murmured.

Anya was on the phone. She said merrily, "Hi, Krelor, it's Anya. Well, it's Anya *now*. I was Anyanka when we were dating. That little vengeance demon you met in the gulag? Yup. The same."

She leaned over Willow's shoulder and said, "It's 'fat.' We need lard to make it work. But Crisco is a fine substitution, if I recall correctly. It's a very versatile product."

She laughed into the phone. "Oh, Krelor! You're too funny! I had forgotten all about that little incident with the butter churn!"

"Huh." Willow continued to read the spell, taking a bite of her sandwich. The consistency was . . . extremely bizarre.

"In fact, I used Crisco in the tuna salad," Anya said to Willow. "Bet you can't even tell it's not mayo!"

Willow worked overtime to swallow the bite, then gingerly laid the sandwich back on the plate.

"So, Krelor. This witch and I are trying to do a Krevalsky's on a shard of clay. There's some kind of residue on it. And we need . . . exactly!" She brightened, smiling excitedly at Willow. "Monkey's paw! The root, not the real paw."

Anya listened some more. "Oh, that's great!" She covered the phone and said to Willow, "He says he's got a local supplier."

"Mmm . . . good," Willow replied, trying to wipe the Crisco off the roof of her mouth with her tongue.

"Go ahead, Krelor. I'm listening. At the Fish Tank? No. I hate that place. Too rough," Anya said. She thought a moment. "How about Willy's?" She checked her watch. "In two hours?"

Willow nodded her assent.

"Two hours. Willy's," Anya said gaily into the phone. "Thank you!"

She hung up. "It's all arranged," she informed Willow. Then she picked up the shard of statue, examining it closely. "With just a smidgen of Monkey's Paw, we can perform our Krevalsky's Titration on this thing and solve the big mystery!"

"We should get some lard too," Willow said. At Anya's perplexed look, she added, "Just in case."

"All right." Anya punched in some more numbers on the phone pad. "I'll let Buffy know what's going on." She grinned at Willow. "I made a salad too. And my own salad dressing!"

Willow tried to smile. "How nice," she said weakly.

Los Angeles

With Qin occupied with the attack on the vampire, Xian excused herself from Shiryah's cloying presence and retreated to her private chambers.

Blissfully alone, she held her magick mirror between her hands. The body she had Possessed was already becoming chill to the touch. Her bones were aching. The freezing problem was worsening.

And she was beginning to wonder if Qin preferred Shiryah's company to her own. She had seen the two kissing on the balcony shortly before the intruders had been discovered. It was a disconcerting thought . . . she had no illusions that if Qin tired of her, he would gladly release her from his court and allow her to make her own way in the world. That was not his way. He was ruthless and heartless, and passion was what mattered to him. It was fortunate indeed that she had to Possess another body so often. It kept her mysterious and intriguing to him.

And if he so much as suspected that she preferred Fai-Lok to him . . .

She shivered.

She wondered how Fai-Lok was faring with the freezing problem, but she didn't take time to discuss it. There was always a danger that Qin would trace the magickal emissions of her mirror and ask difficult questions. It would be highly unusual for her to contact Fai-Lok herself. He was Qin's trusted lieutenant, not hers.

Fai-Lok's handsome new face glowed in her mirror as he murmured, "I have thrown the joss, my beloved. The full moon rises in two nights. It is the most propitious moment for our dream to unfold. My book calls it the Night of Awakening."

Xian clutched the mirror between her hands, holding his face, and said, "So soon?"

"I know it's unexpected, but it is clear we are meant to make the attempt on that night," he replied. "Qin must know it as well. Has he discussed it with you?"

"No," she said. "He is as secretive as always." She flared with anger; she hated Qin. She had hated him for centuries.

"At present, he is attacking someone who got into the temple."

"Interesting," Fai-Lok said. "Do you know who it is?" Before she could answer, he said, "It must be Angel, the vampire guardian of Los Angeles."

"Perhaps," she replied.

"That will keep him distracted. Now listen, let's go through it. I have the Orb," he reminded her. "It will summon Fire Storm here. She will have no choice but to answer its call."

He held up the glittering Orb, which his faithful minions in Los Angeles had stolen from Qin. They had substituted a fake for the crackling blue sphere, and thus far, Bai Ju at the home temple in China hadn't noticed the switch.

"It's beautiful," she whispered. "So lovely."

"Yes. You are," Fai-Lok said to her. "Tell me. Can we count on Jhiera?"

"I doubt it, but Shiryah is loyal," she told him. "I'm still not sure I'll be able to persuade Qin to let us travel to Sunnydale to awaken Fire Storm." She shook her head and glanced furtively around the room, trying to assure herself that she was safe. "I thought I would have more time to work up to it."

"We have a Plan B," he reminded her.

"If he insists that the dragon be sent through to him, you will order the Hellmouth Clan to attack her," Xian said. "If they can either kill or seriously wound her, Qin won't be able to use her against us."

"But he will retaliate," Fai-Lok pointed out.

"Your followers will lay down their lives for you, Fai-Lok," she asserted. The seeping cold numbed her mouth. She sucked in her breath and bit down on her lower lip, desperate to feel.

"Are you cold, my love?" Fai-Lok asked her.

She nodded, her eyes wide and frightened.

"Don't be afraid. I'll figure out how to fix it. I promise."

She took a deep breath. "I'm not afraid," she lied. "I'm Xian. I am fearless."

"Yes, my beauty, you are," he replied. "But we'd better go. Don't be afraid. The God of Thunder is with us."

"*Shr,*" she murmured in their native tongue. "He is with us."

And I pray that He will help you find a way to warm these frozen bones.

She slipped the mirror into the space between her dresser and the wall just as Qin strode into the room. Though she was startled, she didn't show it, but turned and smiled at him, holding out her hands.

He was wearing his sunglasses; it bothered her that she couldn't see his eyes. He cocked his head at her and asked, "Who were you talking to, Xian?"

"Myself." She laughed. "You know I do that when I'm nervous."

"You talk in your sleep too," he replied, still smiling. "When you're nervous."

Her heart turned to ice.

She swallowed hard and said, "Do you catch the intruders?"

Angrily he shook his head. "It was Angel and his people.

192

They have stronger magicks than I realized." He looked frustrated.

"So the war has begun?" she asked.

He didn't answer, only said, "It is paramount that we bring Fire Storm through the portal as soon as possible. I'm going to speak to Fai-Lok."

With that, he turned away from her and strode out of her chamber.

Leaving her very cold and very frightened.

Angel and Company braced for another attack, but none came. Angel had put out queries about Jhiera, and as the night wore on, their errant Fashion Victim informant, Aristide, phoned in and said, "*Alors,* ahm so sorry about the Metro, Angel. I 'ad an engagement with Protar the Unmerciful that I simply could not get out of. But I have some exciting news. Protar said you were looking for these women who can shoot flames. And I just saw one. Very short black clothes—talk about a fashion victim." Aristide chuckled.

Angel glanced from the phone to Gunn. He mouthed *Jhiera,* and then he said, "Where?"

"I'm near the Liang. Do you know it?"

"Yes. I do. Thanks."

"For you, anything, *mon Ange.*"

They disconnected. Angel said to Gunn, "Jhiera's near the Liang."

"Then let's go get her," Gunn said.

Since Angel's car was still back in the alley, they took the drug dealer's car that Lorne had hot-wired. Moving silently, without headlights, Angel drove toward the museum.

He thought he saw a shape move from the recesses of an alley, slowed, moved on.

"Look," Gunn told him, pointing through the windshield.

There she was. And there was a ninja assassin following her.

Jhiera knows she's being followed, Angel thought as he trailed behind the dark-clothed figure who was dogging the princess of Oden Tal. *No freedom fighter would ever walk down the center of the sidewalk like that. She would keep to the shadows from force of habit, and the need to stay vigilant.*

She wants him to think she's perfectly relaxed. And he's buying it. Or else he's just playing with her.

She approached the museum. The ninja followed after.

Angel pulled to the curb and he and Gunn quietly got out.

He said to Gunn, "Let's split up."

Gunn nodded and moved off.

The police had conducted a cursory investigation of the battle at the Liang, but the brisk manner in which they had carried it out made Angel suspect they'd been bought off. Tsung Wei's grisly disappearance hadn't made the news, and Fred had not found any reference to it on any of the law enforcement Listservs on the Net.

Jhiera needed to come up with some answers. Now.

He ticked his glance to the left. He knew Gunn was skulking among the shadows, although he couldn't see him. Gunn was a streetwise guerilla fighter when it came to the war against good and evil.

But Angel could smell him. Gunn was alert but not afraid. Fear had a most peculiar odor.

Jhiera came abreast of the same gate Angel had scaled the night of the fracas. She made as if to open it, then whipped around and shot one of her heat-pulses at the ninja who had been trailing her. He slammed backward onto the sidewalk, and she dropped to her knees beside him.

She raised her palm inches from his face and shouted, "Where is Shiryah?"

"W-who?" the man stammered.

In answer, she directed a stream of heat directly at his face.

He never had time to scream. His head erupted into a ball of flame.

As Angel rushed toward the man, Jhiera jumped to her feet and aimed her palm at him.

"Go away, Angel!" she shouted. "I'll kill you too!"

He ignored her, reaching the flaming body. He had to be dead. All the skin on his face had burned away, and his skull was smoking. The man's clothing was gone; he was outfitted with body armor, but all that had served to do was compact the fire trail underneath it.

Before Jhiera had a chance to fire, Angel pushed from the sidewalk and caught her under the chin with his elbow. She was slammed backward against the gate and was knocked out.

Gunn was already running toward them. By the time he caught up with Angel, Angel had leaped over the gate with Jhiera in his arms. She was already coming to; Angel caught both her hands and flung them behind her back, restraining her from aiming her heat energy at either one of them.

"There's got to be more of them following you," Angel said.

"I have no idea," she replied.

Gunn shook his head. "Didn't see any. I pushed the body into the storm drain. Or what was left of it."

About a minute later, more footsteps sounded.

"Hey," called a voice. "Who's in there? Jake, can you hear me? I think someone's on the grounds."

A radio phone squawked.

"Night security guard," Gunn murmured.

Angel forced Jhiera down. He bowed his body over hers and whispered in her ear, "If you call out . . ."

He didn't finish his sentence. From the top of his chin, down his sternum, across his lower belly, and between his legs, he felt warmth. It was . . . he was . . .

Her spine was glowing. Her *k'o* was responding to his presence, and he was responding to it.

He licked his lips and tried to concentrate. He could feel Jhiera's deep intake of breath. She cleared her throat and said, "Get off of me."

"Don't make a sound," he replied, but he didn't want to move away from her. The contact of her skin on his, her scent, the warmth . . .

The guard said, "I guess it was a false alarm, Jake. I'm moving on."

The radio phone squawked again.

"Hey, man, we gotta move," Gunn said, clearly oblivious to what was going on.

He tapped Angel on the shoulder; Angel forced himself to straighten his back and crab away from Jhiera. As he got to his feet, he hauled her up and pushed her ahead of himself.

The three glided silently across the courtyard toward the museum. Angel didn't want to go back onto the street until he was sure everything had cooled down. So to speak.

He hustled her over to a doorway, thinking simply to stay there for a few minutes. But to his surprise, the door was open.

He glanced at Gunn, who shrugged. Then he tentatively pushed on it, bracing himself for an alarm to go off.

Beyond the door, a field of clay statues marched in frozen rows to an ancient battle. A skylight above them cast moonlight on their heads and shoulders. They were the terra-cotta warriors.

"Damn," Gunn whispered.

He, Angel, and the captive Jhiera strode down the ramp that angled down the exhibit. It led them to the front, where a single figure stood with a raised sword, as if commanding the others to battle. Its face was eerily real, its eyebrows knit over narrowed eyes, its mouth pursed into a thin line.

Angel let go of Jhiera, who sprang away from him and turned around, facing him in a fighting stance. She said, "I'm gathering my women, and we're leaving."

Angel cocked his head. "You were meeting one of them here?"

As if in answer to his question, a dozen Oden Tal females appeared from the shadows. Several of them raised their palms.

"No," Jhiera commanded them. "Leave them alone." Without taking her attention off Angel, she said, "Are we all accounted for?"

"Shiryah is still missing," said a slender female with light brown hair.

Jhiera closed her eyes for a beat. "That doesn't surprise me," she replied.

"Why not? Who is she?" Angel asked.

Then all hell broke loose.

A dozen or more Vigories crashed through the skylight, raining glass and warriors down on the statues and the Oden Tal females as more entered from passages feeding into the room.

"Fight!" Jhiera shouted as her females spread out and assumed attack positions.

She aimed her hand at the nearest Vigory and fired at him. He ducked, executing a snap-kick to the side that would have taken a slower fighter out. But Jhiera had already danced out of his range. Her second volley caught a different Vigory. This time she made contact; and the warrior screamed and collapsed to the floor. Smoke trailed from his wound.

It was a replay of their first battle, and Angel debated over helping the Vigories take her out. Although what they did to Oden Tal females was despicable, they weren't killing human beings. Or helping rich men take over the dimension.

As if he had read Angel's mind, the Vigory nearest him yelled, "Angel! This is not your battle!"

Then Jhiera somersaulted over the Vigory's head and landed near Angel. She said, "Help me and I'll tell you about Alex Liang. I'll tell you everything."

"The Bringer of Chaos is a liar!" the Vigory shouted. "You know you can't trust her!"

Around them, some of the other women were being taken out. Jhiera glanced around with an agonized expression on her face. "Angel, without my help, he will take over your dimension."

And you were going to help him. The Vigory is right. I can't trust you.

"I'm your only hope!" Jhiera pleaded.

"Then we're in big trouble," Gunn intoned as he rammed his fist into the nearest Vigory's face.

"Angel!" she cried.

"Then tell me!" Angel shouted back, taking down a Vigory. He had vamped out; he was feeling savage and feral and he took out another with a one-two punch that sent his attacker flying into the middle of the statues. The Vigory slammed down hard, breaking several figures.

A strange shriek erupted from the shattered statues. It was a high-pitched wailing, like a scream of terror. Angel was startled, but he didn't have time to spare trying to figure out what was happening, as more Vigories rushed him.

He fought them back, then saw that a portal was forming. It hovered in the air about ten feet away. Jhiera had one of her women by the hand, and she was half-pulling, half-throwing her into the portal.

"Hurry!" she shouted.

The Vigories blasted past Angel and Gunn and raced toward Jhiera and her women. Jhiera slammed the front two with heat blasts. Jhiera took the moment to help another female through.

Two Vigories took the places of their fallen comrades. Jhiera shot at them. They fell, and were replaced.

But there were too many.

Angel thought, *Damn it, she's right. She may be my only hope. I have to help her.*

"Gunn, get the women into the portal!" he yelled.

"On it!" Gunn shouted, ramming his way through a cluster of Vigories. He grabbed a petite Oden Tal female and hurled her through the shimmering vortex.

Satisfied that Gunn was on the job with the women, Angel concentrated on the bad guys. There were a hell of a lot of them.

"What's going on?" someone shouted from the open door. It was a familiar voice.

The security guard.

"Stop or I'll shoot!" he warned.

Angel spotted him and yelled, "Get out of here!"

The guard's answer was a bullet, which lodged in the back of the Vigory Angel had just taken on. The man grunted and collapsed.

"They're through!" Gunn said. "Oh no, you don't!" Gunn had his hands around Jhiera's wrists. She had been trying to escape through the portal.

"Let's go!" Angel shouted.

As bullets zinged past him, he gestured for Gunn to follow as he dashed down one of the corridors the Vigories had used to ambush them. Footfalls thundered behind the three of them; Angel grabbed Jhiera from Gunn and dragged her along.

The door at the other end had been pulled shut, and it had automatically locked. Angel broke it down with a swift kick. He bolted outside. Gunn followed.

Outside the building, black-robed ninjas and demons were waiting. Dozens of them. Angel said to Jhiera, "Fire on them!"

She did, cutting a narrow swath through the onslaught. They made it around the corner, where the car was. The top was open, so Gunn pushed Jhiera to climb inside while Angel ran to the passenger's side and jumped in.

Gunn peeled out and floored it toward the hotel. Jhiera turned around and shot heat pulses at their pursuers.

They had driven five blocks when a scream sounded high above them. Gunn looked up and said, "It's that dragon again! The one Alex Liang flew away on."

Angel looked at Jhiera. "Call it off," he told her.

She shook her head. "I cannot."

Angel shouted at her. "Call it off!"

"I can't call off this dragon," she countered. "I can help stop a bigger one. I can't do anything about this one."

"Shoot at it," Angel told her.

Jhiera said, "It's too far away."

"Not for long," Gunn told them.

Emitting another scream, the dragon dive-bombed toward them. Jhiera stood up in the speeding car, bided her time, and then, just as the dragon was upon them, let loose with a heat pulse.

It hit home. The dragon screamed with pain and fury, then plummeted from the sky. Its head missed the side of the car by inches as it slammed against the street.

The car sped away, leaving their attackers in the dust.

Safe inside the Temple of the Hellmouth Clan, Fai-Lok glared at Larry Wong as they stood together near one of two tunnels leading to the sacrifice holding area. Larry had just handed the ornate carved box containing the Orb to his master.

As Fai-Lok cradled the box in his arms, he said to Coach Wong, "I am not pleased with your work here. You have not kept us informed of developments with the Slayer."

"But, Fai-Lok," Larry said, "we've done everything you asked. We're ready to fight."

"The Slayer has a different combination of allies," Fai-Lok said. "You did not tell us that Spike was back, and with a soul."

He surveyed Wong's minions. Mostly younger men, there were approximately a hundred and fifty of them, crowded into the sanctuary beneath the streets of Sunnydale. Their head-quarters consisted of a vast warren of tunnels and rock rooms situated directly beside the Hellmouth. As a vernal spring would warm an icy river, the evil energy of the Hellmouth infused the rooms with an odor Fai-Lok found exquisitely sensual. Evil was heat. There was a reason many religions equated fire with damnation.

The caverns had been dressed in Chinese silks, gold, and jade that reminded Fai-Lok of the encampments he and Qin had lived in during the war years. Ah, those wonderful times. The carnage had been astonishing. The fear of the people was invigorating, as Qin's relentless aggression melded a cohesive nation from small, bitter bands of feuding warlords. The skies had glowed at night as the pyres raged, and Qin and Fai-Lok had warmed their hands over the carcasses of their enemies.

As they had warred, Xian had been left back at court. No tender lotus, she; Fai-Lok knew she ruled the government in her lord's absence with a crueler hand than Qin could ever imagine wielding. That knowledge thrilled Fai-Lok, excited him. He couldn't wait to get back to her, to have her, ravish her. . . .

Soon she and I will be reunited. And we will melt these rock walls with our passion.

"Come here," Fai-Lok ordered Larry Wong.

Perhaps he sensed what was coming; the man took a step back and murmured, "I have been loyal. I've worked hard to get everything ready. I took good care of the Orb for you." He gestured to the box.

Fai-Lok looked at him impatiently. "I said, come here."

"P-please," the man blurted. His eyes widened as he backed away, his arms open wide in a gesture of supplication. He searched the faces of his minions, as if urging them to speak out on his behalf. "I-I've done my best. I always have." He pointed a shaking finger at the nearest minion. "Tell him!"

Screw this, Sam Devol thought. *This has gotten way too weird for me.*

He was standing in the back row, his view partially obscured by a stalactite. That was fine. He didn't want to watch what he figured was going to happen next.

All eyes were focused on the unfolding drama; no one noticed as he slowly crept backward toward the tunnel that would get him the hell out of here.

I'm done, he thought. *All the way done.*

Moving very slowly, so as not to call attention to himself, he backed into the darkness.

Then he ran.

His breath came in short, frightened bursts as he raced down the passageways, grateful that Coach Wong had made them memorize the layout of the entire tunnel system. He'd drilled them on it, just as if they'd been running plays, with tests and everything.

Now Sam hoisted himself up the wooden ladder. He had helped make it, and the wood was still fresh and fragrant; a splinter stabbed his finger just below his Sunnydale High School ring. He ignored it, pushing on the trapdoor above his head.

It flopped open. He scrambled up and out and quickly shut the door behind himself. He was panting. He muttered, "Man. Oh, man," and yanked his red robe over his head.

The warehouse in which he stood was a few blocks from the Bronze. Though the Hellmouth itself was situated under Principal Wood's office, it wasn't that far a walk from the mouth of hell to the hottest spot in town, not that there was a whole lot of town. Sunnydale was dismally lacking in town.

He's going to kill Coach Wong. He might already be dead.

He balled up his robe and stuffed it into the backpack he'd left in the warehouse, just in case. One time Principal Wood had asked to search it for cigarettes, even pulled out the robe and asked Sam what it was for. He'd thought fast, said, "Choir." Luckily, the choir had red robes that year.

But Wood had given him that look of his, and Sam had started to sweat.

Hell with him. Hell with this whole thing.

He decided to leave the backpack there—his name wasn't in it, and it looked like a million other guys'. If that maniac was going to murder Coach, he didn't want anything linking him to that psycho and the other psychos who were still following him.

Leaving it there, he slammed out of the building—and ran right into a chick, knocking her backward.

"Hey!" she cried.

He frowned. She looked slightly familiar. Then he blinked at her, his lips parting, and said, "Willow?"

She frowned back, red brows wrinkling. Then recognition dawned. "Sammy!" She turned to a girl beside her. "Anya, this is Sammy. I mean, Sam. I used to baby-sit him." She grinned wickedly. "He cheated at Scrabble. I let him."

Sam flushed, shuffling his foot in an aw-shucks little-boy way, trying to act like he wasn't fleeing a potential murder scene. But if any of those guys realized that he'd split, he might be next.

"Yeah," he managed, though his heart was thundering so hard, he wasn't sure if he could actually talk. Never knew you knew."

"Oh, you'd be surprised what I knew." She gestured to the chick beside her—blond hair, very pretty. "This is Anya. A . . . friend of mine. We're on a kind of errand." She cocked her head at him. "So. Where you headed?"

He swallowed. "Ah." Hesitated, his gaze darting left, right, while he tried to think of an answer. "The Bronze." He pointed to the entrance. "Heard there's a, uh, hot band tonight."

Willow rolled her eyes. "Nope. It's another 'Depressing Night,' as Xander used to say. You remember Xander, right? He used to do the Snoopy Dance and—"

He shrugged, tried to laugh. It didn't sound right. "Yeah. Listen, I gotta go."

"Oh." Willow peered at him. "Got a hot date?"

"Yeah." He laughed again. It was practically a sob. He raised his chin and smiled at her, but tears were welling. "So. Later, okay?"

"Sure." Willow gave him a little wave. "It was . . . great."

He trundled off.

Anya watched Sam go, then turned to Willow. "What a big weirdo," she said blithely.

"Sam? No, he probably just felt awkward seeing me again," Willow ventured. "All grown up and dating. Plus, retroactively busted for cheating." She sighed. "I feel old now."

"You don't know what old is until you've been a vengeance

demon for a millennium," Anya said, snorting. "Well, let's go get the stuff we need for the titration. Spike's worried the residue will dissipate off the fragment."

"Okay." They started walking.

"You know he's with the traitor," trilled a voice.

Startled, Willow and Anya glanced up.

Seated on the edge of the roof, a little girl with Asian features smiled down on them and swung her legs. Her high-button shoes were shiny with green slime, and her petticoats and black velvet dress were rotten tatters.

"That boy is with the traitor."

Anya jabbed her finger over her back. "That guy? Sam?"

The girl nodded. Then she began to sing, "Ring around the rosy, pocket full of posy. Ashes, ashes, we all fall down."

"What is she, Willow?" Anya murmured.

"Not a clue," Willow replied.

"Only the Master knows about the other one." She smiled brightly at them. "The Master is the one I sing for."

The little girl scooted forward as if she was about to leap off the roof. Willow darted forward without thinking, prepared to catch her. But the girl giggled and raised her hands above her head, drifting slowly to the earth like a moldy little snowflake. Then she pirouetted on her toes and passed directly through the wall of the nearest building. It appeared to be an unused warehouse, judging by the grungy condition of a narrow strip of windows stretched near the top of the front wall.

Willow said, "Let's follow her."

"Okay." Anya licked her lips and straightened her shoulders as she regarded the wall. "However, I don't think I'll be able to pass through the wall. I lost my teleportation powers when D'Hoffryn gave me back my humanity."

"I meant, use the door," Willow told her, quickly testing the door, which was locked. She twisted her hand in a magickal gesture, and the door popped open. She led the way into the warehouse. It was a gloomy, dusty, empty room with cracks in the walls and dust bunnies and mouse poop on the floor.

The little ghost was not there.

But a backpack was.

And it was sitting on top of a trapdoor.

Anya picked up the backpack and unzipped it. She extracted a red robe and showed it to Willow. "Red robes," she said. "Mean anything to you, besides at least one of them is a traitor?" she asked.

"Choir," Willow told her. "Always a diabolical group." She looked down at the trapdoor, touching it with the toe of her shoe. "Do you think the ghost went down there?"

"I don't know." Anya tapped the door with the toe of her shoe. "Should we just open it?"

Willow hesitated. "She's a fairly evil little girl. She might hurt us. Also, this thing could be booby-trapped. I could try to use magick to open it, or see on the other side of it," she mused, looking nervous. "What do you think?"

"Are you feeling veiny and evil?" Anya asked anxiously.

Willow grimaced and moved her shoulders. "I don't know. I felt a little rush when I opened the door, but I think I'm okay. This stuff is hard to figure out, Anya."

"Then let's go get Buffy," Anya told her.

"Let's go get Buffy," Willow agreed, relieved.

They left the warehouse, the backpack in tow.

At the Summers home, Buffy listened to their story while Spike and Xander examined the robe.

"Wonder if it's cursed," Spike mused. "Makes girls go all hot the way Schoolboy's letter jacket did."

Xander scoffed. "Doubtful. There's never been a guy in the history of public education who scored with the chicks because of his fabulous choir robe."

Dawn nodded seriously. "Choir isn't one of your hotcha-hotcha extracurricular."

"Got a point." Spike shrugged and put the robe on the dining room table.

Buffy said, "Well, I'm going to investigate the trapdoor. Xander and Spike, you go look for Sam Devol. Willow and Anya, go on back to Willy's and get your supplies. As her sister opened her mouth, she said, "Dawn, start with the research on the robe, okay?"

"Sure thing." Dawn nodded and hurried to the laptop, murmuring, "Ha! Got out of my homework." In a more cricketlike voice, she called, "Google, anybody?"

"See, he'd make up words like that and I'd give him the points," Willow said. "Sam, I mean. Google. The Scrabble."

"The cheating," Anya said, and flushed slightly. "Cheating at foolish board games, I mean, and not other cheating cheaty things."

There was a beat while everyone tried hard not to remember that Anya had fooled around with Spike shortly after Xander had dumped her.

"So," Anya continued. "Willow used to baby-sit him, and he used to cheat at Scrabble, and now he's just a big weirdo."

"With a yen for scarlet," Xander added.

"Or, he really is a choir geek," Dawn said, hitting "Return" with a flourish.

"He's probably going to turn out to be one of those 'revenge of the nerds' guys," Xander quipped.

"Well, you're one," Dawn said.

Xander looked startled. "I am?"

"Sure." She beamed at him. "You were a total nerd in high school and now you're, like, all cool."

"Some people think so, anyway," Anya said flatly. She inclined her head at Dawn. "Please continue to Google. Try . . . 'magick robes.'"

"Magick *red* robes," Willow corrected. "Otherwise you'll get like a million hits. With red included you'll only get half a million."

"I'm young. I can sit here for years." Dawn sat at the table, powered up the laptop, and started typing.

"Let me go with you," Spike said to Buffy as she picked up a small satchel filled with slayage equipment. It was too hot to wear anything substantial enough to hold stakes. "This ghost girl almost nicked you once."

Buffy scoffed. "Please. She's just a child. A possessed-ghost-demon thing, maybe, but still a child."

"Hey, Chucky was just a child too," Dawn offered as she looked up from the keyboard. "And that girl in *The Exorcist*. Just a child." She raised a fist and said mockingly, "Child power."

"Li'l Bit's right," Spike said. His mouth was pursed into a thin, worried line. Buffy was touched.

"Go with Xander," she said to Spike. "Find that guy. He's the key."

"Key power," Dawn said, raising her fist again. Then she smiled happily. "Only, not. No key here. Just me." She resumed typing.

Buffy picked up her satchel. "Okay. I'm heading out."

"Come home before tomorrow morning," Dawn ordered her. "And call. We may not have much, but we have tons of night and weekend minutes."

Buffy patted the cell phone in her satchel. "Okay. Will do." She headed out.

CHAPTER EIGHT

Sunnydale

After Sam saw Willow and her friend Anya, he broke into a run.

He dashed down the alley in front of the Bronze in a blind panic; he had no idea where he was going. His brain had zapped into overdrive, and his feet were connected to his heartbeat, which thundered at warp factor five hundred. He ran and ran and kept going and didn't stop and—

"Hey!" Principal Wood bellowed as Sam sailed down the main corridor of Sunnydale High and nearly ran him over.

"Sorry, man, sorry," Sam said, dodging around him.

Folding his arms, Principal Wood fixed him with his patented stare and said, "School's closed for the day, Mr. Devol."

Sam didn't know what to do or say. He couldn't tell this man about the Hellmouth Clan, that much was for certain. Couldn't break his oath of silence or—or—

"What's wrong?" Principal Wood asked, lowering his voice.

And oh, God, Sam wanted to tell him, really wanted to. He felt like bursting into tears and grabbing Principal Wood's jacket lapels and screaming, "They're going to kill everybody! It's all magick and it's evil and they can take our bodies and there's going to be a war!"

But all he did was shake his head. "It's . . . it's a chick," he muttered. "That's all."

"Women." The principal nodded. "Enough said. But we're still closed for business. Clubs are over, team's gone home. Coach Wong didn't show for practice."

God. Sam choked back another sob.

"Huh," he said ineffectually. "Well, I gotta go."

"Walk," Principal Wood told him. He pointed a finger at him. "Slow down. World's not on fire."

"Not today," Sam murmured. "Sorry, man. I'll walk." He gave the principal a halfhearted salute and slowly trudged away, as if to prove his point. It took everything in him not to break into another run.

"You might want to make an appointment with Ms. Summers," Principal Wood said after him. "Might give you some insight into your women problems."

"Thanks." Sam kept his back to the man so he wouldn't see the tears streaming down his face. If only it was something that simple.

Sam's such a bad liar, Robin thought, watching the receding figure of one of his favorite problem students. *He's not just upset about some girl. He's scared to death. Wonder what's up.*

Guess I should find out.

Silently, he reached out a hand and tested the knob of the door to the administrative offices, making sure he had locked it. He had.

So he waited a few seconds to put Sam at ease, and began, slowly and cautiously, to follow him.

Los Angeles

Lilah Morgan was working late. As a junior partner in a law firm that provided legal services for various forces of evil, she was often at her desk during the darkest hours there were.

She had her heels off beneath her chair and she was dictating a letter to one of the Archduke Sebassis's underlings about an unpaid bill. One had to be cautious dunning demon nobility for money.

Else one could end up dead.

"Next paragraph," she said into her digital Dictaphone. "'We sincerely hope that the archduke's health is excellent and that he continues to enjoy a full and joyous existence. We look forward to many years of continued service to his house, and to see him, and you, at our next Halloween gala.'"

She clicked off the Dictaphone. "There, that ought to do it." Then she clicked on her Dictaphone and said, "Sign it, 'Sincerely, Mere Smith.'" Mere Smith was her current secretary. Might as well have any repercussions—if there were any—directed at her, not at Lilah herself.

"Okay," she murmured. "That's done."

She reached for the next action item on her list . . . and gasped. She sat upright, shoulders back, breath coming fast. Her eyes lost focus.

"Greetings, woman of the Darkblood," a voice spoke inside

211

her head. "Attend me. I am Lir. I am Lord of all I survey. I am your master."

"Lir," she breathed, not knowing she spoke the name. Knowing nothing of her surroundings, of her self. Only of that name.

"Listen. See. Learn."

The mountains were on fire. The sky was ablaze. And in the center of it, on the only mountain peak that had not been consumed, a lone female demon held a sword in both hands. Her name was emblazoned on it in Solan, a protective magick. Protection or no, she was terrified.

As well she should be.

Lir, magnificent in his crimson glory, stretching high above her, reached into the center of his forehead and pulled forth a glowing sphere. It shimmered a hypnotic blue; it crackled with energy. She knew it was the Orb. She knew what he was going to do with it.

With the Orb in his fist, he cupped his hideous mouth; he bellowed into the conflagration. He screamed a name, and Champion ticked her glance away from him as the firestorm erupted afresh, new flames flapping like wings as something emerged from the destruction surrounding them.

A huge head shot from the walls of fire. It was serpentine, with almond-shaped eyes glowing like coals; its snout was stubby. Its mouth opened, and rows and rows of fangs sparked at her like lightning.

It was the dragon, Flamestryke.

So it is true, she thought. It does exist.

Flamestryke opened his mouth.

She cried out, believing all was lost. She held out her sword and murmured a prayer to the Powers That Be:

I am your Champion. You sent me here to destroy Lir, so that I could reshift the balance. You sent me here; will you allow me to be defeated?

. . . and from the sky came a rumbling louder than the shriek of the creature.

"We send aid, Champion," came a voice from the heavens.

And it began to rain.

Abruptly the vision left Lilah. She shook her head and blurted, "Wow. What the hell?"

Serve me, and after I have conquered your dimension, Flamestryke will serve Wolfram & Hart, the interior voice continued. *Use the Champions of this time to gather the things I need. The things their Champion took for me. They will succeed . . . and one will betray the others, and then I will be free.*

The three things are . . .

Lilah waited. She heard nothing more. She closed her eyes and tried to be receptive.

Nothing.

She said aloud, "Hello? Are you still there?"

But the connection appeared to be severed.

Her phone buzzed. She grabbed it, picked it up.

"Lilah." It was her boss, Nathan Reed.

"Yes, sir."

"Did you just experience something unusual?" he asked.

"You too?" she replied. *What about Gavin?* she wondered, thinking of her rival at the firm. *Did he experience it too?*

"Get on it," he shot back.

"Already am," she assured him.

"The senior partners are interested in this development. They'll be looking for results."

213

When are they not? She asked gingerly, "Did you see anything about three objects?"

"No. I was hoping you had. The vision ending just before that was discussed. Like a bad cliffhanger novel. But I'd venture a guess that the Orb was one of them," Nathan said.

Makes sense. If any of this does.

"It told me to use the Champions of this time," Lilah continued. "That would be Angel. And possibly Buffy." She considered. "Maybe this has something to do with Shanshu Prophecy, about the vampire with a soul and the end of days."

"Perhaps." There was a pause. "Can you handle this? The senior partners have faith in you."

"Yes, of course I can handle it," she said. "You can count on me, sir."

"Very good. Now, there have been some developments concerning Qin. Are you up to date?"

"Ah," she prevaricated, her heart thundering.

"We're wasting time, Lilah," he said. "Let me fill you in."

And he did.

As Angel, Gunn, and Jhiera fled from the dragon, Angel called ahead and warned Lorne that the entrance to the hotel might be under attack. When the convertible neared the Hyperion, the vampire noted fresh demon corpses on the lawn, but no Vigories and no ninjas.

Looking shaken, Lorne stood on the hotel threshold with a crossbow in his arms . . . and very glad to see Angel and Gunn.

"You were right," he said. "The wards are still holding inside, Angel, but I have a bad feeling. I think they're going to give out."

"Got it," Angel said. He hustled everyone inside. Soon, Fred, Gunn, and Lorne stood in a semicircle, watching as Angel handcuffed Jhiera.

"That's not necessary," she said angrily.

"I have no reason to trust you," Angel replied. He stepped away from her and joined the others.

"I could have burned you back at the museum," she reminded him. "I did not."

"And I say again, I have no reason to trust you."

"Okay, Jhiera, give it up," Gunn said. "Why are you here, and what is going down?"

And so she told her story.

"So Alex Liang is really an ancient immortal Chinese emperor named Qin, and you're supposed to thaw out his frozen dragon so he can declare war on us," Fred summarized. "Then he'll help you take out the Vigories and you'll rule your home dimension."

"Yes," Jhiera said.

"Why'd you back out?" Angel asked Jhiera. "Sounds like the perfect arrangement for you."

She exhaled sharply and smoothed her hair back with her fingers. "I know you don't believe me, but I'm not a killer. I'm a warrior. And Qin—Alex Liang, to you—wants us to kill for him. I'm not interested in that. I have no quarrel with the people here."

"You've had a change of heart, then," Fred said coldly.

"I saw you with him," Angel interrupted. He glared at Jhiera straight on. "I saw you laughing with him, kissing him—"

She blinked. "I never—"

"You did. I saw you too," Gunn said, narrowing his eyes at her. "Like some kinda hoochie mama."

"No! I can barely stand the sight of him!" She shook her head. "I did not do that. When did you . . . Shiryah." She closed her eyes. "She has made an alliance with him, then."

"Looked like you," Gunn said, then paused. "You said something was off about her, Angel."

215

Angel took that in. "I did." And they had been watching from a distance. It might have been a different woman. . . .

"Look, I really don't care if you believe me or not," Jhiera snapped. "I can help you."

"In return for nothing more than your freedom." Angel crossed his arms. He wondered if she knew he could feel her warmth. It was emanating from her in waves, and he knew it meant she was aroused. The last time he had seen her, it had been very difficult to stay away from her. . . . Even now, it was a challenge to listen to her words. All he wanted to do was—

"Yes," she said to him. Her eyes were luminous, her lips damp. He felt a thrill at the base of his spine. He kept his face blank. "Yes, I want your help. The Vigories will follow after my women." She looked desperate.

"They'll expect you to follow," Gunn said.

"Yes." She swallowed hard. "I'll get Shiryah and we'll leave."

"If he has Shiryah, then he doesn't need you," Angel observed. "You're superfluous."

Remaining silent, Jhiera looked extremely uncomfortable.

"We should be going after Liang," Wesley said to Angel. "Or rather, Qin."

"We need some more weaponry," Gunn said.

"And magicks," Fred added.

"When is the dragon supposed to come through the portal?" Angel asked Jhiera.

She shook her head. "I don't know. Soon, I think. But I'm not sure."

"What can you do to help us, then?" Angel asked her bluntly.

"I'll locate Shiryah." She looked grim. "And stop her."

"And then you'll leave my town forever?" Angel demanded. "And never come back?"

She walked up to him and stood very close. He could feel the heat emanating from her body as she gazed up at him. "Never," she said clearly. Then she moved her lips as if she was about to say something else, and turned her head. "You will never see me again."

"How can I trust you? You tried to leap into the portal back at the museum, after you gave your word to me."

"They were attacking us. My women were in immediate danger," she argued. "We have a hiding place in our home dimension. I pray that they managed to go there, and that they will be safe for a little while."

"Why do this?" Angel asked her.

"Because she knows that if she doesn't, we'll kill her." Wesley walked up to Jhiera and placed his hand on Jhiera's temple. The Princess of Oden Tal winced and batted at his hand, and he held it open, showing that it was empty. "And now there's a devourer beetle burrowing under her skin. It's a homing device similar to something the old regime used on Pylea. We'll be able to trace her wherever she is. If she tries to use a portal, we can order the beetle to devour her brain."

Lorne looked shocked. But Angel nodded his approval.

"Okay," Angel said. "That works for me."

"Then we need a plan," Gunn said.

Fred, who had remained quiet until then, said bitterly, "We need more than that."

Sunnydale

In case Willow's and Anya's entry had set off some kind of security alarm, Buffy approached the warehouse from behind. Night had fallen, but the Slayer kept to the hidden recesses created by a row of Dumpsters and some round steel trash cans.

A scrawny tortoiseshell cat yowled at her, then rubbed its flank against her shin, and Buffy hissed at it, "Shoo! Shoo!" The cat looked affronted and sauntered away.

Though the six small square windows in the back door had been spray-painted black, Buffy crouched as she tested the lock. It was locked, but hey—*creak*—a good Slayer twist took care of that.

She paused again, in case the noise had been detected by a guard. Funny thing, lots of times the bad guys were thin with the security coverage. She had no idea if it was because they were arrogant or stupid, but either way, it was usually good news for her.

Without warning, the band at the Bronze started wailing. She listened as she slunk. *Whoa. Hot stuff.* Could be Common Rotation, whose work she loved. Maybe Ghost of the Robot. Either way, good news for her, the decibels would cover her tracks as she infiltrated the warehouse; bad news for her, if bad guys were skulking around like she was, because she wouldn't be able to hear them.

Well, slayers weren't built to sit around in idle, she thought.

Still crouched in a squat, she opened the door. It was pitch dark inside. She had a flashlight in her satchel, but turning it on was tantamount to calling out "yoo hoo?" so she moved on in, crabwalking, the satchel under one arm. As soon as she was inside, she set it down and quietly pulled the door closed.

She waited a couple of beats, then rose, still hunching over. It was a lot easier to fight with one's legs underneath one; she flexed her trapezius muscles a couple of times and moved her head, warming up just in case. The Chinese ghostgirl was a loose cannon of evilness; for all Buffy knew, she'd gone to tell Mr. Red Robes's six hundred closest friends and relations that the Slayer was here, and they were currently standing around

218

beneath the trapdoor going "eeny meeny you take her out" as they waited for Buffy to drop down.

And still . . . can't let that matter.

The walls were reverberating from the band. The scent of old dust wafted through the room as Buffy slowly shuffled her boots through the debris on the floor, feeling with her toes for the trapdoor.

There.

She squatted, running her hand along the perimeter. Normal, people-sized door. There was a small metal loop in the center of it for pulling it up.

Fishing in her satchel, she grabbed a stake and hefted it. She got ready to stab it into anybody who sprang up at her. She had a quick, jabbing vision of the night Faith had staked the assistant mayor, but she didn't let that alter her focus or her resolve. Sam Devol was a human being, but she'd learned fairly early in her slaying career that, at least in Sunnydale, evil humans served evil demons. Chances were excellent that beneath her—

It devours.

Buffy blinked. *From beneath you, it devours.* That was what Spike had said the night they saved that girl from her boyfriend, whom Anya had turned into a snake. There had been a weird vibe about that sentence for months.

Is this it? Is this the thing we've been getting the weird hints about?

Her Slayer senses jogged up a notch. If she'd been Homeland Security, her reflexes would be locked and loaded on "severe."

Taking a deep breath, she slipped her fingers around the metal loop and pulled.

Nothing happened.

She pulled harder, with the same negative results.

"Huh," she murmured.

She set down her stake and slid her other hand through the ring. She planted her feet and gave another tug.

She couldn't budge it.

Maybe it's warded, she thought, letting go of the ring. She took a step back and flicked on her flashlight, shielding its diffuse beam from the windows with her satchel.

It was a plain-looking trapdoor.

I'll have to get Willow to check it out, she thought. Willow and Anya were probably at Willy's by now.

She brushed her hands to get rid of as much dust as she could, picked up her stake, put it back in the satchel, and quietly made her way out of the warehouse. She paused on the threshold and slipped out. She had a feeling the broken lock on the door wasn't going to cause much alarm. This was the bad part of town, and breaking and entering was of the business-as-usual bad.

She walked down the dark alley, remembering a night long ago when she had just moved to Sunnydale. It was her first time going to the Bronze; she was nervous and excited, wondering if her clothes were cool enough for a command audience with Cordelia and her Cordettes. And then, that night, she had heard footsteps.

Click-tap.

Then none.

Someone had been trying to play cat and mouse with her. And she'd been irritated at the moron who'd thought he could intimidate a short blond chick walking all alone when in actuality he was tangling with the Slayer. Even if she didn't want to be the Slayer here in Sunnydale.

It had been Angel, coming to warn me about the Master. And now this little Chinese thingie is talking about "the Master." Could it be the same Master? 'Cause I'm thinking he's dust in the wind.

One thing I've learned, though: The dead rarely stay dead in Sunnydale.

But no one came to irritate her or to warn her now, as she walked away from the tantalizing tub-thumping in the Bronze, or to whisper in her heart about a relationship that couldn't be, no matter how much she wanted it. Still, the thought of Angel made her feel warm inside.

She got to Willy's and slammed open the door the way she always did, to give everyone inside a miniature scare, and put the bartender-owner on notice that she wasn't going to put up with any crap.

Willow and Anya were inside the dimly lit bar, seated at a small table with a demon who looked like he'd put his head on inside out. Also, he appeared to be naked, or else wearing an outfit created out of elephant hide.

Ewww.

Willy gave Buffy a weak smile and bellowed in a voice loud enough for all his demon patrons to hear, "Hey, it's the *Slayer!* How you doing, *Slayer?*"

"Bite me," she grunted as she sauntered past him.

Smiling with her red eyebrows raised, Willow unwrapped a hand from around her glass and hailed her over. At her right, Anya was sipping what appeared to be a cola beverage through a clear straw. The inside-out demon was pressing pretzels against a sticky, slimy ridge down the center of its . . . spherical-shaped topmost section.

"What's up?" Buffy asked Willow as she walked up to the table. Then, regarding the creature, "What's that?"

"He's our contact," Anya informed her, slurping the last of her drink through her straw. "Apparently, the Monkey's Paw we want is currently in short supply."

"So he's trying to shake us down," Willow grumbled. "For lots of cash."

Buffy narrowed her eyes at the pretzel-encrusted . . . thing . . . and said, "Obviously you have no idea who you're dealing with. I'm the Slayer."

The creature made a few odd noises. Anya chuckled and batted the demon on its . . . hide.

Looking aggrieved, she turned to Buffy and said, "He says he knows who you are, and that you looked very cute in your chicken hat."

Buffy bristled. "It was a cow hat. With chicken feathers on the back." And her cow hat look was one she would really, really like to send to the cornfield.

"If he knows I worked at the Double Meat Palace, he must know I don't have a lot of money," Buffy said to the creature. "And less patience."

More odd noises.

Anya translated. "He says that we will have to be patient. They only grow that stuff in Tarzana, and things are not very tranquil there right now. Which makes shipping problematic." She frowned at the creature and said, "Tarzana? That's a part of L.A. What are you talking about?"

The thing made growly noises.

"Oh. Not Tarzana." Anya laughed. "Tanzania."

"Huh." Buffy sat back in her chair. "Can you use something else to examine the fragment?"

"We've got this big book," Willow told her. "Actually, several. There's bound to be another spell we can use." She looked at Anya. "At least we can go buy some lard so the night's not a total wash."

"Right." Anya sucked the very, very last of the cola through her straw. Then she made a little happy noise and fished a maraschino cherry from the bottom of the glass. She popped it into her mouth.

"I have another magickal job for you," Buffy informed them.

"I can tie a knot in the cherry stem with my tongue, if that's where you're going," Anya told her.

"No." Buffy looked at them both. "Seems the trapdoor where you found the choir robe is either locked from the inside or magickally protected. I'm wondering if you can take a look on the way home."

"Sure." Willow scooted back her chair.

"Oh. No. She's gay, sadly," Anya said to Pretzel Face.

Willow and Buffy both stared at her. Anya moved her shoulders as she picked up her purse. "He thinks you're cute, Willow. He wanted me to give him your phone number."

"Oh." Willow raised her brows. "Well, it was very nice of you to ask," she told the thing.

It burbled.

Anya caught her breath and gave it a smack on its hide. Then she rose from her chair and grabbed Willow's forearm.

"Let's go," she muttered.

The three walked away from the table. Willow turned to Anya and asked, "What did he say?"

Anya huffed. "You do *not* want to know."

Over her shoulder, Buffy called, "Do you feed pretzels to your mother with that mouth?"

Then she stopped in front of Willy and said, "You need to tell me what's going on around here."

He looked as if his head were about to explode. "Slayer," he said in an undervoice, "haven't I been beaten up enough times for spilling my guts to you?"

"Clam up, and guts will definitely be involved," she retorted. She made a fist and placed it meaningfully on the bar.

The fact that she put her hand on something sticky took a little of the pizzazz out of it, but she maintained her scowl and waited.

Demon heads were swiveling her way. Two Vorlax demons slid off their bar stools and slunk casually toward the door. That happened a lot whenever the Slayer visited Willy's.

Willy whined, "Can we go in the back?"

Buffy raised a brow. "So they can all imagine that the secret you told was theirs, and they'll stand in line to beat you up? Good idea. Let's go."

"Um," Willy said, obviously having second thoughts.

"Let's go," Buffy said again.

They went into the storeroom, which also served as Willy's office. It was cluttered with handwritten receipts, splayed-open paperback Westerns, and an amazing amount of paper. Buffy didn't know how he could stand to work in there.

"What's the news from Lake Woebegone?" she asked him, folding her arms and leaning against a shelf where several large boxes of wine were gathering dust. Apparently there was not a lot of call for wine in a place like Willy's.

"There are lots of disappearing people," he stated. Then he lowered his voice. "Word is they're being nabbed for sacrifices." He twisted his mouth. "Sick world we live in, eh, Slayer?"

"Who's nabbing them?" Buffy asked.

"Do they wear red robes?" Anya cut in.

Willy nodded slowly. "That's what I've heard. Red robes. I don't know anything more." He shrugged. "Only group I know has red robes is the choir."

Moving swiftly, Buffy grabbed him by the front of the shirt. She said, "If you hear anything else, you're calling me."

"Sure, sure I am!" he said anxiously. "You got it!"

"Okay." She released him.

Qin stomped into Xian's private chamber; she barely had time to hide her magick mirror before he plopped down on her crimson satin-covered bed and lay back, throwing his hands over his head and sighing angrily.

"Jhiera has been captured by Angel," he told her. "The Vigories have left our dimension to pursue her females."

The hair on the back of Xian's neck stood on end. She wasn't sure if this was good news or bad. She licked her lips and said, "It's lucky that Shiryah is loyal to us. She can unfreeze Fire Storm for us."

He turned over and stared at her. She tried not to show her anxiety.

Then he nodded and said, "I have thrown the joss. We are not waiting until tomorrow to bring Fire Storm through. We are doing it tonight. Bai Ju and Fai-Lok both agree with me."

He strode to a large carved box that had been arranged in a place of honor in the alcove honoring his demonic father. First he bowed to a seated statue of a winged demon, its face elongated and fanged, and then he picked up the box and opened it. Slowly and carefully, he pulled out a shimmering blue ball.

"The Orb," he said reverently. "It will summon Fire Storm for us."

So it begins, Xian thought nervously, staring at the fake Orb. *One night early.*

Sunnydale

Fai-Lok ended his communication with Qin. His hands were shaking. He was sick to his stomach.

I've been caught off-guard. I thought to have one more night to prepare; did Qin plan all along to bring Fire Storm through tonight?

Then he put away his magick mirror. Deep within the secret cavern where he had gathered his followers, Fai-Lok spread wide his arms.

"My brothers," he said, acknowledging the few women within the fold. Some were still weeping over the death of Coach Wong. Many more were terrified.

Perhaps I shouldn't have acted so hastily. That's my greatest failing.

"The death of Larry Wong was regretful but necessary," he said. "He was a weak man, and these are times that call for strong, clever, brave men. And women." He bowed graciously. "I myself will lead you until a suitable replacement is selected from among you.

"But that is not a priority," he continued. "Our moment is at hand, my brothers. We must arm ourselves for war. This very night we will bring through our secret weapon. And we will rise up against the Slayer and take over Sunnydale!"

The young people in red robes looked stunned. Then a few broke into fervent cheers. Not for the first time, Fai-Lok wondered if this group was up to the task that would be set before them. Their leader certainly hadn't been.

"For generations, I have been currying the friendship of demons in other dimensions, as well as demons who have already made Sunnydale their home," he continued. "I summon them this very minute, to join us in our glorious battle."

He waved a hand, and a portal shimmered into existence. The members of the Hellmouth Clan drew back like one single entity, eyes agog as they observed the swirling green oval morph into an oblong, and then a rectangle.

The quivering doorway hung approximately two feet from

the ground; it was about ten feet wide and fifteen feet tall. Gray, indistinct shapes lurched and bobbed within it.

"Behold our allies," Fai-Lok announced. He snapped his fingers, and the portal shattered.

From it, an army of demons stepped: tall and horned, some quite human-looking; others appeared far more alien as they rolled on footpads or wobbled along in towers of gelatinous goo. They had tentacles, talons, and/or incisors; tails like scorpions, and long, wicked fingers made of bone and congealed blood. They all strode from the portal, pushing back the red-robed humans.

Then from the rock tunnel, more demons entered the cavern until Fai-Lok's followers were nearly crushed by the sheer mass. Gray and mottled trolls marched in a row, axes across their chests.

With a clap of Fai-Lok's hands, blue flames erupted from the backs of his hands. Huge, skeletal fingers took shape in the magickal energy. The cavern shook and thundered. Then the energy-hands fanned wide and descended toward the floor. As the startled acolytes lost their balance, the dirt cavern floor began to lower, slowly, the blue fingers forcing it downward. Large chunks of earth pushed up and spilled over in muddy hillocks. Long-buried bones cracked and shattered. Jagged crevices formed, and the members of the Hellmouth Clan gingerly jumped out of the way.

"What is this?" a Fralox demon shouted in English. "You called us early! And for what? To ambush us?"

Several of the demons unsheathed their weapons—a Flesh-Eater held a sword, a Thrusher, an adze—and rushed Fai-Lok. Before they could touch him, a wall of blue flame shot up, creating a barrier between him and every other occupant of the cavern.

"What are you doing?" a Siltar demon cried in a guttural voice. "Is this a trap?"

The question was so absurd that Fai-Lok almost snapped, "If it were, do you think I would tell you?" but instead he spread wide his arms. The barrier lowered.

"Not at all," he assured them.

"Then what are you doing? What trick is this?" another bellowed.

"I'm simply making room," Fai-Lok replied. He was improvising, but he had to retain his air of competency. He needed these demons. Without them, all he had was a ragtag band of untried humans to fight the Slayer.

"Room? What for?" the Thrusher demanded.

Fai-Lok shrugged as if the answer was obvious. Then, as the excitement of the moment overtook him, his true demonic shape erupted from the body of the young man he Possessed—horns jutting from the boy's scalp, fangs elongating from his upper jaw. His fingers transformed into death-dealing talons. His eyes glowed.

"For our secret weapon," Fai-Lok proclaimed.

The ground on which the demons and monks staggered continued to lower, while behind the blue flame, Fai-Lok's ground remained in its original location. It became an outcropping, in imitation of the overhang of the Los Angeles underground temple.

To allay the panic of his audience, he formed a fireball between his hands and shot it at the right side of the cavern wall. The magickal energy collided with the rock, creating an indentation. He hurled more fireballs in rapid succession. The toeholds in the wall would serve as stairs—by a majority of the creatures in the room, at any rate.

He performed the same maneuver in the opposite wall, and

then on the back wall. Then, with more energy, he created rooms at the tops of each set of toeholds. Blasting them out with energy in much the same way as one might use dynamite, he created a web of glowing blue to catch the chunks of rock as they shot out like cannonade.

The cavern ceiling shook. Fai-Lok wondered if those above-ground could feel the explosions. He wasn't much worried. This was Southern California, land of a thousand earthquakes. No one would wonder why the ground was shaking.

Except, perhaps, the Slayer, he reminded himself. *Best not to get too complacent where she is involved.*

After an hour or so, he was satisfied with his work. He pointed his outstretched fingers three times, and the web disappeared. Immediately, the monks and ambulatory demons hurried up the stairs and into the cavern rooms he had created.

To those still remaining in the bottom of the newly created pit, he said, "Move close to me, toward the front wall."

They complied, and he set a barrier of blue flame between them and the rest of the pit. Then he hurtled more fireballs, creating a floor-level cavern for them.

Once that was done, the blue flame barrier vanished. The demons crowded into the room—all except the Thrusher.

"What the hell is going on, Fai-Lok?" he demanded. "You're penning us up like sheep."

Fai-Lok regarded the assembly. There were perhaps six hundred. He could easily destroy them if he had to, but he needed them to serve as the foundation for his army.

"You signed on to follow me, or so you claimed," he said. "Tonight I will call through the fabulous dragon, Fire Storm, and we will take Sunnydale. We will lay waste to the home of the Slayer.

"And we will kill her."

A cheer rose. He pitied Buffy Summers. She was so intensely hated. He was hated, too, and feared. But he was immortal. He could dodge any number of bullets, as they said. And while it was true that she had been brought back from the dead, she was not immortal.

He could not even fathom the courage it took that young woman to get out of bed every morning; to watch the sun go down; to know that millions of fingers just itched to rip her to shreds— slowly and very painfully, if possible. She was a true warrior.

I will honor her with a clean, quick death.

"Now we will sanctify this place with that which pleases the God of Thunder," he announced.

His onlookers stirred, anxiety rising among them. He smiled to himself, enjoying their fear, savoring their body heat, and clapped his hands.

From small caves in the wall behind him, two beautiful Chinese women in flowing red robes glided forward. He had recruited them from among the coeds of U.C. Sunnydale, and they were exquisite. Their long, wispy skirts dragged in the dirt. Their hair was pulled back and their faces were heavily made up. Each carried a lacquer tray, and on the tray rested a long, curved knife that gleamed in the torchlight.

Fai-Lok clapped his hands again, and ancient Chinese court music began to waft around the room. The stringed *zheng* and the traditional flute, the *xiao*, rose together, playing songs that living people had not heard for over a thousand years. It was glorious, and Fai-Lok thought of Xian, and how she would be with him soon.

Then he said to the coeds, "Escort my offerings."

The two young women kowtowed, dropping to their knees in the moist earth, pressing their foreheads against rocks and roots. He smiled down on them, wishing he could save them to share with Xian, but knowing the two lovely girls had very little time left to live.

They left their lacquer trays and the knives at his feet. Then they rose and backed away, eyes downcast, and disappeared back into their twin caves.

Oh, my God, what is happening now? Roxanne Ruani wondered, as a Chinese chick in heavy makeup clapped her hands three times. Weird, shaggy monkey things emerged from holes in the walls, gibbering and bounding toward the cave where Roxanne had been imprisoned with forty-nine other people in three metal cages. The two other cages had been set up since she had been captured.

She had no idea how long she had been held prisoner. She'd tried to get the other prisoners to make an escape attempt a while ago, and had been savagely beaten for it. A Chinese man had overseen her beating, while two young guys in red robes did the dirty work. One of them whispered an apology to her, but he kept hitting her.

Behind her, a boy of about thirteen was crying and whispering, "Mom. Mommy." It frightened her to hear him. He sounded like he was getting ready to die.

"Anyone who cries out will be gagged," the Chinese chick announced. "Now, stand up."

Roxanne smelled her own fear through the stench of sweat, urine, and mud. Trying to breathe calmly, she looked across to the other row and saw Troy Kelly, a handsome guy she'd seen around. He'd come in all messed up, and there were bruises covering his face.

A lot of bad things happened in Sunnydale. People went missing and never turned back up, or else they turned up savagely mutilated. It got chalked up to the work of gangs on PCP or bad sewer gas or whatever, but Roxanne had always had a feeling it was something more.

And now she knew: It was crazy guys in red robes who hung out in caves with women who wore too much makeup.

"Start moving," the Chinese chick ordered them. "One by one, out of the enclosure."

Cowed like sheep—*that's wrong, somehow,* she thought— they formed a line and slowly began to exit the cage. Roxanne waited until she could be near the end. The toothless old man who had told her they were going to hell was jerked forward by one of the monkey men, who giggled and screeched as the man burst into tears and started singing "Amazing Grace."

"Shut up!" the Chinese woman shouted.

They threaded through the darkness. Roxanne could see a nimbus of light in the distance. Then there was a commotion at the front of the line.

Something in front of her was burning. It smelled like cooked meat.

Oh, God, she thought. *God, don't let it be . . . don't let it be us.*

Blind panic overtook her. She stumbled on, but her mind left the building for a few moments, overtaken by the blood roaring in her ears. Without realizing what she was doing, she tried to turn back.

The Chinese chick said coldly, "Keep going, or you're dead."

Against the rock wall there was a flare of something bright red. Fire.

They're burning us. Oh my God, oh my God.

Someone, come and save us.

Save me!

The line shuffled forward.

CHAPTER NINE

The City of Xian, China

Bai Ju checked his pocket watch, which Qin himself had given him thirty years before, on his ascension as the Number One Vanguard of the Ice Hell Brotherhood of the capital city, Xian. The city had been named after Qin's consort over a thousand years before.

Bai Ju was the most powerful of the sorcerers who served the Yellow Emperor, and he had worked all these years to acquire the magickal powers for this single act.

It was time to transport Fire Storm to Los Angeles. It was night there, and Qin was waiting for her.

Bai Ju put the watch back in the voluminous pocket of his red robe. He wore a spangled, cone-shaped hat atop his free-flowing white hair. With his most trusted lieutenant, Wei Mu-yee, who was similarly attired, Bai Ju walked through the many rooms of terra-cotta warriors. His spirit was soaring.

In one hour he would create a magnificent portal the size of half an American soccer field to send the exquisite dragon Fire Storm to the Most Celestial Qin in Los Angeles. She would materialize there in the Great Hall of the vast underground temple. Jhiera, their confederate from the dimension of Oden Tal, would use her *k'o* heat to free the dragon from her icy slumber.

Then the ultimate battle would begin. Bai Ju had no doubt that it would end very quickly, with humanity surrendering to the reign of Most Honorable Qin, may he reign a hundred thousand years.

And I shall lie down this mortal coil, Bai Ju thought contentedly. *I am an old man, and I shall join my ancestors with great joy.*

He turned and smiled at Wei Mu-yee, who smiled back. The rows of soldiers shifted as they walked past, as if saluting the two imperial servants.

Following a route known only to the two of them, they descended ancient stairs carved by hand into the rock. They carried lanterns, not flashlights, in keeping with the antiquity of the being they were about to approach.

"It is a night to remember, Wei Mu-yee," Bai Ju said.

"Indeed, Master," Mu-yee replied.

With each step, the air grew colder, until their breath was visible. Then they came to the ground floor of the temple that had lain undetected beneath the archaeological dig for the terra-cotta warriors. Columns topped with dragon heads glared down at the two men. Across the room a large, roughly hewn statue of Qin's illustrious demonic ancestor grinned wildly. The room crackled with cold. A brilliant mosaic of flames swirled across the floor, covered here and there by patches of ice. The air smelled blue.

Bai Ju's eyes were closed; he was marshaling his magickal strength. He opened one eye and said, "Prepare yourself."

Then Bai Ju faced the center of the floor, raised his hands, and began to chant. He flawlessly performed the elaborate incantation that would bring them into the presence of Fire Storm.

Wei Mu-yee was preparing himself for something very different from what Bai Ju had planned. Mu-yee had put everything in place, paid off minions and monks, performed his magicks.

But everything was happening one night early!

If this failed . . . if he was discovered . . .

He wrapped his tongue around the false tooth inside his mouth. It contained cyanide, and all he had to do to end his life was bite down on it. It was an old-fashioned method of suicide, but well-tested and highly effective. And painful.

The chamber sank into pitch darkness. Winds howled.

Monkey devils scrabbled from the walls. The feeble-minded creatures skittered around his legs. He simply ignored them, and stared straight ahead.

The blackness began to shimmer and dance. He looked up and glimpsed the stars, just as Bai Ju had told him he would.

Then when he looked back down, he saw that he and the elder magician stood on a mountaintop. They could look down over the whole of China as it had been in the days of Qin.

It's happening, Mu-yee thought excitedly as a rough wind sliced his cheek like a razor blade. *I have waited for this moment all my life, trained for it, and yet, I can't believe it. If only it were happening when I had expected it!*

Bai Ju found and squeezed Mu-yee's hand. "Marvelous, is it not?" he asked. Tears rolled down his cheeks, frozen in their tracks.

The next step was to offer sacrifices. In the magickal dimension in which they currently existed, one thousand terra-cotta warriors appeared in the vast plain below them. Each held in its grasp a struggling, terrified human being or a demon. The clay soldiers stared up at Bai Ju and Mu-yee, awaiting orders. They had been imbued with *p'ai* long ago, and the chanting had helped them marshal it.

Bai Ju chanted in the ancient language. As one, the figures looked stolidly up at him.

Then they began to squeeze.

Mu-yee watched in revolted fascination. The white-haired old man reached out his hands, making snatching motions, as the souls of the living were wrung out of their bodies. The souls were gossamer strands of iridescent blue that wriggled like ghost worms between his fingers. Moving like the God of Thunder, he grabbed them up and sent them hurtling beneath the dirt. The portal began to grow: First the foundation, thick and shimmery; and then the sides, which shot up toward the heavens themselves. Mu-yee assisted, catching souls, their intense heat stinging his fingers until blisters rose. Not for the first time, it occurred to him that Bai Ju might have a trick up his own sleeve, perhaps to seize Mu-yee's soul and add it to the energy necessary to open the portal. He knew it would be idiocy to underestimate his old teacher.

The portal gleamed like illuminated snow. Lights crackled and strobed like lighthouse beacons, throwing huge chunks of light into the black sky and over the piled bodies of the dead.

Then the last terra-cotta general crushed the last soul. The vast plain blasted like a bomb; and the outline of Fire Storm shone like a supernova as she moved through the portal.

Bai Ju threw back his head and laughed, shouting, "Mu-yee! We did it!"

In the cavern deep below the feet of Bai Ju and Mu Yee, the body of Lir, the great demon and father of Qin, strained for movement as his consciousness sought to reconnect with Lilah Morgan and Nathan Reed of Wolfram & Hart. But he could not do it; something impeded him.

He trembled with fear and fury that that "something" might be the Powers That Be.

He gave up and sent out his mind again, seeking another who served him.

It is almost time. Be prepared.

In the Los Angeles temple of the Ice Hell Brotherhood, Dane Hom blinked and heard his master's voice within his head. Images flooded his brain: of an Orb, a Heart, and a Flame.

The Flame is in the ice above me, Lir told him. *Buried in the ice. Seek it. It is a sphere like the Orb. It pulsates with heat.*

Behold, I show you a mystery:

As it rained on the plains of Sol, Flamestryke's flames extinguished. Realizing her advantage, the young Champion drove home her sword into the dragon's chest, dislodging the Flame. She reached for it; it fell, and she let it disappear into the flames, which still blazed across entire dimension.

I will transport you and the others to this frozen place, Lir said to Dane Hom. *I will direct you to the Flame. I will send you the Orb.*

"You said there was a Heart," Dane whispered aloud. "Where's the Heart?"

Others will retrieve it. Be alert. Be ready.

"I will, O great one," Dane murmured.

And the monk beside him thought, *Something's up with this guy. I'd better tell somebody about it.*

When they were dismissed, the monk sauntered from the main hall and then more purposefully wound his way through a number of tunnels to a room marked, SECURITY. Inside, a Mongolian sat behind a desk. He was wearing sunglasses and an earpiece.

When he saw the monk, he raised a brow and said, "What?"

"Um, ah . . ." Now the monk was afraid. *I should have just lain low,* he thought. "There's this monk. He's acting kind of weird."

The Mongolian's expression remained unchanged as he opened a drawer. He said, "What's his name?"

The monk told him.

"Thanks," the Mongolian said. "Anything else? What was he saying?"

"He was talking to somebody he was calling 'Great One.' But I don't think it was the Most Honorable Qin, may he reign a hundred thousand years." The monk kowtowed.

"What's your name?"

"Brian Lee, sir."

The Mongolian pulled up a hefty SigSauer from the drawer and shot Brian Lee in the chest. The young man pretty much went flying in all directions. He put the gun back in his drawer and started writing his report.

The door to his office burst open.

It was a guy from Janitorial. All the cleanup guys had been trained to bring a mop and a whole case of paper towels whenever they heard the sound of the Mongolian's gun.

The janitor got to work.

The Mongolian continued to document the incident. He frowned once and muttered, "Should have asked him if that was B-R-Y or B-R-I. Oh, well, too late now."

Sunnydale

In the cavern of the Hellmouth Clan, an enormous portal flashed into existence in the center of the cavern. Fai-Lok's knees buckled, but he held the Orb high above his head. Fire Storm was on her way through!

It's not even eight o'clock! She should come through at midnight! he thought.

The portal expanded, contracted, then shot out to encompass the entire ceiling of the cavern. The floor and walls shook violently, throwing the demons and humans to the ground again. People began to scream; the demons pulled their weapons and looked as if they were getting ready to charge Fai-Lok's magickal barrier.

He heard screaming in the tunnels but ignored it.

The cavern filled with shimmering blue energy, becoming purple, then green, then blue again. Lights danced and sizzled. Then the blue light of the Orb was blasted by a meteoric, blinding white light, followed by a sonic boom.

And the fabulous dragon herself appeared.

Everyone drew back, except Fai-Lok, who lurched forward. He was speechless. He had not seen Fire Storm for over a century. She was splendid, iridescent, and perfect, encased in ice like a fairy princess, and fast asleep in suspended animation.

"Our secret weapon!" he proclaimed, throwing wide his arms.

The cavern erupted with cheers and applause. The trolls slammed their ax handles on the earth, making it rumble.

Fai-Lok closed his eyes and clutched the Orb against his chest. *Xian*, he thought, *bring Shiryah. Bring her quickly.*

Or else we are lost.

Los Angeles

Qin stared into the magick mirror at Bai Ju, who was kowtowing desperately, tears streaming down his cheeks after he had ascended the stairs out of the temple.

"What happened?" Qin demanded.

Bai Ju prostrated himself, touching his forehead to the stone floor. Behind him, Qin's court executioner stood ready with an enormous hooked knife. One nod from his emperor and the man in the black hood would gut Bai Ju like a carp.

Bai Ju was powerful enough to save himself in any number of ways, but he was a very loyal wizard. He would rather accept death than disobey his master's wishes.

"I-I don't understand it," said Bai Ju. "I positioned the portal around Fire Storm. She slept on, of course. She was frozen. Then I made my sacrifices. They were worthy, Most Honorable Qin. The men were strong. The women were courageous and beautiful."

Bai Ju took a breath. "I made my incantations. It took me all night." He took a breath and extended one hand. It shook like a mouse facing a serpent.

"I activated the portal to the coordinates for Los Angeles. And then I sent her through. To you, Most Celestial Qin, may you reign a hundred thousand years. To the Orb."

"The Orb is useless. And I've been told now she's in Sunnydale," Qin spat. He was livid. The body he Possessed began to smoke. His horns jutted from his head; his face contorted.

"Hold, hold," Xian murmured to him softly in his private rooms in the Los Angeles temple. "Don't leave this body just yet, my love."

Shaking his head, Qin cleared his mind of his anger and fought to calm down.

"Where's your assistant?" Qin asked Bai Ju.

"In hiding. He's terrified."

The executioner who stood behind Bai Ju lifted his eyes and gazed questioningly into Qin's eyes. Qin shook his head. The man gave him an imperceptible nod and held his position.

"What if the Slayer gets control of her?" Qin asked.

"How can she?" Bai Ju asked. "The Slayer cannot generate the powerful heat of the *k'o*."

"Jhiera," Xian murmured, seeing her opportunity and seizing it. "She is in Angel's possession, and Angel must be in contact with the Slayer. We must take Shiryah to Sunnydale immediately."

"Agreed," he said. "I'll alert Fai-Lok. We'll leave at once. I'll contact Alex Liang's assistant and have a private plane readied." He picked up a portable phone.

As he did so, Xian crossed to a bottle of Chinese plum wine on a small lacquer table and poured two glasses. With her back turned to Qin, she emptied a small vial of the same potion used by bokors in Haiti to create zombies into his glass. She was trembling so violently, she had to hold the vial with both hands.

She turned just as he finished the phone call. With a smile, she held out the tray and said, "A toast, then. To a journey we didn't expect, but that will surely end in success."

"*Shr,*" he said in their native language.

He took the glass closest to him—the poisoned one—and tossed it back.

The effects were immediate. He gagged and dropped to his

knees, his eyes bulging. He wrapped his hand around his neck, choking, and collapsed to the floor.

"Qin!" she cried. "What's wrong?"

His breath was coming in short gasps; he reached out a hand to her. His face was turning gray. And then he stopped moving. Glassy-eyed, he stared at her.

They had lived through the death of Possessed bodies, but neither had experienced the paralyzing, mind-freezing effects of a heavy dose of datura, the main ingredient in the potion. But once, in turn-of-the-century Vienna, she had consented to being hypnotized, and she had lost all sense of herself while in that state. During the 1960s, both of them had tried the many mind-altering substances available, and both their consciousnesses had been held suspended during the length of time the drugs were in their systems.

She was betting that datura would keep Qin out of commission until she had time to get to Sunnydale and help Fai-Lok with Fire Storm.

"Qin! I'll get help!" she said, in the event that he could hear her. She would play the innocent for as long as she could. If something went wrong and he came to, she would do her best to convince him that it was not she, but some malcontent in their household, who had doctored his drink.

As fast as she could, she darted down the corridor to the hot tub room, where Shiryah was soaking, and urged her out of the tub. As Shiryah dried off, she said, "Quick! We have an emergency! Fire Storm has been diverted to Sunnydale, and the Slayer is going to use her redheaded witch to unfreeze her. We're going to take a plane there."

"Why not use a portal?" Shiryah asked, putting on her clothes. "I know how to make one."

"Excellent!" Xian cried. "Do it right now!"

Shiryah looked confused. "What about Qin? Is he coming with us?"

"Not right now," Xian told her. "He'll be following in a private plane as soon as he discusses the situation with the Vanguard of the Los Angeles tong. But we need to go immediately."

"All right," Shiryah said. "I'll open a portal."

Sunnydale

Anya's Sumerian book lay open on the floor between herself and Willow as they tried yet another spell to examine the residue in the statue. A metal crucible sat beside the book. They were preparing something Anya had never tried before; something called an essence portal, which was made with common household ingredients—lard being among them, since, when the spell had been written, every decent peasant home-maker had a wooden tub of lard in her pantry.

The theory went that if a spirit was connected with the shard, it would appear in the portal, then Willow and Anya would be able to study it.

"Okay," Willow said, laying a sprig of onala root in the cru-cible. "That ought to do it." Smiling at Anya, she lit a match and put it to the mixture in the bowl.

It began to smoke. Then the smoke swirled and glowed, forming a portal at the top of the ceiling.

They smiled at each other. Willow picked up the shard and said, "Now, I just hold it up toward the portal and the essence will be drawn out."

Willow raised the fragment toward the swirling illumination. The floor beneath them rumbled. The walls shook.

Anya murmured, "Oh God, my downstairs neighbor is going to think I'm having sex."

Willow ticked her attention away from the portal long enough to register surprise as Anya called out, "I'm not having sex, okay? Please don't call the property manager!"

She looked at Willow and held out her hands as if protesting her innocence. "For the record, I haven't been having sex," she announced. "It's just that, in the old days, I could really shake the rafters. Which some people found annoying."

Then Anya's eyes widened. "Whoa," Anya said, grabbing Willow's forearm. "Hold on, Willow. Look at *that!* I think there's a demon inside that portal!"

Kaleidoscopic light carouseled against the ceiling and the top of walls; a violent crack startled Willow. Then she reached out her hands and loudly uttered an incantation of protection.

"What if it's D'Hoffryn?" Anya cried. "Maybe he's sending someone through!"

That was exactly Willow's thinking. She had warded Anya's apartment before, but that hadn't stopped D'Hoffryn from sending assassins to kill the ex-vengeance demon.

Willow tried again. *"Protecte!"* she shouted. Then she launched into a portal-closing spell, barely waiting until it was completed to try another one.

It didn't work, either.

Anya grabbed Willow's wrist and cried, "The hell with the magicks, Willow! If it's D'Hoffryn, he won't let that get in his way! Let's get out of here!"

She hustled Willow out of the apartment as fast as she could, racing down the stairs. Half-turning as she tried to work another spell, Willow blew open the front door with magick, Anya dragging her in her wake.

They raced onto the lawn. Willow glanced over her shoulder. She could see Anya's second-story apartment; the room had grown dark except for a brilliant strobing pulse.

"Get down!" Anya cried.

There was another crack, and then Anya's apartment burst into flames.

Anya dove toward the grass, bringing Willow with her. Willow cried out and hit the ground.

The windows exploded outward, showering them with glass. Willow shouted, *"Protecte!"* again, and a barrier formed above them.

Anya shouted, "D'Hoffryn! You bastard!"

As soon as the glass cascaded to the ground, they both scrabbled to their feet and began to run toward Anya's car, which was parked at the curb. Willow pushed again with magicks to create a containment field as Anya slid behind the wheel. She leaned across and pushed open the passenger side for Willow, who backed up to the car, chanting in ancient Latin, and got in.

She shut the door and put on her seat belt as Anya peeled out.

"We're going to Buffy's, right?" Willow said.

"Where else?" Anya shot back.

Anya floored it, and they shot out of there like a bat out of Sunnydale.

Xian and Shiryah tumbled from the portal into the blazing apartment. Shiryah had shot off one of her heat pulses, which had combined with the magickal energy of the portal, setting the place on fire.

Disoriented and angry, Xian battled the flames and shouted, "What the hell did you do? Where are we?"

"Something pulled us here, something magickal," Shiryah said, dodging the fire as she headed for the door. "I was defending us!"

"So you set the place on fire?" Xian yelled.

The fire raged around her. She knew she was in bad trouble; although the freezing condition was protecting her from pain, the skin on her hands and arms was blistering and beginning to blacken. Shiryah was safe, and she was nearly out the door.

"Come back here!" Xian cried. "Help me!"

Shiryah kept going.

She's going to leave me here, Xian thought, furious. *I'll have to leave this body. I'll be incorporeal until I find another. If she finds out I lied to her about Qin, our plot will be ruined!*

Her horns sprouted. Her mouth pulled back into a rictus of demonic anger. Then the body she Possessed burst into flame, and she flew out of it. Her essence soared into the cold heart of space. She endured it, losing all sense of herself, until she hovered above the burning apartment, watching Shiryah escape the blaze and race across the lawn.

Without another thought, Xian sent herself toward her and slammed inside her body. She hadn't thought it would work—she and Qin had both tried to Possess nonhuman bodies and had never managed it—but she felt Shiryah's high soul struggling to remain. It shrieked wildly as it was expelled, becoming lost in the ether between heaven and hell.

Then Xian was the one racing across the lawn. In Shiryah's body, which was alien, yet blessedly hot; she stopped, panting, as the wail of sirens pierced the air.

I don't know how I ended up here, but I have to get to Fai-Lok.

Becoming accustomed to her new Possession, she walked slowly, noting the address numbers of the apartments and the name of the street. A fire truck flashed past, followed by a police car. One of the officers glanced at her. She kept walking.

The joss has been tossed, she thought. *I must pursue my path. Failure is not an option.*

● ● ●

When they arrived at the Summers house, Dawn was at the dining room table wearing earphones; she hit "Return" on the computer keyboard with a flourish as Anya yanked her earphones off her ears and said, "Where's your sister?"

"Hey," Buffy called from the stairway. The portable phone was in her hand. "What's up?"

"It's D'Hoffryn," Anya told her. "He tried to kill me again."

Willow said, "Maybe it was D'Hoffryn. A portal showed up in her apartment. Something was coming out of it, so we abandoned ship just in time to avoid bursting into flames."

"Your apartment started on fire?" Dawn cried.

"Yup." Anya suddenly burst into tears. "Oh, my God! My apartment just burned down! All my clothes! My furniture! My . . . latex products." She buried her face in her hands. "Will this torment never end?"

"Oh, Anya." Dawn came over and put her hand on Anya's shoulder. "You can share my clothes. Despite my limited budget, I have some hot outfits."

"Minus the one outfit," Buffy cut in as she descended the stairs.

Dawn squeaked, "What?"

Buffy joined them at the research table. "That little slut-tart number you wore to the Bronze when you were under the love spell of R. J.'s jacket? History."

"Buffy, no!" Dawn cried.

"Goodwill," Buffy said.

"You are so mean. That is so unfair!" Dawn turned to Willow and Anya.

"Not meaning to sound superficial," Anya cut in, "but D'Hoffryn just tried to kill me." She shrieked. "Oh, my God! My wedding dress burned up too! Everything I have in the world is gone!"

"Oh, Anya," Dawn said mournfully, gathering Anya into her arms. "Now we've both lost outfits we loved and cherished."

Buffy turned to Willow. "So, after the portal and the flames, what came after you? 'Cause I just talked to Angel about Jhiera and her little flame-throwing girlfriends. Maybe it was one of them."

"Why?" Anya asked. "Why would a girlfriend of Angel's come to my apartment to kill me?"

"Not a girlfriend," Buffy snapped, then thought the better of it. "Okay, maybe a girlfriend."

"Maybe it was an accident," Willow ventured. "She didn't mean to come to your apartment but she did by accident while we were conjuring our own portal. We brought her there without realizing she was already traveling here. Then she set your place on fire. Also by accident."

"What did Angel tell you about Jhiera?" Dawn asked her sister.

Buffy set the phone on the table. "Seems there's a dragon the bad guys have to unthaw so they can take over the world. So they got Jhiera to enlist in their army because she has all this heat energy. She decided not to play, but Angel thinks at least one of her followers has stayed with the other team. Her name is Sheila or something close to that."

She looked puzzled. "But he also said the dragon is going to be unthawed in Los Angeles, not here."

"So there's no reason for the followers to come here and burn up every single thing of mine," Anya said.

Buffy thought a moment, then nodded slowly at Anya. "Maybe D'Hoffryn really did send a demon to get you. Could be this is one of those weird coincidences that can only happen in real life, because in books they sound way too hokey."

Anya sank into a chair and covered her face with her hands.

"Thank God I have renter's insurance. And now I can claim the cost of my wedding dress, which otherwise was a total loss because I could never manage to sell it to anyone. I even advertised it on eBay."

There was a moment where Dawn, Buffy, and Willow refrained from saying anything.

"Speaking of Xander, where is he?" Anya asked, looking around.

"He and Spike went to look for Sam Devol."

"Okay. I'll get my supplies and head out," Buffy announced. "See what I can find and possibly slay."

"Buffy?" Dawn said, half-raising her hand. "Speaking of clothes—"

Buffy turned to her sister. "Dawn, this is not the time to discuss your lack of fashion sense. We'll brawl over it later."

"I found out some stuff about the red robe while you were on the phone with Angel," Dawn said.

"Oh, okay. Talk to me while I'm getting my stuff together," Buffy told her. She turned to go up the stairs. Dawn followed.

"Okay," Dawn began. "Those amulets we found sewn inside belong to something called the Hellmouth Clan. They're Chinese."

"Kicky name," Buffy said. She reached the landing and turned to the left, heading for her room, which used to be her mother's room. "They're here why?"

"I don't know. That was all the information I could find."

"Oh." Buffy was startled. "So . . . that's the stuff you found out?"

"Yes." Dawn made a little face. "I looked through a jillion pictures of amulets and red robes, Buffy. Now, if they had looked a little different, this guy would have been a member of the Ice Hell Brotherhood. There's more data on them." She blinked. "I said 'data.'"

Buffy considered. "Noted and approved of. Data such as?"

"They worship Qin, the Yellow Emperor. Apparently he built the Great Wall of China. And invented money. And burned all the libraries and intellectuals."

"Angel mentioned him," Buffy replied. She opened her weapons chest and started stuffing stakes and crossbow bolts into her satchel. "The Ice Hell Brotherhood has accepted Qin as their personal savior."

"Yeah." Dawn took that in. "Good analogy." She smiled at her sister. "We're learning about analogies in English."

"At last, a Summers who learns the language," Buffy said, sighing as she checked her crossbow and slipped it under her arm. "I am proud."

Dawn preened. "Qin's supposed to come back during the Year of the Hot Devil."

"Then he would be R. J.," Buffy drawled as she walked back out of her room. "And the time would be now."

"You are evil," Dawn groused, grabbing an extra stake and slipping it into Buffy's satchel.

"All big sisters are evil," Buffy told her, giving her hair a toss and acknowledging Dawn's contribution to her weaponry with a quick pat on the side of the bag. "And so, much with the pride again. I am doing a good job of being a big sister."

They went back down the stairs, Buffy in the lead. She strode toward the front door and opened it.

"We've got some clan-type information," Buffy announced to Willow and Anya. "It's not the Hatfields and the McCoys, and they have funny names. Dawn can fill you in while I go on patrol."

"I can drive you," Willow said, joining them in the foyer. "Anya should stay here, though." She grimaced and lowered her voice. "If D'Hoffryn's really after her, Anya should stay in a reinforced bunker surrounded by Doberman pinschers and rottweilers, actually."

"Rottweilers and Dobermans that know how to handle a bazooka," Dawn added.

"I heard that," Anya called from the kitchen. "And I agree!"

"Stay with her, Will," Buffy said to the redheaded witch. "Cast some more wards around the house. Check the ones you've already set."

"Okay." Willow nodded. She wrinkled her forehead. "Much with magick usage, Buffy. I know there's a need and everything, but I don't want to push my luck, you know? Well, not my luck, per se. I'm on good terms with the goddess Fortuna. But, you know."

Buffy put her hand on the redhead's shoulder. "You okay? Let me see your eyes. Are they getting dark?"

Willow widened her eyes and looked earnest. "See anything?"

"You look tired," Buffy said affectionately.

"I'm just hot." Willow made a little face. "It's been hot for so long, I can't remember what it's like to be cold. You know, England was all drizzle and sweaters. I kinda miss the mold and the mildew."

"Maybe there's a hellmouth in Oregon," Dawn said. "We could move there."

"Gray chilly days will return to Sunnydale," Buffy promised, "unless all this heat is some kind of portent of some new flavor of apocalypse."

"Cheery," Willow murmured.

"So very," Dawn agreed.

"Also, on a mission," Buffy said. "Going now."

"Be careful," Dawn pleaded.

"I will." Buffy crossed the threshold, stopped, and turned

back. She cocked her head and smiled faintly. "Okay, Dawnie, I didn't give away your miss hooker clothing. But I did pack it away until you are old enough to wear it. Which will be in the year two thousand and never."

"You are the best," Dawn said, rushing forward and giving Buffy a kiss on her cheek. "That means it's hanging in the left side of your closet." She turned to Willow. "That's where she keeps all the stuff she doesn't want me to use."

"Be careful with the snooping, or you will also learn the truth about Santa." Buffy smiled more broadly at her. "Lock the door after me. Will, take care of her."

"Will do," Willow said.

"Bye," Dawn called.

Willow shut the door.

Buffy slipped the satchel strap across her chest and rested her hand on the heavy bag. She looked over her shoulder, walked quietly behind a privet hedge, and studied her house. She saw Willow move behind the picture window in the living room. Dawn followed behind her with what looked like a sprig of laurel and a pewter goblet in her hands. Good. They were going to work right away on the magickal wards guarding the house.

After a few minutes, she continued down the street. At the chain-link perimeter of Weatherly Park she slowed down, attentive and alert. The park had been the site of a lot of bad Sunnydale juju, from werewolf and vampire attacks to more mundane murders and drug dealing. But she heard nothing unusual, and detected no movement in the eucalyptus and palm trees or the bushy clumps of geraniums bordering the fence.

She moved on.

CHAPTER TEN

Sunnydale

"Let's go home," Spike grumbled to Xander. "I'll bet you kittens Sam Devol's home in bed in his ducky jammies with his night-light on. We've not found him, at any rate, and I fancy a bit of something, don't you?"

"No," Xander sniped. "Not the kind of something you're fancying, Spike-ula." He grinned as he found his childish name-calling groove. "Spike-feratu."

Spike flashed him his patented *I'm-so-unimpressed-and-you're-so-boring* scowl and stuffed his hands into his duster. "Sticks and stones, *Alex.*"

"Hey," Xander huffed. Then he let it go. It was just Spike, after all. Hence, meaning not so much.

"Okay, let's pack it in," Xander conceded. "But we'll stop off at Buffy's first."

"Slayer HQ. Right." Spike pulled out a cigarette and lit it. Puffed out his match and dropped it on the parched ground.

Xander frowned. "Hey, careful. This place is so dry, it could go up like the *Hindenburg*."

"That was a Resistance plot," Spike drawled, sucking in smoke. He let it out. "Didn't have to happen."

"Oh, I see, Mr. Bond."

"I was there," Spike said.

"Right. And on the *Titanic*, too. You're so grandiose."

Spike lifted a brow and cocked his head. "Grandiose. There's a word costs a farthing. You get one o' those word-a-day calendars for your birthday or something?"

"Don't forget I'm your landlord, Spike," Xander said, shaking his finger in the vampire's face. "I can uninvite you anytime I want."

Spike took a drag. "Slayer wouldn't like that." He winked at Xander. "So come on, bad puppy, let's go see her." He gestured. "We can cut through Shady Hill."

Shady Hill was one of the twelve cemeteries within the Sunnydale city limits. Xander hoped the dead were quiet tonight. And that their target had not recently joined their ranks.

Spike pushed open the creaking metal entrance gate. His heavy boots crunched on dried-up leaves and twigs. The trees jittered in the Santa Ana wind; Xander could practically see smoke rising off the branches. It was so friggin' hot. He wiped his brow and crunched on, wondering idly what the hell had happened to Sam Devol.

Then Spike stopped and said cautiously, "Hello?"

Xander came up beside him. In the moonlight, a petite

figure faced them, her hands held slightly away from her sides like a gunslinger. She didn't look like a zombie, a vampire, or any other night-bumpy thing, but looks could be deceiving and she was concealed by darkness. If she so much as smiled in his direction, she was evil, guaranteed.

The woman stared back at them. Then she took a step forward, and the moon shone down on her.

Surrounded by a curtain of shiny black hair, her face appeared to be ridged. So, either not human or bad plastic surgery.

Spike took another step toward her.

Then she raised her hand and something radiated from her, waves of energy or magick that zapped Spike square in the chest.

Spike cried out, "Shite!" and fell on his ass.

The woman turned and broke into a run.

"Hey!" Spike shouted.

Xander started to chase after her, but Spike reached out and grabbed his ankle, flinging him onto the dirt. Xander smacked facedown in the dirt.

"Hey!" Xander shouted. "Spike, what the hell—?"

Then he saw Spike's chest. His black T-shirt had been burned away, and the flesh beneath was a smoking mess of extremely gross proportions.

"Oh, my God!" Xander blurted. "And may I say, yuck?"

"Yeah." Spike stared down at his ruined torso. "Lucky thing it wasn't you. Saved you, didn't I? Again?"

"Yes." Xander made a face at his wound. "That is so incredibly disgusting."

"Hurts, too, thank you very much."

"Can you walk?"

"Gimme a minute." Spike smoothed back his hair; Xander

figured he was trying to act nonchalant, mostly to cover the gasping. "Maybe you should go on, tell Buffy. I'll be along."

"No way." Xander studied the wound.

Spike looked moved, so Xander hastily added, "If that chick is anywhere around here, she might go after me instead of finishing you off."

The jab worked; absorbing the fact of Xander's enlightened self-interest, Spike rolled his eyes. "Ought to warn Buffy as fast as possible."

"Warn me about what?" Buffy asked.

Xander and Spike turned. Buffy hopped down from the top of a tomb styled like a Grecian temple with the name CLANCY emblazoned on the side.

"Check out Special Effects Guy," Xander said, pointing at Spike's chest.

"Oh, my God." Buffy dropped to her knees as she examined Spike's burn. "What did this?"

"A bird," Spike said. At her look of confusion, he elaborated. "A girl. She had heat powers or something." His smile was joy-filled as Buffy continued to touch him. "Didn't see her all that well."

"I did," Xander said. "She had these really high cheekbones. They were flared." He gestured to his face. "Demon."

Buffy took that in. "That confirms it, then. It's got to be one of the Oden Tal women from Los Angeles. Probably named Sheila or Shirley." As she examined the wound, she added, "We briefly thought it might be a hit demon sent from D'Hoffryn to kill Anya."

Xander's mouth dropped to his kneecaps and beyond. *"What?"*

Buffy moved away from Spike, flashing him one more sympathetic grimace. "She and Willow were doing some research at her apartment. They created a portal, and it looks like one of the heat-missile women Angel's working with used it to escape from L.A. While she was at it, she burned down Anya's apartment."

She held up a hand as Xander sputtered. "Anya's fine. She's at my house."

"And that's what we ran into?" he asked, his voice shrill. "A demonic heat chick? What if she heat-afies someone else? Like Anya, at your house?"

"I'm on the job, Xand," Buffy reminded him. "I'll get Heat Chick before she gets anyone else."

"I'll help you with that," Xander insisted.

"You going to be okay?" Buffy asked Spike.

"S'pose." He pursed his lips and remained on the ground. His hollow cheekbones were like sockets in the moonlight. "Remind me never to die by immolation. Can't imagine a worse way to go."

"Okay. If it ever comes to that, I'll remind you," Buffy promised.

She got to her feet, and she and Xander broke into a run. He stayed up with her as she jogged along at a good clip, rounding a headstone and avoiding a tree root.

She maintained her pace and said, "Any more details you can give me on Spike's attacker? Something I can use to defeat her in battle?"

"No." He looked over at her as they jogged passed a statue of a weeping angel. "Buffy, if Spike had been human, he'd be dead. Not that he's not dead. But you know what I mean."

"I do," she said seriously, leaping over another root. "We have to pick her up and stop her as soon as we can."

Xander's only answer was a steely eyed gaze as he fought to keep up with her. Then he said quietly, "Buffy, there she is."

Buffy looked to the right. There, standing beside a headstone, was the female demon. She was wearing next to nothing—speaking of tarts on wheels—which did nothing to warm Buffy's heart toward her.

"I'm taking her," Buffy told him. She unstrapped her satchel and handed it to Xander, then moved off toward their adversary.

The demon spotted her. She began to run.

Silly evil person, Buffy thought grimly. *I'm like the Terminator, and you're Sarah Connor before she started working out.*

The woman was fast. Buffy was faster. She punched on the turbo and easily caught up with her. The Slayer threw her arms around the female's waist and tackled her, forcing her to the ground. The female struggled, kicking her legs and thrashing beneath Buffy, but the Slayer held her fast. Whatever this chick's power, Buffy was betting—okay, hoping—that she could only use it effectively when she was facing her victim. On the other hand, if she set the foliage on fire, the graveyard would go up in a flash.

"Who are you? What are you doing here?" Buffy demanded. She had no idea if her captive spoke English. The woman didn't answer, but she did try to turn over.

So Buffy slugged her.

The woman slumped. Buffy wasn't about to take any chances, so she slugged her again. Her quarry didn't so much as groan.

Satisfied that the demon was unconscious, the Slayer got to her feet, hoisted the woman up, and threw her over her shoulder firefighter style. Buffy started walking, trying to decide if she should bring Heat Girl to her house or not. She wanted her under constant surveillance, and her own house was probably the best place for that.

Xander caught up with Buffy, her satchel strapped across his chest.

Buffy said, "Xander, my cell phone's in there. Could you get it, please?"

"Sure." He reached in. "Call your house?"

"Thank you."

He dialed, and said, "Hey. Hi, Anya. Buffy's here." He pressed the phone to the side of her face.

"Anya, I think I have your attacker here. I want Willow to get the basement ready for company of the Firestarter variety." She sighed. "It's not very well fortified, but maybe she can do something to keep it from bursting into flames. And ask her to give it a more abandon-all-hope-like feel. And if you want to leave . . . okay, hold on." She looked at Xander. "She wants to talk to you."

Xander took the phone back and said, "Hey." His face changed, grew solemn, tense, and his cheeks reddened. At least, by moonlight standards, they appeared to redden. Or else he was dying. "Sure. No, it's no problem. I'll take the couch. Okay." He disconnected and put the phone back into Buffy's satchel.

"She wants to spend the night at my place," he told Buffy. "I said it was okay." He looked at her, the red traveling across his face. "Do you think it's okay?"

"I think it's okay," she said softly.

"Because it might be safer if she stays at my house."

"Three sets of fists are better than two," Buffy pointed out. "With Spike there."

"Spike? Please. He'll just leave wet towels around," Xander riposted.

"Then I'll keep him at my house to deal with the hottie."

"I think that's best." Xander's voice was carefully neutral. "Anya will be safer with me."

He sounded very sad about that.

Oh ho ho, what have we here?

A blue-skinned demon named Orlando moved from the trees beyond the Shady Hill Cemetery, quietly observing the Slayer as she carted away the female she had subdued. Orlando had passed through en route to the gathering at Fai-Lok's when he had caught sight of the Slayer, and hidden. He had heard enough to put two and two together, and he knew he needed to let Fai-Lok know what had happened just as soon as he possibly could.

He waited until the Slayer was safely gone, and then he ran like hell to Fai-Lok's secret hideout.

Orlando realized at once that it was what the Slayer had been talking about. The woman she had subdued must be the one who was supposed to come here and unfreeze the dragon with her heat powers.

As Orlando anticipated, Fai-Lok was completely freaked out when he told him what he'd seen.

"They were taking her to the Slayer's home? Just the one female?" he demanded.

"Yes," Orlando replied.

Fai-Lok looked stricken. He turned away for a moment as if composing himself. Then he turned back to the assembled gathering with a fierce, wild look that made Orlando feel a little peckish.

"Hellmouth Clan!" he thundered. "We're going to the home of the Slayer to retrieve the match that will light our cannon!"

On the way to Buffy's street, Spike caught up with her and Xander, moving with obvious pain, but able to keep up. Buffy was sweating profusely by the time they reached her home. The heat debilitated her less than the average Joe, but it still drained her.

Xander got the door. Spike stepped aside for Buffy to go in first. She headed straight for the basement.

Willow was at the bottom of the stairs with a hammer in her hands. She pointed to a coil of heavy chain on the floor; also, what looked to be a cattle prod. Heavy batting had been nailed into the walls.

"Fire-retardant material," Willow said as Buffy laid the unconscious female on the basement floor. "We've been keeping busy." She pointed to the ceiling, where there was another similar piece of batting. "I'll try to minimize her powers, but I wasn't very successful before."

"You were taken by surprise," Buffy pointed out.

Willow nodded. "Let me take a look at her." She bent over the inert woman. "Hmm. Look at the ridgey things. That'll help narrow it down."

"Google 'Oden Tal female' first," Buffy suggested. "Even better, call Angel."

"Okay," Willow replied. "You keep her unconscious, and I'll figure it out."

"Thanks, Will." She picked up the cattle prod. "Am I supposed to use that?"

"That was Dawn's contribution." Willow gave Buffy a look. "Why do you guys own a cattle prod?"

"I have no idea." She walked to the other side of the basement and pulled over a chair. She sat down on it and hung her hands over her knees, staring down at her prisoner with grim satisfaction.

"What does she look like?" Anya called from the top of the stairs.

"You can come see. She's unconscious," Buffy called back.

"Don't go down there, Anya. Please." That was Xander. How had D'Hoffryn referred to him? Gallant. Buffy smiled.

There lived no one more gallant than Xander.

Willow said to the Slayer, "Are you going to be okay down here?"

Buffy nodded. "I'm good."

"Okay." Willow hesitated. "Want some iced tea?"

"Sure. That would be nice."

A few minutes later, heavy boots sounded on the stairs. Buffy glanced over her shoulder to see Spike still doubled over, hanging on to the banister as he carried a glass of tea. A cigarette dangled from his fist, and with each step he took, he trailed ashes onto the stairs.

She flashed him a smile and he crossed to her, handing her the glass. His chest was still a mess, and she was surprised to see him up and about. He healed quickly, but the wound was terrible.

He took a drag on the cigarette, sucked in his cheeks, and said, "Sorry. No smoking in the Slayer's house."

"Basement's okay," she told him.

"Good." He exhaled, then took another drag and let the smoke out slowly, formed a ring, and chuckled to himself. "Simple pleasures." He cocked his head as he surveyed the unconscious female. Buffy had chained her wrists and ankles together. "Another one would be to bash her head in."

Buffy handed him the cattle prod. "We own a cattle prod."

His left brow raised lazily. "Too bad we didn't know about this before."

She closed her eyes and shook her head. "That would have been too much, even for us." She averted her gaze and moved to the other side of the demon.

"There wasn't a thing invented was too much for us, luv. In our day." He sounded wistful. Then he tentatively touched the prod to the demon.

The female bolted awake and attempted to sit up. But the heavy chains held her down against the floor.

"No ouch," Spike remarked, patting his head. "Chip didn't go off. You got a demon here, Buffy."

"Hi," Buffy said cheerfully.

The woman's eyes shifted. She ticked a wary gaze from Spike to Buffy.

Then she said, "Hello."

"Oh. English." Spike smiled at Buffy. "Interrogation's gonna go a lot easier."

"Hope so. For her sake," Buffy said to him.

"Where am I?" the woman asked. "Tell me at once."

"Sorry. Doesn't work that way," Buffy told her. "*I* ask *you* questions."

"And demand answers," Spike added. He gestured with the cattle prod.

"Don't, Spike," Buffy ordered. She put her hands on her hips and leaned forward, hoping to violate the woman's personal space in a moderately annoying way. "So, are you one of Jhiera's happy harpies? Is your name Sheila, by any chance?"

Inside Shiryah's body, Xian was quaking. She was quite aware that this blond woman was the Slayer, and that Buffy Summers had more of the puzzle pieces than she and Fai-Lok would have liked.

It can't end like this, she thought. *I need to think of something to tell her. I've lied to save my skin before. I can surely do it again.*

"Who are you?" Buffy demanded again.

CHAPTER ELEVEN

Ancient China, before accurate maps existed

It was said that Qin's human father, whose name was Lo Wei, was attacked by a demon while he was planting rice. When Lo Mei next lay with Mei, his wife, the demon inside him impregnated her, and she gave birth to Qin.

From there, Qin's story was shrouded in myth, until the documented fact that on the eve of his fourteenth birthday, Qin led a coup against his guardian, who was a warlord in a southern province. How he became the warlord's foster son is not known. But it is recorded that Qin buried the man up to his neck in salt, then invited the local children to saw at his neck with dull knives made of serrated bamboo.

He was said to be a demon, like his real father. That his

touch was like ice. That he was evil and depraved. He was never seen in public without a golden mask called the Dragon's Mask. Wearing it, he waged war on every tribe and every clan he encountered. It was said that the Gods of Hell were with him, and he never lost. The defeated soldiers were given a choice: a painful death, or service to Qin. The majority chose to join his armies.

Within three years, he had amassed a fighting force greater than the population of many of the provinces he invaded. Qin was insatiable. He subdued the Dai people, and the Bouyei. He took their most beautiful women as his concubines, installing them in tents guarded by eunuchs. His women tried to give him male children, for only by holding on to the hands of her sons could a woman rise to greatness. But it was said that his seed was made of ice, and turned to steam when it entered their bodies.

In a mountainous region of the great Yellow Land, the concubine of a great warlord watched Qin's progress, and she knew the warlord was doomed. She also knew that Qin walled up the concubines of vanquished enemies and let them starve to death.

Her name was Xian, and the warlord's name was Yinzheng.

Fai-Lok, Yinzheng's court magician, had worshipped her from afar. As she was the property of his liege lord, he had never dared to speak of his love.

So while there was still time—a year, perhaps, before Qin reached her lord's stronghold—she sought out Fai-Lok, and she very deliberately seduced him. He was enraptured. He became her slave. If Yinzheng knew of it, he was far too distracted by the approach of Qin's war machine to do anything about it.

Then Qin hovered at the borders of Yinzheng's territory, and Xian knew the time had come to ensure her survival . . . and

Fai-Lok's, too. She did love him, in her way. He was savage, and he was clever. And he was hers.

She prevailed upon him to imprison her inside an enormous vase, using his magicks, and to leave it where Qin's forces would discover it.

Sure enough, one of Qin's most trusted lieutenants found it; the flames of Yinzheng's palace played over the damascene surface as he loaded it on a cart and presented it to Qin.

Seated on a throne he had fashioned from the skulls and bones of Yinzheng and his sons, Qin examined the vase. He said to the lieutenant, "I've raided Yinzheng's treasury, and I laid claim to incredible treasures. You may keep this vase."

As the grateful man carted the vase away, Xian's voice rang out from inside it. "I will not belong to a lesser lord! I will be the great Qin's, or I shall be no one's!"

As the lieutenant backed away in terror, Qin laughed sharply and leaped down off his throne. He climbed onto the cart, shouting, "Bring me a torch!"

One was given him, and he held it over the mouth of the great vase. The flames flickered over a shape; he moved in more closely and squinted against the bright orange-and-yellow light.

Xian smiled up at the dreaded Dragon Mask. She had taken pains with her appearance. Her skin was white; her eyes were as shining black as her hair, which was the color of Mongolian ink. Her lips were brilliant crimson, so red it looked as though she had bitten them and broken the skin.

"Greetings, my great lord," she said boldly, although she was terrified. "I am Xian, and I will belong to no one but you."

"Oh?" He was amused. "But you belonged to another man. What if I do not want you?"

"Then I will remain inside this vase and starve to death, like the other concubines," she replied. "I will die weeping that the great Qin did not appreciate true beauty when he saw it."

"But by the time you die, you will be very ugly," he retorted. "Skin and bones. Those red lips will wither."

"It won't matter what I look like after I am dead." She leaned her head back in the curve of the vase's neck. He tried to see beyond her neck to the swell of her bosom, but that joy was denied him by the shape of the vase. "It matters now, and I am as beautiful as the moon."

"Then crawl out of there and let me see you," he ordered her.

"Alas, I cannot," she told him. "I have been placed inside this vase for you, and you alone can extricate me. And if you do not, I will die."

He drew one side of his mouth up in a lazy grin. He liked this game. None dared to deal lightly with him. "How am I to extricate you?"

"With magicks, my lord," she told him. "Performed by my former master's court magician, Fai-Lok."

"Indeed." He turned to his lieutenant. "Have we beheaded this Fai-Lok?"

Xian's heart nearly stopped, but she continued to smile.

"I don't know, Celestial One," the lieutenant responded, kowtowing.

"Search for him, and if he lives, bring him to me."

"Yes, Most Honorable Qin. May you reign a hundred thousand years." The lieutenant made obeisance and left.

Qin leaned into the vase and said to the woman, "What if he's been killed?"

"Then my fate is sealed," she replied, forcing her voice to keep steady.

"Who is your father?" he asked her.

"Dead long ago, like my mother. Of no consequence, at any

267

rate," she told him. There was no emotion in her voice. "I am beautiful, not warm-hearted."

"You are ambitious."

"That too." She chuckled.

"You should have been born a man."

"You won't say that once you have freed me."

He was clearly astonished, and why not? Who else dared speak so cheekily to the demon lord Qin?

He shivered with delight. "Are you naked?"

"That remains a mystery for my lord Qin to solve," she told him with an air of insouciance. Her large, liquid eyes made promises. Women's eyes often did.

At last Fai-Lok was brought in. Xian knew Qin would see a handsome young man dressed in robes of vermilion.

"Celestial Qin, I am ready to pledge my loyalty to you," Fai-Lok declared in a loud, firm voice.

"You pledged your loyalty to Yinzheng, and he is dead," Qin said.

"That is true, my lord," Fai-Lok replied. "But a sorcerer is like a kite. I can fly and I can command lightning, but I need an anchor point. Otherwise I will drive in the wind, masterless."

Xian chuckled, amused by Fai-Lok's boasts. Like other sorcerers, he claimed powers he did not possess.

Then Qin asked him, "Can you get her out?"

Fai-Lok said bluntly, "Yes."

"Should I allow it?" Qin asked. "Is she an assassin, seeking revenge on behalf of her former lord's family? Or a ghost, perhaps, eager to suck my qi out of my body?"

"Neither, my lord," Fai-Lok replied. "She seeks to preserve her own life by joining your household."

"How do you know so much about her?" Qin demanded, leaning forward suspiciously. "Are you her lover?"

"No." Xian and Fai-Lok knew that Qin would ask. Fai-Lok had practiced for this moment, and his performance was flawless. "But the whole court knows of Xian. She is brilliant, and she is very beautiful."

"Will she give me sons?"

Xian held her breath.

"I have not cast that fortune, Lord Qin. I cannot say."

"She has not given Yinzheng sons?"

Fai-Lok shrugged. "To my knowledge, sire, he never lay with her. He favored Mongolian women. He believed them better able to bear children, like their ponies."

Qin snorted in derision. "All women are alike. If they die giving men children, they die. It is their fate, or it is not."

"With all due respect, Most Honorable Qin, that is not so. Some are more likely to survive childbirth than others. It has to do with the way they bear weight through their hips."

Xian stifled a giggle. She knew Qin would be stunned that Fai-Lok dared correct the man who could order his death with a wave of a single finger.

There was a pause. Then Qin said, "Release the woman from that vase, and I will consider sparing you both. The rest of the household will be killed."

"Of course." Fai-Lok paid more kowtow. "With your permission."

Xian heard Fai-Lok walking around the vase. Then lights exploded above her head, swirling with the colors of jade and night, and crimson.

She was lifted up, up, and then the vase shattered in mid-air, releasing her. She tumbled with the shards of metal. She was indeed naked.

The court sorcerer touched both middle fingers and third fingers to his thumbs, and a gown of gold appeared, held by tiny misshapen dwarflike creatures who tossed it into the air. As Xian fell, the gown wrapped itself around her. Bright scarlet flowers dressed her hair.

The dwarves vanished.

She landed softly on the ground, kowtowing, her long, white fingers barely visible at the ends of the voluminous sleeves of her gown.

"Leave us," the powerful warlord said to everyone else in the tent. "All illumination must be extinguished. No one dare look inside this tent. If he does, his eyes will be put out before he is burned to death."

He looked at the court magician and added, "Fai-Lok, you have done well. You may live."

"You are most gracious, O Qin," the man replied. He doubled over and walked backward from the tent.

And so it began.

Qin took off his clothes and joined Xian on the floor. He left on his Dragon Mask.

And she was glorious. She shimmered and undulated in his arms like a fish, like a serpent, like a dragon. She made no comment about his coldness. She teased and tantalized him and pleasured him, and herself as well. Like Fai-Lok, he was mesmerized.

"You will be my chief concubine," he told her. "You will reign over all the women in my pleasure tents."

Something passed through her eyes, and then she smiled at him.

Time went by, and Fai-Lok endured his jealousy while Xian wove her own spell around Qin's heart. But that heart was very, very cold.

Of a night, his bones ached with cold. He ordered larger

braziers and bigger fire pits. Night and day, he kept fires burning, and when he made war, he set entire villages aflame, hungry for the heat.

He turned to Fai-Lok, the magician, for help. Fai-Lok mixed potions and unguents and cast spells for him. They brought some measure of relief . . . and then they stopped working. Fai-Lok tried again, creating new heat magicks, and they worked for a time as well.

Xian did all she could to warm him, but truth to tell, she was terrified of him. She had heard stories that the great Qin was not one man but many; that he stole men's bodies from them when his own had become to cold for him. Although he blindfolded her when they went to bed and he always wore his Dragon Mask, a concubine knows her lover's body, and his was often different.

The stories were true.

"If you speak of this to anyone, I will kill you," he told her, and she believed him.

At last Qin had conquered all the Yellow Land, from the Yellow River to the White, and he was supreme ruler of a country that had never been united before. Using Yinzheng's destroyed fortress as a guide, he built the most impressive palace the world had ever seen—an enormous pagoda of rooms and outbuildings, underground dungeons and high-flung astrologers' towers. His banner, the orange and yellow dragon, flapped in the overheated nights for which his castle became renowned. Night and day, fires burned. The forests were denuded as he sought to keep himself warm.

He had made incredible numbers of enemies along the way; and though he had slain many of them, he knew that others had hidden themselves away and were plotting his overthrow.

He said to Xian, "Fear chills people's hearts and freezes them into inaction."

So he sought to keep his enemies very afraid. He tortured their religious leaders and emptied all their libraries and burned their books in his braziers.

Fai-Lok and Xian kept their distance from each other. Yet Xian knew she must keep Fai-Lok faithful, so she burned him with her looks, let her bosom rise and fall with a lover's sigh when he glanced her way.

The time came for Qin to take an empress, and he was surprised that Xian took it badly when he married the daughter of one of his greatest enemies.

"You are my love," he told her. "You will always be my love. But we need sons to rule after me."

"We?" she had demanded, dumbfounded. *"We?"*

"You and I. We are a team," he told her. "We are as one." He gave her a look. "But you have failed me in that area. You have given me not one son."

She went insane with fury that was born of fear. She threw things; she broke things; she stomped around his private bedchambers without a thought to his displeasure.

"You have thought all along to be my empress," he said. "But don't you understand that marriage is only a legal maneuver? You will always have my heart."

She would not be consoled. "I don't know what you are, Qin," she said, dropping all pretense of polite forms and conversation. "But you are more than a man. You are like a god. And I am not. You have many enemies, and as I am your concubine, so do I.

"I will not have the legal protections a wife has. If your enemies come after you and her, you can thwart them."

She wept bitter tears. "But Xian? Alone in her chamber in the pleasure garden? If they come after me, who will stop them?"

"You are well guarded," he reminded her. "Well cared for. And since you will not be my wife, you will actually be safer."

"Safer to be walled up and starved to death?" she screamed at him.

"It did not happen to you before," he reminded her. "You are a survivor, Xian. Like me."

"You are casting me out," she moaned. "Another woman will live with you intimately. She will learn your secret, and you will think I am a liability."

"No. That will not happen," he told her.

"Women are dispensable. Especially women who have no sons." She turned away from him.

He grabbed her hand and said, "Then let me give you power. First I'll cover your eyes—"

"No!" she cried. "Not now!"

"This is not for pillowing," he informed her. "This is for a different sort of joy."

Xian took a breath, held it, and reached down inside herself to find her qi, her central life force. Many things could happen in the moments after Qin blindfolded her. He could ravish her. He could kill her.

He could reveal his true nature.

She knew that she had no real choice but to submit to her karma. So she let him cover her eyes with the silken dragon scarf. A tear coursed down her cheek, wetting the delicate fabric. Either he didn't notice it or didn't care, for he ignored it. He took her hand and said, "Trust in me."

She didn't trust in him. She trusted in no one but herself. But she inclined her head and let him lead her.

They walked for some time, making twists and turns. It was blazingly hot; her silk robes clung to her skin as sweat rolled down her forehead. Smoke ticked her nose; flames crackled in her ears; her heart raced. Was he walking her to her own funeral pyre?

The polished wood of the palace floors gave way to polished stone, and then uneven stone. Then stairs. Several. More.

Dozens.

Hundreds.

She reached out a tentative hand and jerked it back. The wall was made of stone as well, and it burned her fingertips. The air became close and very hot; she licked her lips and sent a prayer to the Goddess that if she was about to die, it would be quick and painless.

She stepped down again to discover that they had reached a smooth surface again. He walked her forward and her knees gave way slightly; she quickly righted herself and squared her shoulders. It was almost too hot to breathe, and she was having difficulty staying alert.

"Xian," he said. She turned her head in the direction of his voice. "No one has ever seen what you are about to see, not even Fai-Lok. I must swear you to secrecy. You must promise you will never divulge to another person what I am going to show you. If you tell, I will know, and I will kill you."

She consented with another nod of her head.

"Very well," he said.

The scarf dropped from her eyes.

This time, when her knees gave way, she collapsed to the floor.

She was standing in the middle of a vast underground temple. Columns of stone rose like dragons' backs, ending in fierce demonic faces topped by horns. Almond-shaped eyes glowed red from flames inside the columns; the noses were stubby snouts resembling those of bats. The mouths leered at her, with long rows of fangs overhanging the jaws.

As she stared up at them, they appeared to move, tilting down at her the better to inspect her. She looked away, then realized that the floor was a huge picture made of tiny bits of colored stone. She was surrounded by flames.

Across the room, a blackened statue sat in the lotus position, one knee over the other. Its stomach was a brazier in which embers glowed. Its hands were claws, and its face resembled the demonic visages of the statues, although it was far less detailed. Wings spread from its back to span the length of the wall facing Xian. Each wing was at least three times as long as she was tall.

Qin bent low and whispered into her ear, "Meet my ancestor, Xian. This is my father."

Xian swallowed. Her skin crawled as she stared at the statue; the hair on the back of her neck rose, and ice water filled her veins. Despite its roughly carved appearance, a palpable evil emanated from the figure as if it were a real being. If it had reached out one of its claws and grabbed her, she would not have been surprised.

"Now," Qin continued, "look from father to son."

He reached his hands to the sides of the Golden Mask. She caught her breath; she had both dreaded and longed for this moment. So many times she had wanted to see his face. Now she was going to, and she was no longer sure that she wanted to. She sensed that everything in her world was about to change.

It has changed before, she reminded herself, *and I have not only survived, but thrived.*

His face was that of an ordinary, handsome man. She relaxed for a moment . . . until she recalled the ordinary, handsome servant who had held the stirrup of her horse only that morning.

Qin smiled at her with that man's lips, gazed at her with that man's eyes.

Somehow that was more frightening than if he had shown her a demon face.

"It is how I survive," he told her. "As my father survived. He came to this plane from another place. But he knew he couldn't stay here. He was not made to stay here. He attempted to Possess my mother's husband, but he knew he could not stay inside him either. It is too cold here. His kind needs heat."

"His kind. Your kind," Xian said shakily.

"Yes. My mother's husband took her. Lust is heat. Wonderful heat." He leaned in and kissed her, pressing the stable boy's mouth over hers. She forced herself not to recoil, although she wanted, very much, to scream.

"His qi mixed with the seed of the man he Possessed, and he impregnated my mother. And I was born."

He beamed at her. "But I grew cold inside the shell of my first body. I began to freeze. I could feel it. And so . . . I learned to leap into the bodies of others. To Possess them. Thus, I am immortal."

Her eyes widened. She studied his face, touching his cheek, his forehead, the ridge of his brow. "How can this be?" she asked.

"I told you." He took her hand and pulled her to her feet. "And now you have a choice. You can become like me, or you can remain as you are." He waved his hand. "Either way, you live in my heart. At least, while you are young and beautiful. I need never age. But you are mortal, Xian."

She reeled. It was too much to comprehend. She understood the choice, but that was all she understood. The rest was too bizarre, too unworldly. It was like a children's tale.

"The Yellow Land has never seen one such as I," he boasted. "I can Possess body after body. I can escape assassination attempts, and cheat death."

She made herself speak. "What . . . what is to prevent you from Possessing my body?"

"I have attempted it." At her stunned expression, he shook his head and chuckled. "Not you. I have attempted to Possess other women. I cannot enter. I believe it is because I am male power. I am yang. Females are yin. Additionally, I can only Possess certain male bodies. Not all.

"I assume it will be the same for you, with female bodies."

"What will you do to change me?" she asked quietly. Her mind was spinning, but she was able to consider the possibilities, weigh the pros and cons. Endless life!

He pulled her against the young man's body. "I can feel your blood rising at the thought," he said to her huskily.

"Yes," she replied, hearing the uncertainty in her voice. She forced warmth into it. Though he had said she had a choice, she wasn't at all sure that he would let her live if she refused his offer.

"I'm glad. I knew you would welcome this." He held her close again. "Ah, Xian. I have read Fai-Lok's books of magicks. I have attempted this before, and failed." He pointed to the brazier. "The bones of my failures warm this room."

She shuddered, but he kissed her cheek. "You will be the first female of my kind."

"So . . . you have not succeeded at this yet?" she ventured.

"Trust in me," he said, smiling at her.

As she watched, he crossed to a low stone table and picked up a curved knife and an ornate mirror. The gleam from the blade matched the gleam in his eyes as he sliced it across the vein in his wrist. The blood streamed from the wood, droplets plinking onto the mirror. Her face gazed back at her.

Then he held his wrist over her mouth and said, "Drink."

She was repulsed, but she did as he asked. She dozed,

awakening to find him performing magicks over her. In the blackened room, lights shimmered.

As she watched in horror, horns sprouted from the crown of his head. His fingers became talons. He was monstrous, horrible.

Then he bit hard into her chest, as if to devour her very heart. He growled and moaned, and then he pulled slightly away, as if forcing himself not to savage her. She screamed and struggled, to no avail.

She passed out from the pain and the terror.

When she awoke, she was alone in the chamber, and terribly cold. She shook so hard, she was afraid she would split her lip with her teeth.

Then a figure stepped into the darkness. Once more, Qin wore his golden mask, and he was dressed in an orange and yellow robe. He reached behind himself and pushed forward a beautiful young woman whom Xian had never seen before. She wore red and gold; she was gagged, and her wrists were bound in front of her. He pushed her again, roughly, and she fell to her knees.

"Think of yourself melting into her," Qin told Xian. "Think of yourself being warmed by her."

"But . . ."

"Obey me."

As she closed her eyes and tried to envision what he was describing, he took his bloody wrist and wiped his blood over Xian's naked body. He spoke incantations over her, and then he had her look into a mirror as he sliced her belly open, releasing her human qi; as she writhed, she began to see double, then triple: she saw her own face superimposed over the face of the terrified girl.

Something ripped from her body. It didn't hurt, but it was disorienting, dizzying; and then she was looking at the man in the golden Dragon Mask from a completely different vantage point.

The girl's vantage point.

Xian screamed.

"I have made you what I am," he told her. "You are a Possessor, as I am. You have my gifts, and my deficiencies. You are no longer a mortal. You will live forever."

"Qin," she breathed. "What have you done to me?"

"But you will be cold. You will need a lot of heat. You will use up the qi of the body in which you reside—the heat of creation, lodged in the body's abdomen—and you will have to find another body in which to live, and to warm yourself."

"By the gods," she murmured, touching her face, her body. She stared down at her old body, and cried out.

It was blue and crystalline, as if it were made of ice.

"This is the fate of each body as you use it up," he told her.

"I'm dead," she blurted. She recoiled from him. "You have killed me!"

"It will take some getting used to," he said gently. "And remember this: You can only enter the bodies of those who carry yin qi. Feminine energy. And they must carry Dark Blood."

"What?" Tears streamed down her face. She was barely able to make sense of anything he was saying.

"I have learned much of my special nature," he told her. "I am the son of a demon. I carry evil blood in my veins. But so do many human beings. You can only enter the bodies of females who carry this evil blood, which I call Dark Blood."

"But . . . what if there are none to be found?" she asked. "What if I need to . . . Possess . . . a new body, and I cannot find one?"

He gestured to the statue of his father. "I have discovered that I can reside inside the likenesses of living beings, which are also separated according to yin and yang. First I smear them with my blood."

She didn't ask any more questions. She sat down awkwardly on the stone, rested her face in her hands, and began to weep.

CHAPTER TWELVE

Sunnydale

In the basement of the Slayer's home, Xian, wearing Shiryah's body, gazed up fearfully at Buffy Summers.

"Hello? Needing some answers here," Buffy said, hefting the cattle prod as the Slayer's little sister screamed and shouted, "Buffy! The high school choir is attacking us!"

Glass crashed. There were loud thumps. The shouts of men. Then Xian heard the voice of the man she loved.

Fai-Lok bellowed, "Xian! Where are you?"

The redheaded witch named Willow rushed forward and clamped her hand over Xian's mouth. Xian tried to bite her, but the witch grabbed her hair and yanked back her head.

The Slayer raced up the stairs, calling over her shoulder, "Watch her, Willow!"

A Chinese guy in a red robe barreled past Buffy as she reached the top of the stairs. She let him barrel, preparing to catch the next one as he charged across the broken front door, which had fallen to the floor. She unhappily registered the fact that evil choirboys had broken through all of Willow's wards.

She intercepted Barrel Guy, grabbing him around the middle and hefting him up off the ground. Then she used him as a bowling ball to knock down more evil choirboys who were thundering through the front door. He went flying, and Buffy got a strike as guys dropped like pins. She grabbed another one, and he was halfway to being a gutter ball as he smacked against the doorjamb with a loud groan.

"That's gotta hurt," Buffy muttered. "At least, I hope so." Then she yelled, "Dawnie! Where are you?"

"I've got her upstairs!" Anya yelled back. "Watch your head!"

Buffy glanced up as Anya hurtled a brass coatrack down the stairs. It caught three red robes on their way up and tripped them handily. As they tumbled end over end, Buffy yanked them out of her way and grabbed up the coatrack. Then she raced back to the front door with it and used it like a quarterstaff as a seemingly endless mass of guys poured into the house. There were just too many of them, not that a slayer should think like that; she yelled to Anya, "Get Dawn out of here!"

"No, Buffy!" Dawn cried.

"I don't have time to argue!" Buffy shouted.

"Window!" Anya ordered.

"Buffy!" It was Willow, from the basement.

There was a tremendous explosion. The house shook; pieces

of plaster fell from the ceiling. Buffy thought, *Oh, great, Xander's gonna love this.*

Then she hung a U, plowing through the busy sea of scarlet, pushing guys out of her way and fighting for each stair down into the basement. A strong wind was blowing across the basement floor, throwing chairs and cattle prod against the wall at the foot of the stairs.

Willow was crouched down with her face pressed against her knees. A gaping hole had taken out about a third of the basement wall behind the Wicca, and Buffy ran to her.

"Will!" she cried.

Willow looked up, and Buffy was startled. Willow's cheeks had been raked with long fingernails. Her eyes were dark gray. And she was panting hard.

"I'm okay," Willow told the Slayer.

Buffy was not convinced, but she had a job to do. She raced to the hole and dove through, then scrabbled up to a standing position. She was unarmed, but that was not usually a huge problem.

Across the street, a man in a red robe was dragging Buffy's former captive along behind himself and racing heading toward Weatherly Park. As if the woman sensed Buffy's gaze, she looked over her shoulder and grinned at her.

"Whoever hurt Willow gets hurt first," Buffy muttered, and moved into full-pursuit mode.

She cut the distance in half, then in fourths. She was gaining on them, and to add to the joy, Xander and Spike showed up from rounding the corner, took in the sitch, and joined in the chase.

Buffy caught up with her boys and they ran three abreast, Buffy in the middle. Spike yelled at her, "Couldn't find the choirboy. What's this, then? He rescue her?"

"With about three bazillion of Sam's closest friends," she said. "Kick it up! We're losing them!"

They ran for another minute or so. "Gotta bow out," Xander huffed, slowing down. He waved as the vampire and the vampire slayer hit turbo and left him in the dust.

Buffy waved back, then got down to business. Heat Chick and Red Robe reached the entrance to the park. Buffy put on a burst of speed, as did Spike, and by mutual unspoken consent they skipped the main entrance and roared on down the fence, planning to overtake the couple at the exit.

"Cor, luv," Spike gasped, pointing to the tall palm trees within the park.

The man and the woman rose into the air and began half-running, half-flying across the tops of the trees. It was eerily beautiful, like something from that movie directed by Ang Lee and starring Chow Yun-Fat, whose title escaped Buffy at the moment.

"That would be *Crouching Tiger, Hidden Dragon*," Spike cut in, staring at the leaping figures. "What'd I say? Chinese magicks. It's all that opium they smoke."

"Can you read my mind now?" Buffy shouted at him as they galloped along.

He gave her one of his patented grins of ultra-arrogance and shouted back, "Always could, Slayer."

That was enough bantering; Buffy put on another fresh burst of speed, figuring that sooner or later her prey would have to land back on planet Sunnydale. Then she and Spike could capture them in some clever nonexplosive way . . . that she hadn't thought of yet. For the time being, however, all she could think to do was run after them the same way a kid would run after a runaway kite. Much with the running and staring upward . . .

The two soared up and out of the park; having run out of

trees, they half-landed on the ground and took off running and semi-gliding in a very familiar direction. . . .

The Hellmouth.

Robin Wood caught up to Sam Devol in Shady Hill Cemetery. The boy was sprawled up against a headstone that read MINEAR, and his Razorbacks T-shirt was soaked through with sweat.

Robin couldn't tell if Sam was panting or sobbing, but he advanced on him and stood with his hands at his sides in a non-threatening gesture.

"All this for some girl?" Robin asked gently.

Sam shook his head. "No, man. I . . ." He started to hyper-ventilate. "Oh, my God, Principal Wood!"

Robin sat down beside him and said, "Easy, Sam. Talk to me."

"They killed Coach Wong. They're going to kill more people. Even football players." He was shaking. "I thought . . . I thought it was like a fraternity. That's what they tell you to get you to join. Like Amway, only eviler." He sucked in air and rubbed his face with his T-shirt.

"Who?" Robin asked. "More to the point, where?"

Sam shook his head. "I'm not going anywhere near that place. If they see me . . ."

"I'll go with you," Robin said. At the boy's look of horror, he said, "Just show me where they are. Then I'll get help. I won't implicate you."

"They'll know. They . . . they . . ." He sobbed. "Please, Principal Wood, just get me the hell out of Sunnydale!"

"I will," Robin said. "Show me where, and I'll drive you to the bus station myself."

Sam stared at him. Robin stared back. Then Sam dropped his head to his chest and nodded.

"Let's go," Robin said, rising.

Sam got to his feet.

From their position on the roof just outside Dawn's window, Dawn handed Anya another crossbow bolt and said dazedly, "Rock, Anya."

The former vengeance demon was pretty good with a crossbow. She was shooting choirboys left and right, in basically non-fatal places, and they were dropping all over the lawn like strange, oversized, unconscious garden gnomes. Others of their kind were still on the rampage, and Dawn was worried about Willow.

Then someone got a signal or a phone call or something, because one of the choirboys yelled, "Fai-Lok says to retreat. They're safe!"

There was a lot of cheering and then a shriek as Anya shot another red robe, this one in the leg. Like a herd of buffalo, they wheeled around and started running away from her house. There was more shouting, more passing the word about someone called Fire Storm, and more choirboys emerged from the house.

Less than a minute later, the house was quiet.

Then Dawn heard Willow cry, "Dawnie? Anya?"

"Here!" Anya shouted. She said to Dawn, "Come on."

Anya led the way back into Dawn's room and into the hall. They were at the top of the stairs when Willow appeared. There were twin lines down her face, as if she had been crying tears of blood.

Dead or unconscious red robes lay all over their house, which was in its familiar state of ruin. As they walked past them, Dawn suppressed an urge to go all crazy and kick a few of them as hard as she could.

"Our prisoner was liberated," Willow said unnecessarily. "Buffy went after them."

"Then let's go after her," Dawn piped up.

"Buffy wouldn't want that," Anya told her. "She would want you to stay here."

"Where it's so safe," Dawn retorted sarcastically.

They looked at Willow, who turned her head and said, "Hey, Xander."

Sure enough, the former center of Willow's existence hung in the doorway, panting. He said, "You held a rave and didn't call?" Then, to Willow, "Spike and Buffy went on ahead to catch Ridge Chick and her boyfriend. On account of they have speeding powers not unlike those of the Flash. Buffy and Spike having Flashlike powers, that is. The other two are more like the Bionic Man and Lindsay Wagner."

"Where did they go?" Anya asked.

"Last I saw, they were heading for the park." He frowned at the red-haired witch. "Jeez, Willow, the lipstick goes horizontally, and on your mouth."

"Let's go," Dawn said. "Buffy may need our help." At the hesitant looks of her elders, she shifted her weight and jutted forward her lower lip. "Come on. How many times have we gone after her and we've ended up saving the day?"

"More than even on episodic TV," Xander admitted.

Point made, Dawn raised her chin triumphantly.

"Okay, but we're going armed," Anya told the group. "We'll have more arms than Shiva. I'll go get some more things out of the weapons chest."

"I'll drink enough water to fill a bathtub," Xander announced. He looked at Dawn and Willow. "And everyone should go to the bathroom before we hit the road." He raised a finger and regarded Dawn with a stern face. "You may *think* you don't have to go, but wouldn't you hate to wet your pants in the heat of battle?"

"It's extremely embarrassing," Anya said. "Back when I was with Olaf . . ." She trailed off. "I'll get the weapons."

They left heavily armed, which made them slow. Xander was too tired to go fast, anyway, so it didn't make much difference.

They reached the park. No Buffy, no Spike, no nobody; and Xander said, "Okay. I suggest we fan out like in the war movies and search—"

"Hold on," Willow said. She took a breath and murmured an incantation that sounded like the singing on a Hindi movie sound track.

Above them, trails of glowing red and yellow powdered the night sky. They hung above the tops of the palms, then dipped toward the ground on the opposite side of the park's chain-link fence. Then they hung in the air about street-level.

"Follow that magickal jet stream?" Xander asked Willow, impressed.

Willow nodded.

They continued on.

Xian and Fai-Lok crashed into the warehouse, breathless and pumped. Fai-Lok was in ecstasy. His beloved had not died! She had cleverly body-jumped into the Oden Tal woman, and with that act, their success was assured.

Horrible music pounded from the nearby club with the metallic name; it was difficult to concentrate on the appropriate spells to unlock the trapdoor.

But Fai-Lok managed it. Then he grabbed Xian's hand, and they dropped into space. Landing easily, they dashed through the tunnel, to find portions of it blocked. The dragon's arrival had wrought a lot of damage.

Inside the cavern, the beautiful creature lay encased in ice at least ten feet thick. It glistened and gleamed, but it was magickal ice that would never melt. Like characters in a play, Fai-Lok's demon generals and the members of the Hellmouth Clan had backed away, still rapt.

"We must hurry," Fai-Lok told Xian, kissing her hungrily. "Do you think you can produce the *k'o* energy?"

"I know I can," she said proudly.

She stood at the top of the cavern and regarded the dragon for a moment. Fire Storm, the ancient dragon, the wondrous creature who would free them from the yoke of Qin's rule forever . . .

She aimed her hands at the dragon, took a breath, and let the body of Shiryah do the work. Her spine heated; her *k'o* energy shot through her like a hot wind.

Heat streamed from her hands; she felt the force of it as an exhilarating, heady whoosh of unimaginable power. The heat hit the ice with a loud sizzle, and immediately the ice began to melt.

Then there was a lot of noise in the tunnel, and Fai-Lok realized that the Slayer might have already caught up with them.

Sure enough, he turned his head to see the Slayer and Spike the ensouled vampire rushing toward him and Xian. He shouted, "Hurry!" and turned to face the Slayer.

"What the hell is goin' on here?" Spike demanded, quickly taking in the scene. Then there was no time for chitchat as a rather nasty-lookin' seven-foot-tall reptilian-styled demon in leather armor rushed him, drawing a sword as it did so. Spike didn't get it; here he was, living—in a manner of speaking—in the twenty-first century; yet all the heroics seemed to require weaponry invented during the bleedin' Middle Ages.

Be that as it may, swords could do just as much damage as guns, only not usually as quickly and efficiently, so Spike shifted into kickin' mode and got it going. He loved the battle; he lived to deliver blows. Being stifled with that Initiative's soddin' chip had nearly driven him insane, but now with the soul and all, he wasn't much for hurting human beings, anyway.

But this big, lizard-skinned bloke was another matter entirely. All fangy with the mouth, and then tentacles erupted from around his head and snapped with teeth as they shot toward Spike. He dodged them one-two-three, then executed a magnificent sidekick that clipped the thing behind its left kneecap. It bellowed and staggered, and Spike grabbed the sword and gave it the old heave-ho, landing it directly in the solar plexus. Where, as he expected, the demon's body armor was thinnest—another anomaly of current life: Why wasn't everyone wearing Kevlar, swooping in on the Slayer in black helicopters?

Speaking of the Slayer, she was doing fine, slicin' and dicin' as she went, likewise armed with a sword she'd lifted off one of the enemy. Then the sort-of king bloke moved his hands, and fireballs erupted from his hands. Buffy deflected them easily. She charged at the wizard or necromancer or whatever he was, and he moved into battle posture.

Spike kicked the snot out of the next demon that came at him; then a swarm of the oddest sort of monkey demons chittered and loped his way. Not for nothing did he prize the boots he wore, nicked from one of the finest Goth shops in Oxford Street back home. Always fancied the way they looked with his duster, trophy from his run-in with a Slayer back in New York, and *wham!* Ol' William makes one for Manchester United!

"Buffy?" he shouted.

She was head-to-head with the wizard, who was really givin'

her what-for with various magicks. Fire, blue bolts of energy; and his girl was handling herself well.

She's not my girl.

"Get Heat Chick!" Buffy shouted.

"On it!" he assured her.

Then three of the monkey demons grabbed his duster in various locations, holding him fast. He struggled, but it was no good; more than irritated, he yanked his arms out of the sleeves and left them with his treasured garment.

Punching and kicking and ha! another sword, picked it up, skewered a few assailants, kept goin', kept goin'—

"Protect her!" the wizard screamed.

Spike figured he didn't mean Buffy, and he was right: His order galvanized the assembly—*cripes, must be a thousand of 'em, how's he feed 'em all?*—and Spike knew it was time to take out Demony Woman or something even worse was gonna happen.

Roxanne had been pushed back into the cage, and she was cowering in the corner as sounds of a battle echoed back to her and the other prisoners.

Then the tunnel ceiling collapsed. Piles of dirt and rock crashed down on her, burying her.

She fought to free herself, crabbing and scrabbling at the huge piles of earth. She opened her mouth, and dirt poured in; she was beyond thinking at that point; just a pair of lungs and reptilian brain . . . needing air.

Some vestige of her rational mind murmured, *It's better than burning. . . .*

"Keep going," Robin said to Sam as they raced toward the warehouse. Then the street beneath their feet shuddered, and the warehouse door fell off the hinges. Streetlight poured inside.

"No way!" Sam cried.

"We're going in there. Now!" Robin told him, flinging the door out of his way.

As he crossed the threshold, the floor collapsed on the other side of the room. Sam jumped away from the building. "You're crazy, man!" he shouted, and raced away.

"Sometimes I wish I were," Robin said to himself. "It would make this stuff a little easier to do."

Then he took another step into the warehouse, and that part of the floor gave way as well.

He landed inside a tunnel, which was shaking all around him.

Bet we have a cave-in, he thought, and headed on into the belly of the beast.

Out of the corner of her eye, Buffy saw Spike racing toward the woman with the energy pulsing out of her hands. She had a moment where she wanted to shout "No!" because she didn't want to see his chest go away completely. But she took advantage of the confusion to grab her sword, spring into the air in almost as cool a fashion as the Chinese guy had done, and race toward the female.

The woman was standing at the edge of a cliff with her back to Buffy; and when Buffy landed beside her, she took just long enough to peer over once and see the fabulous dragon.

And Buffy arced back her sword, took aim, and whacked the woman's head clean off her body.

A tremendous geyser of heat energy shot from the woman's neck. The force was unbelievable; the heat even more so.

Then the headless body tumbled over the edge.

"No!" Buffy shouted; she raced to the side and looked down. The corpse landed on top of the ice-encrusted dragon, and then it exploded.

The light was blinding, and as Buffy doubled over, she was thrown backward by waves of energy. Demons and guys in red robes flew everywhere, many of them in pieces. She couldn't see Spike anywhere.

The wind knocked out of her, she squinted in the direction of the pit where the dragon lay.

A tremendous roar emanated from the hole. A ragged cheer rose from the chaotic masses still able to make sounds.

Then the entire cavern went up like a volcano.

"Oh, my God," Robin breathed, as the tunnel blew into the air. A comet of flame headed his way. He relied on the survival skills his mother had drilled into him, curling into a ball and attempting to remain as limp as possible. He shot into the air as if from a cannon, but he kept his face and head protected with his hands and tried not to fight it.

"Buffy!" Dawn shrieked as half the street ripped away from the ground and as buildings, sidewalks, streetlights, and people rocketed into the air. The Sun Cinema sign launched; rooftops and furniture and cars spiraled wildly as they went screaming upward. "Buffy!"

A fissure erupted in the street. Another. The blacktop buckled and shook; parts of it sank and others pushed upward. The buildings that hadn't careened into space were shaking.

Earthquake.

Then fire, as structures ignited as if a large invisible hand had poured gasoline all over them and lit them with a match.

Within seconds, blocks of the bad part of Sunnydale whooshed into a firestorm.

"Come on!" Xander shouted, grabbing her wrist. He clamped on to Anya's as well. Anya seized Willow's forearm, and the four took off, running as fast as they could in the opposite direction.

The power lines above them sizzled as flames traveled along them. Chunks of burning debris catapulted into the street around them. Dawn's face burned. Her hair stank.

"Dawn!" Anya cried. She batted at Dawn's hair. "You're on fire!"

Dawn screamed and ran harder. Xander grabbed her up and rolled her on the ground. She flailed at him, then realized he was putting her out, and cooperated with him.

"Okay," he said, yanking her to her feet.

They ran.

As she was jerked along, Dawn glanced over her shoulder at the chaos and moaned, "Buffy!"

"I'm sure she'll be okay," Anya shouted.

Then the section of street split open and swallowed her. Just as quickly, an outcropping piece of the same street slammed over the hole, burying her.

"Anya!" Xander shouted. He got to his knees and started digging. Dawn did too. Then Willow.

The earth shook wildly. It was another earthquake. An enormous swath of ground to Dawn's right collapsed.

"Sinkhole!" Willow cried.

Then the sky was ripped in two by a shrill, deafening roar. As Dawn and the others looked in its direction, the head of an enormous monster emerged from the ground. Its face was covered in shimmering blue-green scales; it was stubby-snouted; fangs lined its mouth. Almond-shaped eyes gleamed red and hot.

The face rose into the sky, perched on a long, scaled neck. It flew upward; more was revealed—short forelegs that ended in claws; a long midsection. Scales on the back; another set of stubby legs—

Dawn stared at it in disbelief. *It's a dragon!*

With another roar, the monster wheeled in the sky, hovered there a moment, inclined its head. A burst of fire gouted from its mouth, spraying fire in every direction.

"Get down!" Willow shouted. She threw herself across Dawn.

There was another huge explosion. Followed by another.

Then every single building behind Dawn crumbled and collapsed.

Sam ran.

The world was ending, and he ran.

The earth shook, fires ignited all around him, but he kept going. He ran down the center of Main Street before he realized that cars were caroming around him. Then he climbed into the back of a flatbed truck until a sinkhole swallowed the vehicle and he jumped off, just in time.

I'm going to live through this, he promised himself as he put more and more distance between himself and the convergence of disasters that was taking out his hometown. *I did the right thing and now I'm going to be spared.*

He had outrun the fires.

He had avoided the sinkholes.

The buildings that were falling down had missed him.

But Sam had forgotten about something.

Sunnydale had a dam.

Perched high above the highway, the bowl-shaped concrete bulged and contracted with the ripples of the quakes. Back and forth, back and forth, it bulged like the doors in the Haunted Mansion at Disneyland, only less obviously because, well, tons and tons and tons of cement.

But unlike the controlled special effects of a theme-park ride, the forces of nature overtook the Sunnydale Municipal Dam.

It broke.

Millions of gallons of water raged into the valley below the dam. Pine trees snapped, were uprooted; the wild animals never knew what drowned 'em. The waters engulfed the water department's outbuildings and the water department's employees; security guards; and a man who had just decided to commit suicide by loading up his pockets with rocks and leaping into the dam.

Good timing.

The brand-new river slammed itself a new channel and a new set of embankments as it cut through the land like a diamond-tipped saw about three miles wide.

And it picked Sam Devol up and carried him away, away, away, bobbing like that poor fisherman at the end of *The Perfect Storm*—not George Clooney, who went down with his ship on purpose, but that other guy, the one who was in love.

Life flashing before his eyes, Sam thought sadly to himself, *Damn it, I'm gonna die a virgin.*

CHAPTER THIRTEEN

Los Angeles

In the lobby of the Hyperion Hotel, Angel and company stared in disbelief as Kelly Andrews, the TV anchor, concluded her report on Sunnydale.

". . . the entire town lies in ruins. Fires, floods, it's . . . apocalyptic." Kelly held her serious face a beat, then softened up and added, "The weather is next."

"Oh, my God," Fred whispered.

"Buffy's okay," Angel bit off. Not that he knew that. Not that he felt that. Just that she had to be.

She had to be.

"Of course she is," Fred said to him. "After all, she's Buffy."

"Hey," said a voice from the doorway. It was Cordelia. Angel looked at her, then around her. She had come alone. No Connor in sight. He was relieved. He couldn't have handled seeing his son at the moment.

"Hey," Angel said gratefully.

"I came as soon as I heard." Cordelia swallowed and walked toward Angel. "They should . . . should stop letting people live there, don't you think? The insurance premiums alone . . ." She faltered. Her face was pale, and her hands were shaky.

"Buffy's okay," Fred told her.

"Oh, did you hear something?" Cordelia asked, her voice rising with excitement.

"No," Fred confessed. "We just want it to be true."

Then Cordelia slid into Angel's arms. It was an unexpected move; he jerked slightly, then put his arms around her. They held each other a moment. Angel was thrown. Cordelia had never cared much for Buffy.

But Cordelia had changed a lot since . . . she had changed.

What are we doing, mourning Buffy together?

Gently, she moved away. She smoothed back her short hair—he liked it longer better—and took a breath. She rubbed her forehead. "My visions . . . is this what they're about?"

"I hope so, sweetcakes," Lorne told her. "Because if there's more, I don't really want to know about it."

"Ditto that," Gunn said grimly.

Feeling numb, Angel moved away from them and stared out at the night. This was a waking nightmare. So many times he had thought Buffy was dead. So many times she had proved him wrong. He had begun to get complacent, assume she was immortal, as he was.

It couldn't have finally happened. I had gotten used to it never happening.

Fred came up beside him. "Want some tea?" she asked in a sweet voice. Tears were welling in her eyes.

He didn't. But she looked as if she needed him to, so he said, "That would be nice. Thanks." She looked relieved to have something to do.

"Knock, knock," said a voice at the door. It was Lilah, dressed in a black silk blouse, a short skirt, black stockings, and high black heels. She wasn't invited in, but vampires of her sort didn't need to be. She sauntered into the lobby as if she owned the place. No surprise there: Wolfram & Hart had tried to take it away from him before. Blink, and Lilah would succeed where others had failed.

"Sunnydale has fallen," she informed them. Then she glanced past Angel to the TV. "As you know."

Angel found himself thinking of the time he had locked Lilah, Lindsey, Holland, and a whole lot of other Wolfram & Hart attorneys in Holland's wine cellar with Darla and Drusilla. Right now he missed those dark days . . . with a vengeance.

"I'm so glad we had this little chat," Angel said coldly. "Now get out."

She ignored him. "But what you don't know is that the reason it fell is because the dragon—Fire Storm—has been activated."

Angel and the others looked first at one another, and then at her. "And *you* know this because . . . ?" Angel asked her.

She gave him a sly grin. "Because we're Wolfram and Hart."

"That you are," he said, his tone cold, flat, and filled with hatred.

"Activated how?" Wesley asked, stepping between the bloodsucker and the vampire.

"Where's Jhiera?" Lilah asked.

"Looking for someone," Angel said. He glanced at Lorne,

who nodded. He and Fred had executed a finder's spell on Jhiera, and she was still in the Los Angeles city limits.

Unless she had found a way to trick them . . .

"Seems we underestimated Xian," Lilah told him. Then she ticked her glance past him to Fred. "May I have some tea too?" She smiled at Wesley. "Tea for three?"

"No tea," Angel said. "Say what you have to say and leave."

"Wes," Lilah whimpered, smiling broadly to show that she was mocking him, "aren't you going to tell your friends to treat me with more respect?"

"No," Wesley replied.

"Okay." Lilah moved her shoulders. She sat down on the round sofa and crossed her legs high above the knee. "My God, it's hot in here. Aren't you using the air conditioner?" She gestured to Angel. "Since you always run at room temp, you must be feeling a little peaked."

Angel didn't so much as blink.

"Lilah, no one is interested in fencing with you," Wesley snapped at her. "I have no idea what you're up to, but get to the point."

"All right, *dear*," Lilah drawled.

Angel watched Lilah square off against the man she was sleeping with. Then he watched her let it go. Angel figured he understood dark passions like theirs better than they did. Connor was alive because of Angel's own dark passion for his mother, Darla.

"Xian body-jumped—or whatever they call it—into one of Jhiera's followers. Then she went down to Sunnydale and thawed out Fire Storm. The dragon woke up, and off she flew." She wrinkled her nose. "If it makes you feel any better, we think Xian died while she was doing it. And she rendered Alex Liang comatose, but he's recovering nicely."

"You mean Qin," Fred said.

"Oh, there's a yay," Cordelia said sourly.

Lilah looked amused. Then she said, "Had any good visions lately?"

Angel moved toward Lilah. "Leave Cordy alone."

"Ah. We're back to 'Cordy.' How nice for you both." She patted her forehead and exhaled theatrically. "It's so hot. I'm not certain I'm going to like roasting in hell after I die. Oh well, I made my choices."

"What was the dragon doing in Sunnydale?" Gunn asked. "Word we had was she was being sent through a portal to Qin's temple here in L.A. to get defrosted by Jhiera."

"That was the plan." Lilah nodded at him. "This was the counterplan. Miss black widow spider Xian's plan. We're pretty sure she and Fai-Lok have turned against Qin. That they stole the dragon out from under him.

"Additionally," she purred, "we think they're going to try to destroy him." She paused dramatically and added, "In a nice big war."

"Here's your tea," Fred murmured, coming up beside Angel. He took it from her.

"Is that what you want?" Angel asked Lilah, his voice hard and sharp. "A war on the streets of Los Angeles?"

"It could prove interesting," Lilah replied.

"Then why come to us?" Wesley asked, also looking to Lilah for an answer. "Why let us know?"

Lilah held Wesley's gaze for a moment. "'Come to *us*'? Wes, is there something you haven't told me?"

He clamped his mouth shut. Lilah looked approving.

"Smart. That's the way I like them. Oh, what a fabulous solicitor you would have made. Barrister. Whatever you call them in Jolly Olde. With one of those curly wigs . . ."

Then she turned back to Angel. "I know you want time to grieve your loss, but unfortunately, you don't have that luxury. There's another dragon up for grabs. With a name just as poetic as the other one's. Flamestryke. And whoever gets hold of it . . . might win that war."

"Is it loose in Sunnydale too?" Cordelia asked. She exhaled slowly. "No wonder the whole town's been destroyed."

"No. Flamestryke has not been detected within the Sunnydale city limits. We believe this second dragon is still back in an interdimensional prison deep below China," Lilah said.

Gunn half-raised his hand. "So . . . I'm thinking Qin will get it shipped here, then activate it with Jhiera's help the way he planned with the first dragon, and then each side will have one," he said. "They'll have equal strike force."

"Wrong." Lilah patted her forehead again. "You know, I really could use a glass of water."

No one moved.

"It wouldn't be equal strike force. It would be escalation," she filled in. "Flamestryke is far more powerful than Fire Storm."

"'Far more' is how much?" Gunn asked her.

Lilah looked at each of them in turn. "Megatons."

She let that sink in as the others reacted, glancing at one another and connecting the dots.

Fred furrowed her forehead. "You're talking nuclear capability."

Lilah gave her a wink. "Yes. I am."

Stricken, Fred turned away and hurried off.

"Where are you going, lambchop?" Lorne called after her.

"To get Lilah a glass of water," Fred replied.

"Good idea," Lilah said. She looked back at Angel. "We've

known about both dragons for . . . a long time. Here's the best punch line so far.

"We also know that Qin has no idea that Flamestryke even exists."

Off their looks, Lilah smiled lazily. "He thinks there's only one dragon. Both sides are grabbing after Fire Storm, but Flamestryke is the real prize. And Fai-Lok is equally ignorant."

"Then how do *you* know?" Fred asked, returning with the water.

Lilah only smiled. "Thank you, Fred." She took the water from Fred and sipped it. "No ice?"

"No," Angel cut in. He folded his arms. "I'm asking you again. Why are you telling us this?"

"There's still going to be a war between these two factions," Lilah said. "Each side will do its best to obliterate the other. We don't want that. This entire plan has gotten far too unpredictable. We thought it would go a little smoother than this." She wrinkled her nose. "But the fact is, none of us can afford to let Qin or Fai-Lok go near Flamestryke."

"Then why don't you just kill both of them?" Fred asked.

Wesley's cheeks colored; Gunn glanced away. Angel noted both reactions and filed them for later inspection.

"Oh, I proposed that. The senior partners said no. It really wouldn't do the job. Can you imagine why not, Wesley?" She smiled at him as if he were a favored pupil.

"I'll give you a hint," she continued. "These beings were originally Chinese. Ancient Chinese."

"Known for their secret societies, and their secret societies within those secret societies," Wesley added, taking up her thread. "It's the tradition of the tong and the triad, beginning with the Hung societies and the Ching lodges. One has no idea whom to trust. There are traitors, and traitors within the ranks

302

of the traitors. The grappling for power is endless. In this case, Wolfram and Hart can't simply kill the principal players and assume they are safe."

"Because there are other players in their rank and file making side deals and running their own games," Gunn added. "You'd have to kill every single one of them. And you guys are good," he said to Lilah, "but no one is that good."

"No one is that good," Lilah concurred.

"So the first order of business is to stop both sides from getting hold of Flamestryke," Fred put in.

"Yes." Lilah beamed at her. "You're so smart, Fred."

Fred was clearly not fooled. She knew Lilah detested her.

"Why not get Flamestryke yourselves?" Angel asked.

Lilah sipped water.

"They can't, for some reason," Cordelia said. "You know what? I'm really getting tired of twenty questions. Why don't you just spell it out and then you can get out of here."

"Ah, temper, temper." Lilah raised a brow at Cordelia.

"There's something about this extraction, then," Cordelia pressed on. "You need Champions. You guys are too evil to do it."

Lilah smiled at her over the rim of her glass as she drank down the rest of her water.

"So, you want to spread the risk. You want us to join forces to retrieve Flamestryke," Angel filled in, "and then what?"

"You're getting, dare I say it, warmer," Lilah said, raising her glass of water in Angel's direction.

"Then Wolfram and Hart will kill us," Fred concluded.

Lilah chuckled throatily. "Come now. You know we won't do that. We haven't yet. And we've had plenty of chances." As she said this she looked back over at Wesley, who remained stone-faced.

Gotta hand it to you, Wes, Angel thought. *When you play on the dark side of the street, you take all your toys.*

"Where is Flamestryke?" Fred asked.

"Well, apparently there are a number of things one needs to gather, then take to Lir, who is Qin's father," Lilah told her. "Once the three items are in his possession, a portal will open and Lir will awaken Flamestryke himself."

"What are they?" Fred asked.

"Well, we don't have complete information on that," she said. "We know about two of them. One is the Orb. We're assuming that's in Sunnydale, from our research. And there may be a sword. . . ." She looked a little uncertain.

"But you don't know what the other two objects are, or where they are?" Wesley asked.

"How do you take them to Lir once you have them?" Angel added. "Where is he?"

Lilah shrugged. "That's a little unclear. According to . . . our best information, Lir's body is still imprisoned in the Ice Hell dimension beneath a city in China. We surmise that may also be where Flamestryke is. The city itself called Xian. It was Qin's capital, back when he ruled China. He named it after his faithless concubine." Her smile was cynical.

"Xian is where the terra-cotta warriors were exhumed," Wesley volunteered. "In the seventies."

"Interesting," Lilah said, gazing at him. "The earliest files we have on the subject date from the seventies." She gave her head a little shake. "Is my law firm the best, or what?"

"So we get to Flamestryke before it can be activated," Angel said. "We destroy it."

"And we keep those things outta Lir's hands by getting them first," Gunn added.

"It's a he," Lilah said. "And I wouldn't be so hasty. It might not be killable."

"That's a chance I'm willing to take," Angel replied.

Lorne raised a hand. "Okay, so Angel cakes goes off to slay one dragon. We do some research about the other two objects and figure out how to retrieve them. Then I suppose the rest of us—and I have no idea how we are going to accomplish all this—are on tap to take out Fire Storm when Fai-Lok attacks L.A. with her, and—"

"Oh." Lilah held out her empty water glass. No one moved forward to retrieve it. She cradled it in her hands and cocked her head. "Did I say Fire Storm was coming to Los Angeles? Because that would have been a lie. Fai-Lok's diverted her, just like a hijacked jet."

"But you know where Fire Storm is," Angel said. It was not a question.

From his vantage point above his father and the others, Connor listened hard. He had come in search of Cordelia, furious that she had left him back at his place and trotted back to his father.

". . . our sources indicate that Fai-Lok has taken Fire Storm to the Mojave Desert," Lilah was saying. "We're not precisely certain where, but we'll find them."

Connor pursed his lips. His eyes shone.

Not if I find them first, he thought.

Good, very good, a voice said inside his head.

But Connor didn't really hear that voice.

Just as silently as he had entered the Hyperion Hotel, he left it.

Sunnydale

As Xander, Willow, and Dawn huddled in the car Xander had stolen, Xander turned around in the driver's seat and said to Willow, "It's so good that you tried to destroy the world, Will.

305

Otherwise I might not have known the quickest way to Kingman's Bluff."

Xander had dragged Dawn and Willow into the nearest vehicle, hot-wired it, and driven it out of town as fast as he could. He'd sped straight for the highest point in Sunnydale, where Willow had raised a Satanic temple out of the ground in preparation for flaying the earth's crust off its body and incinerating everyone who was not Tara.

Willow, whose eyes were bloodshot—not from evil magicks but from intense crying—was huddled in the backseat with Dawn. The Slayer's little sister was sobbing against Willow's chest. All three of them were in shock. They had seen the fires, the quakes, and most recently, the flood. And down there somewhere in all that high-budget destruction lay their best beloved ones: Buffy and Anya.

Oh yeah, and Spike too.

"Buffy," Dawn whimpered brokenly. "Oh, my God. She can't be dead."

"She found a way out," Willow murmured against the crown of Dawn's head. "She's okay."

Dawn looked up into Willow's eyes. "You really think so?"

"Of course I do," Willow said, putting on her best resolve face. "She's the Slayer."

"She's Buffy," Xander added. His voice broke. "And Anya isn't Buffy."

"But she's a survivor, too," Willow told him. "Anya's okay, Xander. I feel it."

"Even though the earth opened up and swallowed her whole," Xander replied dully. "Will, you don't have to spare me." His voice grew hoarse. "Because if I knew she was still alive, and needed help, I couldn't stand it that I was up here and not down there digging with my bare hands—"

"Xander, don't leave us!" Dawn begged. Her eyes were wide; she was frantic as she pulled herself out of Willow's embrace and grabbed Xander's shoulder. "Please!"

"He won't," Willow said calmly. "He'll stay here with us."

"Here." Xander squeezed Dawn's hand. "I'm here, Dawnie." He tried to smile, but couldn't quite manage it.

Then his cell phone rang.

All three of them were so tense that they screamed at the sound.

"Yes!" he shouted, connecting.

"Xander?" It was Buffy.

"Oh, my God!" he shouted. "Buffy?"

"Buffy?" Dawn cried.

"We're okay. We're in Happy Memories." That was the cemetery farthest from Main Street.

"But you're not dead," Xander said cautiously.

"No. Well, Spike still is." She took a breath. "My sister?"

"Dawn's fine. She's right here. And Willow too." He handed the phone to Dawn.

"Oh, Buffy!" she cried. Then she broke down into fresh tears. "Buffy, when I saw the explosion, I thought . . ." She listened. Then she said, "No. We haven't seen Anya. The . . . there was a big split in the road, and it . . . she went in. Then more dirt swallowed her up." Dawn took a deep breath. "Kingman's Bluff," she replied, as if to a question. "In a car. Yes, we'll wait here."

Xander took the phone back. "Xand, I'm sorry about Anya," Buffy told him. "We're coming to you. Spike's hot-wired a car."

"Same as me," Xander murmured. "Okay." Then his brows shot up. "Buffy, you'll let him drive, right? You won't try to drive."

"No. I don't have a death wish," Buffy assured him. "Well, I did when Willow brought me back, but—"

"But nothin'!" Spike's voice crackled through the phone. "Slayer, let's go!"

There was the sound of squealing brakes. Then a crash.

Then dead air.

Xander closed his eyes and disconnected the call. *What just happened?* he asked himself. Then he told himself, *Don't answer that.*

"What? What's wrong?" Dawn demanded.

"Nothing," Xander told her. "We wait here for Buffy."

God.

In the hell that was the outskirts of Sunnydale's downtown, Spike backed away from the car that had slammed head-on into theirs and jerkily swerved around it. The other vehicle had been driven by a ferocious-looking gray demon with a purple-black one riding shotgun.

"Damn foreigners," Spike bit off.

"Floor it, Spike," Buffy ordered.

She turned around and looked through the rearview mirror. Her stomach churned.

Through the fire and the water and the roiling smoke, thousands of demons capered down the street. Tall, elegant, Gentlemen-style demons; stumpy trolls; Lubbers; a few creatures she had never seen before that looked like Ferengi on *Star Trek: DS9*; and a cast of many, many others. It was a sight no TV show or movie could ever hope to duplicate: the budget for CGI effects and latex masks would be astronomical.

They motored on. The new high school still stood; much of everything else lay in ruins. And everywhere, demons danced the funky chicken dance of joy.

"There's so many," Spike muttered, scanning their surroundings. "Call me crazy, Buffy, but I think the Hellmouth blew."

She sighed heavily. "Well, you used to be crazy, but I think you're right."

They looked soberly at each other. Spike pressed his lips together and returned his attention to the road. Buffy looked back through the rearview mirror. The Slayer part of her longed to leap from the car and kill evil creatures; the rest of her understood that it would be a futile gesture that would get her killed, no doubt of that.

"Anya didn't get out," she said to Spike.

He nodded as if to himself. "Figured that," he told her. "Rest in peace, Anya. Or pieces, whichever." He added mournfully, "She was a great kisser. Not as good as you, of course."

"Please, Spike. Now is not the time."

To the shrill melody of a tune by Nerfherder, her cell phone went off. She answered, saying, "Dawnie?"

"Buffy?" It was Angel. "Buffy! Oh, my God!"

"Angel, I'm okay." She looked at Spike, who rolled his eyes.

Angel said, "I called and called—"

"My bad. I've been keeping it off to conserve the batteries." Her face flushed at the sheer happiness she felt in talking to him, and his obvious joy that she was alive. "I should have called—"

"It's all right." She could hear the deep relief in his voice, and it warmed her. "Listen, something's happening."

"Well, yeah," she retorted. "You guys have a TV, right? Watched the news lately? Probably they didn't see the dragon. But there was one, and—"

"Buffy, there's more," Angel cut in.

She immediately stopped talking.

"Tell me," she said.

Buffy and Spike arrived at the rendezvous site on Kingman's Bluff about twenty minutes later. Dawn's total joy at seeing her sister alive lasted about five whole seconds. Then Buffy told her that they had to go to Los Angeles. Going to L.A. was okay; it was *why* they were going to L.A. that was not.

"No," Dawn told her older sister. "No way!"

"Angel and I have to go after the other dragon," Buffy explained.

"No more going after anything," Dawn insisted. "You almost *died,* Buffy. *Again.*"

Buffy ran her hands through her hair. "I know. I'm sorry. I'll try not to do it anymore."

"Then don't go with Angel anywhere!" Dawn shot back. "Let's just go to L.A. and hang out with those guys and—"

"Dawn," Buffy said sternly, "unless Angel and I retrieve that dragon, Los Angeles will be no safer than Sunnydale. No place will be safe."

Dawn's eyes filled with fresh tears. "I don't care! I don't want to lose you again!"

She flung her arms around her older sister. Buffy looked above Dawn's head and said, "Will, I think you should come with us."

Willow nodded. Her face was still streaked with red, and with the dirt and the wild hair, she looked like a voodoo priestess.

"We'll stay here, try to do what we can," Xander said, including Spike with a jerk of his head.

"Excuse me?" Spike demanded. "There is nothing we can do here! Sunnydale is finished!"

"There is a hellmouth here," Xander reminded him.

"And it's busted wide open," Spike retorted. "If *you* want to die a useless hero's death, be my guest. But I'll be gone before . . ." And then he turned to look at Buffy.

She gazed steadily at him. His features softened. He sighed. Then he said to her, "I'm no Champion, luv. You know that."

She said nothing, only continued to look at him.

He sucked in his cheeks and stared back.

"Bugger all." He shook his head. "Life was a lot simpler before you came along, Slayer."

She smiled faintly at him. "I know, Spike. I'm sorry."

He glared at Xander. "All right. I'll lend you a hand. Just don't get in my way."

"Hey," Xander began, then rolled his eyes and said, "Fine."

"All right, then." Buffy spoke to the left-behinds in a stern, commanding voice. "Lie low. No heroics. Wait for instructions." Then she faltered, just a little. "Just stay alive, okay?"

"I've got no problem with that," Spike told her earnestly. "Unless he pushes me to do 'im in. *Kidding*," he blurted at Buffy's angry scowl.

"My whole life is this weird road movie with Spike," Xander muttered. "Like Hope and Crosby."

"More like Toot and Puddle," Dawn teased through her tears. She turned to her sister. "Buffy, why is this happening?"

"Because I'm being punished for atrocities I committed in a past life?" Xander guessed.

"That would be me, being punished," Spike cut in.

"No, I mean all of it," Dawn pressed. "All this blowing up and exploding and the fires and everything. Plus the high school is still standing! It's all wrong."

"We'll try to make it right," Buffy told her, smoothing her sister's dark brown hair. "Except we won't try to blow up the high school."

"Drat." Dawn smiled weakly. "I was hoping the notion of my having an education would, you know, just fade away in all the chaos."

"Sorry, Dawn," Buffy said. "Even in our insane world, you need good grades, or it's the cow hat of doom for you."

311

Strained smiles all around. As was their stock in trade, Buffy and the Scoobs made lame jokes when things were at their direst. But they had lost the heart for it.

Anya was dead.

Sunnydale was overrun with evil.

The Slayer lowered her arm and regarded the small group. "Okay, I guess this is it. For now."

"Yes. For now." Then Buffy turned to Xander and put her hand on his forearm. "Xander, I'm so sorry about Anya."

"Yeah. I know." He swallowed hard. "I just always had this feeling . . . I thought we'd both be in the last episode of all this. She and I."

"Maybe this is the last episode," Spike ventured. "Maybe this is the way the world ends." He stuffed his hands in the pockets of his black jeans. "Wonder if I can get a refund on this soul. Might not do me much good in the hereafter." He gazed hard at Buffy. "Do you know those answers, luv? What's waitin' for me?"

"I don't know what's waiting for any of us," Buffy answered soberly.

"Angel is waiting," Willow reminded her. "We really should get going."

CHAPTER FOURTEEN

Los Angeles

In the garden of the Hyperion Hotel, Angel waited for the Slayer to arrive.

He paced, hands behind his back.

She is not coming to see me. Or to be with me. She's coming to help me save the world, he reminded himself. *We're old soldiers now. Not lovers.*

And yet, the thought of Buffy's imminent arrival warmed him as little had in his long, chilly life. Just to see her again. To smell her scent. To touch . . .

Someone stood behind him. He squared his shoulders and turned around.

Jhiera of the Oden Tal stepped from the shadows.

She was a study in white and black. A halo of moonlight shone on her raven-black hair. The ivory light bleached the color from her skin, accentuating her dark brows and eyes. She was wearing the same abbreviated black leather clothing he had seen her in before. Her face was stern, and her expression, guarded and hostile. As he approached, she held up her hand, in warning.

"I had nothing to do with what happened in Sunnydale," she said quickly.

He glared at her. "You had everything to do with the dragon that got sent there."

"Fire Storm was supposed to come here." She crossed her arms over her chest and stood with her legs spread apart. He reminded himself that she could hurt him. He kept his distance.

"And you were going to reanimate it for a demon who planned to take over my dimension with it."

She gave her head a quick shake. "We were going to steal it from him."

"You're lying, Jhiera," he flung at her. But he wasn't sure of that. Not that it mattered too much. Their private quarrel was going to have to wait.

She sensed his change of subject and drew near him, cautiously. "We can still get it back from him," she said. "We'll need it or he'll use it on Los Angeles. We won't be able to defeat him."

He sensed the heat coming off her. Felt . . . warm. Felt like a man. His interest intensified, and he took an involuntary step closer to her. He knew it was her power, her $k'o$, that was affecting him, like physical signals from an animal in heat. But knowing that didn't make much difference; he was responding in ways he didn't want to, as if she was putting a spell on him.

She looked over at him; her eyes dewy, her pupils large. Her lips parted; they were moist, and very red. She was being affected too. She raised her chin and took a slow, deep breath as if steadying herself against the strength of her attraction to him.

"I did not go to Sunnydale," she reminded him. She closed the space between them; he felt her breath on his chin as she looked up and he looked down. "I did nothing to your people there."

"I don't . . . have people there. My people are here." He sighed and shook his head, moving on from thoughts of Buffy. "You were supposed to find Shiryah and stop her. You failed. And the devourer beetle in your brain—"

"Is a myth," she interrupted, sneering at him. "Your friend made it up, feigned putting something in my head. She nicked my temple with a poorly concealed stiletto."

Angel processed that. No one had filled him in. "If you knew that, you could have left. But you came back."

"I came back," she said softly, and she gazed up at him with her deep, luminous eyes. "I am an honorable person."

He resisted touching her. He remembered a term Cordelia had once used, back when she was new in Los Angeles, still trying to become an actress, and she was very lonely. *Skin hungry.* When one is not touched, not embraced, not caressed and made love to, one becomes hungry for contact, for connection . . . for that heat. . . .

He closed his eyes.

"Angel, I needed help," she said, putting her hand on his arm. "You wouldn't help me."

Opened them.

"I helped you escape."

"I wanted you to continue the fight with me. Join with me."

"You know I couldn't do that," he said flatly.

Her luminous eyes studied his face. "Why not?"

"Because you kill human men." He gritted his teeth. "I told you not to bring your battles back here, Jhiera."

"We had nowhere else to go." Her voice was haunted. Her touch . . . exquisite. "They had run us to ground in our dimension. My own father ordered my execution. The Vigory who brought proof that my *k'o* had been severed would become my husband and his heir."

She dropped her hand and half-turned from him. As she did, the moon highlighted the delicately arched ridge of her backbone. It glowed white-hot.

"Angel . . . ," she said.

And then another voice said softly, "Angel."

Angel turned his head. Buffy stood on the threshold into the garden. Dressed in a skimpy T-top and white trousers, she was covered with blood and dirt, her hair disheveled. He had never seen a more beautiful sight in his life.

"Buffy."

He walked to her, and Jhiera dropped back into the shadows a few steps, giving them space. Buffy came up close but did not touch him, and he was even hungrier for contact.

"Did they call you with any word on Anya?" she asked him. "I haven't heard anything and I was hoping maybe—"

He shook his head. "I'm sorry."

She lowered her head, nodding. "Maybe she'll show," she said halfheartedly.

"Yes, maybe she will."

Then Jhiera stepped into view, and Buffy's eyes widened. She looked from Angel to Jhiera and back again.

"Angel," she said, "who the hell is she and what's she doing here? Her best friend just destroyed my town."

316

Jhiera raised her chin. "I am Jhiera of Oden Tal," she informed Buffy. "And the being you saw was not one of my people. It was a shapeshifter."

Buffy assumed a battle position. "What a stupid lie," she flung at Jhiera. She prepared to attack, raising her fists kung-fu style and spreading out her stance.

Angel held up a hand. "Buffy, it's true. Let me explain the rest."

In the lobby, Willow and Dawn acknowledged Fred, Cordelia, and Wesley as they walked toward the circular couch. Everyone looked and felt dazed and miserable.

Lilah had left, and Wesley was glad of it. It sickened him to realize that she had probably played a part in the destruction of Sunnydale, whether directly or not. He had to stop this madness with her.

But why? Why not indulge myself. There is no black or white anymore, no right or wrong. Am I to deny myself the fire that rages inside me when I'm with her, for the sake of "right"?

"So, portals," Willow said shakily. A tear slid down her cheek and she staggered, worn down to the nub.

"Oh, poor Wicca woman," Lorne moaned. He took the turquoise polka-dot handkerchief out of his jacket pocket and daubed her cheek with it. Grimaced at the dirt he picked up and folded the handkerchief inside out, and gingerly replaced it in his pocket.

"We don't have to talk about portals right this very minute," Fred ventured, looking to Wesley and Lorne for agreement. "We can get you and Dawn upstairs and into bed, and in a couple of hours—"

"How fast can you get a portal working?" Buffy asked Willow as she strode back into the lobby with Angel and Jhiera. Wesley was surprised to see the Princess of Oden Tal with Angel and the Slayer, but only mildly. She was a resourceful field warrior; she seemed to have the ability to evaporate into thin air, then reappear at will.

Rather like those body-jumpers Lilah blamed for Sunnydale.

Willow looked exhausted, but she rallied, sitting up a little straighter as she answered Buffy.

"Depends. Portal to where?"

"China," Buffy said.

"Xian, China," Angel filled in. "We think it's the closest place in our dimension to where this Flamestryke is stored."

"Imprisoned," Jhiera corrected him.

"We'd have to heavily ward such a portal," Wesley said to Buffy, then turned his glance toward Willow. "They'll be expecting attempts to infiltrate and retrieve the dragon."

"And now it's not such a big mystery why Wolfram and Hart want Angel to go," Cordelia drawled. "They'd love nothing better than to see you both dead somewhere in this exciting adventure."

Willow yawned. Dawn's head bobbed onto her shoulder, and the witch put a companionable arm around the Slayer's little sister.

"She needs to rest first," Fred informed the others. "She's exhausted. She could make a mistake and then . . . poof."

"Another Sunnydale," Cordelia said. "My God, I wonder how many of my old friends are dead."

"They never wrote you," Lorne said plaintively. "Not that that means they deserve to die."

Cordelia gazed down at her hands. "In the old days, I would make some crack about how they had no taste or were horrible dressers or something."

Dawn stirred and asked, her eyes still tightly closed, "Why are you guys talking about furniture?"

Fred blinked at her and said to the others, "See? They're all just too tired. They need to sleep."

Angel walked forward and scooped Dawn up in his arms. Buffy looked on, and her features softened. It had been before Wesley's time in Sunnydale that Angel had reverted to Angelus and had threatened to kill Buffy's loved ones. Before Dawn's time, too, though no one remembered the past without her being present in it. The Monks had equipped the Key— Dawn—with a false past that everyone remembered as being real. Now that Dawn was no longer the Key, her past was even more solidly lodged in their memories as one they had all shared.

As Angel carried Dawn upstairs, Willow rose and said, "I'm sorry, Buffy, but Fred's right. I'm just too tired to be of any use." She shrugged unhappily. "I must be getting old. Time was, I could run for my life and still have enough energy left over for homework."

"We're all getting older," Buffy murmured, smiling at Willow. "Look at Cordelia."

"Hey," Cordy snapped.

"I'll lie down for just a couple of hours. Then I'll be all shiny and new," Willow promised the Slayer. "First I'm gonna call Xander and fill him in on the new stuff."

"Rest well, Willow," Wesley said. He smiled gently at her. He had a soft spot for her. She was an intellectual, like him, and she had chosen to study the occult, as had he. There would never be any chance of a more . . . intimate relationship developing between them, as she was not interested in men.

And besides, though I'm presently . . . occupied . . . with Lilah, I am still most pathetically carrying a torch for Fred.

"Everyone rest," Buffy ordered. "Except for the people who don't need to." She turned to Jhiera and said frostily, "Do your people shut down for a while, or do they wreak havoc twenty-four/seven?"

Before giving Jhiera a chance to respond, she turned her back and followed Willow up the stairs.

"Does she need directions to your room?" Jhiera whispered to Angel.

"Stay away from Buffy," Angel shot back. He glanced at Wesley. The party was breaking up. It was time to go back to his flat.

Wesley wondered if Lilah would be there.

As Wesley turned to pick up his weapons, he caught Cordelia studying herself in the glass of the weapons cabinet.

You're still very beautiful and very young, he wanted to tell her. But it would speak of older, gentler times when they were friendlier to each other. These were not those times.

He had crossed halfway to the double doors when Gunn called out, "Watch your back, man. Those Vigories are out there, and the Chinese dude's minions too."

Wesley glanced over his shoulder. "I'll be careful," he said to Gunn, and Gunn alone. "Thank you."

"Wait," Cordelia said. "Can you take me back to Connor's?"

Wesley looked surprised. "If you really want to go, yes."

"Thanks." She glanced up at the stairs. "Buffy's here, and . . ." She looked wounded and uncertain. Not a good look for her. Nor for anyone for whom Wesley cared. And he did care for Cordelia.

The two left in silence, Cordelia's shoes echoing on the marble floor.

Fred glanced quickly at Gunn, then down, and murmured, "I'm going up too."

Gunn hesitated, nodded, said nothing.

That left Lorne alone in the lobby with Jhiera. She was one

scary lady, and Lorne had met a number of scary ladies in his day. His mother, for one. But this Jhiera . . . brrr. Very strong. Very driven. One could practically say possessed and that would not be taking it too far.

He said to her, "I'm an Anagogic demon. Don't suppose you'd like to sing for me, would you? After a few bars, I can read your aura, tell you things about your future."

But Jhiera was busy taking note of the weapons cabinet. As she crossed over to it, she asked Lorne distractedly, "Are your aura readings accurate?"

"Indeedy yes," he informed her. "Just as accurate as a slayer with a crossbow." She glanced at him. "Or a winsome member of the Oden Tal with a zappy palm."

"Do I have to sing a song native to this dimension?" She gazed at the vast array of weaponry with what could only be described as hunger.

"Nopers," he told her. "You can yodel whatever dimensional ditty strikes your fancy."

"All right." She gave the cabinet another glance, then turned to face him. She stood very straight, squared her shoulders, and took a deep breath.

Then she began to sing.

Lorne didn't know the words; he didn't know the tune. But her voice was as clear and sweet as a piece of Pylean shame crystal. It was so beautiful, it nearly took his head off.

Enraptured, he closed his eyes . . . until he remembered that he was supposed to be reading her aura. Then opened his eyes and scrutinized.

Yikes. She's going to have sex with Angel!

"That's so lovely," he said to her, holding up a finger for her to stop. "Really, really nice. If this were a contest, you would get an enormous . . . ah, trophy. Really . . . huge." He gently shook his head and closed his eyes, wishing for a trapdoor or, failing that, a juicy Seabreeze.

"What did you see?" she demanded, looking put out. He couldn't decide if she was angry that he'd stopped her, or irritated that he was fumbling around with such an incredible lack of enthusiasm.

He rubbed his palms together. "I have excellent news. You're going to live to fight another day."

She scowled at him. "That's it?"

"Sometimes . . . things are hazy around the edges. What I can tell you is that you are not going to get killed or wounded tonight. Or even fight. No fighting for you!" He tilted his head and flashed her his baby reds in a manner he hoped she found both reassuring and perhaps a little attractive.

She clenched her teeth. If her eyes could shoot fire energy, he would soon be charcoal.

"You're lying," she said.

He waggled his shoulders, all innocence. "Sometimes it just doesn't work very well." He lowered his voice and said, "But *please* don't let that get around. I have a reputation to maintain, you know."

She narrowed her eyes at him and he flinched, fingers crossed that nothing was going to emanate from them except an expression of her massive contempt for him.

"You're a fraud," she accused.

He drew himself up. "Hey, there's some folks in Vegas who would beg to differ."

With a dismissive shake of her head, she dropped the subject. Case closed, no prisoners taken or charred.

Then she peered up the stairs. "I'm going to stay here tonight. It's too dangerous to move around the city."

Stay here? No, no, no! There may be musical beds going on

up there already. No need to add to the melody line or the back-beat with another, er, warm body.

"Which rooms are vacant?" she added.

"That might be a little hard to tell, unless someone starts singing." He shook himself and added quickly, "And even then, who knows, with these limited abilities of mine."

She kept looking at the stairs. "Does Angel bed with the Slayer when she's in town?"

"Ooh! So direct!" He swallowed, smiled brightly. "Apparently they're just friends. Right now. Today."

"Oh." She walked toward the stairs.

Oh, my God, she's going to march right up there and do what I saw!

"The couch is always good." He patted the circular sofa and smiled invitingly. "Very comfortable."

She sneered at the couch. She disdained the couch.

And mounted . . . er, ascended . . . the stairs.

The Mojave Desert

It was hot.

Very, very hot.

For a drowsy moment, Anya thought D'Hoffryn had managed to burn her up after all, the way he had torched Halfrek when Anya had asked him to take back the vengeance she had committed on the frat boys at U.C. Sunnydale. Then she rolled over on her back and stared up at the blazing sun, in a sky so yellow that it was hard to tell which was sun, and which was sky.

Her throat was parched. She felt positively dried out. When she licked her lips it was like running an emery board across them.

Where am I?

She turned her head. She was sprawled on hot sand, and there were some outcroppings of rocks to her left and right. She figured she was lying in an arroyo, in a desert. A disjointed Joshua tree crooked its neck at the sky; seeing it, she knew she had somehow wound up in the Mojave Desert. One of the perks of her former life as a dispenser of vengeance on mortal men was a hell of a lot of travel. Joshua trees grew in one place and one place only on the planet—the Mojave.

There were other unique objects in her range of vision, however. One of them was the smashed remains of a purple Volkswagen Beetle. Another was a twisted mass of metal that may have been a fire hydrant. Beyond that lay several heaps of cracked pavement, bonded together like s'mores, with melted asphalt standing in for the chocolate.

There were pieces of buildings and their contents: tables, chairs, cell phones, and boom boxes from the electronics store; a shattered newspaper stand. Plates, dishes, and, oh God, at least six human bodies lay scattered in the wreckage.

Accent on scattered.

Seeing the death, Anya got nauseated. She woozily raised herself to a sitting position and bent forward. Nothing came up. She had the dry heaves; she was too dehydrated for good vomit. She managed to crawl beneath the stubby, twisted tree, which did very little to shield her from the sun. Then she turned around and saw a big gray boulder, and wondered if she could manage to stagger toward it and—

Oh, my God. That's not a boulder!

It was an enormous reptilian body, rather snakelike, probably thirty feet long. The part closest to her was the tail; its head was on the other end. She figured it for Asiatic; it had that look, with the batlike nose and the almond-shaped eyes. It was covered

324

with deep cuts like sword slashes, and parts of it were burned. Its eyes were closed, and it looked like it was dead.

Then it took a breath, the flesh bulging about a sixth of the way down the body. Slowly it exhaled, and it groaned. It was obviously in a lot of pain.

A young man in a red robe rose from behind it. He, too, had been burned; his dark hair was singed practically from his head, and his face was smudged with charcoal. On another day, he might have been good-looking; it was difficult to tell beneath the grime and his red complexion.

He was speaking to the dragon in Chinese, apparently trying to comfort it. That made Anya feel a little more charitable toward him, but she knew she'd best keep her distance. She had no idea if he was friend or foe.

Then, from the outcropping to her right, three very bizarre creatures emerged; they were about four feet tall, and they loped along like chimpanzees. Their faces were a mixture of dwarf and demon, with more monkey thrown in. She wasn't up on her Chinese demonology, but she figured them for minions. Not a good sign. People with minions were usually evil.

The minions started hooting at the man, who spoke to them very gruffly. While they were distracted with each other, she took the opportunity to dart from the tree toward a large steel crate that was part of the destroyed electronics store tableau. There was a debris field of gadgets and gizmos that was really quite impressive, and she slid on a boom box that had been crushed, then stepped directly on an iPod. No one noticed her, and she crouched down, thinking, *Okay, how the hell am I going to get out of here? Everyone back in Sunnydale—if there is anyone back in Sunnydale—probably thinks I'm dead. If I could just check in . . .*

She stared down . . .

. . . on one of these very many cell phones . . .

They were packed in boxes for the most part. She wasn't certain if those would work; she knew one had to activate the service somehow.

But there were at least half a dozen that were lying around loose. She reached down and selected the one that looked least damaged, flipped it open, and pressed it on.

There was a dial tone.

Yes!

She rapidly punched in Xander's number. Waited.

Waited some more.

There was only silence.

Pooh.

She was just about to give up when someone connected and said, "Hello?"

"Xander!" she cried.

"Anya?"

"Yes!"

"Are you dead?" he asked.

"No!" Grinning, she moved her head back and forth the way she did when she was happy and said, "Can you believe it?"

"Where are you? How did you—?"

The dragon groaned. It was an amazing sound that rolled over the landscape, making Anya jump.

She lowered her voice. "I'm in the Mojave Desert. There's a guy here with a *dragon*, Xander. And these monkey trolls." She looked around. "And lots of electronic gear and broken dishes."

"Oh, my God, Anya!" Xander said. "Okay, we need to stay calm. Think." Then she heard his voice grow a little distant as he shouted, "Spike! It's Anya! She's alive!"

Though Anya couldn't hear Spike's reply, she could tell that he was happy. *I sleep with the best,* she thought.

"Listen," Xander said to her. "Maybe there's one of those

326

global positioning units there. Or maybe we can find one. We might be able to triangulate where you are. Do you have access to more cell phone batteries?"

"I don't know." She clutched the phone with both hands. "Is everyone else all right? What the hell happened?"

"It was that dragon you're staring at. Bad guys were defrosting it, and I guess when Buffy killed one of them, the place blew. We're fairly certain the Hellmouth opened too."

"What makes you think that?" she asked.

From his vantage point on Kingman's Bluff, cell phone pressed to his ear, Xander stared down at the sizzling, burning town of Sunnydale, populated by more demons than he had ever seen in his entire life combined.

"Oh, just a hunch," he said to Anya on the other end of the line. "Just a little theory Spike and I cooked up. But we're all accounted for," he assured her. "Buffy, Dawn, and Willow went up to L.A. Looks like there's another dragon, only worse than the one you've got, and they need to find it before the bad guys do."

In the burning desert, Anya sagged with relief. "I'm so glad everyone's okay. Which is weird, because just recently I wanted to kill them all. Well, not all of them. Just Buffy, and—"

"An, don't forget about your batteries," Xander said gently.

"Right. Right." She took a deep breath. "I'm scared to disconnect, Xander." Then, before he could say anything, she took another deep breath. "But hey, what's the worst that could happen? Now that I'm a human being again, I'll die in what seems like a pitifully quick amount of time whether it's fifty years from now, or fifty seconds."

"Just stay hidden," Xander urged her. "Put the phone on vibrate, and I'll get back to you."

"Roger," she said. With a shaky sigh, she did as he said.

She held the phone against her chest, feeling very, very lonely.

Angel paused at Buffy's closed door and remembered how he used to watch her sleep. As Angelus, and as Angel too. How he had sketched her, traced every curve of her features . . . the softness of her cheek, the sweep of her hip beneath the bedclothes.

She didn't remember the twenty-four hours they had spent when the Mohra demon had rendered him human. Didn't feel deep in her bones and muscles and in her blood the passion they had shared when, finally freed of his curse, he had made love to her for hours on end.

Buffy.

She was here. His love. His one true love. And they were going to work together.

To save the world, he reminded himself. *So focus on that. She is not here for you.*

Move on.

And yet, he lingered at her door.

"Are you going to bed her?" Jhiera asked, coming up to him. She gestured to the door. "Buffy?"

He shook his head. "We don't do that."

"But you did." She smiled. "I can tell. The heat between you two is very strong." She placed her hand on the door in an almost protective gesture. "The Slayer must stand alone. I appreciate her devotion to duty. I know how that feels."

She glanced up at him; there was a warm glint in her eye. "But warriors must take pleasure where they find it. The battle is long and wearying."

She moved to him, standing so closely that he could feel the heat emanating from her body. Not the heat of her *k'o,* but of being alive and vital and filled with energy.

"Angel," she said softly.

"Good night," he answered.

She touched his chest. "I won't burn you," she murmured. "I will take away some of the chill."

"Good night," he said again. He put his hand over hers and lowered it to her side.

Her mouth rose in a crooked half-grin. "There are no men on my planet who would refuse to sleep with Jhiera of Oden Tal. But first, they would take away my *k'o* and make me a slave. But you are a vampire. You savor the hunt."

He made no answer. She chuckled and said, "Good night, Angel."

Then she walked past him. Her spine glowed white-hot as she sauntered down the corridor, experimentally opened a door, and went inside.

"Oh! There you are!" Lorne said jovially as he appeared at the top of the landing. "How you doing, Angel cakes?"

"What's wrong, Lorne?" Angel asked, his voice hushed so as not to waken Buffy.

"Nothing. Just . . . on my way to my room, and here you are in the hall with Jhiera . . . in front of Buffy's room. . . ." He smiled way too brightly. "Such a full house."

Angel got it. "Good night, Lorne," he said patiently.

"You going to hit it too?" the Pylean asked. "We could walk down the hall together. To our rooms."

"Lorne, we're not in high school," Angel drawled. "Not that we ever were in high school. Either of us."

"Okay." Lorne dropped the happy face. "I read Jhiera," he said. "She's . . . her future is looking rosy as far as having sex with you goes."

"What?" Angel stared at him.

"She sang for me. Which is a lot less than she's gonna do for

329

you, Angel." Lorne moved his hands as if to say, *Whaddaya gonna do?*

"You have to be wrong," Angel said.

"Haven't ever been yet. Of course, you can change your destiny. We know that. You've done it before. But . . . mmm . . . do you want to?"

"Lorne . . . ," Angel said, then trailed off. The discussion was beyond him. "Let's just go to bed."

"*Us?*" Lorne chirruped, chuckling. "Sorry, boss. I'm not trying to make your life complicated. It's just turning out that way."

Vampire and the Anagogic demon headed on down the hall.

Unaware that Buffy had been standing on the other side of the door listening to every word.

Then her door opened, and she said, "Hey."

Angel and Lorne turned around. Buffy smoothed back her hair, looking awkward, and said, "I was thinking. While we're waiting for portal creating . . . how about some recon at this temple you told us about? We need to know what's going on with Qin."

Angel pondered that. "Good plan."

Lorne frowned. "Hey wait, kids, that's *not* a plan. That's an idea. But not a plan."

"I'll go," said a voice at the end of the hall. It was Wesley's.

As everyone looked at him, he walked toward them and said, "Angel, I came back to tell you that Connor's gone. Cordelia thinks he left, judging by things of his that are missing."

"Left?" Angel asked.

"Where to?" Buffy asked.

"Cordelia says she has no idea. She was quite concerned." Wesley inclined his head to Buffy. "But I think Buffy's right. Some recon would be appropriate. And I volunteer to do it."

"Why not just ask Lilah, kids?" Lorne asked them. "She

brought a lot to the table tonight. Cold cuts and condiments. Wolfram and Hart probably has that place bugged."

"I think she's told us everything she's prepared to," Wesley replied icily.

"I want to go with you, Wesley," Buffy announced. "I'll go get my shoes."

"No, Buffy. It's too dangerous," Angel argued, frowning at her.

She paused with her hand around the doorknob, giving him quite the look. "Excuse me? Too *what*?"

"We have to go to China," he said reasonably. "If anything happens to you before then—"

"Has anyone even gone to the temple?" she asked.

"Once. Briefly. And we were discovered," Angel retorted.

Gazing at Angel, Lorne, and Wesley in turn, she shrugged and said, "Then it's time to go back. Maybe Willow can ward us with some magicks."

"Wesley can go alone," Angel ventured.

"No." Buffy's face hardened.

Wesley nodded at Buffy, who nodded back. "All right, then. We'll go together."

Angel exhaled, looking frustrated. "I can't stop you, Buffy. I can only ask you not to."

"That's right." She gave him a crooked smile. "You're not the boss of me."

He held out his hands, gesturing down the hall where other warm bodies lay in other beds. "At least let Jhiera help you with a portal."

"No," Buffy said. "I don't trust her. And besides, she should stay here and help Fred and Willow with creating the portal to China."

"Okay." Angel sighed. "It's your call."

"Let's go," the Slayer said to the former Watcher.

"Let's go," Wesley echoed.

CHAPTER FIFTEEN

Los Angeles

Buffy woke Willow, who sleepily cast spells of protection and deflection on the Slayer and Wesley. Lorne also called the Furies back in, who cooed over Angel as before, then augmented Willow's work.

Eager to avoid detection by either demon followers of Qin or the Vigories of Oden Tal, Buffy and Wesley took the service elevator to the basement, then headed into the sewers. Standing point, Buffy had a crossbow out, alert for attackers. Wesley gripped his Bavarian fighting adze and moved cautiously behind her, facing backward as he scanned the perimeter.

Eventually they reached St. Alexis and traced their way to the portion of the sewer Angel had described.

"Lucky thing my clothes are already disgusting," Buffy muttered.

Wesley didn't so much as crack a smile.

Wow, he's changed, Buffy thought. *If a guy could scare me, I'd say he was scary.*

In fact, I still say it.

They slogged through the drainpipe and eventually into the rank water, neither saying much. After a time they reached the wall Angel had told them about, the one where a portal had opened to admit the creature that had eaten the museum curator, Tsung Wei.

They took turns rapping on the wall, which was solid and evidently portal-free. Buffy looked at Wesley and said, "You got some hocus-pocus for this?"

Wesley murmured a few words in Latin. Nothing happened.

Then suddenly a rectangular shape began to glow; it vibrated and shimmered, becoming an oval. Buffy and Wesley moved on opposite sides of it, giving each other a nod to show they were on the job—

—and two guys in red robes came flailing out of it, splashing into the water.

They were both young, probably college age. Buffy grabbed one and Wesley took the other, clamping their hands over their mouths.

"You want to drown?" Buffy asked her captive. His eyes were huge as he shook his head. "I'm going to take my hand away and ask you a few questions. If you scream, I'll dunk you and I won't let you up."

He nodded. She pulled her hand away.

"Who are you and where are you going?" Wesley asked him.

"Oh God, please just let us go," the guy said, looking from

Buffy to Wesley and back again. "Qin's just found out about Fai-Lok and—"

Above Wesley's hand, the other guy's eyes bulged. He shook his head wildly.

"Do you serve Fai-Lok?" Buffy asked.

The guy—Jason—stared at her nervously.

Wesley said, "We're no friends of Qin's, I assure you."

"Yes. I serve Fai-Lok," Jason murmured. "So does he." He jerked his head at Wesley's prisoner, who nodded.

Wesley uncovered his guy's mouth. He sucked in air and then he said, "Fai-Lok promised to get us out of there, but we don't think that's going to happen." He started to cry. "We just want to get the hell away from all this!"

"Then give us your robes," Buffy said.

Wesley made a face. "Buffy, they're disgusting. They're dripping wet and they stink. We'll be noticed for sure."

"You got a better idea?" she asked. He looked defeated; she turned her attention back to her prisoner and said, "How long will that portal stay open?"

"Another minute or two," he told her.

"How did you open it?"

He gestured to the wall. "You hit that brick. On this side or inside the temple, it works the same." He touched a brick, and the portal closed. Touched it again, and it opened.

"Is someone on the other side wondering what the hell you're doing?" Buffy asked.

"Fai-Lok taught some of us how to make ourselves invisible," the guy responded. "We're both pretty good at it."

"How do you manage it?" Wesley asked.

"It takes a while to master. You have to learn some spells, burn some herbs—"

"No time," Wesley said.

"Maybe we should make you come back with us," Buffy said. "Show us around while you're invisible."

"Too risky," Wesley argued. "We should go alone."

"Okay," Buffy agreed. She turned to the guy. "We're going to take you back to higher ground. Then we're going to take your robes and go wash them . . . somewhere, and tie you up inside the sewer. We'll go in, we'll come out, you'll come with us. Got it?"

"Can't you just let us go?" Young Guy begged.

"Sorry. Better luck the next time you join an evil cult," Buffy bit off. "Now, come on, let's go."

Qin's cry of fury echoed throughout the Temple of the Ice Hell Brotherhood. Xian had betrayed him, poisoning the body he had Possessed. Through sheer luck, one of his minions had come to check on him, seen the comatose body, and realized that Qin was still inside. One of the magicians slated for incineration had arrived, fallen to his knees, inviting the great lord to Possess his own body. Luckily, Dark Blood had moved through his veins, and Qin had quickly moved inside the warm shell.

Now Qin held in his hand the tangible evidence of further betrayal: a missive, delivered anonymously to the Temple:

> Know this, Great Lord of China,
>
> I, Fai-Lok, challenge you in the arena of battle. I have stolen the dragon, Fire Storm, and hidden her from you. I shall meet you on the field of war in Los Angeles. I shall wipe the streets with your blood. My army marches to engage you. The gauntlet is thrown down.
>
> Fai-Lok,
> Leader of the Hellmouth Clan

In his new body, wearing the Dragon Mask, Qin screamed for vengeance as he looked out over the hall. He sat on his throne, raging, as the fires in the braziers roared and smoked. Gongs rang throughout the complex, summoning the inhabitants to the Great Hall. The red-robed monks jostled one another as they hurried to answer the summons, finding places in the throng.

Soon the mosaic floor was covered with monks.

Two of them wore slightly damp robes: Buffy and Wesley had successfully infiltrated the Temple, and were allowing themselves to be swept along with the crowd.

One of the unsuspecting minions of evil whispered to Wesley, "Oh God, what now?"

Qin rose from his throne and opened his arms. The throne beside his was empty, the glittering Dragon Crown resting on the seat.

The monk next to Buffy whispered, "Something terrible has happened. Where is Lady Xian? Why are we being summoned? What if Qin—"

"The war has begun!" Qin cried over his questions. "But not the war against Angel and the Slayer! The traitorous Fai-Lok has issued a challenge to us, and we shall answer it!"

The monks gaped at him. There was murmuring, a number of monks looking at one another with stricken faces.

The one who had spoken to Buffy was coming unglued.

"I have to get out of here," he begged her. "Help me."

Buffy gave him a piercing look. "Are you a Fai-Lokian?"

"I didn't say that!" His eyes huge, his face chalk white, he grabbed his chest and collapsed in a heap.

The others drew back, startled.

Wesley knelt beside him, rolling him over. The man's face was gray; he was gasping.

Then one of the other monks strode up to them and hissed, "What the hell is going on?"

"He's sick," Wesley said, his voice low and his face hidden by his hood. Then he added, "He has medicine in his . . . locker. For his . . . condition. I'll go get it."

"All right," the monk told him. "Hurry up."

"That monk there, ah, knows the locker combination," Wesley said, gesturing to Buffy, who also kept her face hidden as she nodded.

The monk gestured for them to go.

They pushed their way through the throngs, Buffy wondering how on earth they would ever find lockers in this enormous place. She was both amazed and grateful that Wesley had actually hit upon this little escape plan.

They got through the crowd. She scanned quickly, figured Wesley was doing the same.

And there, on the wall directly ahead, was a white sign with black letters that read DRESSING ROOMS and an arrow pointing to the left.

At the end of the corridor, banks of tall lockers hung open in dim light. Seemed Qin liked to save money on electricity.

Then Buffy noticed something hanging inside one of the lockers, and peered inside.

"Huh," she muttered. It was a shiny metallic backstage pass for a band called Darling Violetta.

That was when a huge wrestler-type guy in wrap-around sunglasses stepped from the shadows and grabbed Wesley by the throat and put a gun in his ribs.

"Who are you?" he demanded as Buffy made herself as small as possible, wedging herself into the locker and concealing herself with the door. She peered through the grating.

The wrestler guy dragged Wesley down the hall.

From his sanctuary in the blistering desert, Fai-Lok opened a satin bag and enclosed the magickal herbs in his left fist. Closing his eyes, he murmured words that had not been spoken in centuries. Through time and space, his incantation spoke to the *p'ai* of the terra-cotta warriors in the museum in Sunnydale.

One by one, the clay soldiers awakened to his voice, obeyed his simple commands:

March south.

Kill everyone you see.

Stirring, awakening, moving, the army began to move. Left, right, weapons drawn . . . they were not so much conscious as alert; not so much aware as activated, like ancient robots, timeless killing machines. Without fear, without malice, without mercy.

He had created them for Qin, back in the day when the Yellow Emperor ruled all of China.

Fai-Lok remembered the first time Qin had taken him down into the secret chamber and told him of his father, Lir, who had been imprisoned miles below them, in a frozen hell dimension.

"He freed his soul, but his body and the bodies and souls of other demons still dwell there," Qin had told him. "I have seen them in dreams. I want to free them. I want them on my side. My enemies are gathering. I need warriors who cannot be defeated."

They set to work. First Fai-Lok transported political enemies of Qin to the Ice Hell, strapping magick mirrors to their foreheads so that he and Qin could see what they saw. Though the men died en route, as they were weak, they were able to observe the cavern.

"It is exactly like my dreams," Qin murmured.

It was a vast, desolate place. As Qin had said, the bodies and souls of horrifying demons from many dimensions had been sent there to suffer. They dwelled beneath huge sheets, under frozen lakes, and inside cubes of ice. They were demons of all sorts: blue, black, human-looking, leathery—some for which Fai-Lok had no words to describe.

In the center of the barren, frozen wasteland towered the enormous, winged body of Lir, Father of Qin, Lord of the Ice Hell. Lir's leathery skin glowed scarlet; his massive wings stretched from one side of the cube to the other. His face was a nightmare, features elongated and covered with pustules; his oblong head was crowned with horns, and he was taller than three men standing on one another's shoulders. Talons curved from his fingers and toes, and his eyes glowed through his eyelids like the braziers his son burned to stay warm night and day.

He was terrifying.

"His awareness, his soul, are not there. They have flown back to his home dimension," Qin told him. Fai-Lok had no way of knowing if that was true, but Lir seemed to gaze at him through his closed eyelids with a malevolence that shook Fai-Lok to his core. He wished desperately that Qin would allow him to stop investigating the Ice Hell.

But Qin was not to be dissuaded. Fai-Lok experimented in his halls of magicks, until at last he conjured demons that should withstand the conditions in the nightmarish cavern. But his envoys were discovered by the guardians of the Ice Hell dimension, and brutally killed. Then the guards reinforced all the passages to and from Ice Hell.

"Is there a way to send something that cannot be killed?" Qin asked Fai-Lok.

Something stirred in Fai-Lok's mind, almost like a whisper from outside it.

He listened.

A thing that is not alive cannot be killed.

He scoured books of magicks; he conferred with spirits and other magicians. It was as if he was magickally guided. He learned of a desert land where kings were able to place their souls into figurines for safekeeping, and he read their sacred texts. There was another tribe of desert people who conjured figures to do their bidding by placing sacred texts in their mouths.

That was when Fai-Lok hit upon the idea of creating lifelike images of clay and imbuing them with volition. He created a full-sized dozen replicas of Qin's fighting troops, down to the exquisite detail of their weaponry and their armor. After Qin wiped his magickal blood on them, Fai-Lok shredded the lower souls of men and minor demons and fed them to his beautiful terra-cotta warriors.

Then he marched them down to Ice Hell; they did battle with the guards, freeing several demons. Then several more.

Then another dozen.

The souls of some of the demons were placed into terra-cotta warriors, while others joined Qin's retinue in their original forms.

Then he heard whispers again.

He dreamed of dragons.

Then one appeared over Qin's Forbidden City. It was a serpent dragon, with a body as long as a rice paddy and four short legs that ended in claws. Its teeth were long and curved, and it shimmered like a fish. Glowing golden eyes flashed in the moonlight, and when it opened its mouth, fire sprayed from it.

Place p'ai *into her,* the whispering voice told Fai-Lok. *Use the soul of the most valiant demon you have freed.*

Fai-Lok did so.

The resulting creature was a fantastic war machine, a female dragon, whom he named Fire Storm as she danced and arched against the moon. He told Qin about it, and the emperor was pleased.

And she is mine now, Fai-Lok gloated as he sat beside the dragon on the floor of the Mojave Desert. *And the terra-cotta warriors in Sunnydale now answer to me. Pity that I cannot control the ones in Los Angeles as well. I didn't have a chance to use magicks on them before I left. Or on the ones in Cleveland, Tokyo, or Germany.*

But when the time comes . . . I will. Qin's time is ending. Mine has just begun.

As if in reply, the dragon threw back her perfectly formed head and roared.

Los Angeles

Jhiera couldn't rest, not while her women were scattered and the Vigories were in pursuit. She appreciated Angel's ability to compartmentalize his worries in order to marshal his energies, but she had lived a resistance fighter's life for so long that she had forgotten how to do that. For her, there was very little strategy involved; her battle was constant, and she rarely had time to regroup.

She rose from her bed in Angel's hotel, slowed at his door, and went outside, into the night. She scanned the hotel garden, which was, for the moment, free of Angel's enemies. It was hot; crickets scraped, and a Santa Ana wind flapped through the trees like a predatory bird.

That was when she saw the hand.

It was extended a few inches behind the silhouette of a round bush with small leaves, and in the moonlight it looked gray.

Jhiera ran to it.

"No," she murmured, when she found the body.

Blue eyes stared up at her as if to say, *Where were you?* They belonged to one of her own, a young woman named Mirali. She had last seen the blonde woman at the Liang Museum, and watched her leap into the portal to safety.

Or so I had assumed. What if all of them are dead?

Swallowing back her grief, Jhiera turned the body over. Someone had attempted to remove Mirali's *k'o*. Portions of her ridged spine were covered in blood, and the *k'o* had been cracked.

Had she died escaping, trying to get to Jhiera? Or had she been left here as a warning?

Jhiera took the dead girl's hand in her own.

"No one else will die," she murmured to Mirali as a promise.

The blue eyes stared at her.

"I swear it."

Then Jhiera of Oden Tal closed Mirali's eyes, bowed her head, and wept.

When she was done, she found a shovel and dug a shallow grave. It was the best she could do for her fallen comrade.

But I can do better for the others, she thought. *I can do whatever it takes.*

And I will.

Her resolve hardened, she returned to the hotel and spoke of what had happened to Mirali to no one.

Lir laughed. He had found the Champion who would surely betray the others. The one who would bring the Orb, the Heart, and the Flame to him. But, just as important, the one who would free him from the ice.

What the others had not known was that Fire Storm had

been a necessary component of his quest to be free. The heat that she could generate was the heat he needed to melt his frozen prison. He had been working to have her brought back to him . . . had sent young Connor to the desert for that purpose.

But now there was an alternative: this beautiful woman, capable of enough heat to do the work of Fire Storm.

Jhiera of Oden Tal was his . . . and all he had had to do to secure her loyalty was cloud the mind of a certain Anagogic demon who happened to be wandering in the city, seeking fame, but finding death.

Under Lir's influence, Honnar of Pylea had murdered this girl, this Mirali, and had brought her where her mistress would find her.

And now she is mine, Lir told the Powers That Be. *And she shall help me tip the balance.*

Sunnydale

The theory was, Spike didn't have to sleep. So he would stand watch while Xander got some shut-eye.

The problem was, he was Spike.

Easily bored and not particularly thrilled to be stuck in Sunnydale, which was, as far as he was concerned, a lost cause, he got up and wandered over to the site of the Satanic temple. As far as he could tell, it had completely disappeared; he squatted to examine where the foundation ought to be, and—

Bloody hell, he thought as the ground under his feet began to shake. *Another earthquake.*

He rose unsteadily and called, "Xander? Time to wake up now."

Making his way back to the prone body of the Slayer's

343

number-two man, he frowned as he realized that the shaking was not the random chaos of a quake, but something very regular in its rhythm.

"What the hell?" Xander shouted, muzzing awake. He looked at Spike over his shoulder. "What's happening?"

"Dunno." Spike walked unsteadily toward him. Xander got up, and the two of them hurried to the edge of Kingman's Bluff.

"Oh. My. God," Xander murmured.

Through the smoke and the haze, they both looked down to see the terra-cotta warriors from the Sunnydale Museum of History marching down what was left of the ruined streets of Sunnydale. Hundreds strong, faces contorted and fierce, they moved in silence, except for the thunderous noise of their feet hitting the ground.

"Orio, oreeeeo," Xander chanted breathlessly, mimicking the song of the guards of the Wicked Witch of the West.

"Be a damn sight happier if those buggers were in Kansas and not here," Spike bit off.

Los Angeles

Buffy could have fought the temple wrestler guy for possession of Wesley, but a quick glance over her shoulder revealed that more monks were spilling into the corridor—she had no idea why—and the better part of valor was keeping their presence under wraps—er, robes—for as long as possible. There were way, way too many people around, even for the Slayer.

Keeping out of the man's line of sight, she trailed after him as he yanked open a door and threw Wesley into a room filled with other red-robed monks. As he wheeled around, Buffy scooted in behind him.

Not noticing her, he slammed the door shut.

"What's happening?" one of the room's occupants asked Wesley as the ex-Watcher got to his feet. The questioner was short and wore a goatee.

"Are you with Fai-Lok?" another guy asked. He stared at Buffy. "Hey, you're a woman."

"News flash," Buffy said, wrinkling her nose. "That's not your biggest problem."

Wesley looked back at them. "Are *you* with Fai-Lok?"

Everyone nodded, but Buffy noted that a couple of them were a bit hesitant in their responses.

"Yes . . . we, um, follow Fai-Lok." A wiry monk who was a very bad liar looked down at his hands.

"Well, I myself am on a mission to retrieve Flamestryke," Wesley said boldly, taking a chance that these monks already knew of the second dragon.

No one showed any recognition. Then Goatee Guy cleared his throat and moved in close. He looked around the room as if trying to make a decision. In a tense voice, he said, "My name is Dane Hom. I'm the leader of the Lodge of Sol. There are some here who are with me."

Another man across the room blurted, "Who are you talking about? We're Fai-Lok's acolytes. Qin's rounded us up to kill us."

"I'm not," another informed Wesley. He looked at Dane Hom. "What's he talking about, Dane? What's Flamestryke?"

"We serve Lir," Dane Hom continued, speaking to Wesley. "But among us, I am the only one who knows about . . . the one you mentioned."

"Flamestryke?" Wesley echoed.

Dane caught his breath. "I have never heard that name uttered aloud before. Only in my mind."

The other monks traded confused looks. Then one of them said, "Who's Lir?"

Dane looked proud as he said, "Lir is the demonic father of Qin. Lir is the true lord of this dimension. Flamestryke is the dragon he will summon, and he will lay waste to this city and all the other cities of the world."

Oh, way bingo, Buffy thought.

The Slayer said brightly, "Could you be more specific? Since we're all gonna die, anyway?"

That works on TV. Wonder if it works in real life.

"All right," Dane Hom said. "Here's the story."

CHAPTER SIXTEEN

Time Unrecorded, in the Dimension of Sol

His name was Lir, and he destroyed an entire race.

It was said he was the product of an unholy liaison between a hellgod and an ambitious female demon. She beguiled his father with potions and love spells. They wore off. After Lir was born, his father had his mother killed. Slowly.

His father was nearly twenty feet tall, with a wingspan nearly that wide. His body was covered with crimson leather; his face was contorted into a rictus of fury. Barbaric cruelty emanated from him like an odor.

His father had had thousands of enemies. Hellgods usually do. When it came time for Lir to assassinate his sire, it was an easy task.

Lir's savage reign over his home dimension, which was called Sol, destroyed nearly every living being in it. Once he had tasted the power of death-dealing, he could not be stopped. His rampages blotted out entire species of animals, vegetation, and demons. He was insane with sadism.

Pockets of green-skinned, horned resistance fighters cowered in caves and underground caverns, their fear practically unendurable. Those who were not the spawn of hellgods and demons, the rabble, looked much like their cousins in Pylea, and there were many vain attempts to open a portal and leap into that dimension for safety.

Lir heard of these attempts and realized that with a means to open portals, he, too, could travel to other dimensions. Pylea sounded as good as any other, if there were beings to conquer and riches to plunder. But all the attempts to open portals had failed, and Lir captured and tortured the Solans for the secret of how to do it, but they all died without being of any use.

So for the moment, Lir contented himself with picking off the few Solans who were left. One group continued to elude him: a hereditary line of resistance fighters had sprung up. They were called the Home Group, a ragtag but highly effective army of perhaps one hundred souls. They had tunneled into the mountains, but Lir could never discover precisely where.

The Home Group held on, sometimes welcoming a new member through a birth, more often mourning the death of a fine, young warrior in a skirmish with Lir's armies. Their numbers dwindled with the years. Few joined them. There were not very many Solans left, and though Lir hadn't located them, he had succeeded in cutting off the roads that led to the Home Group's bunker.

Then, one midnight, there was a clamor at the bunker's magickally warded entry door. Though the door was hidden from outsider's eyes, appearing as part of the rockface of a cavern, someone or something pounded heavily on it, and a voice rang out, "Let me in! I'm a Champion of Good!"

It was a female, from the sound of her voice. She spoke with authority. The sentries, seven of them, stared at one another in confusion. No outsider had ever located their bunker before.

"Get the First Leader!" she cried. "I've been sent by the Powers That Be!"

The First Leader himself arrived, a tall Solan wearing fatigues, alert despite being roused from sleep. As the sentries watched, he approached the carved door. The names of all the fallen had been etched into it, with the warm rays of Sol bathing their memories. He put his hand on it, as if he would be able to tell who stood on the other side.

Within a minute, others quickly gathered, flame-robed magicians and warriors in battle gear, each prepared to defend the bunker with their lives. Children huddled behind their parents. Babies' mouths were covered.

Had Lir finally brought the battle to them?

She said through the door, "I've been sent to fight for you. I won't allow anyone to wound me or kill me."

There was a stir among the elders.

"I was a Higher Being," she announced. "I'm a Champion of Good."

"It's a lie," one of the other fighters grumbled. "It's a trap. Lir seeks to wipe us out and turn this world into Hell."

"That is true," she agreed. "But after I defeat Lir, you will be allowed to go to Pylea. They will help you. You will be warm, and free from fear."

With that, they opened the door, and invited her into their bunker.

Her name was Hannah.

"She fought Lir, and she managed to wound him," Dane told the followers of Fai-Lok, who were grouped around him like children listening to a bedtime story. "She thrust her sword into the body of Flamestryke's body and extracted the Flame. It has been revealed to me that it lies buried in the caverns near the body of the Great Lir. As he was weakened, she subdued Lir himself, and the Powers That Be sent him to an icy hell dimension, from which he could not escape—or so they thought." He smiled proudly.

"He was encased in a block of ice large enough to cover three city blocks, and that block was placed inside the coldest hell imaginable. Lir was frozen solid. His consciousness slowed, dulled. But it was there.

"Gradually, he realized that he could detach a part of his consciousness and place it inside one of the many guards. Then the higher soul of the one he Possessed would be cast out. Lir would use the lower soul, the *pa'i*, to move the body, but it was his higher soul that would control the body."

He waited for a reaction. The others were gaping at him, and urging him to go on.

"This icy dimension is located deep below the heart of China. When one of the guards had completed his term of duty and was allowed to return to our dimension, Lir possessed him and came with him. Once aboveground, he found another body to Possess, and mated with the mother of Qin."

One of the others said, "We all know that Qin was part demon. So is Fai-Lok."

"No, you're wrong," Dane replied. "Fai-Lok is only a long-lived wizard."

The monks Buffy had identified as Fai-Lok groupies shifted

uncomfortably, but no one contradicted their informant. She wondered if he realized that he was giving up a lot more information than he was getting.

As if sensing what she was thinking, Dane drew himself up. "It doesn't matter anymore. Lir is the king of all these pawns. He will retrieve the Flame and use it to bring Flamestryke to life."

"Indeed," Wesley said. "That's precisely what we're doing. And we're given to understand that there are two other things, one being an Orb and the third is . . ." He paused.

"The Heart," Dane said. Then he raised his hand over his head and pointed. "Here it comes!"

There was a strange humming sound, low and vibratory; the hair on the back of Buffy's forearms prickled as if someone had touched her with cold fingers. Faint colors danced in the center of the room, flickering over the rapt faces of some of the others. Most of them were frightened and confused.

The monks pushed themselves against the walls of the room, leaving the center open. One of them pulled Buffy alongside him, then looked toward the open space with a look of anticipation. Wesley did the same.

The colors grew darker—orange, yellow, red—and then they snapped into a glowing ring.

"Go!" Dane shouted. "Hurry!"

One by one, about six monks raced toward the ring, leaped into it, and disappeared. It was a portal.

Dane turned to Buffy, dug into his pocket, and pulled out a small satin bag.

"Have you been prepared?" he asked her. "Lir told me how to ensure our survival during the teleportation." He reached into the bag—

—and at that moment, heavy footsteps thundered in the

hallway outside the room. Dane looked stricken. "They're coming for us!" he cried. "Hurry up!"

The door began to open.

Guards in body armor burst into the room.

Dane panicked.

He grabbed Buffy and flung her toward the portal.

Lights flashed, swirled. There was tremendous heat, nearly broiling the skin off Buffy's face. A yellowish-white light bloomed around her. She looked for Wesley but could see nothing.

And then she found herself hovering in the night over another part of Los Angeles. She hung level with the second story of a high-rise; a bird flew past, squawking.

Then she tumbled downward, just like a character in a cartoon.

Down she went, down, down, the fall broken as she landed in the fronds of a palm tree.

"Buffy!" a voice shouted from the bottom of the tree. It was Wesley.

"Wesley! I'm fine. You?" she called to him. She looked through the fronds to see him standing at the base, staring up at her.

"Landed quite easily," he said. "I've no idea why."

"Like Lorne says, gift horse, mouth," Buffy told him. Then she began to shimmy down the tree. "What the hell happened?"

"It seems the followers of Lir were rescued by means of that portal. They must have been prepared for transport in some way. Perhaps they had specific amulets in their robes . . . or had talismans or something. At any rate, it seems we were found wanting, and therefore . . . disgorged."

"We're rejects," Buffy muttered, and she dropped down

beside him. "But at least our recon wasn't a loss." She grinned at him. "We have cool information for Willow. We now know what the three, two, one was about."

"Yes. As well as the missing bit of information that's been bothering me."

"The bit that goes like this? If Qin and Fai-Lok don't know about Flamestryke, how do their followers know? And how does Wolfram and Hart know?" Buffy asked.

"Indeed," Wesley said. "I'm guessing that Lir is still very much a player in all this. And Qin and Fai-Lok don't know about that either. I do wish they'd happened to discuss the Heart more fully. If this were a badly written movie, they'd have spilled their guts explaining things to us even though they assumed we knew them."

Wesley looked at his watch. "According to this, we've been gone four hours. There's that time anomaly again. We should discuss—"

He cocked his head. "Do you hear that noise?"

Buffy listened a minute. It was a distant, rhythmic booming sound, almost like cannonfire.

"Yeah, I do."

They headed toward it, running a few blocks to the north. Wesley took stock of their surroundings and said, "Buffy, we're near the Liang Museum."

"Oh, my God," Buffy said, looking past him and pointing. "Look."

The terra-cotta soldiers were crashing through the gates of the museum complex and marching down the street. In ranks and files, their clay feet thundered against the blacktop. Their faces were fierce but their eyes were eerily blank. Their weapons were drawn.

They were accompanied by demons of all shapes and sizes, and strange monkey-creatures that bobbed around them.

Several very large Asian-looking men in body armor strode at the head of their ranks, and each was carrying a rocket launcher.

"Let's get back to the hotel," Wesley said. "We need to tell the others."

Buffy nodded, and they ran.

Nearly colliding with a short Pylean who looked very much like Lorne and who screamed at the top of his lungs, "All I wanted was to be a singer!"

Buffy and Wesley brought the Pylean, whose name was Honnar, back to the Hyperion with them. Lorne was thrilled to see him, fussing over him and asking for gossip about their home dimension. He was digging the intense compliments over his latest ensemble, which included a peach shirt and darker orange-based trousers.

But the visit was cut short as everyone watched the latest developments of the marching terra-cotta army on the TV news. Things were not good: Three office buildings in the vicinity of the Liang Museum had just been reduced to rubble.

A police officer who had tried to interfere with the warriors had been trampled to death; some street kids with submachine guns tried to save him, and they had been slaughtered.

"They whacked off Mikol's head!" a sobbing woman told the on-screen news anchor.

When there was a lull, Buffy and Wesley told them everything they'd seen and heard in the temple. Lorne listened carefully, and his expression got soft and kind of goofy.

He looked at Honnar, who was also looking goofy.

"That guy was talking about Hannah of Pylea," Lorne said reverently. "I can't believe it. I thought she was a myth. This all fits. This . . . this is too amazing." He wiped his brow. He was sweating. "Oh, my God. I'm twitching."

"But . . . but that's why I'm called Honnar!" Honnar said excitedly. "I'm said to be a direct descendant of hers. So that means you are too, Krevlorneswath!"

"Oh, my God, do you think?" Lorne asked shrilly.

"Talk in longer sentences, please," Buffy said. "Either or both of you."

"Not big with the patience, are you?" Lorne said to her. He regarded the group with misty wonder. "Well kids, see, there used to be a Pylean heroic quest story. Very Joseph Campbell." He thought a moment. "Which proves, by the way, that Jungian archetypes about heroic figures are accurate, and universal."

"*Please,*" Buffy huffed.

Lorne shook himself. "You see, there's a story in Pylean mythology that a brave Champion arrived on Pylea from 'another place' with a band of heroes and a protective amulet. It was called the Heart of the Demon."

"Yes! And it's said to be buried in the castle in the center of the world," Honnar cut in.

Lorne's mouth dropped open. "Get out."

"It's true." Honnar grinned. "It's supposed to be in the lowest basement, near the mutilation chamber. I've never been there, but—"

Lorne looked at Angel. "Guess what, Pale Rider. *We've* been to that castle, and I've been to that basement."

"The one where Cordy was the Cow Princess?" Angel asked.

Buffy stared at him. *"What?"*

"Yes," Lorne said. "The champion brought the Heart of the Demon from her home."

"Okay," Buffy said, "the Heart of the Demon has to be the heart she yanked out of Lir. And there's the Orb, and then that monk guy Dane said the Flame is buried in the ice above Lir."

Lorne smiled. "And again, we have liftoff! The Hannah myth

also mentions three gifts. And I'm willing to bet they weren't gold, frankincense, and myrrh." He spread his hands wide as if he were back on the stage at Caritas, about to sing "Lady Marmalade." He continued between them. "So we have the Heart of the Demon, the Orb, and the Flame! And the Heart is on Pylea."

"Wow," Fred said, her eyes wide. "Witness the power of folklore."

"It's often very useful," Willow agreed. "We've used folklore and mythology to destroy quite a few evil beings down in Sunnydale."

"Okay, let's get the research machine going," Lorne suggested. "Pin down those clues. Get solid data. This Orb—is that what Lilah was talking about? We have so many threads we could weave a tapestry! And those Lir-followers portaled somewhere, kiddies," he reminded the group. "As much as I hate to say it, someone should go to Pylea as soon as possible, just in case they're one giant leap ahead of us."

"Not alone," Fred said uneasily. "No one should go there alone."

"I . . . I'll return with him," Honnar said, looking, well, terrified.

"Not meaning any offense," Fred interjected, "but if you two are attacked—"

"Fred's right," Angel cut in. He looked around the room. "Gunn?"

Gunn nodded. "I'll go with Lorne and Honnar." He looked at Fred. "You still remember the magick words?"

She closed her eyes. "Sometimes at night I wake up mumbling them."

"*That's* comforting," Lorne drawled.

"All right," Buffy said, rising. She bobbed her head at Gunn and Lorne. "Let's do as much research as we can before you take off."

She turned to Angel.

"I'm thinking we'll still need to go to China. Flamestryke is there. We'll have to destroy the three artifacts as soon as our side gets our hands on them. And Wesley . . ."

She glanced around the room. There were a few blank stares. "What?" she asked.

"Just that we're kind of used to Angel being in charge," Fred said, ducking a little. "So, it's . . . different having you issue the orders."

"I'm the Slayer," Buffy said, then looked around the room at the expressions that did not change with that announcement. "Okay. Sorry. My bad. Angel, please. Be my guest." She extended a hand in invitation.

Angel looked at the others and said, "Do what she just said."

The Mojave Desert

The dragon's roar shook the desert floor. Anya clutched her cell phone and two dozen packs of batteries as she fell to her knees. She bit her lip so that she wouldn't cry out and possibly reveal her location. Then she realized that was ridiculous. No one would be able to hear anything above the dragon's roar.

And she wouldn't be able to hear Xander if he called her back.

She scoured around and found several pairs of earphones and plugged one into her phone. Then she realized there was a cool auxiliary port for an extra earpiece and took advantage of the opportunity for stereo.

Not far away, Connor muttered, "Bingo," as an enormous, thundering roar boomed across the barren wasteland like a sonic boom. It startled him as he sped along on a Harley Fatboy through the Mojave Desert. He had stolen the bike and the helmet. The jacket, he had owned.

The racket had to be the roar of an enormous creature.

Like a dragon.

He sped along, wondering how close he could get to the source without alerting anyone with the noise from the Harley.

Only one way to find out.

The roaring grew louder, which meant either that he was getting closer or that, well, the dragon was roaring louder. While it was noisy, he put the pedal to the metal, jammin' down the highway. It was blazing, and he was sweating inside the helmet. He wanted like anything to take it off, but he didn't want to spare a second to do it.

The roaring grew fainter, so he screeched to a halt, put down his foot, and turned off the machine. He peered into the blinding expanse of white.

In the distance was an outcropping of rock.

Maybe some kind of magickally created oasis, he thought.

Now he did take off the helmet, leaving it beside the bike. He unpacked the saddlebags and got out the pack he had found among Cordelia's things. It was loaded with water and some protein bars. Connor was hungry and thirsty, and he was also so hot, he wanted to scream.

He slipped on the pack, adjusting the straps. Then he reached into the other saddlebag and got out the rocket launcher.

Okay, he thought. *Locked and loaded. Won't my father be surprised when I tell him I took this dragon out.*

Maybe he'll even treat me with a little respect . . . and leave Cordy and me alone.

Sunnydale

Xander and Spike stood on Kingman's Bluff and watched the procession of terra-cotta warriors stride down the street.

"Five hundred terra-cotta warriors on the wall, five hundred guys of clay, you take a few out and smash 'em all about, and that's the hokey pokey of doom," Xander sang.

"Shut *up*," Spike said through his teeth. "You are going to annoy me to death."

"We can always hope." Xander flashed him a smile. "So. Let's have a mission statement. Big, heroic gestures of saving . . . or sitting up here safely while lots of people die?"

Spike swiveled his head toward him. "You have got to be kidding."

"Yeah." Xander rubbed his hands together and nodded. "I figured you'd go with the saving."

Spike snickered. "Not bloody likely. Not with that group trottin' about."

"See, there's that thing again that always puzzles me," Xander said, gazing down at the soldiers. "They're not trotting. They're just marching. Like the Mummy. So why did anyone worry about the Mummy? It just lurched along, lurched along . . . a Chihuahua could have outrun it. What was all the fuss?"

"Well, see," Spike began, then frowned. He stuffed his hands in his jeans pockets. "I'm sure there was a reason."

"Hah." Xander preened. "My Earth logic defeats your vampire logic."

"Please." Spike kicked a pebble.

And at that precise moment, the terra-cotta warriors went all crazy. They broke formation, yelling and screaming. Their faces contorted into fierce, feral grimaces of extreme aggravation. Clay hands reached for clay swords and clay lances and clay bows and arrows.

They loaded clay arrows.

They turned and fired at Spike and Xander.

And about a third of them started charging toward Kingman's Bluff with murder in their clay eyes.

"Oh, crap!" Spike cried. "All right, no safe sitting!" he bellowed at Xander. "We'll be doing some saving, shall we? Of our own arses?"

"Roger that!" Xander shouted.

They ran down the other side of the bluff, which led into a valley. Or what was usually a valley. Now it was a river about twenty feet wide and twenty feet down, which had been created by the breaking of the Sunnydale Dam.

"Do a Butch and Sundance?" Xander asked.

"What the hell are you talking about?" Spike demanded, scowling at him.

"This!" Xander yanked Spike's arm and leaped.

Spike yelled something that was not suitable for prime time, and the two plunged into the churning river.

It was cold, which should have been good news on such a blistering day. But Xander wasn't prepared for the iciness of it, and he gasped as he went in. So, no air in the lungs; he realized that Spike didn't have to worry about that. The vampire could stay underwater for months and probably nothing would happen to him.

But Xander was a human, and he had to get up to the surface.

That much he managed, but as he broke the waterline, he saw that the soldiers were leaping in after him and Spike.

"Oh, my God!" he shouted.

"What? Oh, my God!" Spike bellowed as he breached the surface.

The soldiers started swimming for them. Xander started swimming, too, but the current was too much for him. He was swept along, end over end, struggling just to keep his head out of the rushing water. He lost track of Spike.

A clay warrior splashed toward him. *Why doesn't he sink?* Xander wondered, but his world was all askew, and he went under water again.

Then someone grabbed his arm and started dragging him toward the surface. He struggled, figuring it was one of the soldiers. Then he caught sight of a face. It was a guy, not Spike, and he looked astonished to see Xander.

"Oh my God, oh my God!" the guy shouted. He was on the verge of hysteria. He had dragged Xander to the opposite bank of the river; he was young, soaking wet, and banged up.

He helped Xander stagger away from the water. Then he shouted, "I'm Sam Devol! Follow me!"

"Wait!" Xander cried. He looked around. "Spike?"

"Come on! They're coming!" Sam shouted.

And they were. Dozens of them, dripping wet but still fully intact, racing after the two of them.

Xander and Sam tore the hell out of there.

Just then, the cell phone in his pocket trilled. Startled, he grabbed it and said, "Buy stock in Verizon. This thing still works."

"Xander? It's Willow," she said. "Are you okay?"

"Kinda busy, though I think I'm with that kid you used to baby-sit—oh, and I heard from Anya. She's fine. Just transported," Xander answered anxiously.

"Oh, thank goodness. And weird. Listen. Wesley, Fred, and I have been doing research. Together. And we're good at it! There was an orb that attracted Fire Storm to the portal in Sunnydale instead of coming through the one in L.A. It's called the Orb. Which, duh. And it's blue."

The warriors were gaining on him and Sam. Xander said, "Okay, Will! Talk to you later!"

"No, wait, Xander!" she cried. "You need to find that orb.

Buffy saw it in the cavern beneath the warehouse by the Bronze. Spike probably saw it too. You guys have got to retrieve it before anyone else does. Buffy and Angel really need it!"

"Okay! Later!" Xander shouted.

He disconnected and stuffed the phone in his pocket just as a warrior leaped at Sam. Sam curled into a ball, and the warrior tumbled over him, slamming stomach-first on the ground. Xander trotted up beside Sam, grabbed his arm, and helped him out of the way.

The soldier rolled over on its back as if in preparation for sitting up. Xander had no idea what to do, but his instinct for self-preservation took over: He picked up a giant rock and held it over his head, preparing himself to slam it into the face of the soldier.

Then he lost his balance and dropped the rock. It landed with a crack on the soldier's lower abdomen.

The warrior made a strange hissing noise, like a balloon losing all its air. Its face sank in; its head deflated.

Then it exploded.

Shards of clay flew everywhere. Xander whirled around and hit the dirt, covering his head.

It was over in a couple of seconds, like a vampire dusting, only with larger fragments.

"Hit 'em below the belt!" Xander shouted to Sam.

They picked up rocks. As two more soldiers approached, both guys aimed for the solar plexus. Both made contact.

The two attackers exploded.

"Wow!" Sam shouted. "That's so cool!"

"We've got to get out of here," Xander shouted back. "There's just too many of them!"

The bad guys were swarming out of the river. There were fifty of them, maybe more. And they were coming too fast for Sam and Xander to make a getaway.

"Hold on!" That was Spike, who had just staggered onto the embankment about ten feet downriver from them. Soaking wet, he rushed to their aid, employing massive amounts of vampire strength as he punched and kicked at the soldiers.

"Get their stomachs!" Xander yelled. "It makes them blow up!"

"Got it!" Spike shouted back. "Even though it's weird," he muttered.

Times past, this was what Spike lived for: the fray, the melee. All the hittin' and the bruisin' and the breakin'. It was glorious, was what it was. Still quite enjoyable, even if he had learned there was a bit more to life than destruction.

Xander was right about hittin' the clay buggers in the stomach; it was the only thing they could do to stop them permanently.

As he battled, Xander and the other guy got in their fair licks. Xander yammered on about some orb or other, and the three began making tracks back toward the ruins of the cavern where Spike and Buffy had seen the dragon.

There was too much fighting to do to argue with Xander about the lunacy of going back there, so Spike wound up back at ground zero rather by default. By the time they reached it, they had managed to leave the clay army behind; presumably the lads were marching south toward Los Angeles. At any rate, they had abandoned their pursuit of Spike and company, and that was just fine with Spike.

The place was no lovelier than before: piles of dirt, chunks of buildings on fire; lots of bits of dead things, human and demon. The smell rivaled any charnel house in old London Town, back in the day when he had been William and his mum had admired his poetry.

Truly, she had. Was only after I bit 'er she went off on it.

As it was, there were demons about, but Spike guessed that they were the laggards stumbling out of the Hellmouth. He'd seen most varieties before on other adventures: Vorlax, Drokken, Haxil Beast—*uh-oh, hide the women*—Durslar Beasts, and many others. Some of 'em could be quite ferocious, but for the moment none of them were looking for a fight. They stumbled about as if they had hangovers.

He, Xander, and this new Sam person crouched behind a pile of burning rubble, spying on the demons. The cavern's roof had collapsed, and to the right, the warehouse Sam had described was a pile of kindling.

"Orb's in there somewhere," Spike told them. "Unless the sorcerer took it. Which would make more sense than looking for it here," he said under his breath.

"Well, what are we supposed to do, find some shovels and dig?" Sam asked. "Let's just get the hell out of here."

"*You* can," Xander told him. "But Spike and I have to do this." He slid his glance toward Spike. "*Right?*"

"Blimey," Spike groused. "I'll look for shovels."

CHAPTER SEVENTEEN

Los Angeles / Pylea

Gunn, Honnar, and Lorne stood side by side in the lobby, waiting for the happy words that would whisk them off to Lorne's not-so-happy home dimension.

Everyone in the hotel had assembled to bid them bon voyage: Willow, Angel, the adorable Dawn and Buffy, Fred, and the formidable Jhiera in her dominatrix outfit.

Lorne said brightly, "Anyone need anything from my home-sour-home dimension? Pylean kalla berries? Crug grains? A finely honed decapitation ax?"

"Just the Heart of the Demon," Buffy said. "Get it and come back."

The Slayer has no sense of humor, Lorne thought privately. *She really needs to lighten up.*

Then Fred read the magick words, and *whoooooooosh!*

There they were: the suns, the meadows, the unattractive castle looming in the background. Pylea, a mirthless dimension where music was forbidden and his mother hated his guts.

"Well, we made it," Gunn said. "Let's go."

I need a Sea breeze, Lorne thought, trailing after him with Honnar in tow.

On the whole, I'd really rather be in Tarkna.

The Mojave Desert

"Oh, my God," Anya whispered as she peered from behind the ruined sales counter of the electronics shop.

The man with the dragon was climbing atop it as if he was preparing for takeoff. That was probably bad news, but Anya had no way to stop him.

And no water, if he leaves me out here alone.

But I have lots of cell phone batteries, she thought anxiously, clasping her cell phone against her chest.

Then someone came up behind her, pressed a hand over her mouth, and said, "Ssh."

She tried to scream; the hand pressed hard, and a voice said, "I'm armed."

It's just like in the movies, Anya thought dismally. *The incredibly beautiful-looking damsel in distress gets distracted watching one bad guy, forgetting that bad guys usually come in pairs. There's a reason people say, "Watch your back."*

Then her cell phone vibrated. She shifted anxiously as the man muttered, clearly torn about letting her answer it.

He said, "Give me your left earpiece," and took it off her ear. She assumed he was pressing it against his own ear.

"Take the call," he said. "Don't give anything away, or I'll shoot you."

He removed his hand from her mouth. Anya slowly raised the cell phone to her mouth. "Hello?" she said nervously.

"An, we're looking for this orb that acts like a homing beacon for the dragon. We're thinking that if we find it, it might somehow call her back to Sunnydale. If she takes off, I want you to call me as soon as you can, all right?"

"Sure, Xander," she said.

"Man, I wish Buffy was here. There's a whole lotta evil goin' down."

"Yeah."

"Are you all right?" Xander asked.

"Um, well . . ."

The man grabbed the phone and said, "Are you Xander, the Slayer's friend?"

"Who's this?" the voice on the other end of the phone demanded.

"My name is Connor. I . . . I live in L.A."

"You do," Xander said skeptically. "And you know about Buffy because . . ."

"I fight . . . like she does."

"With Angel?" Xander asked.

Connor paused. Then he said, "Yes. I came here to stop Fai-Lok from taking this dragon."

"Well, we're on the same side, then," Xander told him. "You got a plan?"

"I have a rocket launcher," Connor said.

"You have a rocket launcher?" Xander repeated, chortling. "You really *are* one of us!"

367

"He's lying!" Anya cried. "He doesn't have a rocket launcher!"

"It's with my Harley," Connor explained.

At that, Anya turned around. "You have a Harley?" she said excitedly. "Let's go!"

"After we take out the dragon," Connor said.

"Sure! Great!" She beamed at him.

"Help me carry the launcher?" he asked her. He took the earpiece off his ear and handed it to her.

"Absolutely!" She said to Xander, "I'm going with this nice young man to get the rocket launcher."

Xander said, "Good. Tell Connor that . . . what, Spike? Oh." Xander paused. "Connor is Angel's son."

Angel has a son? There is so much I don't know, Anya thought. *And everyone is having sex but me.*

They took off, slipping and sliding in the sand. She attached her phone to the waistband of her pants, saying, "I guess you're not a vampire, out in the sun and all."

He glanced at her. "You know who I am?"

"Yes. Um, but *what* are you?"

His face clouded. "I don't know."

"Oh." She smiled at him. "Don't let it get you down. I don't know what I am either. I've been the honey of a troll—only he wasn't a troll when we hooked up. And a vengeance demon— twice. Then I got jilted at the altar. I thought I was going to be a missus. But I'm just Anya, which isn't even my real name, and—"

"Here," he said, walking her over to his bike.

"Ooh, a Fatboy," she said appreciatively. "You know your Harleys."

He flashed her a quick, shy smile that was too adorable and popped open the lid of one of the saddlebags. He started passing her the pieces of the launcher, and she gathered them up in her arms.

"Oh!" she cried, nearly dropping them. "I'm vibrating again!"

She dropped the pieces to the sand and grabbed up her phone. "Xander?" she said.

"It's Angel. Xander just called me. Is the dragon still there?"

"Yes." Anya nodded even though he couldn't see her. "And so is Connor."

"Put him on."

"It's for you." She held the phone out to Connor.

He frowned at her. "Who is it?"

"Your dad." She thrust the phone toward him. "Hurry. We have a dragon to shoot down."

His face went all sullen. He took the phone and said, "What?" as if he would rather drink gasoline than talk to Angel.

Anya went back to gathering the pieces of the launcher, trying not to eavesdrop, but if it was something dishy, well . . .

"Yeah. Still here," Connor bit off. "Rocket launcher. Sure."

He disconnected. Seeing that Anya had her hands full of weaponry, he slid the phone into his jeans pocket. Then he picked up the rest of the launcher and said, "Let's hurry. We need to be ready."

"Sure thing."

They hurried back toward the debris field.

Another roar shattered the still desert air like a sonic boom. Connor muttered under his breath and said, "I think we'd better get the launcher ready. Right here."

"Okay." She dropped to her knees and began piecing it together. He passed her the main section, and together they stabilized the tripod.

There was a tremendous whirring and flapping. Sand pelted them; Anya ducked down her head and said, "It must be taking off!"

"We can't let it get out of here!" Connor cried. "Okay, then, we won't!" Anya yelled. The wind was rising; it was like a terrible sandstorm, and they were caught in the middle of it. "Put in the payload."

She sprawled out on her stomach and aimed the launcher high. She kept her eyes tightly shut against the sand. Then Connor patted her shoulder and yelled, "Fire!"

Anya deployed the weapon.

She peered through her eyelids, watching the projectile streak toward an enormous shadow moving across the sun. She realized she was seeing the dragon fly through the sandstorm.

The payload went nowhere near the target. All she saw was a streaming burst, and then nothing.

But apparently the man riding the dragon had seen it: a blue fireball slammed into Anya and Connor, knocking them both to the desert floor.

Something tumbled to the ground next to them as well: a small satin bag.

The sand continued to whoosh over the bag, and over Anya and Connor, and began to bury them.

Anya's cell phone vibrated.

No one answered.

Los Angeles

After finally responding to several phone messages from Wesley, Lilah showed up at the Hyperion about twenty minutes after Gunn, Honnar, and Lorne had left for Pylea. Angel had Fred and Willow share what they had discovered, and Lilah went on the computer when they were finished.

"I'm pulling up records," she told them. She shook her head in frustration. "I can't believe we started all this without an arrangement with Lir. Compared with him, Alex Liang is tiny potatoes." She sighed. "If I can deliver a client of his caliber, I'll be a senior partner in no time."

"There's something to aspire to," Wesley said coolly.

"Oh, snap out of it, Wes," Lilah drawled. "You know my endless ambition is a turn-on."

A muscle jumped in Wesley's cheek. Otherwise, he showed no emotion.

"Well, I think you were right about the Orb," Lilah said, scrolling down a screen. "Looks like that's how Fai-Lok managed to divert Fire Storm to Sunnydale. And the Heart"—she tapped away, then nodded—"we have a cross-reference to that. Hmm, all it says is that Hannah of Pylea was originally from another dimension called Sol."

"Anything about the Flame?" Angel asked, looking over her shoulder.

She poked around, then shook her head. "I have no idea what it is. You seem to know more than we—I—do."

"Then we go with as much as we know, now," Buffy said emphatically.

"I agree with the Slayer," Jhiera chimed in. "We can take a portal."

Lilah made a face. "Your Vigories are all over portals hunting your followers. You should take one of the Wolfram and Hart private jets."

"I'd rather walk," Buffy interjected.

Lilah gave her an amused smile. "Well, Buffy, things aren't quite so . . . binary around here. It's not 'bad idea, good idea.' It's what's expedient. Isn't that right, Angel?" She looked to the vampire for agreement.

"We'll take the jet," Angel said. He looked hard at Buffy. "We need to get there as soon as possible."

"In one of their planes?" Buffy crossed her arms over her chest.

"Would you rather stick out your thumb and hitchhike?" Angel asked.

"*She* should do it," Buffy shot back, gesturing to Jhiera. "The way she's dressed, she'd get rides quicker."

"Ooh, bitch fight," Lilah said. Her eyes shone. "Shall we start a betting pool on who will win?"

"All I know is that the Vigories of the Oden Tal are pursuing my women, and war has come to Los Angeles. And I have people to protect," Jhiera said. "I don't care how we get this done, as long as my people are safe."

"And we're back to expediency," Lilah said to Buffy.

A Wolfram & Hart limo took them to the private airstrip just outside downtown L.A. A demon was their pilot. There was no copilot.

Buffy strapped in and crossed her arms across her chest. Seated facing her, Angel did the same. Jhiera sat on the opposite aisle, parallel to Angel.

"We're wasting time doing it this way," Buffy said.

The jet began to taxi down the runway.

"That may be, but that woman had a point," Jhiera said. "We want to arrive there in one piece. If Lir knows that his presence has been revealed, he will do everything he can to stop anyone from approaching."

The jet picked up speed.

"I still say a portal would work," Buffy said.

The jet left the ground.

They were off.

Buffy sulked. And dozed.

Then Angel was gently shaking her awake. "We're here," he said.

She stirred. "What? We just took off."

Jhiera was scowling. "It was a trick. We went through a portal after all."

"No. We just flew very fast," said a voice from the front of the plane.

It was their tall, dark, and demon pilot. He was carrying three large white rectangular bundles. "You'll need to put these on now," he told them. "Parachutes."

The Mojave Desert

Fai-Lok smiled grimly as he rode Fire Storm away from the desert. Whoever had tried to harm the dragon was dead now. He didn't know who it was, but he was certain they had been sent by Qin. Who else?

I have to be careful. There may be other factions attempting to take control of the Ice Hell Brotherhood.

Whatever the case, it's time. My soldiers are marching toward the battleground. I'll make a portal and lead them down the streets of Los Angeles. I'll ride at the head of my army on this fantastic creature.

And we will wreak such death and vengeance as has not been seen since the fall of Qin's Forbidden City. . . .

THE PALACE OF QIN:
Ancient China, the City of Xian

Hell Night—the opposition had one mandate: to wipe the floors of the palace with the blood of the tyrant, Qin. To put him to the sword and make his people suffer as the Yellow Land had suffered beneath his yoke.

The first phalanx of the massed armies of Qin's many enemies crashed through the gates of the Yellow City. Dressed in armor and carrying the banners of dead warlords and decimated noble families, they raced toward the inner courtyard.

The terra-cotta warriors had been massed against the attackers. Silently, they thrust long, wicked blades into necks, arms, thighs, eye sockets.

But Fai-Lok had woven spells around them, weakening them, and throwing off their aim.

Above them, Fire Storm swooped and spewed flame . . . also missing most of the attackers, as Fai-Lok had arranged.

From his rooms in the upper pagoda, Fai-Lok smiled at the unending stream of fighters, illuminated by the torches they carried. The emperor's forces were severely outnumbered.

Yes.

He raced down the halls to the emperor's private quarters and kowtowed, forehead pressed to the floor. Fai-Lok said, "They are here. We cannot prevail, my lord. You must leave here."

Qin scoffed. "Surely you're joking, Fai-Lok. What of my terra-cotta armies? And the demons who serve me?"

"There are too many," Fai-Lok insisted, kowtowing. He kept his face hidden. He feared he would betray himself at the last: This attack had been engineered by him and Xian, to topple Qin from power.

"What about Fire Storm?" Qin continued.

"I think she's been bewitched," Fai-Lok said. "Or weakened in some way. She's not hitting very many targets."

"My liege lord, we must leave immediately. The palace has been compromised, and the assassins are on their way."

"What?" Qin was visibly shaken. "How can that be?"

"I don't know. They must have a weapon we don't. Or outside help. But Most Honorable and Celestial Qin, that doesn't matter now. You can live forever. You can fight another day. Take the empress and—"

"The empress? What do I want with her?" Qin asked him contemptuously. "Go to Xian. Tell her to come to me. Now."

Alarmed, Fai-Lok bit his tongue to keep from shouting in jealousy.

Over a year ago, Xian had wept bitter tears, telling Fai-Lok that she had been abandoned. Qin cared only for his empress now.

"Then our time has come," Fai-Lok had said, pressing his advantage.

"Then our time has come," Xian agreed.

She had kissed him then, and thus had their conspiracy been born to force Qin from the throne and seize power for themselves. The first order of business was to transform Fai-Lok into a Possessor, something that neither he nor Xian were certain could be accomplished. Xian was a second-generation Possessor, and Qin had told her she was a creature of yin, and must Possess only females.

Together they stole into Qin's secret magick chambers and read all his books and practiced his incantations. They experimented on other human men, killing each failure . . . and when they were finally successful, they killed that man too.

Then the Goddess smiled on them, and Fai-Lok was granted immortality. But lest Qin discover the truth, Fai-Lok prepared a glamour, which he wore at all times: Anyone who looked upon him saw Fai-Lok, unchanged. He wore the same outward face, no matter how many bodies he Possessed. Thus, all thought him simply a wizard who had mastered long life. Xian wished she could do the same—her original body was so beautiful!— but she knew that she would have to continue to enter bodies, as Qin did.

Their scheme worked. Qin did not suspect a thing. And the terrorized courtiers of Qin's household tried their hardest not to know, not to see, and to stay out of danger.

Now Fai-Lok found Xian in her rooms, exulting over the downfall of Qin. Fai-Lok hurried her into a private chamber, kissed her long and hard, and said, "He wants you to accompany him out of the palace."

She stared at him. "He's forgotten me," she said.

He shook his head. "He told me he will abandon the empress, but not you."

Her heart pounded beneath his hand. "But . . . the armies will raise us up, you and I. It doesn't matter if he knows."

"Let me think," Fai-Lok told her. "But for now, come with me."

They hurried across the courtyard; then a figure staggered from the shadows. His face was coated with blood.

"Fai-Lok," he said, slurring. He was dying. "We are betrayed. The generals mean to assassinate you. They want no one from the Yellow Emperor's house left alive."

Xian paled. Fai-Lok put his hand on her arm and said, "But they know I will make them immortal. They know I have magicks, and—"

"The tide has turned against us, Fai-Lok," the man said. He dropped to his knees. "If Qin does not know, flee with him now before the generals reach the gates. Wait for another chance. This is the wrong time."

"No," Fai-Lok insisted. "This is my hour!"

But it was not. The man was right; and as the battle unfolded, Fai-Lok accepted the truth.

The palace was ablaze as he walked the 105 steps to the secret caverns. He called the terra-cotta soldiers to the caverns, knowing they would soon freeze. Then he summoned Fire

Storm with the Orb he had created years ago just for that purpose, and magickally surrounded her with ice.

"Sleep well, beauty," he told her, and she laid her head down very gently and patiently.

At the border of the Yellow Land, Qin bade him farewell. "Create a brotherhood," Qin ordered him. "And dedicate the monks to a new world order, in which I shall rule not only the Yellow Land, but every place in the human world."

He reverted to his demonic aspect and added, "Do not fail me, Fai-Lok. I will have spies everywhere, ensuring your loyalty. You do not want me for an enemy."

"Of course not, Celestial One," Fai-Lok had answered steadily. Inside, he quaked.

Inside, he thrilled.

May you live in interesting times, he told Qin. *And may I one day prevail over you, with your woman at my side.*

Los Angeles

Three hours passed, and Los Angeles was in huge trouble. Skyscrapers burned. The Hollywood sign blazed and smoked. People fled down the streets, some on fire, all shrieking as the terra-cotta warriors marched in relentless formation.

On the steps of the Hyperion, Willow stood beside Cordelia—who had come back—Wesley, and Fred. Dawn had been left behind, in the lobby. Wesley held his Bavarian fighting adze across his chest. He was thinner and tougher than when he'd been a Watcher back in Sunnydale, plus kind of mean. Fred, who had seemed all giggly when Willow had first met her right when she came back from Pylea, had an edge now too. Willow figured it was part and parcel of grappling with the dark. Sometimes the shadows stayed with you.

She knew all about that.

Cordelia showed just as they were assembling to go outside. Her face had whitened when Wesley told her Angel had left on a mission with Buffy and Jhiera. Then she had smoothed her short hair (Willow preferred it longer) and said, "Well, I'm here, and I'm ready to fight."

She was so different from the cruel high school girl she had once been. Willow was grateful for her presence.

Fred was armed with some spells Willow had taught her; also, a crossbow. Her hair was pulled back in a ponytail, and she wore all black, as did the others. They were ready to fight, to lay it all on the line. It was the way of Champions—and of people who had gone terribly wrong and had to make things right again: people like Willow herself.

"Now, remember," Willow told them as the soldiers marched toward them, "Xander says their weak spot is the solar plexus. The lower abdomen."

"In Oriental medicine, the lower abdomen is where one's life force is stored," Wesley said. "Makes perfect sense."

"If walking statuary makes sense," Fred said anxiously. "And, unfortunately, it does."

"The quest for power makes you do the wacky," Cordelia mused.

From the ranks of the soldiers, strange gibbering creatures emerged. They looked like evil monkey-trolls, and they began dancing and frolicking along the sidewalks. They grabbed fleeing passersby and began biting them and dragging them along. Two of them wrestled a man to the ground and pummeled him in the face.

"I'm not sure we're going to make much of a difference," Willow breathed.

"If we can just hold them off until help arrives," Wesley said. "Wolfram and Hart are on their way. As are my private forces."

"Back in the olden days, Gunn had homeys," Fred said. She licked her lips. "We could use their help."

"Maybe they're trying to get here," Willow said. "Listen, we've all done this Alamo thing before—just a handful of us and a whole lotta them, and we're all still here." She smiled weakly at Fred. "So, it can happen again."

"Yay, team," Fred enthused.

Wesley said quietly, "Here they come."

At that moment, the terra-cotta army broke ranks. The marchers became runners. Their stiff features shifted; horns sprouted from their heads; fangs extended from their lips. They raised their weapons over their heads and picked up speed.

Facing them was terrifying. It took every ounce of Willow's resolve to not wheel around and run into the hotel.

"Here we go," she whispered.

"Yes," Wesley replied quietly.

Willow glanced at him. He was utterly fearless. She was beyond impressed; his courage gave her hope.

The footfalls of the terra-cotta warriors shook the ground. Willow smelled the fires burning the city, the stench of sizzling flesh. Human screams rose and fell in the distance like sirens.

Nothing was louder than the beating of her heart.

The warriors approached—fifty feet away; forty. Willow blinked and thought of Tara, and Buffy, and Xander, and even Oz . . . and prepared herself to do battle.

Then a roar boomed overhead, shattering the sky. All the windows in the front of the hotel exploded; in the shower of glass, Willow grabbed Fred and pulled her to the ground, praying to Hecate to erect a protective barrier around all of them.

The magickal shield was created; Willow looked up through the sheen of green energy to see an enormous dragon flying through the air. Its long head extended forward.

"It's Fire Storm!" Wesley shouted.

A man was riding on the dragon's back. Willow assumed it was Fai-Lok.

The dragon roared again, and flames shot from its mouth, engulfing the clay warriors closest to the hotel. The figures lurched forward for a few more steps, and they exploded into thousands of fragments. Some of the shards impacted with the demon monkeys; at least a dozen of the weird creatures dropped, shrieking in pain.

"Inside!" Wesley ordered.

They retreated, racing into the lobby just as Fire Storm delivered another plume of fire at the terra-cotta army.

As the three stood together, heavy footsteps sounded from the opposite end of the hotel ground.

"Fai-Lok's warriors have arrived," Wesley announced.

"God. Is there going to be anything left?" Fred asked.

Willow closed her eyes and invoked Hecate again.

"Goddess, protect your own," she murmured.

Beside her, Cordelia murmured, "Angel."

The Mojave Desert

"Hey, kid," Anya murmured, wiping the sand from her face as she stood over Angel's son. She jiggled his shoulder, and he coughed hard, spewing sand and spit, and jerked his eyes open.

"We're alive," she told him. She showed him the satin bag. "This protected us. Burrowed us out all by itself. I saw it fall from the sky as the dragon took off."

Connor sneered at it. "I hate magicks."

"Well, magicks just saved your butt, mister," she said sternly. Then she softened. "So, you got enough gas to get us back to Los Angeles?" She moved her shoulders. "Of course, we're probably going to have to dig your hog out of a sand dune. But I'm up for it if you are."

"Hell, yes." He grinned at her.

She reached out her hand and helped him stand.

"You're cool," she said appreciatively.

Connor swaggered.

Anya thought fondly of a young man she'd once eviscerated. This boy looked a lot like him.

Strange world, she thought pleasantly.

En Route to China

Inside the Wolfram & Hart jet, Buffy finished slipping on her black flight suit as Angel and Jhiera did the same. She put her hands through the straps of her parachute and buckled the restraints, then helped Angel inspect Jhiera's.

"I could still open a portal," Jhiera said, clearly put off by the bulky object on her back.

"No, not here," their demon pilot said quickly. "I've just had confirmation from the China branch office that the rescued followers of Lir are en route from Los Angeles. There are too many magicks in the air already. It's too unpredictable."

Jhiera glared at Buffy. "You should have taken them out in the temple."

"You didn't have to come," Buffy said pointedly.

Jhiera's back stiffened. Which was saying something.

"What I'm trying to tell you," the pilot said, "is that Fai-Lok is no longer your prime adversary. Lir is."

"Lir, who can't even enter this dimension," Buffy said. "If you mean the humans and demons who worship him, we can take care of them." She looked to Jhiera and Angel. "Right, guys?"

"I can't speak as to whether he is present in this dimension," the pilot replied. "I only know what I've been told. And that is to advise you to be very careful."

"I don't suppose that advice comes with some kind of ground support?" Jhiera asked, raising her chin. "We are expected to do all the work alone?"

"Let me guess," Angel said, before the pilot could answer. "Wolfram and Hart have cut some kind of deal with Lir."

"Witness my surprise," Buffy drawled.

The pilot smiled politely. "I have no knowledge of that. I only fly the plane."

Buffy shook her head in disgust. "I can't believe how cozy you are with these guys, Angel."

"It's the nature of the beast," Angel replied.

"The beast being Los Angeles?" Buffy said sarcastically.

"In a manner of speaking," he said.

"Excuse me?" the pilot said. "I'm sorry to interrupt, but you're going to miss your jump window."

"Fine," Buffy huffed. She hooked the static line to the overhead wire. She knew a seasoned soldier like Riley would never use a static line, but she had no idea if Jhiera would be able to time the pulling of her ripcord so that she would land with her and Angel. Once she jumped, the static line would extend and open the chute automatically.

Buffy looked at the pilot. "Can I open it?"

"Yes. The cabin pressure will be magickally maintained," the pilot replied.

"Figures." Buffy looked at Jhiera, then at Angel. "You two good to go?"

Jhiera and Angel both nodded.

Buffy baled out of the plane. She plummeted for a few seconds, then was yanked up into the air when the ripcord opened her chute. Angel went next, and then Jhiera; their forms were outlined by gauzy moonlight.

Soon they were descending slowly toward the darkness.

We should have asked for walkie-talkies, Buffy realized.

She sank downward, the moonlight bouncing off the other two chutes, until they descended farther down and darkness swallowed them up.

We basically have no idea what we're doing, Buffy thought as she concentrated on keeping her legs loose and flexed. If she landed with locked knees, she would probably break something.

Shadows shifted beneath her, signaling that she was nearing terrain. She took deep breaths to stay relaxed, her gaze shifting from directly below herself to the horizon and back again.

Shapes formed in the distance, breaking the blackness with dark gray zigzags. *Mountains.*

And then, the blackness beneath her became more solid. More solid still . . .

. . . *Ready for landing* . . .

. . . but she kept going.

A whoosh of chill air hit her from below; then, as she continued to descend, the chill air became cold, and then icy, and then freezing. Her teeth were chattering.

She could see nothing below or around her. Above her, blackness.

Great, she thought. *This is probably a trap. What a surprise.*

She found herself uncommonly irritated with Angel, as if this was all his fault.

Then she touched down, and her feet slipped out from

under her. Her chute began to descend on top of her and she rolled out of its way.

This is ice, she thought. *I've landed on ice. I'm Buffy the Vampire Slayer on Ice, the new hit skating show.*

And then she became aware of something reaching out to her mind, something cold and dark and wrong and evil. Tendrils crept inside, tugged, urged her to pay attention.

Come, something whispered.

There was a moment as Angel drifted where he felt incredibly strange, overcome with vertigo and a little sick to his stomach. Then it passed; he landed on cool sand and expertly rolled to his side. He heard Jhiera do the same. Deftly he unhooked his chute, then hurried to help her with hers. But Jhiera had already figured out how to free herself from the alien apparatus, and was rising lithely from the ground as he approached.

She seemed a creature of the night in her black flight suit and hair and eyes as she looked at him, knowing he could see her even if she couldn't see him. Since Angel was a vampire, he could see quite well in the dark.

She said, "Where is the Slayer?"

Good question. Angel looked around, but Buffy had not yet landed. He looked up.

The sky was empty, save for stars.

Softly he called, "Buffy?"

There was no answer.

"We've been separated," he told Jhiera. "We'll have to find her."

Her face scowled. "We've lost the Slayer. This is a foolish mission," she said angrily. "You were idiots to trust Wolfram and Hart. We've been tricked."

You're probably right, he thought, but he said, "We'll find her. And then we'll stop Lir."

Jhiera jerked as if he had slapped her. Angel had no time to ask what he'd said to offend her. It didn't really matter, anyway. They got this done, and they were history all over again.

Together they bundled up the parachutes and hid them behind some rocks. Jhiera was jumpy and irritated, and he didn't blame her. He was too.

The parachutes taken care of, he led the way through the surprisingly rocky terrain. There was a large mountain ahead; maybe it housed the local Temple of the Ice Hell Brotherhood.

Jhiera grumbled, "We're going to be attacked. I just know it."

Again, an assessment he shared. It made perfect sense for this to be ambush.

For Angel, it wasn't the most important aspect of the mission.

The problem with being a hero is that we have to do what other people can opt out of. Self-preservation makes sense only if it allows us to live to fight another day.

I'm here to stop Lir because he's endangering the people I've sworn to protect. Same with Buffy.

But Jhiera's reasons are more complicated. Sure, she wants to snatch this secret weapon right out from under our noses. But she stayed when she could have left. . . .

Ahead, an entryway had been cut into a mountain. He could make out the outlines of a tall rectangle. As Angel neared it, he realized that it had once been a door. The door itself had been blasted away or had decomposed with time, leaving the entrance unguarded.

He gestured ahead, even though Jhiera couldn't see anything, and said, "There's some kind of entrance ahead. Into that mountain."

She muttered something under her breath, but continued to follow him.

They crossed over the threshold, which told Angel either that this was a public place or that everyone who had inhabited it was dead. Otherwise, he wouldn't have been able to enter without an invitation.

They were standing in a room that, by the size of it, had housed a lot of people. Some kind of military outpost, judging by the swords and crossbows scattered on the ground. Everything was thickly coated with dust and cobwebs, including a rusted metal table and some chairs that might have been partially made of wood or fabric. Those sections had rotted away.

The scene was not unlike that of a long-submerged shipwreck. Angel felt another flash of queasiness, this time from the memories of his ordeal trapped inside the metal coffin at the bottom of the bay.

His boot tip nudged a particularly beautifully forged sword. Angel knelt in the dust and picked it up. He blew some of the dust away, to read runes that resembled the Pylean written language. Angel had learned the basic alphabet from Lorne.

"Jhiera," he said, "this may be the bunker where Hannah lived."

She came up beside him.

"Why do you think that?"

He held out the sword, then realized that, in the blackness, she couldn't see it.

He took her hand and placed it on the sword. There was a moment of silence, and then he realized the runes were being illuminated by a soft orange glow.

He glanced at Jhiera. Her *k'o* was glowing.

She took a deep breath and closed her eyes. She swayed a

386

little as she stood beside him. Her body warmed his shoulder and the side of his face.

What was radiated from her was desire. For him. Like a glass of warm brandy, her *k'o* energy slowly suffused his body. He became warm himself. Desirous, himself.

Not now, he thought. But he also thought, *At last.*

His chest was tight; he tried to keep his focus on the sword, and the reason they were here, but all he could think of was Jhiera. *It's just a physical reaction,* he told himself. *A distraction. Ignore it.*

The warmth intensified throughout his body. He could almost feel his still heart beating. His blood, soaking up the fierce heat, the need that overpowered women from Jhiera's home dimension . . .

"Angel," she murmured, squeezing his hand. "Oh . . ."

Despite himself, he wrapped his other hand around hers. She was warm, so warm; and he had been cold for so long. . . .

This is insane. He fought against his reaction. He knew the women of Oden Tal elicited this reaction in men. It was one of the reasons they were so feared in their home dimension, their *k'o* taken from them.

"Not now," he said through clenched teeth. "Jhiera, get away from me."

"I cannot." Her breath was hot on his earlobe as she bent toward him. Her lips grazed his cheek. He flinched, stood, and moved away, shutting his eyes tightly as he fought the sensations moving through his body.

She followed. She put her hand on his thigh, and he swallowed hard. Shook his head. "Jhiera, stop."

The glow in the room became brighter.

"I burn for you," she whispered. "Angel, if we are to die, let us love first . . . oh, I long for you. . . ."

Summoning all his strength, he moved away again. He kept hold of the sword and said, "Jhiera. We have to find Buffy. We have to stop Lir."

He glanced at her, saw her head dip, and how her shoulders moved.

Then her *k'o* stopped glowing.

She was silent for a moment. Then she said, "I apologize, Angel. I . . . I didn't control it."

Not "couldn't." Didn't. He didn't know if her choice of word was significant. Or honest.

Then she cleared her throat and straightened, standing beside him. "Where are we?" she asked him. "Not this room, but this place. I felt sick for a moment as we descended, and we have been separated from the Slayer. . . ."

"You were sick too? I felt dizzy." He thought a moment. "I think we slipped through a portal."

"Or we were sent through one," she said suspiciously. "Perhaps to retrieve this sword?"

As she spoke, another wave of dizziness passed through Angel. He heard her gasp . . .

. . . and then they shifted through the darkness into another cavernous space, this one very cold but lit with a low blue glow that seemed to come from the ice itself

. . . and Buffy was there.

"Buffy," he murmured, coming toward her. He felt strangely as if he had been unfaithful to her. And yet, that claim was gone. That relationship was laid to rest.

"Where'd you go?" she asked him, taking in both him and Jhiera. She gestured to the sword. "What's that?"

"This place is evil," Jhiera said, hugging herself as she looked around. "I can feel it."

Angel gazed at Buffy, still unaccountably ashamed at how he

had behaved with Jhiera. He and Buffy had no allegiance to each other; there was no call for his fidelity, and yet . . .

Buffy is my soul mate. Unattainable, yes. But I haven't moved on the way that I thought I had. Yes, I was in love with Cordelia.

But that's very different from what Buffy and I had . . . still have. . . .

"This place is very evil," Buffy agreed, nodding her head at Jhiera. "It's so evil, it speaks to you in evil-ese." She gestured behind herself. "It wants me to go over there. I was about to do just that when you two magickally appeared. Like leprechauns."

"This is a sword we found in a bunker," Angel told her. "I think Jhiera and I got sent to Lir's dimension to retrieve it."

"Maybe we are still in Lir's dimension," Jhiera observed.

"Maybe it's one of the things Lir needs to summon the dragon, so he sent us here to get it," Buffy said, smoothing back her hair. "Maybe we're just errand boys on a big scavenger hunt of the bad." She winced. "Errand persons."

"We were thinking that same thing," Angel told her. "That we're being manipulated every step of the way."

"And yet," Buffy said wryly, "a hero's gotta do what a hero's gotta do."

"Yes," Angel replied.

Buffy groaned. "It's just . . . if it's not a math test, it's a hero's quest. To do my best for slayage and my country, I had to drop out of not only math and psychology, but Lit 101. Which was fun. And then I had to wear that cow hat. How about that." She grimaced. "Erk. I've been possessed by a bad-poetry demon."

He couldn't help his grin. "The world is the poorer."

She scrunched her nose at him. "I think I'll leave the just-gotta-rhyme-it stylings to Spike."

Angel sighed heavily. "He was a terrible poet."

"Yeah. Really *sucked*, so I hear. Loud and clear."

Oh, this is part of what I miss so much, he almost told her. *Tortured soul mates, yes, but we were also such good friends. Comrades on the field of battle, plus puns.*

Jhiera stepped forward and said, "Are you two insane, joking at a time like this? We have a mission to fulfill."

Angel suppressed a momentary defensive urge to say to her, *Well, you wanted to have sex at a time like this.*

Buffy took the sword from Angel and gave it a run through some basic moves. "Okay, if this is one of the things we need, I wonder how everyone else is doing. Xander and Spike need to get the Orb, and Gunn and those two green guys—"

"Lorne and Honnar," Angel supplied.

"Yeah. Are off on Pylea getting the local Pylean Heart of the Demon. And about the third thing, we have no idea."

Come, the evil whispered. *Come to me.*

Buffy glanced up at Angel as he cocked his head. Behind him, Jhiera looked left and right. "You guys hear that?" she asked.

He tapped his head. "In here."

Eyes wide, Jhiera silently nodded. Buffy could see that she had a wiggins on, and the Slayer couldn't help feeling a little bit superior. Maybe back in Jhiera's home dimension it was all fighty-fight-fight. In Buffy's line of work, lots of weirdness iced the gingersnaps.

"We must leave here at once," Jhiera said.

"Well, that's the thing," Buffy began. "We really can't, because—"

That was when the walls exploded.

Guys in red robes and guys in street clothes came crashing through the walls of snow and ice, yelling for all they were worth as they rushed Jhiera, Angel, and Buffy. At once, the three fighters defended themselves, going back-to-back in a tight circle without a moment's discussion.

Buffy still had hold of the sword. She got it ready as her first attacker launched himself at her; judging by his face, he was a human being, and she had a mandate to spare human life even at the cost of her own. But these were times that tried a Slayer's soul; she had a lot more at stake than her own personal safety if this guy got the upper hand.

So she whapped him hard in the chin with her left elbow, crowning him with the heavy handle of the sword. She grabbed him by the front of the robe and tossed him backward, a reprise of her bowling-ball maneuver back at her house. The force of his momentum successfully toppled at least six more adversaries before he skidded on the icy cavern floor.

There were plenty more where he came from, however, and three guys leaped into the air and executed decent 360s before extending their legs with perfect timing and slammed their street shoes into Buffy's chest. She was thrown backward; she let herself fall to the floor, then pushed herself back up to a standing position, lunged forward in a classical fencing posture with the sword extended, and skewered the nearest circle-jumper in the arm. The next one got it in the shoulder; the third, his thigh.

An eight-feet-tall, scaly green demon approached, flanked by six human combatants. The demon, she stabbed in the neck; then jerked him forward and flung him at the three humans to her left. The other three, she took out *cha! cha! cha!* with three side snapkicks.

Good thing I'm a skater, she thought as she balanced like a flamingo on the slippery ice.

"Angel! You good?" she cried. Everything around her was a blur of red robes, fists, and feet; it was a drag being short.

"Yeah! I've missed this!" he called back, sounding almost

jovial. It stung a little to realize he had way lightened up since moving to Los Angeles.

"Space ranger!" she shouted. "Jhiera! You okay?"

There was no answer.

"Jhiera?" Angel echoed. Then he said, "Wait!"

Wait? Buffy wondered.

A supercharged blast of heat slammed into the floor about a yard away from where Buffy stood. Suddenly the icy floor beneath her swamped with water. Then it gave way completely.

Down she tumbled, like Alice in the rabbit hole, if a waterfall had been involved, surrounded by drenched guys in robes and a guy in a red USC T-shirt being pummeled by the deluge of ice water; and a guy in a soaked orange T-shirt that read FREE WINONA RYDER; and a guy in a Spiderman T-shirt swallowed up by the torrential waterfall before she could reach him. They were all riding gravity's extremely wet rainbow to the next level down; and through the savage water forces, Buffy punched bad guys who got too close, and also she stayed loose so that when she landed, she wouldn't break something belonging to herself, such as an ankle.

The waterfall kept coming, swirling and crashing at the bottom of the pit.

Not a pit. It's a temple, she thought as she fell toward an enormous hall decorated with extremely tall jade columns of dragons and snubby-nosed demons. A vast mosaic of red-and-orange flames fanned below her. High-budget, high-concept, and a long way to fall.

Then, as she and the rest of the party crashers approached splashdown, red-robed guys swarmed into the hall, wading knee-deep in the water. Ducking the monster spigot action, they were shouting and shaking their fists at Buffy and tumbling company.

Some of the guys in the water carried weapons—*ew, guns*— and a number of them let off a few rounds. The falling bad guy nearest Buffy screamed, and his chest gushed blood. Another guy took a round in the leg, and his blood added to the shower of crimson as it bathed Buffy and the others.

She concentrated on avoiding the gunfire while trying to observe what was going on around and beneath her.

So not what I was expecting, she thought.

Apparently Jhiera had attacked the newly arrived red robes with heat energy, melting the cavern. On the other hand, Angel, Jhiera, she, and the red robes were cascading into another, previously undetected cavern, so maybe it was the right thing to do, who knew.

As they landed, she recognized Dane among the fallen. At least some of the newbies were the followers of Lir who had been teleported out of the Los Angeles temple.

Huh. We actually beat them here.

Getting to her feet, she spotted Dane and his fellow Lir pals racing down a narrow corridor on his left like firefighters toward a blazing building.

Maybe they're going after the Flame! Buffy thought.

Then a gusher of icy water tinged with human blood poured down from above with such force that Buffy was knocked off her feet.

Angel saw Buffy take off after the monks who were racing down the corridor, then go down beneath the weight of cascading water. He went after them, slogging his way through the chaos, wondering who was who. Everyone was wearing the same color robes, except for some young men who were succumbing to hypothermia in T-shirts. The fight was like a huge pub brawl, everyone hitting one another sloppily and falling. In this case, water, not ale, was the reason for the awkwardness; it was nearly up to Angel's waist.

Which would mean that if this kept up, Buffy would be treading water very, very soon.

CHAPTER EIGHTEEN

Pylea

In Pylea, Lorne, Honnar, and Gunn donned the catchy post-modern roughly woven garb of the average Pylean. Lorne avoided a reunion with his mother and siblings, but he did connect with his kinsman, Landokmar of the Deathwok Clan. As Honnar had told Lorne, Landok had fully recovered from the Drokken demon's bite, and he told Lorne he would be happy to help them infiltrate the castle to find the Heart of Demon.

Now, by moonlight, the quartet skulked along the castle walls, and Lorne was awfully depressed. Landok had filled him in on the many Pylean current events that Honnar had not gotten to. The Pyleans had chucked most of the plans for the dimension that Cordelia and the Groosalug had dreamed about.

"All that work to create a People's Republic; you kicked out Groo; and then you guys went and crowned another cow princess?" he asked.

Landok shrugged. "We of the Deathwok Clan have remained true to the ideals of Princess Cordelia. We are working to reestablish the People's Republic."

"Exploding heads on servants, bad monks in robes, and worst of all, still no music." Lorne looked at Gunn. "Let's get this demon heart and get the hell out of here."

"There has been some progress in our reclamation of the Cow Princess's dream," Landok ventured. "Our bad monks are not of the Covenant of the Tromboli. They belong to a new order, and they are mildly evil."

"And we have hopes of a fashion industry," Honnar chimed in. Then he blushed. "Or at least I do. And we have a stock market, and financial products to help make our money goals a reality."

"'Financial products.' The only reforms of Cordelia's that you folks kept," Lorne accused him. "Numfar's not the only one who should be doing the dance of shame."

"Don't be too hard on your cousins," Gunn said to Lorne. "They're helping us, aren't they?"

Lorne sighed. "You're right."

"And together with my brothers of the Deathwok Clan, I *am* plotting the destruction of the present regime," Landok added. "We seek to re-establish liberty and justice for all."

"And maybe, someday, even music," Honnar said.

"All right, all right," Lorne said, giving a little. "Things are practically perfect in Pylea." Landok frowned at Honnar. "We will never have music. Do not dream that dream, young Honnar."

Honnar looked crestfallen.

"But you have the Heart of the Demon, and we need to find that as quickly as we can," Gunn reminded them.

"So it is said," Landok replied. He gestured to a boulder. "This is the secret entrance to the castle. We in the resistance have been planting bombs in strategic locations throughout the castle for the past few months. We are nearly ready to destroy the entire despotic infrastructure."

"I'm really sorry we won't be here for that," Lorne said earnestly. "When's it gonna happen?"

"The word will be given," Landok said, his voice mysterious. Then he elaborated. "We have a secret code, and when the proper word is spoken, everything will blow up."

"You never told me that!" Honnar accused Landok.

Landok looked at him fondly. "Why do you think I urged you to find Krevlorneswath?"

"Oh." Honnar flushed. "How kind, Landok."

"Well, good luck with that." Lorne ducked his head and prepared to enter the secret tunnel. "You sure you don't want to come along?"

"My presence is required at base camp," Landok told him. "The struggle is never-ending."

"Well, if you ever get fatally poisoned in my new dimension again, be sure to look me up." Lorne smiled at Landok.

"I will. Thank you, my cousin." The Pylean embraced Lorne, then Honnar; hesitated, looked at Gunn, and said, "Farewell."

Landok trotted away. Gunn, Honnar, and Lorne entered the tunnel, Lorne on point so that if they were discovered, he would be seen first; Honnar trailing for the same reason. Their Pylean appearance would not raise as many questions as Gunn's lack thereof. It might buy them some time to escape.

They wove around and through and down and up. As luck

would have it, Lorne had had a very nice tour of the castle on his way to the mutilation room the last time he'd been here. He recalled seeing a number of promising locations for the Heart. Honnar filled in the blanks, showing him and Gunn several small alcoves with tiny runes in ancient Pylean that read THE GIFT etched above them. Also, a statue of a Pylean girl holding a spear. He had just figured it all for religious icons, never dreaming it would be real.

"It is real," Honnar assured him excitedly. "It's fate that sent me to you, Krevlorneswath! So that I could help you with this quest!"

"Fate," Lorne said, "or the Powers That Be?"

"I do not know," Honnar said. "Are they different things?"

"Good question," Lorne replied.

"Let's start with this statue," Gunn suggested, moving to the figurine, which stood in one of the many alcoves. It was about a foot tall, and it appeared to be made of dark gray clay. "We can examine it to see if there are any hidden drawers. Or maybe it's hollow, like a chocolate Easter bunny."

"Okay, but careful," Lorne cautioned. "Around here, it's not 'You break it, you buy it.' It's 'You break it, we decapitate you.'"

"Okay." Gunn picked the statue up and gently tapped it against his open palm.

It shattered into hundreds of pieces.

"Whoops." Gunn glanced at Lorne and Honnar. "Sorry." He heaped the fragments back in the alcove, then glanced around and noted a small woven basket on the ground, which he placed on top of the fragments.

"Oh, that hides it so well," Lorne drawled.

Gunn squared off. "Hey. I'm improvising, same as you."

"Okay. You're right." Lorne raised his hands in a *don't shoot me* gesture. "Sorry, sorry."

They moved on. The first of the alcoves was a dud. So was the second. But the third . . .

. . . had a secret drawer set into the alcove ledge.

Inside lay an oblong object made of what appeared to be black metal. Etched into it were two words in something very close to Pylean: LIR and HEART.

"Bingo," Lorne murmured, clutching the object to his chest.

And the alcove exploded.

"Bingo must have been the word!" Gunn shouted as he, Honnar, and Lorne covered their heads and dropped to the floor.

Then the roof exploded.

"Guess it really was bingo!" Lorne bellowed.

Then the roof exploded.

"Stop saying bingo!" Gunn bellowed back as they raced for the tunnel.

Then the room burst apart and started on fire.

The three would have been toast, except for the fact that the tunnel they ran into was set deep in the earth and was well-fortified above. Say what you wanted about the old regime, they knew how to build things.

They hightailed it through the twists and turns, Lorne yelling, "Fire is chasing us!" as flames tickled his, um, fancy. He hazarded a glance behind himself and saw the terrifying sight of an enormous fireball rolling after them, just like in the Indiana Jones movie that they made into a ride at Disneyland.

"Come on!" Gunn shouted, punching on the turbo. Clark Kent would have been impressed with the speed he applied to save his life. He glommed onto Lorne and half-carried, half-dragged him along behind.

That was when he realized that Honnar was missing.

• • •

The vision had hit Honnar like a thunderbolt:

He was wandering the streets of Los Angeles, in a stupor . . . a young woman appeared . . . she wore ridges, like the men he had seen . . . she was frightened . . . suddenly, he saw a wicked blade on the ground . . . and something urged him, ordered him . . .

Attack her. Kill her.

Take her body to the hotel, where Jhiera will find her.

"I didn't do that. I didn't do that," Honnar gasped. But he knew he had.

He had to tell Lorne. And the man named Gunn. He had to . . .

. . . and that was when the fire washed over him. And the sin of Honnar was burned clean, clean as bones, clean as hell . . .

In hideous, all-consuming heat.

Lorne was shouting, "That way! The other way!" and Gunn had no idea which way the Host was talking about, so he just kept running and doing his best.

Then the floor beneath him gave way, and he leaped over it like a freakin' gazelle, yanking Lorne along behind. They arced majestically over a geyser of fire and then smacked solidly into a pile of sizzling horse manure.

"Oh! My! God!" Gunn shouted.

Lorne plopped—so to speak—down beside him. He looked like he was wearing jungle camouflage makeup.

"Well," Lorne began.

There was another horrendous explosion, this one the Mother Bezoar of the other two; the battlements behind them shot straight into the air, followed by the crenellations and the ramparts and all the other parts. Bricks and stone and mortar screamed upward.

And whatever went up, had to come down. . . .

"Where's Honnar?" Lorne cried. "Honnar?" He looked around wildly.

"Let's go!" Gunn cried. "Go, go, go!"

They scrabbled like cartoon characters through the muck; Lorne found purchase first and he hauled Gunn right out of there.

"There they are!" someone shouted. "After them!"

Uh-oh. Gunn figured out they were the most likely "they"s around. They who attacked the castle, most likely.

He hoisted himself out of the manure and took off after Lorne.

"Say the words! The words that will get us out of here and back to L.A.!" Gunn demanded.

"But, Honnar . . . okay, okay," Lorne said, heading for a copse of trees. "Let me think—"

But before he could utter a single syllable, Lorne started shimmering, like someone standing in the transporter on Classic *Trek* wearing a rather hokey "alien" outfit, and disappeared.

"Hey!" Gunn shouted.

Then he went all swirly too.

Ice Hell

Aware that he was being followed, Dane listened to the voice of his master roaring in his head.

Left, go right, go forward. Go on. Yes!

Images of Lir's battle with the green-skinned Champion flashed through his mind; and then of Lir's capture and imprisonment. How he had struggled; how, in the struggle, one of his captors had dropped the box containing the Flame; how it had disappeared into the caverns of ice and snow.

401

And how Lir had successfully clouded the minds of his tormentors so that none of them ever found it.

But here it was! And he, Dane Hom, had found it!

Dane dropped to his knees and stared for a moment at the patch of glowing snow. When he touched it, magickal energy burned his fingers. He grimaced, but took hold of it.

"They're coming," one of his fellow Lodge members warned him. "Want me to help you carry that?"

"No way," Dane replied.

Come, Lir called. *I am waiting.*

"Yes. Yes, I hear you," Dane replied aloud.

He flew like the wind.

Sunnydale

"Take it easy," Robin said to the girl as they limped along together in the ruins of the cavern. Her name was Roxanne, she was a student, and he had dug her out of a huge pile of dirt. All he had seen were her fingers, illuminated by the glow from a strange blue sphere, which he now had cradled under his arm.

The tunnel that was twin to this one had not collapsed, as Roxanne's had. She and he had freed the hysterical captives inside a metal cage, and they were filed behind her and Robin now.

The cavern itself had been leveled, the demons and redrobed humans killed. The place stank of bad deaths. Many members of Robin's escape party were covering their mouths with torn-off pieces of clothing. Others were choking on the dust and particles of debris.

Then they reached the end of the tunnel opposite the cavern, and Robin felt a pang of despair. It had collapsed. He and approximately fifty other people were essentially trapped inside a tube containing a limited amount of air. How long it would last was anyone's guess.

A few people broke down. A few more prayed.

Roxanne bent down and said into the blue sphere, "Mayday, mayday."

"You get those things at Sharper Image," a man said. "They work off batteries."

Robin glanced down at it.

Somehow, I don't think that's correct, he thought.

On the site of what had been the warehouse and the cavern, shovels hadn't helped much so far, except to uncover a lot of bodies. Spike had a strange feeling of déjà vu, which he could not identify, and watched as Xander leaned on his shovel and said, "I thought I got out of this part of the job. I'm the guy who holds the blueprints, doesn't get blisters." He gazed up at the moon. "It's so damn hot."

Spike cocked a look at his digging partners. Sam looked worn out and very frightened. Xander just looked worn out.

Then someone called, "Help." Very softly.

"You hear that?" Spike asked.

They both shook their heads.

"Dig faster," Spike urged them as he hefted a shovel full of earth and demon parts. "Someone's down there, alive!"

Sam and Xander stared at him. Then they returned to digging, really puttin' their backs into it.

Before long, Spike's shovel penetrated a hollow space. Screams emanated from it, and a lot of bad smells . . . and something that sent out beams of blue magickal energy.

"Gotta be the Orb!" Spike cried.

He leaped down, crashing through the layer of earth and into a space crammed with human beings. He was astonished to discover that the principal of the high school was holding the Orb.

Robin Wood stared at Spike. Spike stared back at him and said, "Lovely basement you've got. Not this one. The other one." Then he realized he'd better shut up about that, and grabbed the Orb.

"He has it!" a voice said from above him.

Spike looked up. The weird little Chinese girl from the cemetery and the Sunnydale Art Museum was kneeling over the hole he had fallen through, staring down at the lot of 'em. She was lookin' a bit decomposed, and she had a bizarre grin on her face.

"Master Lir, he has the Orb!" she shrieked as she leaped onto Spike's shoulders.

"Bloody 'ell!" Spike shouted, staggering from the impact. He nearly dropped the Orb.

Robin's eyes got really wide as he reached out toward Spike—who was suddenly flying out of the tunnel.

"Wheee!" the Chinese girl screamed, bucking his shoulders as if she were riding a horse

—and hurtling through time and space.

The City of Xian, China

The portal that had sucked Lorne out of his home dimension flung him against a wall of ice. Dazed, he slammed downward and landed on his keister, suddenly up to his neck in ice water.

He was immediately surrounded by a semicircle of young men in choir robes. One of them, so much a fashion victim with his goatee, grabbed the black metal object out of Lorne's underwater grasp and held it above his head. He was already holding a round glowing sphere.

"The Heart of the Demon!" the guy shouted. "Now we have it and the Flame!"

Next there was a flash, such as a portal makes when it's opening up, and Spike the vampire from Sunnydale tumbled into the floodwaters beside Lorne. There was a bizarre little girl sitting on his shoulders, who whooped and kicked at the water just like a regular little girl, except she was wearing a rotting turn-of-the-century dress and her skin was dropping off in chunks.

She was holding a glowing blue ball, which she tossed to the same goatee guy. He caught it in his arms and cradled both it and the Heart, and the other glowing ball.

It's the Orb, Lorne realized. *That must be one of Lir's followers. Now he has the Heart, the Orb, and that other sphere must be the Flame. And it's uh-oh time, kiddies. . . .*

"Give those back!" Lorne shouted. "Spike, don't let her have that!" He scrambled to his feet and half-sloshed, half-swam toward the monk with the prizes.

The little girl dove into water, swam up at him, and bit him on the shin. Very, very hard.

"Ouch!" he shouted.

More red robes swam into the cavern, followed by Angel. He nearly collided with Spike.

"'Ey!" Spike cried. "Fancy meetin' you here. What the hell is going on?"

"Spike," Angel bit off. "What are you doing here?"

"Had this glow-ball Willow wanted. Got teleported here. This your doing?" He gestured at the chaos surrounding them.

"Glow ball?" Angel echoed. "Do you still have it?"

"Ghosty girl gave it to one of those blokes," Spike replied.

"Spike!" Angel cried in frustration.

"Angel!" Lorne shouted, but his words were, ah, drowned as water-fighting commenced.

"What the bloody hell is going on?" Spike demanded as he staggered to his feet beside Lorne and started swinging. Lorne got in a beautiful uppercut on the nearest minion's jaw, who fell backward into the water and disappeared beneath the surface. Grimacing as he put his weight on his wounded leg, Lorne kicked at the little girl beneath the water. She rose to the surface like a bloated corpse. She was still decomposing, gibbering and laughing in a high voice, "The Master! The Master!"

Angel yelled at Lorne, "What are you doing here?"

"Heart! Glow-ball orby thing!" Spike and Lorne both shouted back.

Damn it, Angel thought, vamping as he fought his way through the melee. *Lir must have brought Lorne and Spike here.*

He spotted the red robe who was holding the—three objects. Two of them were glowing, so the monk wasn't hard to miss. Angel slogged toward him. About twenty demons, or maybe a hundred, blasted in from another entry into the cave and positioned themselves between Angel and his quarry. They hunkered into attack position.

"They've got all three!" Angel shouted to Lorne and Spike.

Jhiera, who had seen Angel run after the red robes, trailed after him, and was about to come to his aid when she heard what he was saying.

Lir has just won, she realized. *He can call Flamestryke.*

A red robe launched himself at her. She shot heat at him; he sizzled and screamed. She completely ignored him, half-running and half-swimming scanning for the monk with the artifacts.

There!

The blue globe was being spirited around a corner, surrounded by a dozen red robes or more, and a huge clot of demons.

She blasted through the wall, ducking as more water gushed everywhere. Then she sent another surge of heat at the feet of the minion holding the globe. He was holding two other things, one of them glowing as well, and she knew she had succeeded in getting to them first. Steam rose around him.

She hurtled herself at them, announcing, "I follow Lir! Take me to him!"

Angel felt Jhiera's heat blast; then he was sprayed with steam and ice water. He turned his head just in time to see Jhiera joining the throng that had possession of the three artifacts.

Damn her. I knew I couldn't trust her—

"Angel!" That was Buffy, who had also entered into the cavern and was dropping down from the ceiling. As she hailed Angel, she rammed the hilt of the sword into the abdomen of a tall, green-skinned demon, stood back, and said, "Huh. Must only work on the clay guys." Then she repeatedly thrash-kicked her opponent until he collapsed.

Buffy leaped over the inert body and took on another adversary, this one a scrabbling monkey-thing. She made short work of it.

She battled through to him; he did the same, concentrating on anything that moved. When they were facing each other with no bad guys between them, she flashed him a worried look and said, "What's going on?"

"They've got the artifacts. They must be taking them to Lir," Angel told her.

"That's bad!" she cried. "We have to stop them!"

"With you on that!" he said.

"So are we," Spike informed them as he joined their foe-free space. He turned around and waved at Lorne. The Pylean was doubled over, rubbing his leg. He waved back. "Cover your ears!"

Then Lorne straightened up, tossed back his head, and threw out the most piercing high C of his entire life.

The cavern shattered, just like a piece of Pylean shame crystal.

Down everyone fell, a reprise of the fall from the first cavern into the Temple. Like ragdolls, or corpses, they tumbled end over end, water and blood and huge chunks of ice and now and then some mosaic tiles. It was a whole *Alice in Wonderland* thing.

Buffy's ears were ringing, but they weren't bleeding, like some of the red robes who zoomed past her. They were in agony, and she was pretty glad about it.

So call me petty and mean.

Down, down, down the rabbit hole . . .

Jhiera had been taken prisoner by several of the red robes, who had tied her hands behind her back and rushed her to higher ground to escape the floodwaters.

When the piercing note had been sung, her captors screamed and put their hands to their heads, crumpling to the ground. The demons with them did likewise.

She stepped away from the carnage, sent a pulse of heat through the rope, and grabbed up the Orb. Moving swiftly, she searched among the fallen humans and demons and located the metal object they had identified as the Heart.

Then she looked until she found the other glowing sphere . . . the Flame.

As soon as she touched it, she was surrounded by a ring of flame. It circulated around her, sending out arcs, until it became a boiling, living sphere like a miniature sun. Jhiera clamped herself into a ball, pressing her face against her knees, sensing the heat yet not really feeling it.

The sphere began to spin, and then to burrow down into the ice.

• • •

"Angel!" Buffy shouted as she landed on top of him in the melee. He was on his back, and he grabbed her torso, easing her fall, as they sprawled on a heap of unconscious or dead red robes and demons.

Together they watched a small burning sphere shoot past them and disappear into the ice water.

"It's the Flame!" Angel shouted.

As one, they both leaped into the water, swimming downward and following it. Although the sphere was fully submerged in the water, it was still burning.

It burrowed a hole in the bottom of the new cavern and disappeared. Buffy and Angel were sucked through the hole, fell a few feet, and landed on a huge chunk of ice.

Inside the ice stood a massive red demon. It was as tall as maybe five Buffys, with arms and legs that ended in talons, and wings wider than a jumbo jet. Its face was grotesque, as if someone had melted a *Scream* mask and stretched it out twice its length. Horns protruded from the skull. Its eyes were closed, but they gazed at Buffy as if they were fully open.

She unwillingly gazed back. Dimly she heard Angel shout something, but she couldn't look away . . . couldn't look away . . . the sword fell from her hand and clattered to the floor. . . .

And then she was Hannah, battling on a vast, lonely plain. The stars glowed purple-black above her. She had to keep Lir occupied until the rest of the Home Group could enter the portal and leave for Pylea.

But he was so big, and so fierce. He towered over her, a fearsome giant. The sight of him made her quake. It was all she could do to stand and fight. Every instinct for her survival screamed for her to run.

The demon Lir swiped at her with his talons. She leaped away from him and aimed her crossbow at his eye. She loosed the bolt; with a haughty laugh he caught the bolt and flung it back at her.

She dodged it. It came dangerously close.

For hours, she fought him. She used a sword, a mace, a standard bow, a crossbow. She sweated blood; she wept with exhaustion.

Then he plucked her up like a doll, bringing her toward his mouth. His laughter shook the plain; the stars wobbled.

And she dove into his mouth.

Holding her breath, she swam down his throat and into his chest cavity; she located his hearts—one, two, three—and grabbed the smallest. It was black and hard, metallic, and she pushed herself back up through his throat and jetted out of his mouth before he had a chance to react.

He threw back his head and screamed as he staggered and tumbled to the ground. The earth shook as he fell.

Hannah ran for the portal. It flashed into existence; she leaped into it, and was gone.

Buffy dreamed.

It was China during the Boxer Rebellion. Smoke and fire hung in the air, but she was safe. She was dressed in a beautiful jade-colored robe that hung loosely around her, and Angel was there.

He had his soul. He sucked on the opium pipe, smiled lazily at her, and handed it to her.

Light shimmered around them; beyond the walls of the opium den, the world raged and blazed. But here . . . here was safety. And love.

They were lying in a bed and it was very soft and silky; a fire roared. Everything was woozy, and soft, and very, very good. He took down her hair, kissing the tendrils at her forehead. Slid the robe down her shoulders, kissed those too.

The fire was warm, and inviting. His touch grazed her.

"Angel," she whispered.

"Stay with me," he whispered back, his dark eyes flashing. His mouth was soft, his smile kind. "Stay here forever with me . . . Darla."

And as she said drowsily, "Not Darla, not," an old Englishman dressed in the garb of an Anglican priest walked past the entrance to the den. His hand was wrapped around the hand of a little girl. She was pale, and cold.

Perhaps he didn't realize she was dead.

She sang softly in heavily accented English, "'I have peace like a river in my soul, in my soul.'"

And he made the sign of the cross over her and said, "Very sweet, my child."

Perhaps he did not see the crazy spinning in her eyes as Lir found the crevices of madness insider her dead brain, and whispered to her of quests and secrets.

While inside the den, Buffy sobbed, "Not Darla."

And Angel murmured, "Buffy. I know you are Buffy. I was dreaming . . . of another time. A time that does not have to happen. Ever.

"Let's make a baby, my love. Feel the heat inside me. Feel me burn."

And she did. She did, and she loved him so. . . .

Angel had fallen beside Buffy on the frozen demon's icy prison. Seeing her lose herself, he reached for her. Then the monster's eyelids shifted and gazed at Angel; and Angel lost himself, lost . . .

Lost . . .

He reclined on a bed of black and silver hangings, and a fire that blazed in a hearth in the center of the room.

Jhiera was with him, straddling him . . . he moaned with pleasure, and she smiled and said, "Stay with me."

"Cordy," Angel whispered to her.

And then it was Buffy. Always and only Buffy. Her hair, her skin, the softness of her shoulders. Heart to heart, soul to soul.

Love was hotter than lust. It could melt anything, change everything . . .

. . . But not for us. Not for us.

His tears sizzled.

Her tears turned to steam.

My love is the fire. My love is the sun. My love is the only heat I need in this cold eternity. . . .

They say that vampires burn in the sunlight the way evil men burn in hell: tyger, tyger, burning bright, who can take that much pain?

Who should have to?

Buffy the Vampire Slayer staggers among the ruins of Sunnydale. Buildings smoke, huge piles of rubble. The street is a mosaic of asphalt, cement, and body parts. Blood rushes into the gutters.

The Sun Cinema blazes behind her; the burning marquee reads A SUMMERS PLACE, *until the flames lick at the S and it disappears. Then the entire sign goes up in flames.*

Armageddon has come, and it has struck the Slayer down.

The earth sizzles under her heeled boots. Her hair is silver with ash; her cheeks are tinged with soot and blood; and her black tank top is burned half away. Her black trousers are ripped on both sides from thigh to ankle so that they hang in tatters like a Celtic warrior woman's skirt.

She staggers, hand over her heart, as she bends down to pick up a tattered teddy bear. Tears are for victims and people who have time to cry; With dry eyes and trembling hands, Buffy surveys the bear's damage.

I bleed for her.

Her Slayer senses pump up, and she knows she is not alone; she turns her head and stares straight at me. Her eyes widen, and I know it is almost too much for her to see that I have come.

That means it's over.

"Oh my God, Angel!" she cries.

She flings open her arms.

And I move from the dancing red shadows.

I lost my soul to have you, I tell her as I approach, as I drink in her beauty, richer than any blood I have ever tasted in my long life.

Then I lost my humanity. For twenty-four hours I was a man, your man, and then I gave it back, to save you. I would do anything to save you.

I love you, Buffy Summers.

But I can't save you, my love.

No one can.

Not even I.

I move from the red shadows into the smoky day; the sun blazes red in the sky, but it is there.

It is there.

And it burns me as I walk toward her. My hair ignites first, and then my shoulders; then my arms and hands, and finally, my face.

Tyger, tyger, the flames shred my body with razor-sharp inci-

413

sors, but I move toward Buffy, moth to the flame. Candle in the firestorm.

One burning soul reaching toward another . . .

Tyger, tyger, she screams; and runs toward me, shrieking, "Angel! No! Go back!"

But there is no going back. I love her. I cannot live without her another night, another hour, another flame-bright breath.

Since it's all over, I'll die with her.

That pain sears me far worse than this one.

Carrying a torch, becoming one . . . what is the difference, if I can't be with her on the last day of the world?

"Angel!" Buffy screamed.

She ran to him and threw her arms around his burning silhouette as the red sunlight devoured him. Then her hands went through him, and there was nothing left but ashes. A hero's funeral, a hero's cremation, and his ashes sifted through her fingers to sprinkle the sidewalk. The fierce fiery wind picked them up and carried them away.

"No!" Buffy cried, staring at her empty hands, then screaming at the sun. "No, no, no!"

"Angel!"

Then he was there, glowing in a ball of flame. His arms were open, and she ran into them. She felt the heat; this was the center of Angel; oh, her love, her love, the core of his soul . . .

The ball of flame extinguished itself, and Jhiera sprang out of it with the Heart, the Orb, and the Flame still in her arms.

She was standing directly before an imprisoned demon. Buffy and Angel lay unconscious on top of the cube in which it stood immobile.

Come, it called to her.

It has to be Lir, she thought.

Lir, the interior voice affirmed.

So here it is, then, she thought. She kept Mirali's image firmly in her mind. She made herself see her bloody spine, the jagged crack from the attempted removal of her *k'o*. She remembered her vow to her slain friend outside Angel's hotel. She vowed that no one else among her followers would die.

This is the moment I betray Angel in order to save my women.

"I have the things you need," Jhiera announced. She carried the objects to the base of the ice and laid them down. "The Orb, the Heart, and the Flame. I will give them to you. I want to make a deal with you. I want you to help me save my people. I am Jhiera, Princess of Oden Tal, and I—"

Electricity arced, leaping from the Heart to the Orb to the Flame. It jittered and sizzled; then it gathered up into a concentrated rush of energy that flashed upward to the top of the cavern, then to the sides, caressing the icy expanses with blue fingers; they swept along the floor. Within seconds, the room was bathed in blue; all the other demons who had been imprisoned for centuries began to stir.

Burn me, then, Lir ordered her. *Now.*

And Jhiera, Princess of Oden Tal, burned him. She raised first one palm, and then the other, and heat shot from her. Her *k'o* burned as it had never had before. The power emanating from her both thrilled and terrified her; it was as if she was free, finally, to give herself over to the heat inside her, the fabulous heat—

Yes, Lir urged. *More.*

She gave him more. And more. Sweat rolled down her face; she was panting. The power inside her, the ecstasy—

415

I could burn the entire world! she thought jubilantly. *No wonder our men fear us!*

Yes, more! Lir commanded.

Beneath sheets of ice and in frozen lakes and in blocks of ice like Lir's, the eyes of the damned ticked open.

Steam rose around their bodies as the ice melted. Blue flame danced along a hundred sneering, brutish faces, flickered along glazed reptilian eyes, short snouts, huge fangs greased with frozen mucus. Tentacles and claws twitched quivering shapes and skeletal shadows. The enormous cavern creaked and groaned as the nightmares of a hundred races began to realize that their prisons were falling down.

And she gave still more heat; she couldn't stop herself. It was flowing from her like a river, a volcanic geyser of heat so intense that it could vaporize worlds—or so it felt, to Jhiera.

Yes! Lir exulted. *I will move! I will vanquish! I will destroy!*

"You will!" Jhiera shouted. "Yes!"

And then she dropped to her knees, exhausted, bursting into tears.

CHAPTER NINETEEN

Ice Hell

In the melting confines of Ice Hell, Lir opened his eyes.

At last. I will return to my own body, and I will crush this place.

His soul had dwelled for eons in the destruction of Sol, which he had wrought: scorched earth, smoky skies. Everything dead. Everything.

He reveled in the absence of life, in the ruins. His Dark Blood raged and seethed and boiled; he was mad with hatred and crazed with evil.

Chaos was the very essence of him.

But there was nothing more he could do to Sol. He had waited all this time for fresh worlds to destroy; his son's was as good as anyone else's, and likeliest for him to smash. . . .

As the ice melted from his body, the Slayer and the vampire slid from his shoulders into the slush below. He still held power over their minds. He wasn't sure how long he would be able to control them. He had to take advantage of their stupor while he could.

The ice dripped from his wings; he unfolded them, allowing them to flap slowly. Frigid winds whipped up from the movements, blowing the ice off the demons who had been his companions in misery all these long centuries. Drokken, Sphrarer, Del-h'aNial and Lubbers—he had visited their minds; he knew them each by name. He had curried their loyalty, made deals and threats.

If he freed them, they would march with him.

And then, my crowning achievement: Flamestryke!

From a distant part of the cavern, the dragon silently answered the summoning of his name. He had kept Flamestryke a secret for centuries, only recently allowing knowledge of the dragon to seep into the consciousness of the few minions he needed to serve as his arms and legs. Only when he had seen that Qin and Fai-Lok were preoccupied with each other had he launched his bid to free Flamestryke and ride him in the final battle—the war he would wage to overtake first this dimension, and then as many others as he could. It would not be as it was on Sol, when a single Champion had defeated him.

He had learned much since then.

He would have slaves, several species of them. And he would have a hot-blooded mate to warm him after his eternity of imprisonment. Perhaps this bold woman with the markings over her eye. She lay drained and sobbing on the ice, but he could already feel the heat inside her recharging, rebuilding. She would provide him with fire and heat for a long time, if he chose to let her live.

He sent out his mind, alerting those faithful to him, sending out his commands. . . .

Frankfurt am Main

It was very late. Gisela Von Bischoften paused at the threshold of the installation of the terra-cotta soldiers and pressed her hand to her chest. They were magnificent.

Getting them for the Stadtmuseum was the achievement of a lifetime. The warriors were splendid, and sought after, fought after: Dozens of museums had vied for the honor. She had courted the Chinese government officials like a Japanese geisha, and she had no idea why, in the end, she got the soldiers. Her colleagues in Berlin were crying foul and demanding a full accounting for the slight.

"Na, du," she murmured, smiling brightly as she walked up to the lead warrior, whom she'd nicknamed Der Kommandant. His brows were drawn together over a long nose, and his thick, sensuous lips were capped by a mustache. He was tall, and thickly built. His arms were veined. He looked half-alive as she stared into his vacant eyes. *"Du bist wunderschoen."* You are wonderful.

Laughing at herself, feeling a little guilty because touching was *verboten,* she put her arm around his shoulders and kissed him lightly on the lips.

"I can die happy now," she told him in German.

So he obliged her.

Cleveland

The front facade of the Cleveland Museum of Art resembled a Grecian temple, and Doris DeWitt felt as if the gods had indeed smiled down upon her. Seated in her office, she focused the beam of her desk lamp on the catalogue for the terra-cotta army of the dead exhibit.

Her reputation in the art world was secure. She had worked hard to get the warriors for Cleveland, and she knew that other, more prestigious museums were scratching their heads and wondering, *Why Cleveland?* And some of them were going to decide that it had nothing to do with the worth of the museum, but the persuasive charm of its Oriental Holdings curator, Dr. DeWitt.

Doris smiled as she doodled a square around the photo of her warriors on the front cover of the catalogue. She had thought "Army of the Dead" was a little over the top, too horror-movie. But the marketing department had insisted on it.

"I'm too sexy for my job," she sang softly to herself.

Then something clunked behind her.

Startled, Doris turned.

And the moment hung out of time for her. It was as if everything was a blank, or a blur; it didn't really register that one of the terra-cotta warriors stood before her; or that he raised up a terra-cotta sword and slammed it across her face so hard that her head detached from her neck like a top-heavy, overripe piece of fruit. End over bloody end, it sailed across the room and smashed into a glass display of Japanese dolls decked in festive brocades and silks.

Doris was dead, so she never saw that the fierce but very human face of the warrior had transformed into a hideous demonic mask. That the horns of the demonic soul living inside it sprouted from the crown of its head.

Tokyo

Tohei, the janitor, didn't like to walk among the terra-cotta warriors late at night. They frightened him. He would be horribly embarrassed if anyone realized his secret, but the fact of the matter was, he couldn't wait for them to be boxed back up and sent back to China.

"No offense, honorable soldiers," he murmured, flushing as he ran his carpet sweeper down the long aisles beside them. He felt ridiculous talking to them, but they were so lifelike! Sometimes if he looked at one of them, then back again, he was certain that it had moved.

Like that!

Tohei caught his breath. Surely that time, the tall warrior to his left *had* moved. . . .

He glanced at the solder, glanced away. Glanced back.

And screamed.

The terra-cotta warrior was staring straight at him!

"Aieee!" Tohei screamed, stumbling backward.

The soldier grinned at him.

It took a step toward him.

The soldier to its left ticked its head toward Tohei, and moved its hand to the scabbard on its hip.

"Help! *Abunai!*" Tohei shrieked. He turned and ran.

The soldiers burst into action, chasing Tohei as he got to the door, as he opened it.

They trampled him, then crashed through the door, moving swiftly into the dawning day at Ueno Park, in the center of Tokyo. Early-morning vendors selling chestnuts and soup shrieked at the sight of six hundred Chinese fighting men of clay trotting toward them.

They marched in a wave, in a phalanx. And then, as more Tokyoites rushed to see what the noise was about, hideous monsters appeared out of nowhere, joining the army, shaking swords and spears above their heads.

Within minutes, every human being in Ueno Park had been slaughtered.

The Army of Lir marched on. The monsters capered and danced. Their faces were splattered with blood and human brain tissue.

"For Lir!" one shouted in Japanese.

"Banzai! Banzai! Banzai!" the others chorused, raising and lowering their arms.

CHAPTER TWENTY

Ice Hell

Angel awoke and found himself on the floor of the cavern.

What? Buffy?

Then he saw that Lir was free.

The enormous red demon seized the three objects he had last seen in Jhiera's arms. The vampire sprang into action and rushed the creature, managing only to be slammed out of the way by his fist as he straightened back up. The demon sneered at Angel and let out a guttural laugh that echoed throughout the cavern.

It was answered by a hundred others. The ice was melting. Demons by the scores, freed from their prisons, were crashing through the walls and disappearing.

Angel whirled around, shouting, "Damn you, Jhiera!"

She was nowhere to be seen.

"Buffy!" Angel shouted. He spotted her a few yards away, unconscious. "Buffy!"

Her name awakened her like a magick spell. Lying on the icy cavern floor, the Slayer sat up. She took a moment to assess the situation; then she leaped to her feet and bounded toward the demon. Lir laughed at her as he had at Angel, pulled back his hand, and swiped at her. The talon on his forefinger rammed her against one of the melted walls of ice, which crashed in on her, burying her.

Angel ran toward Buffy, but she had already dug herself out and was scrambling to her feet. He reached out a hand to help her. It wasn't needed.

Facing him, her eyes grew huge; she pointed over his shoulder and murmured, "Oh. My. God."

The entire back of the cavern was glowing. Then it vanished. Steam rolled away from the enormous empty space.

Encased in ice, a massive head was curled around a body so huge, Angel couldn't take in its full size. It was a shiny ebony color, the under portion of each scale tinged a glowing scarlet. Its eyes were closed. Blue light shimmered around, as more mist and ether roiled around it, as if caressing it.

It was a dragon.

Flamestryke, Angel realized. *We're reaching the final act.*

Lir gazed contemptuously over at Angel and Buffy, then turned and strode toward the dragon on his well-muscled legs. With each tread of his foot, the ground shook.

The three objects were clutched against his chest.

"No!" Buffy shouted. She looked around as if for a weapon. Then she narrowed her eyes at Angel as if to say, *You're the best weapon I've got.*

Acting as one, they sprinted toward Lir. Their movements flowed together like a dance, like tai chi, which they had practiced together so very long ago. Their strides were exact; the way they pumped their arms was identical. Slayer and vampire, Champions both . . .

As they neared, Lir flapped his wings, which were steadily drying out. It sent Buffy and Angel spinning. The wall they hit dissolved before they hit it, and the wall after that. They were melting in sequence.

Jhiera is doing that, Angel thought, seething. *If I ever see her again, I'll kill her.*

Through wall after wall, Jhiera dissolved the barriers, essentially ejecting Angel and Buffy from the cavern. Then, sailing over the edge of a precipice, he and Buffy arced into the air. They fell, down and down and down, and landed in an ice-cold, underground lake.

It was the coldest water yet. Even Angel's dead body reacted with shock.

Buffy broke the surface, gasping and flailing in her flight suit. "Angel," she breathed. "Oh God, I'm freezing!"

She had already been cold for so long, but at least they had been able to keep moving for the most part. But this was something different. This could well prove to be an inescapable trap.

She'll get hypothermia, he realized. *She may be a Slayer, but she's still a human being.*

He quickly swam toward her, gathering her up with one arm, and heading for the side of the cavern. She was gasping. With his vampire sight, he could see the rock. There were no handholds, no way to pull himself out. If he couldn't do that, Buffy was going to freeze to death.

What am I going to do?

• • •

Lir raised the Heart and breathed his own breath on it. It warmed, began to glow.

Began to beat.

Then he smashed it into his chest, breaking through the skin and thrusting it inside his ribcage. The blood sizzled and cauterized; and his heart burrowed in beside its brothers like a litter mate. His head fell back from the wholeness and pleasure of it. He reached out his hand and red energy coursed from it, coursing along the ice that had protected Flamestryke all this time.

Fai-Lok had the right idea with Fire Storm, he thought, if in miniature. But then, he got the idea from me. I spoke to him through the blood of my son, which was given to him by the traitorous beauty, Xian.

I'm delighted that they're distracting Qin. He will clear the world of the offal, and then I will subjugate him and his minions. He has forgotten who is the true lord of this dimension.

I will help him remember.

Next, he picked up the Orb. Flamestryke chuffed like a horse and opened an eye. Lir waved the Orb back and forth, and the blue glow changed to orange, emanating warmth toward the huge dragon.

The ice began to melt. It cracked into chunks; and into shards and into small cubes; and it glittered like jewels and tears and stars.

Flamestryke realized what was happening. He began to shift eagerly beneath the evaporating shroud of ice.

Yes, my beauty.

Then Lir held up the object that would completely free Flamestryke. Appropriate name: the Flame.

The dragon growled. Flamestryke didn't have volition yet, and he could not produce fire as yet. But once the Flame had

426

been pressed into his chest, the Dragon would be a living death machine, spewing a conflagration that would turn every city in this dimension to ashes.

Lir turned to Jhiera and said in a gravelly voice, "For this, I will spare your people."

"Just my women," she told him.

Then, finally, dozens of red robes dashed into the ruined cavern. Most of them were wet and bloody, their robes half torn off. When they saw Lir, they fell flat on their faces, kowtowing to him.

"Oh, great Lir," said one of them, a man wearing a goatee. He sobbed with joy. "I can't believe it! We're here! With you!" He raised a hand. "You have the Flame! O Master!"

Lir held it up for all to see. Then he walked toward the dragon, turning his head to gaze at Jhiera as he said, "Flamestryke will make your own powers of heat seem like the warm breath of spring."

Jhiera was chilled by the contempt in his voice.

Sunnydale

After Spike disappeared, Xander reached down and helped Robin Wood and the other prisoners out of the tunnel. As Principal Wood thanked him, Xander said, "If they'd had me build this place, it wouldn't have collapsed."

Wood didn't smile.

That was when a pack of flesh-eating trolls about five feet tall rounded a pile of smoking rubble and thundered straight for them. The other humans screamed and scattered while Xander and the principal fanned out in preparation for taking out as many as they could.

Huh, kung fu guy, Xander thought as Wood assumed a fighting position. The butt-ugly troll nearest Xander brandished a club. Xander glanced at it and licked his lips. His heart was pounding. He was scared, but he was ready to go.

Robin wondered if the fight that was to come would reveal his secret. He was an excellent street fighter and he was going to be able to take out at least four of these creatures on his own. Plus, he wasn't bothering to act afraid or ignorant of the forces of darkness by turning to the Slayer's friend to say, "What *are* these things?" Questions were luxuries the two of them didn't have time for.

He'll tell her how well I did, and then she'll be the one asking questions.

"Harris," he began, keeping his eyes on their targets.

There was a grunt to his left, where Harris was standing. Robin turned to see what was going on.

"Oh, my God!" he shouted.

A tall, skeletal creature had pounced on Xander's back. It screamed, "Kill one this time! Kill!"

Then it crossed its bony hands over Xander's temples, gave his head a sharp twist, and broke his neck. Robin heard the crack from where he stood.

The skeleton dropped him to the ground and capered away. Xander tumbled onto his side, his sightless eyes staring at Robin.

Then the trolls attacked.

Los Angeles

Gunn tumbled out of the portal from Pylea and into the lobby of the Hyperion Hotel, where the Slayer's little sister let out a shriek and jumped away from him. Then she said, "Oh good, it's you!"

"Where's Honnar? Where's Lorne?" he asked her, getting his bearings. "Where is everybody?" Then he frowned at the booming noise coming from outside. "What's that noise?"

They didn't come back," she said. Her face was pale, her eyes enormous. "Those are the terra-cotta warriors. And their friends. They're fighting!"

"Damn," Gunn said. He turned to go, turned back, and said to her, "Stay here!"

"Already told to, already doing it," she said wanly. She gave him a wave as he headed back out.

Gunn raced to the entrance of the hotel. He pushed open the door and stopped dead in his tracks. "My God," he breathed.

The world was on fire. The sky was a brilliant orange, and sparks and cinders showered him like snowflakes. The palm trees lining the street looked like Fourth of July sparklers.

In the middle of the firestorm, a Chinese-style dragon swooped across the horizon, dipping into canyons of blazing high-rises. It was shooting flames at hundreds of terra-cotta warriors battling hundreds of others. Along both sides of the road leading up to the hotel, dozens of skyscrapers rattled as their windows exploded outward. Black, oily smoke rose and smothered the moon.

There was a figure riding the dragon, but Gunn had no idea who he was. Sure as hell wasn't one of the good guys. . . .

Black helicopters hovered at a safe distance from the dragon; as Gunn watched, one of them launched a missile. It shot straight for the dragon, which hitched higher into the air and spewed the missile with fire. The payload exploded with such an enormous burst of energy that Gunn was thrown to the ground.

He stared straight into the eyeless sockets of a charred

demon skull. Human bodies were strewn everywhere, many of them on fire. Burning skeletons of demons draped the curbs. Across the street, a dark blue Montero blazed, then exploded as the flames hit the gas tank.

Gunn got up. He dodged clay arms and clay swords as he wove through the melee searching for his friends. Then he looked up, in the opposite direction of the dragon, and saw a man in a long red robe wearing a golden mask and floating about thirty feet in the air.

Dude was some kind of sorcerer—might be Qin; whoever it was, he was sending out waves of energy from his hands, which the dragon was deflecting. Gunn figured the sorcerer to be the head of one army and the guy on the dragon to be the head of the other army.

Then one of them is Fai-Lok.

As he watched, the dragon launched a huge fiery column at the sorcerer, and he, in turn, kinda swooped downward and aimed some magickal bolts at something on the ground. Gunn strained to locate the guy's target.

Oh, my God! It's Cordy, Wesley, and Fred! He's shooting at them!

Gunn tried to move toward them. The terra-cotta pressed all around him, immersed in combat. One took a swing at Gunn as he lurched past, and was beheaded by an assailant for his trouble.

Gunn smacked another clay soldier upside the head, then got in a jab to his abdomen. And wham! the sucker blew up!

Get 'em in the gut, Gunn realized.

Armed with the knowledge, he began to clear a path toward his friends. As he charged through, a man in a SWAT uniform stepped up beside him, spraying all comers with submachine fire.

Yo Mama! Gunn exulted as he ducked and covered his head. Clay shards rained down, smacking the backs of his hands and his elbows. He didn't give a damn.

As another entire line of warriors exploded, the man clapped Gunn on the shoulder and bellowed, "Wolfram and Hart Special Ops."

"Gunn, Angel Investigations," Gunn suspiciously yelled back.

"I know, sir," the man told him. "I'm here to escort you through the hot zone."

With that, he turned, pulled a grenade out of his pocket, yanked the pin out with his teeth, and tossed it toward a cluster of warriors. He went way kaboom. The man didn't so much as flinch.

"Let's bounce," Gunn said.

Sunnydale

Crouched behind the hulk of a burned-out Toyota Camry, Robin wretched as the trolls ripped Xander Harris's body to shreds and ate it.

Sunnydale was burning; Sunnydale was drowning. Screams and explosions pummeled his ears. The people he had saved had run off . . .

. . . leaving Robin alone to witness the most unnerving, revolting sight he had ever seen in his life.

Ice Hell

Lir held the Flame and the Orb in his hands as he continued to examine the dragon; the Heart beat in his chest.

The creature was beginning to stretch and move.

Jhiera was unnerved. She had made a miscalculation. This monster was not going to help her.

I don't know that.

She reminded herself that she had made her choice; she wasn't certain if she could unmake it. Or should. After all, Angel had never changed his mind about helping her women.

I made a vow to Mirali. No one else will die. And Mirali will not have died in vain.

If it turns out that he will not help, I can leave this dimension to Lir. These people are not mine. We can close our portals against him and we will never even know what happened here.

What happened to Buffy.

Or Angel.

Damn it.

Gritting her teeth, she crept out of Lir's line of sight. She gazed at the void she had created with a blast of heat, essentially flinging Buffy and Angel out of the cavern.

She looked back at Lir, who was busy with the dragon. The huge, fantastic heat machine of a creature; she closed her eyes and imagined herself riding it into Oden Tal, terrifying the men into surrender. The joy! The triumph for the Princess of Oden Tal, and all women everywhere!

She held that image for a long time.

And then she let it go.

She walked softly, and then she began to run.

Jhiera felt for an illumination device in her black flight suit. She found a small piece of plastic. She fumbled with it and accidentally broke it. It began to glow. She smiled briefly, amused, and held it aloft.

A series of melted walls provided her with a trail. She sent through slushy piles of ice, scanning for Angel and Buffy. She found another glowing stick. And another.

As she moved on, she nearly fell over an outcropping and into an underground lake.

At the center of the lake, Angel held Buffy in his arms. Her head was back in the water, and she looked dead.

Jhiera gazed at them for a moment. Looked at the Slayer, at her fresh face and slack, soft mouth. Buffy was a young girl . . . like Mirali.

Angel looked up at Jhiera. She knew that he could see perfectly well in the dark.

He said, "Help."

She stood with her legs apart. "You made me leave this dimension. You threatened me. Do you have any idea what it was like for us after we left Los Angeles? How many of my women died?"

"You can leave me here," he said. "But help Buffy. She's never done anything to you."

Jhiera gazed at him. "You love her."

He was quiet for a moment. And then he said, "Yes."

She was moved. And envious. Her warrior's life had no time for love.

She held up her palm and shot heat toward the lake. And more. And more.

It began to steam. It grew hot.

"Enough," Angel warned her.

She nodded, looked around. Then she took off her flight suit and began to shred it, tearing it into long strips. In the pocket she found a coil of plastic rope. She used that instead, unrolling it and securing one end to a nearby outcropping of ice. She tossed the other end down to Angel.

He grabbed it and began to hoist himself and Buffy up with it. She held the other anchor end, just in case it gave way.

Angel somehow managed to find enough traction to get

them up and out. Steam was rising off his body as he appeared at chest high, then leaned forward as Jhiera half-pulled, half-dragged him the rest of the way.

"Warm her," he said to her.

Jhiera gazed at him, at the way his wet clothes clung to his body. Her *k'o* began to glow.

She put her hands on Buffy's face, on her chest. The Slayer began to stir.

"Thank you," Angel said.

Then he stepped forward and slugged her across the face as hard as he could.

As Jhiera fell backward, the space around them began to shake. The vibration increased until Angel was thrown off his feet. A subterranean rumbling fwommed throughout his body, crescendoing into an explosion.

The dragon! he thought.

With one last look at Buffy, he took off, heading back toward the cavern containing Flamestryke and Lir. Through the dissolved walls and channels of ice water, he ran as fast as he could.

There was more rumbling; pieces of ice hit the ground like bombs.

There was a roar so loud that Angel shouted from the pain to his ears. Then he raced around a corner and stood at the back of the cavern.

The red robes were lying facedown on the ice. Angel couldn't tell if they were alive or dead. Some demons were still imprisoned in their icy cages; others were breaking free of them, like chickens pecking their way out of their eggshells.

And Lir was pushing the Flame into the chest of Flamestryke with both hands. The dragon was glowing with crimson heat, and its eyes were burning and smoking. It threw back its huge heat and shot fire into the roof of the cavern.

It dissolved immediately, leaving no ice, no steam.

Lir leaped onto the dragon's black-and-red back. The creature undulated; black-and-red dancing. Smoke and embers puffed from its hide as if it were a huge bellows. The dragon rose onto its tree-trunk limbs. The red robes didn't move. Angel figured them for dead.

Then Angel raced toward the dragon; Lir saw him but only laughed, extending his hand.

"There's nothing you can do!" he announced.

His wings spread and flapped; he patted the dragon's back, and Flamestryke began to rise into the air.

Angel leaped at the monster, grabbing the last bit of the tail as it soared upward.

Up, the creature flew, fire spraying the icy barriers. Angel didn't know if Lir realized he was aboard.

At last the dragon cleared the last level of ice, and Flamestryke shot into the night sky. Angel assumed they were above present-day China, judging by the number of lights he saw on the ground.

As Flamestryke raced toward the stars, the demon raised both his hands above his head and laughed triumphantly. Then he began to shout words in a language Angel didn't know.

A portal burst open, and the dragon flew into it.

Lir, Angel, and Flamestryke soared out of the portal above hell.

No, it's Los Angeles, Angel thought, horrified, as he held on tightly to the dragon's tail.

There was no part of the cityscape below him that was not on fire. Everything was burning up. It was an inferno.

"Some say the world will end in fire," he thought, quoting the poet Robert Frost.

There was another dragon in the sky, much smaller. Its rider saw Flamestryke and wheeled toward it.

Lir called out, "Fai-Lok! Surrender!" and kicked his heels against Flamestryke's sides. Flamestryke flew at Fai-Lok and his mount. Both dragons spit fire at each other. Angel felt the heat. As for Lir, he was bathed in flames, and he was still laughing.

Fai-Lok sent out magickal bolts of energy. Lir absorbed them. Flamestryke spewed more fire at Fai-Lok, and Lir threw back his head and laughed uproariously.

In the ice cavern, Buffy wiped her face and looked around. The space around Jhiera and her lay in icy ruins.

"Where's Angel?" she asked.

Jhiera shook her head. "I don't know."

"And you don't care," Buffy said angrily.

Jhiera's face hardened. "I care more than you can imagine, Slayer." She gestured with her head in the direction Angel had left. "Perhaps we can help him."

Buffy was still very, very cold. Her bones ached. But she made herself move. She caught up with Jhiera, then passed her up. She got to the cavern first. Except for a lot of dead minions and some half-defrosted demons, it was empty.

"You did this!" Buffy shouted at Jhiera. "You let that thing escape!" Buffy ran from her, looking for a way to catch the dragon, get out of there, do something.

Then she saw something in the ice.

It was the sword Angel and Jhiera had found.

The sword they had been taken to another dimension to get.

Buffy grabbed it up.

Jhiera cried, "Buffy, look!"

To the far right a small dragon about the size of a pony was wriggling free of an ice block. Buffy and Jhiera both raced toward it. Buffy grabbed it by the head, and Jhiera leaped on. Then Buffy vaulted over its head, using it like a gymnastics horse as she performed a 180 and landed facing straight ahead.

"Portal us!" Buffy shouted. "Los Angeles!"

"But we don't know where Flamestryke went!" Jhiera argued.

"I have a theory," Buffy replied. "It's a good one!"

She held the sword at her side as she, Jhiera, and the dragon went out in a blaze of glory.

CHAPTER TWENTY-ONE

Los Angeles

*P*op goes the Slayer!

Jhiera could be an interdimensional navigator, she was so good with the triangulation.

She and Buffy and their little dragon, too, were soaring over Los Angeles like the boats on the Peter Pan ride, which was about a fifteen-minute walk from the Haunted Mansion ride, and ten minutes from the Indiana Jones ride. It was completely e-ticket, as they flew through a curtain of smoke and flame.

On their extreme left, Qin of the golden mask hovered in the air, but his shoutin' days were pretty much over; Fai-Lok, too, who was riding a smaller dragon, which had to be the one Lilah had told them about. It was a whole sky-based family reunion of the losing side.

And the winner and so-far reigning champion was there as well: As Buffy had predicted, Lir had come for the showdown. A truly gut-wrenching sight astride the enormous Flamestryke, the pair had stolen the skies, executing more loop-di-loops than a Sopwith Camel at an air show.

As soon as the red demon saw Buffy and Jhiera, Flamestryke's head whipped in their direction. The creature let loose a cannonade of flame that nearly cooked their, ah, geese, though Buffy managed to get the dragon to plummet downward. The heatwave rocked them; it dealt Buffy a body blow that nearly unseated her. She held on tight.

Jhiera did the same.

There was another blast, and if they had been any closer, they would have ignited like a piece of dried-up wood.

"This is fun, but I'm not sure it'll be going anywhere," Buffy shouted into Jhiera's ear. "We're outmatched. On the other hand, we may have a whole King Arthur thing going here. Excalibur," she added brightly, hefting the sword.

Jhiera frowned at her. "What are you talking about?"

"So many things, on so many levels," Buffy replied. Then her mouth fell open.

Angel was clinging to the Flamestryke's tail, and he looked as if he might fall at any second.

CHAPTER TWENTY-TWO

Los Angeles

Protected by a circle of Wolfram & Hart Special Ops forces, Willow, Cordelia, Wesley, and Fred stood together, hands clasped, as Lilah Morgan said, "All right. We've done the research. I've got the protocol. We're going to do a sort of reverse-the-polarity portal regression, all right?"

Willow muttered, "And no Crisco or lard will be involved."

Cordelia was strangely quiet. She seemed very distracted.

She's worried about Angel, Willow decided.

"Let's begin," Lilah said.

Willow closed her eyes and began the simple chant that Lilah had taught them. Fred did the same. Wesley, however, kept his eyes open and his adze at the ready in case they were attacked. In traditional forms of Wicca, it was the job of the high priest to protect the priestesses while they did the magicks.

Apparently, this portal-regression was part old European magicks and part Chinese. Lilah had already told them that it was this precise set of circumstances that made them work. Once this war was over—*please, let us end it!*—the spell would be over too.

"Thar, shr, qi!" Everyone chanted together. Except Cordelia.

With a brain-rattling explosion like a sonic boom, a large portal blossomed into existence about fifty feet away, directly above a clump of battling warriors.

"Now!" Lilah instructed them.

"Qi, qi!" they chorused.

Wind and smoke poured out of the portal, mixed with white light and a weird, subaudible humming sound like a motor. The portal wobbled and vibrated; the white light shot down and enveloped the solders. The terra-cotta warriors froze.

"Their energy has been removed," Lilah explained. "They're just statues now."

Then the clay soldiers winked out of existence.

"Yay!" Fred cried.

"Let's do it again!" Lilah ordered them.

"I'm so on board with that!" Willow told her.

They created another. It took out some more soldiers.

They cheered again.

And another . . .

The Wolfram & Hart Special Ops guy and Gunn had cleared a path to the Special Ops encircling Lilah and the others. Looked to be some of Wesley's men had shown up too.

At the sight of Gunn's escort, they moved aside. Gunn was

just about to run up to Fred when something blurred straight toward them; the guys with the guns took aim, and Wesley yelled, "No!"

Gunn and his Special Ops dude leaped back just as an extremely phat Fatboy Harley roared up and stopped with a squeal of brakes.

Connor and some chick Gunn didn't know got off the Fatboy. The woman was holding a small satin bag, and both of them were dusty and filthy. Girl's hair looked like a fright wig.

"Gunn," Connor said over the noise. He looked up and pointed. "You were right, Anya. Fai-Lok beat us here."

"And he's got company," Anya added, following Connor's pointed finger. "Look! Is that Angel?"

Gunn looked at Connor. Kid's eyes widened; his jaw clamped down. It was difficult to tell if he was worried about his father or sorry that Angel hadn't already died. So to speak.

"We tried to take that midsized dragon out with a rocket launcher," the chick named Anya told Gunn. "Look," she added, extending her hand. "This satin bag protects the holder from harm. Or from dragon-ic harm. We don't precisely know. Except that it's a good thing. It saved us from dying."

Gunn looked up again worriedly. "Maybe we can send it via weather balloon up to Angel."

"Um, except I'd like to keep it," Anya protested. "For *my* protection."

Gunn gave her a look, then took the bag. "Thanks," he said. "Come on."

Then they hustled over to Fred and company.

"Gunn!" Fred cried. She looked damn happy to see him, especially for someone who had stopped acknowledging him when he walked into a room.

"Hey." He went ahead and hugged her.

Then he extended the satin bag toward Willow and said, "Can you use this? It's some kind of Chinese protection thingamabob."

Willow opened the bag and examined the contents. When she looked back up at him, her eyes were completely black.

"Sure," she said.

Her smile was terrifying.

CHAPTER TWENTY-THREE

Los Angeles

Maybe it was the pointing and gesticulating between Buffy and Jhiera. Or the fact that even enormous demons bent on destroying the world can't be stupid forever.

Whatever the case, Lir finally turned around and saw Angel hanging from Flamestryke's tail.

He roared with anger; then he put his clawed feet to the flags of the dragon and he shot straight down. Angel held on, just barely; he had his limits, and Lir was just about to figure out what they were.

They were rocketing toward the burning hell that was L.A. Flames as tall as skyscrapers raged and shook their fists; there was so much windshear, Angel could hear nothing. But he knew

Lir would pull up on the stick and the dragon would soar back skyward. He knew there would be a whipcrack effect, and he knew it would probably snap him off the dragon.

And then he realized that that might not be a bad thing.

Buffy had already spotted him.

Buffy was smart.

At the moment, he probably had more control over his trajectory than he would again.

Buffy, pay attention, he thought.

And he let go.

Wesley saw what Angel was doing.

"Willow," Wesley said firmly. His voice was steady.

Everyone else, including Lilah, looked very nervous.

"Willow, come back to us."

He put his hand out, took the satin bag, and opened it.

"Murmur words of protection into this bag," he ordered her. "Now."

She looked at him with her black, evil eyes. Her mouth parted in a horrible smile. *"I have killed,"* she said to him.

"Do it now." He grabbed her by the chin and made her look into the bag.

"Don't you touch me!" she screamed.

Lightning cracked above them.

And more lightning.

"Wait a minute," Gunn said.

The sky cracked open.

And it began to rain.

It rained on the burning skyscrapers and it rained on the dragons and it rained on Angel, who was plummeting into flames.

And it shocked Willow back into herself. She staggered forward into Wesley's arms and blurted, "Oh, Goddess! I'm so sorry!"

He held out the bag, and she murmured an invocation to Hecate over it.

Then he turned to one of the Special Ops forces and said calmly, "Put this in a launcher."

Willow nodded. "It might help a little," she said.

"Hurry up!" Buffy screamed through the rain at the little pony dragon.

It was flying as fast as it could, but Angel's descent was faster. She'd seen him let go, didn't know if he planned it. She was doing everything she could to get to him.

We have to save him . . . oh God, Angel—

"We need to go at a sharper angle!" Jhiera shouted in her ear.

Buffy yelled at the dragon, "Got that? Do you speak English? What do you speak?"

Then, something from the ground blasted directly at them. Buffy couldn't tell what it was, only that if they didn't duck, it was going to make direct contact with the dragon's face.

The dragon let out a screech and shot downward just as easily as if Buffy had said, "Could you possibly accommodate my need to save the love of my life by altering your flight plan, my good dragon?"

They were hurtling downward. Flames were everywhere, and smoke; Buffy looked up, around, and saw no falling Angel.

Then Jhiera shouted, "There he is!"

And Angel slammed onto the little pony behind the Slayer, nearly unseating Buffy, who cried, "Angel!" at the top of her lungs.

"Hi. Sorry to drop in like this," he said breathlessly, putting his hands around her waist to stabilize himself.

Buffy couldn't speak. Tears mingled with the rain and streamed down her face.

The dragon tried to swoop back up, but it faltered a little.

"We're too heavy, we three," Jhiera said. "It's too small."

"Hang in there, baby," Buffy muttered.

Then suddenly the dragon put on a fresh burst of speed and—

"Jhiera!" Angel shouted. "Stop!"

"Wait?" Buffy asked him, turning her head. She couldn't see Angel's face in all the smoke. "What happened?"

There was silence.

Then Angel said, "She jumped."

Buffy's dragon ascended the sky, lifting Angel and the Slayer from the blankets of smoke that the rain could do nothing to thin. There was no time to process Jhiera's sacrifice.

They had a dimension to save.

Buffy still held on to the sword. She said to Angel, "This was given to you guys for a reason. I'm thinking it's a 'Powers That Be' kind of thing."

He took the sword from her. Hefted it.

Nodded.

"All I can think of to do with a sword is stab someone with it," Buffy continued.

"Me too," Angel said, managing a weak smile.

"Okay, then. Let's stab."

Soaked with rain and surrounded by flames, Wesley and the others craned their necks as Buffy and Angel flew for Lir and Flamestryke.

Lir looks exactly like Dante's description of the Devil in The Divine Comedy, Wesley thought. *And he was imprisoned in ice, the Ninth Circle of Hell. Is this the apocalypse at last? The one that will end us?*

If so, how do I acquit myself and my actions?

He slid a glance toward Lilah, who was grinning eagerly as if she were having the time of her life.

Then he stared back up, his lips moving.

Am I praying? he wondered.

I truly do not know.

Time to end this, Lir thought. *Time to kill them all.*

He closed his eyes and saw in his mind the terra-cotta warriors in the other cities: Cleveland, Tokyo, Frankfurt. They were overrunning those cities. The citizens were panicking. And dying.

Death would be welcome.

And the death dealer, crowned with glory . . .

Lir was laughing; each time he laughed, the skies shuddered. The rain was a waterfall; the sky was like mud. And through it, Buffy and Angel flew at him, and he laughed.

Buffy threw off her fear like a wet sweater. She didn't get to freak out. She was the Slayer.

She shouted back to Angel, "Lilah mentioned megatons. We've seen lots of big fire, but no thermonuclear action—"

"Spoke too soon," Angel said.

Over his words, Flamestryke began to glow eerily. Then, from head to tail, the dragon burst into orange flames that vibrated and pulsated. Lir sat among the strobing rhythms, and the huge smile on his face made Buffy's heart sink.

There was a *whummmm* just like something activating, and huge blooms of fire mushroomed in the sky above Lir's head. They were as big as buses, and as Buffy stared at them, they expanded to the size of tugboats. And then . . .

. . . Oh my God . . .

• • •

If this had happened back in the day, Angel thought, *I would have become a good Catholic priest.*

I may still.

Spheres of flame miles wide blistered the sky. Lir was silhouetted against them, and the dragon Flamestryke was a glittering mass of heat.

"Buffy," Angel said, "I think we have to stab Lir now."

"I think you're right."

"I think that's why our dragon is flying toward him."

"I think you're right," she said again. "I think we're getting some help. From the Powers That Be."

Help with dying a hero's death. Oh, Buffy . . .

He pressed his hands against her lower abdomen. He felt warmth there.

He blurted, "I didn't think I could have children. Darla and I . . . Connor . . ."

"I know." She was crying. He could hear it. "I'm glad you got to have that."

He could almost hear her adding, *Even if it wasn't with me.*

"Buffy," he said, "you know that I would have given anything to stay with you. You have to know that."

"Angel . . ." Moving the sword, she pressed her hands tightly over his hands. "I do know. I know." She took a breath. "I think I'm going to really die this time. I mean, again. Even I only get so many chances to come back."

"Don't be afraid, Buffy. I'm here. I'll go with you." He managed a wan chuckle. "It's really not so bad."

"Okay." She raised up the sword. "Let's go."

And something guided that weird little dragon pony straight for the killing field . . .

. . . and something made Lilah's team erect a regression portal that opened up above the heads of both Fai-Lok and Qin.

The two Possessors stared upward, each seized by this moment, rendered motionless:

I was the First Emperor of China. When I spoke, millions trembled.

I was to come again, into my glory. But I forgot about my ancestors. I disdained the demon who gave me life.

Lir, I beg of you, do not forsake me! I shall be your son! I shall be your lapdog! Only, save me!

But there was no answer. Only silence, and a sudden, horrible cold that engulfed him. It grabbed hold of his bones, and his flesh, and his Dark Blood; and in one instant, his physical body shattered into brittle shards of ice.

And then it flash-froze his *p'ai*, the upper soul of the Most Celestial Qin, may he reign a hundred thousand—

Fai-Lok saw it happen: the final, true death of his rival and enemy, Qin.

First Qin's body burst apart, and then he and Fai-Lok soared out into space. And Qin's essence solidified; it was horrible to see, more demonic than anything Fai-Lok had ever seen. Dark and evil; it was unknowable. And he knew that it lived inside himself as well.

It hovered for a moment, its face a rictus of terror, and then it shattered.

And the pieces were flung throughout time and space.

Then the cold came for him. And he was almost glad of it. If such evil lived inside him . . .

His last thought was of Xian. Had this happened to her? Had she suffered when she died?

Where was she now?

And a voice whispered inside him, *Because your last thoughts were of another, because of that tiny moment of living outside your self, you will not suffer as Qin will suffer.*

But where you go, you will be very, very hot.

Forever.

. . . and something made lightning zap into Lir's chest at just that moment.

And while he was momentarily distracted, Buffy and Angel took their one shot, their single and only opportunity, to slam their dragon directly into Flamestryke's chest. They leaped off the little creature as it impaled itself into the dragon . . .

. . . not realizing at first that the object of their quest was the Flame, embedded in Flamestryke's chest. That's what the sword was for.

As the little dragon smashed into it, the flame ejected from Flamestryke. It was like a shimmering piece of celestial magick, the brightest, whitest light Buffy had ever seen. As it hurtled straight at her, she raised up the sword, brought it down.

The flame shattered.

The sky exploded.

Buffy and Angel were blasted away, far away, into warmth, and joy, and being finished, and being . . .

. . . in love.

Her lips on his, his arms around her.

Oh, my darling, oh, my own . . .

And both of them had the sense that they could stay there, and be together. Maybe it was a reward, or a temptation, but they could have it.

They kissed, long and hard. They kissed as if they would rather die than leave this place.

Then they pulled back, and gazed longingly at each other, and let it go.

They let it go.

And then, they were tumbling into the mess and panic and the horrible realness of the present moment. . . .

Then, invisible hands surrounded them, and brought them gently to Willow's side.

She threw her arms around Buffy and Angel, crying, "We did it!"

Buffy looked at Angel, and Angel looked at her; Angel found himself thinking of a song from the musical *West Side Story:*

"There's a time for us, somewhere . . ."

"We did it," he said to the Slayer, and a single tear—of farewell?—coursed down her cheek.

EPILOGUE

Los Angeles

Cleanup was so boring.

There was only so much Lilah could do with portal regression, and now that Lir, Qin, and Fai-Lok had been eliminated, those magicks didn't work anymore.

If only I could have retrieved those objects, she thought. *Oh well, they're gone now.*

Something interestingly evil is bound to show up soon. I'm still in the game.

Having been warned about the condition of the sewer near the Temple of the Ice Hell Brotherhood, Lilah had opted for a rowboat. Two other boats accompanied hers, each filled with six Wolfram & Hart technomages.

Oh, and Wesley was with her.

"It's this brick," he told her.

"Okay." She tapped it, and the portal opened.

The technomages sprang into action, taking readings and measurements on their arcane equipment, making notes, taking names.

About an hour later, one of them—a rather thin, nebbishy guy—reported to Lilah, stretching from his rowboat to hers.

"We think we can manage it, but only once," he said. "If we make a mistake . . ."

She smiled brightly at him. "You won't."

And it worked: Harnessing the time anomaly that the temple had somehow created, Wolfram & Hart bought Los Angeles and Sunnydale, Tokyo, Frankfurt, and Cleveland a full week. Time rewound. There were no fires, no explosions, no floods.

Xander Harris was not devoured.

The terra-cotta warriors returned to their exhibits, their masters whisked off to gods knew where.

Doris DeWitt lived.

Alas, Gisela Von Bischoften stayed dead. Who knew why?

Tsung Wei made it, and lived a long time after that to spend his millions . . . before he went to hell.

And a cast of thousands lived also. R. J. teased Sam Devol about tackling some chicks after school. Roxanne Ruani broke up with Johnny Heybeck and hooked up with the painter Troy Kelly.

As Robin Wood watched the Sunnydale High School buses take off for the museum to see the terra-cotta warrior exhibit, he wondered when he should tell the Slayer who he was.

Angel didn't precisely remember that lost week, but he had documented everything so he could prevent it from happening again. When he tried to thank Lilah, she gave him a long look and said, "I didn't do it for you, Angel." Then she walked over to Wesley and slid her arm through his. "Or you."

Then she sauntered away with Wesley as if he were her just reward for what she had accomplished.

Sunnydale

"Some say the world will end in fire . . ."

"I'm so hot, I can't even think," Buffy the Vampire Slayer said to Spike as they patrolled Shady Hill together. "If we find anything, I'll be too hot to kill it."

"Then we'll let it go. Plenty more where it comes from." He glanced at her. "It's still botherin' you. Gettin' yanked out of heaven."

She turned and gazed hard at the vampire with a soul.

"I was safe. I was warm. I was finished," she said to him. "And here—"

"You're warm." He winked at her, and his smile was filled with affection.

Buffy sighed. "I'm warm."

The two old soldiers moved on.

". . . and some, in ice."

What she precisely was, not even the little Chinese girl knew. Centuries of magicks had swirled through opium dens, and in the secret societies dedicated to Fai-Lok, and Qin, and Lir.

She popped into existence in the place where Ice Hell had been, tiptoed over to the Orb, which sparkled on the scorched cavern floor, and tossed it into the air like a toy ball. Up and down. She knew she had something precious in her hand. Something the Master would have use of.

"Ashes, ashes, we all fall down." She touched the side of her head and said, "Another time, Master."

Inside her mind, Lir answered, *Yes. Another time, indeed.*

And the voices of the Powers That Be chorused: *Never.*

Angel stood against the glittering nightscape of Los Angeles and found himself thinking, oddly enough, of Doyle. He remembered his old friend asking him if he was game to fight the good fight against the forces of evil, or if he planned to spend eternity brooding about the past.

So much time had passed since then, and Doyle was dead.

Was there a special heaven for martyrs? Was that where Buffy had gone before Willow brought her back? Where he and she had gone, and willingly consented to leave?

"We all got something to atone for," Doyle had told him.

Jhiera certainly had. But her death . . . was that her atonement?

What of his own atonement? His own death?

I have a child, he thought. *I don't know why Connor is here, but he's my real immortality. Buffy . . .*

He glanced out at the nightscape and felt her name inside him. Felt his love for her, and felt not the heat of the Santa Ana, but the comforting warmth of a place for them, a time for them.

Buffy.